Many good people helped in the preparation of this novel. They know who they are and I thank them. In particular I wish to express my gratitude to Brian and Nelli Hitchen and Gordon Lindsay who provided shelter. To Ross Mark who introduced me to Washington. To Peter Worthington who introduced me to a defector. And to Donald Seaman, my mentor.

AUTHOR'S NOTE

The period is 1968. A year that embraced the assassination of a black and a white leader, a lunar space shot, the election of a new American President, race riots of unprecedented fury, the Russian invasion of Czechoslovakia. A savage, tragic, momentous year. In the interests of the narrative I have jockeyed a few dates, a few occasions, a few moods, and I apologize to any students of contemporary history who may be offended. It should also be noted that some of the speeches in the sequence dealing with an actual meeting of the United Nations Security Council are interpretations published by the UN and not precise translations.

THE RED HOUSE

The true Charlie Hardin. She thought: I expected weakness but not deceit. In the climax of love, even. Inside her. Still plotting. Disbelief and disgust shouted dumbly inside her.

She thought: So I was the poor little peasant girl. Easy prey for a plausible Russian-speaking seducer. She saw herself in her awkward clothes and came as near to crying as she would that night.

Hardin lit another cigarette. Natasha Zhukova lay on her back and gazed beyond the stars . . . She raised herself on one elbow and said, "It seems to me that perhaps you were given two alternatives. One to enlist me as a spy, sneaking secrets from my own father and mother. Or, if that failed, to persuade me to defect. Am I right?"

"None of it matters. I love you and want to marry you . . ."

By Derek Lambert

ANGELS IN THE SNOW
THE KITES OF WAR

The Red House

Derek Lambert

A BERKLEY MEDALLION BOOK
PUBLISHED BY
BERKLEY PUBLISHING CORPORATION

To Blossom with love

Library of Congress Catalog Card Number: 74-172637

SBN 425-02410-5

BERKLEY MEDALLION BOOKS are published by
Berkley Publishing Corporation
200 Madison Avenue
New York, N.Y. 10016

BERKLEY MEDALLION BOOKS ® TM 757,375

Printed in the United States of America

Berkley Medallion Edition, September, 1973

PART I

Chapter 1

7 A.M. on New Year's Day. Beneath the aircraft the lights of Long Island probed the ocean with disciplined jeweled fingers. The lights of Moscow, Vladimir Zhukov thought, had been more abandoned: scattered nebulas of milky neon. Symbolically, the lighting plans of capitalism and Socialism should have been the other way around.

Zhukov swallowed his vodka as if it were the last drop of Mother Russia's milk; there had been many vodkas on this special Il-62 flight from Moscow to New York.

Beside him his wife closed her handbag with the finality she instilled into most movements. "Please excuse me," she said, standing up.

"You are going to prepare yourself to meet the decadent, bourgeois imperialists?"

"I am more concerned with making myself presentable for the representatives of our embassy."

"It was only a joke," he told her retreating figure as it stumbled, uncharacteristically, with the descent of the aircraft. He watched her with affection, then moved into her seat.

The affection melted into many emotions. Expectation, curiosity, pride at what he represented. And a vague, uncatalogued apprehension, as cold and disquieting as a first snowflake smudging the window of a warm and complacent room.

He gazed down at the avenues of lights, the pastures of snow luminous in the darkness, the black oil of the ocean extinguishing the lights. Coney Island? Long Beach? The old movies on which most assessment of America was based—forgetting propaganda for the moment—had an-

7

other revival in the auditorium of his mind. Jack Oakie, Alice Faye, George Raft. Cops with caps and nightsticks, black shoeshine boys, double-breasted suits with lapels as flat as cardboard, leaning tenements and jostling skyscrapers, ice-cream sodas, bourbon on the rocks, girls with lovely legs and afterthought faces, the drawling South and the snapping North, submachine guns, King Kong. That's my America, that's the America of the most humble apple picker in Kazakhstan. There it is spangled beneath me. True or false?

And, returning inevitably to the propaganda, he thought: New York—the fount of decadence, the blood bank of criminal aggression. True or false?

Vladimir Zhukov, aged forty-four, newly appointed second secretary at the Embassy of the Union of Soviet Socialist Republics in Washington, gripped his empty finger-greased glass tightly and regarded the accelerating reality with awe.

His wife returned smelling faintly of Russian cologne. The smell of our soap, our pomade, our scent. The smell of the audience at the Bolshoi. Turn the serpent head of the aircraft around and fly it back to Moscow. New Year's celebrations—the children with presents from the toy shop in Kutuzovsky, Kremlin parties with clowns and storytellers, Georgian wine, Stolichnaya vodka, bear hugs, skating in Gorky Park, women singing with lemon juice in their voices. From his pocket he took a New Year's card —foreigners in Moscow sent them as Christmas cards— and examined the Kremlin. Two red stars and a flag perched on pencil-sharpened spires and golden baubles. Plus the new Palace of Congresses completed in 1961 and seating six thousand, his statistical mind recalled. And somewhere in the center of this symphony of architecture the big growling bears.

He glanced at his wife in case she was listening to his thoughts. But she was busy fastening her safety belt, pleating the waist of her black suit inside it.

Vladimir Zhukov said, "We're fortunate to be flying direct to New York instead of Montreal."

8

"We're very lucky," Valentina Zhukova agreed.

He patted her hand because of adventure shared and she smiled with a glint of gold; the glimpse of sunlight she sometimes regretted.

"Do you feel nervous?" he asked.

"Not at all. You shouldn't either."

"I didn't say I was," he lied.

"But you aren't completely happy at the prospect of our arrival."

He shrugged his big torso. Over-shrugged. Who would ever suspect the fragility inside such a big frame? The poetry drowning in statistics. His stomach rumbled as the vodka passed on, depositing the last of the alcohol into his blood.

Valentina said, "You shouldn't have drunk so much."

"It's the first day of the new year. Back home we'd be celebrating and Natasha would be singing to us in our apartment."

"Are you sure you didn't drink to give yourself courage?"

Did a man of his stature need liquor to armor-plate his guts? Would the party have permitted such a "degenerate" to be posted to Washington, the enemy capital? Only Valentina could have asked such a question: only a wife with nocturnal knowledge, only a wife observing after sex, after a loss, after disappointment . . . "Don't be ridiculous," he said.

"I'm sorry."

He held her hand. "Let's feel this together. Would you have dreamed when we first met that one day we'd visit America together? Even now I find it hard to believe that Manhattan, Brooklyn and the Bronx are down there."

Mickey Rooney, the East Side Kids, Al Capone, organ-grinders with monkeys on their shoulders. Upton Sinclair, Sinclair Lewis, Steinbeck, Dreiser, Mark Twain.

"I know what you mean," she said leaning across him to look down, her large breasts comfortable against his chest.

"Africa wouldn't have this effect on me. Or China or

9

India. But this—I don't think I really believed it existed. All those tourists in Moscow, those unlikely diplomats, those businessmen. All straight out of the movies."

The lights swarmed up on them, streaking past the windows. The half-dozen passengers on the jet loaded with provisions and equipment for the embassy in Washington and the mission to the United Nations in New York waited for the landing with theatrical nonchalance or honest rodent fear. A bump and the lights were slowing, the white ranches of Kennedy International Airport braking. Dawn began to ice the skyline.

Ponderously the plane trundled toward the New World. The stewardess, plump-plump in threadbare blue, stood up and peered out a window as if she were hoping it were Khabarovsk or Leningrad. The passengers pointed, nodded; the aircraft stopped.

Inside reception it was a bewilderment of glass, marble, neon, plastic. Black porters, movie voices, no guns that Vladimir Zhukov could see. His head ached at the base of his skull and a vein throbbed on his right temple.

Somewhere a man addressed another as "pal" and was, in turn, referred to as "a lousy son of a bitch." He had arrived. He was in America.

Or was he? Two men wearing gray fedoras and black overcoats with clothes-hanger shoulders came up. "Good morning, Comrade Zhukov," one said. "Welcome to New York."

Nicolai Grigorenko occupied half the front seat of the black Oldsmobile, his companion and the driver the other half. Grigorenko was a large man, Siberian-faced, not unlike Brezhnev, ponderous but authoritative, a chain-smoker, fiftyish, throaty. One of the growlers. Mikhail Brodsky was a sapling by comparison; soft-haired, smiling, with a cold lodged high up in his nose, gold-rimmed spectacles, nervous hands and a habit of prefacing answers with two singsong chords. *Uh-huh*—D flat rising to E flat.

The Growler spoke. "Ordinarily we would have driven direct to La Guardia and boarded the shuttle to Washing-

10

ton. But there's a blizzard in Washington and you'll have to stay the night at the mission in New York."

Excellent, Zhukov thought. Everyone should spend his first night in America in New York. "What is this shuttle?" he asked.

"Like a regular bus service. You buy your ticket on board."

"That sounds very progressive," Zhukov rashly observed.

The silence in the car throbbed.

Grigorenko turned his big polluted face around. "You will learn, Comrade Zhukov, that much of what appears to be progress in this country is achieved at the expense of far more deserving causes."

Brodsky removed a bullet-shaped inhaler from one nostril and hummed a two-bar introduction. "An Aeroflot pilot wouldn't have been deterred by the sort of blizzard they have in Washington."

Zhukov leaned back in his seat and, with two fingers on the vein in his temple, observed the approaches to New York.

With the deep snow on the ground and flakes peeling off the sky it might have been Sheremetyevo Airport. Even a few pine trees on the perimeter. Except for the cars. Acres of them bonneted in white in a parking lot. In Moscow it took more than a year to get delivery of a stubby little Moskvich or a Volga of ugly and ancient design at prices few could afford. Automobiles, he told himself, are my first impression. Uniform, luxurious, decadent, asleep in the comfortable snow. But so many . . . Did anyone walk?

Grigorenko followed his gaze . . . or tuned in to his thoughts. Perhaps one day they would even achieve that. He pointed up to the sagging sky. "It's the automobiles that cause the pollution. Every year it kills thousand of old people in New York City. It's typical of the American mentality that comfort of the middle classes should take precedence over the welfare of aged."

"The senior citizens," Brodsky hummed. And giggled.

11

Grigorenko continued his recital while Zhukov thought briefly of the pollution over Kiev and decided not to make the comparison. He was a second secretary and his guides were inferior in rank. But not, he guessed, in that other hierarchy in which a third secretary could outrank a minister counselor. Perhaps even an ambassador.

The houses on the left looked English; dozing villas alive inside with occupants preparing for breakfast. Silver buses and ruthless trucks spraying the windshield with brown slush; highways wheeling and diving beneath each other; wires and roads and signs glaring and guiding. The mind panicking a little; the panic masked by the impassive trained exterior.

Grigorenko, official Soviet guide on the nursery slopes of first impressions, turned again. A single hair grew from the end of his suet nose. "You have been celebrating on the aircraft, Comrade Zhukov?"

"It *is* the first of January."

"Certainly. And there will probably be a small celebration in New York. But it was, perhaps, a little unwise to drink so early in the morning?"

"You lose all sense of time between Moscow and New York."

"True." The big puppet head nodded slowly.

Valentina squeezed Zhukov's hand. "Look, Vladimir."

Ahead, Manhattan assembled itself in the young, snow-tattered light, blurred coyly, then reasserted itself—a postcard so familiar that it was again difficult to accept the reality.

Grigorenko isolated the Empire State from the rest. "The world's greatest TV tower," he said reluctantly.

"That's correct," Zhukov agreed without thinking. "And the whole building weighs three hundred and sixty-five thousand tons—that's fourteen tons to support each occupant."

Grigorenko glared at him suspiciously. "You seem to know a lot about one American building? Perhaps it's you who should make the introductions." He felt for the hair on his nose.

"Not just one American building. The most famous of

all. I read my tourist literature. And," he said apologetically, "I have this facility with figures and statistics. They lodge in my brain. Often annoyingly."

Which was true. There was Manhattan, floating as serene as a reflection, and he had to toss three hundred and sixty-five thousand tons of concrete into it. Such training.

"It's very impressive," Valentina said. "Especially beside all this." She pointed to some grubby miniatures along the road.

"Uh-huh." Brodsky tuning up. "But it seems to me that we should not forget the squalor and corruption that exists behind those façades. Drugs, drunkenness, violence, vice." He ticked them off on the fingers of his dogma, his voice lingering and slavering over "v-i-c-e."

Only the driver said nothing, and Zhukov wondered how his young peasant brain reacted—if his training had left him with any reactions.

I want to feel and savor it by myself, Zhukov thought. I want my own private instincts which I have so carefully and privately nurtured. To feel and judge and file.

They lingered beneath a red light before entering the Kremlin of capitalism.

Manhattan's streets and avenues opened up and the sky narrowed—gray canals high above. He saw a Hollywood cop feeling his nightstick as if it were a damaged limb and thought of the Soviet militia with their dramatic topcoats and irritable toothpick truncheons. Discovery and nostalgia fought each other. Steam billowing from vents in the city's bowels and lingering in the icy, lacy air; felt boots crunching fresh snow on Arbatskaya Square.

Discovery won the battle without deciding the war; the shops the storm troopers. Windows of nonchalant plenty. Furniture in theatrical sets, beds of jewelry and dormant watches, racy clothes and gossamer fabrics, skis and golf clubs, package tours to Las Vegas, Miami, Dublin or Tokyo, a coffee carafe of Pyrex and silverplate like a contemporary samovar, beckoning beds, busty, gusty displays of brassieres and corsetry, a garden window with simulated grass being cut by a mower (plan ahead for summer), czarist perambulators, floods of shoes ready to quick-march, toys Russian children couldn't dream of because they couldn't imagine them. Everything cheaper than everything else, every store flaunting infinitesimal advantage.

And the Christmas tableaux in cavernous windows. Dwarfs and children and fairies strutting and dancing and blessing; a carousel carrying dizzy teddy bears; a rocket bound for the moon with Santa Claus (Grandfather Frost) astride the command module. And Christmas trees (*yolka*) buttoned onto the haunches of the elephantine buildings with white electric bulbs.

Grigorenko interrupted as he had done with many other newcomers. "I know just what you are thinking."

"You do? You presume too much, comrade."

"You are wondering what can be wrong with capitalism if it produces so many fruits."

The vein had subsided, the ache at the base of his skull fading. "Is that what *you* wondered when you first arrived?"

Grigorenko's pattern was disturbed. "Not I. But you. Is that not what you are thinking?" The growl lost a decibel of menace. Brodsky felt the bridge of his sinus and made a noise that could have been a simper, a giggle or a sneeze.

Zhukov said it wasn't, enjoying the transient authority of unexpected attack. He was, after all, a second secretary.

"Then what *are* you thinking?"

"Just remembering that in the shops in Gorky Street you can see nothing in the windows."

"You are commenting unfavorably on the commerce of the Soviet Union?"

"On the contrary, Comrade Grigorenko. I'm surprised that you should interpret a remark so prematurely and so incorrectly." He gestured toward a windowful of lingerie threaded with tinsel. "If you judge a woman by her jewelry you may find a whore."

"Just so, comrade." Grigorenko made notes in his mind. "You speak very well—but of course that's your job."

"Surely yours as well, comrade."

Valentina's elbow nudged his ribs, warning.

14

Brodsky said, "Perhaps Zhukov's words are as empty as those shops in Gorky Street."

Zhukov said, "But the shops aren't empty. Only the windows."

"You will make a very good diplomat," Grigorenko observed. "You're smart with words."

"I *am* a good diplomat."

"Forty-four? Second secretary? Perhaps your capabilities have been underestimated." The doggy face regarded Zhukov with total seriousness; in the bruise-colored pouch under one eye there was an incipient growth.

If I were a man, Zhukov thought, I'd reply, "But you're only a third secretary." But you had to be smart with not saying words as well as saying them.

The city was slowly on the move, the snow like the fuzz the morning after too much Stolichnaya.

A Buick fanning wings of slush hove past bearing the legend SAVE SOVIET JEWRY.

From what? Ah, diplomacy . . .

A street sign said TOW AWAY ZONE. Another said SNOW EMERGENCY STREET. They turned into East Sixty-seventh Street. No. 136—the Mission of the Union of Soviet Socialist Republics to the United Nations. And those of the Ukraine and Byelorussia. And, across the road, down the street from the red-brick Nineteenth police precinct clubhouse a synagogue.

Chapter 2

BUT THE SPIRIT of goodwill and New Year's resolutions hadn't penetrated the pale and clinical building at 136.

In the foyer Zhukov's body turned clammy in the artificial heat. A woman with graying hair forced into a bun, and a lackey in a miserable suit and thin tie regarded him suspiciously. A plastic Grandfather Frost and the Snow Maiden beamed in the corner in spite of it all.

"We shall stay here until they open Washington airport," Grigorenko said. "You would perhaps like to get some sleep?"

"I'd like to have a look at New York while I'm here," Zhukov said.

"It would be better if you got some sleep."

"I should like to see New York. It might be my only chance."

Valentina sided with Grigorenko. "I'm very tired, Vladimir."

You couldn't make a scene within minutes of arrival; nor could you relinquish all authority to a couple of third secretaries protected by the ghost of Beria. "Perhaps later," Zhukov said.

Outside they heard scuffling. Russian oaths involving mothers. A voice with a Uzbek accent screaming *"Smarsky!"*

The doors sprang open. A blast of cold air followed by a young man held by two squat captors. They pinioned him easily, his feet just touching the ground. His hair was black and curly, badly cut; his skin dark, his body slight and struggling.

Grigorenko strode across to them and growled as softly as he could, showing the squatter of the two an identification card.

Grigorenko spoke to the young man.

"Go and fuck yourself," screamed the young man. His dark face was frenzied with fear—a man being carried to the hangman's noose.

Grigorenko nodded slowly, as if abrupt movement might dislocate the big head from his neck. "Put him down." The hunters released their quarry. "You haven't made a very good start on the new year," he observed.

"Shit on you," said the prisoner.

Grigorenko stepped forward, kicking hard and down

16

the shin, crunching on the instep, bringing his knee up into the crotch as the man gasped forward, finally rabbit punching the side of the neck with the blade of his hand.

The young man, doubled over in pain, was carried away.

"Tomorrow," Grigorenko said, "he will be on the plane to Moscow."

"And what was that all about?" Zhukov asked.

"It's nothing for you to worry about," Grigorenko replied.

Brodsky, who'd been watching with his inhaler held up one nostril, said, "Just another drunk, probably. They will insist on drinking scotch when they're used to vodka."

"That man wasn't drunk."

"It affects different people in different ways."

"And now," Grigorenko announced, "it's time for bed."

He was, Zhukov thought, very avuncular. As avuncular as Stalin.

Only Grandfather Frost who had once been on the receiving end of denunciation—a puppet of the priests, no less!—saw any humor in the situation.

He allotted himself two hours' sleep and lay down on one of the two single beds in the small bedroom. A bowl of fruit and a picture of Lenin dominated the decor.

He listened to his rapid vodka heartbeat and told himself to calm down. About the priorities shifting around in his mind. About the tests of loyalty ahead.

Although I am a good citizen, Vladimir Zhukov assured himself. A good party member. I believe in our crusade. His trained brain recited, unsolicited: "From each according to his ability, to each according to his need." The last lecture in Moscow surfaced. "We know that an accelerating, unmanageable national debt will effect civil collapse and open the floodgates of Socialism." The lecturer's fanatic face peered closer. "This is now happening in the United States of America. It is up to you. . . ."

They had observed him over the past five years and he had passed their surveillance. Not for them to penetrate

17

the secret sensibilities that are a man's soul. The coil of poetry unsprung. Not for them to glimpse the doubts on which true strength are founded.

He lapsed into an excited doze, limbs twitching, eyelids quivering. Yellow cabs vanishing down narrowing vistas of skyscrapers, Manhattan a mirage behind a veil of snow. When he awoke he was confused about reality; he had dreamed so often about this arrival in a celluloid city projected on his private gray screen.

He climbed out of bed carefully, still in his underwear. It was exactly two hours: such damned precision. His wife slept serenely. Through a slit in the curtain he looked down on the synagogue, on the blue cap of a guardian cop.

In the bathroom down the corridor he shaved, drawing blood from his tired skin. He pressed his eyelids and his eyes ached back at him. He massaged a little pomade into his sleek hair and watched the wires of silver fade. He returned to the bedroom.

Valentina said, "Where are you going, Vladimir?"

"I thought I'd take a stroll. I can't sleep."

"You mean you've stopped yourself from sleeping." She knew him so well.

"I may never see New York again."

"They don't want you to go out alone, Vladimir. You know that. Why defy them on our first morning in America?"

"I'm not their slave, Valentina."

"Don't be foolish—remember how you've worked for this day." She sat up in bed, hair loose, the brown aureoles of her nipples visible through white cotton; in her waking moments she was more feminine than she cared to be.

"A servant, maybe. But, I repeat, not a slave. I must assert some authority now before it's too late."

"Come and lie down with me." She stretched out warm arms.

Vladimir Zhukov silently apologized to his wife for rejecting her comforts and put on his new dark-gray suit with the wide trouser bottoms which Western fashion was beginning to acknowledge. Except that with his trousers the width extended to the thigh.

18

Valentina said, "If you insist, then I shall come with you."

But he wanted to see it by himself. Gary Cooper walking lone and tall down Fifth Avenue. Compromise—the dress sword of the diplomat. "I'll meet you later and we'll have lunch together."

"Meet me? Where? We don't know anywhere in New York."

He reacted swiftly. "At the top of the Empire State Building." He laughed aloud for the first time since the aircraft touched down at Kennedy Airport.

He felt as if he had been released from prison and was vaguely ashamed of his exhilaration. But a lot of conformity lies ahead, comrade.

It was midday. The snow had stopped and the sky above the rooftops of Lexington Avenue was polished blue. A few jewels still sparkled on the edge of the sidewalk but in the gutters the slush was ankle-deep. They had a lot to learn about street cleaning, he decided proudly.

The Gallery Drugstore, Marboro Books. Sixty, 59, 58 . . . 53, 52. He enjoyed the drugstores. "Meet you in the drugstore, buddy." Sulky-faced girls with bobbed hair wisecracking with chunky athletes with greased or chopped hair (Hollywood 1935–50). But it needed courage to enter one. They would call him mister and ask where he came from.

Bookshops, delicatessens, restaurants . . . the luxury seemed cozy and refined in this particular avenue. East Side, West Side. Which was which? Grand Central Station, Central Park, Times Square, Fifth Avenue, the Waldorf-Astoria, Harlem, Greenwich Village—that was all he knew.

He found courage and bought two newspapers from the front stall of a drugstore. The New York *Times* and the *Daily News*.

"Thank you," he said.

"You're welcome." The girl sighed, yawning and chewing and talking simultaneously.

He tucked the papers under his arm like a baton won-

19

dering if he could be mistaken for an American. He looked behind to see if he was being followed. It didn't look like it, but you could never tell.

What strikes me most? he asked himself, seeking first impressions for the album. It had to be the shops with their abundance of consumer goods; *this* he had been warned about—the products of exploitation, late participation in wars, geographical advantages, twenty million Soviets killed conquering the Hun. But the briefings hadn't fully prepared him for the profusion, the multiplicity, the permutations of plenty. (How many variations of salad dressing could there be? How many odors of deodorant? And who wanted to smell of lemons or Tahitian lime anyway?) In Moscow he had queued for a ball-point pen with a sputnik that slid up and down the stem.

And again, the cars—the automobiles. New Yorkers paraded in their cars. Vladimir Zhukov, crunching down Lexington Avenue with the enemy all about, lusted guiltily for a big tin fish with automatic drive and power-assisted windows. He was startled by the number of female drivers —girls with long, straight hair, smartly coiffured old ladies steering their vehicles like tank commanders. What happens to the *babushkas?* Do they have them put to sleep? Or let them drive their tanks over the cliffs like lemmings?

He reached Forty-second and turned right past Grand Central, remembering faintly from another life the stations of Moscow—cathedrals, fortresses, terminals of turreted grandeur where immigrant peasants wandered like bewildered insects.

He looked at the street numbers and know with his mathematical certainty that he could never be really lost; just the same at that moment he was, gloriously and excitingly. Like a child trying to get lost and fearing the chilly second thoughts of dusk.

Courage, comrade. He said to the cop frowning at the unplumbed depths of slush on a street corner, "Excuse me, please, can you tell me the way to the Empire State Building?" His words froze and hung between the two of them.

The patrolman who had long sideburns and a squashed face said, "How's that?"

20

Zhukov expelled the rush of words again, hating the sense of inferiority that accompanied them. Put this cop in Red Square and see how *he* managed.

"Where you from, fella?"

"Moscow."

Enlightenment shifted the crumpled features around and Zhukov realized that it was a friendly face.

"No kidding. One of those émigré guys, huh? And you don't know where the Empire State is? How about that."

Zhukov waited.

The patrolman said, "Two blocks down. Turn left down Fifth. You sure as hell can't miss it. I guess that's the one building you can't miss."

"Thank you." Zhukov crossed the slush, wishing he didn't look so conspicuous. Even though no one seemed to pay him much heed.

"Okay, pal," said the patrolman. "Any time. Any time at all. Have a good day."

The City Library (four million volumes). Blacks, Italians, Poles, Swedes, Germans, Puerto Ricans (he presumed), hippies, producers in camel's hair coats, soldiers to be sacrificed in Vietnam, women in furs and boots as arrogant and vapid (he was sure) as fashion models, businessmen with slim black attaché cases—one there munching a hot dog. All intent on something on this white melting day.

One thing he did not do: He did not walk along staring up at the narrow sky because that was the hallmark of the greenhorn. Which I am not, he thought. I am a representative of the greatest power on earth. It's just that I'm a stranger. At which point he discovered that his head was tilting upward like a peasant seeing his first airplane.

So there it was—a colossus of play bricks beneath him. Massive and vulnerable. You could crunch them, swipe them aside with one bear paw.

On the 102d-floor observatory, nicely placed at 1,050 feet, Vladimir Zhukov surveyed the enemy camp with awe and got annoyed about the awe.

He gazed southwest where the vanguard of the buildings

21

gathered for approaching tourists. With the Statue of Liberty on sentry duty. He moved and sighted north toward what he thought was the Bronx, beyond a phalanx of skyscrapers. Difficult to believe that in one section of one story of one of those obelisks, a business, and existence, a saga, could exist without awareness above or below.

To the northeast the metallic, ostentatious thrust of the Chrysler Building with, he surmised, the pygmy-giant of the United Nations close by.

The city, so beautifully exhibitionist, within the ice-blue perimeters of its rivers.

"Sometimes snow and rain can be seen falling up."

"I know," Vladimir Zhukov said. "And the rain is sometimes red."

He turned without surprise and faced Mikhail Brodsky.

The breakfast was called The Heavyweight. It consisted of a wafer of bacon, two rheumy fried eggs and three pancakes covered with maple syrup and crowned with a dollop of whipped cream. For your one dollar and twenty-five cents you also got a small glass of orange juice, toast and coffee. It was, Zhukov thought, good value and totally disgusting. He ate it with relish.

Brodsky ordered coffee, tapping the last grains of sugar from the paper sachet with his forefinger, leaking the last drop of cream from the tiny carton, his actions the legacy of a needy youth. Although the delicate bloom on his cheeks seemed to have bettered bread and potatoes and blinis.

Brodsky tuned in with two bars and said, "I think this is more our style."

More than what?

Brodsky cat sipped at his coffee. "I feel at home in these places. With these people." He indicated the coffee shop's occupants: a gaunt, white-haired man in Stetson flirting grotesquely with the woman behind the counter; a starved little guy in a red-checked lumber jacket continuing his life's search for winners with a chewed fingernail; a bearded black in a cowboy jacket riding his chair like a horse;

22

mother and son spooning banana splits; a salesman inside an overcoat collapsed by rain and snow.

The statement seemed to Zhukov to be an admission of inferiority. But he let it pass. "How did you find me up there?" Either the room had been bugged or Valentina'd told him or he'd been followed. Any one explanation wearied him.

"It was not so remarkable. Your wife was still feeling tired and suggested that I meet you instead." He wiped his glasses, looking myopic and vulnerable. "And it's good that we become friends because we shall be seeing a lot of each other in Washington. I think we should have a chat now before we leave. You see," he explained, "the weather has cleared and we shall be taking the shuttle this afternoon."

"So soon?"

"Washington *is* your destination." He glanced around the café with a furtiveness as natural as sleeping and breathing.

"So we are going to have a frank and open talk, are we?"

"I hope so, comrade. I really hope so." The girlish hair fell about.

He pressed his loaded sinus with finger and thumb; nails pared and clean, hands hairless. His lashes brushed the lenses of his spectacles. He wore the same dark overcoat, the same woolly scarf that mothers made you wear, a thin gray tie.

"Then tell me what happened at the embassy this morning."

"It was all most unfortunate."

"I could see that. It is never fortunate for a man when he is kicked in the crotch and rabbit punched. But why, Brodsky? Why?"

"He was a very foolish boy."

"What happened?"

"You need not concern yourself. It was a small irritating incident and you have the great task of adapting yourself to life in this self-indulgent society in which we find ourselves. It was the foolishness of youth. A girl, too much whiskey—watch the whiskey, comrade. He will wake up in Moscow and be dealt with there. A small punishment, probably, plus the knowledge that he has ruined his career."

"I think he tried to defect."

Brodsky sighed, holding up one delicate hand as the woman came to clear the table.

"More coffee?" she asked.

"Please," they said.

"Coming up."

She was blond and Germanic and smiling, but she moved like an automaton, like the girl who sold him the newspapers. A symptom of being a menial in an affluent society, Zhukov supposed. She brought more coffee and they thanked her and she said, "You're welcome."

"Did he try to defect?" Zhukov asked.

"That is a very dramatic and contemporary word. He simply decided that he would like to stay with this American girl." Brodsky reached for his inhaler. "I suppose you might as well know the full story." (Which meant he would be lucky to hear a half-truth.) "He arranged to meet an American in a café in Queens. She was going to help him disappear for a while. But we were waiting for the unfortunate Boris Ivanov in the café."

"You mean you made some sort of deal with the Americans?"

Brodsky shrugged delicately. "It really isn't my business. I can only tell you what I have heard. He was only a boy, after all. I suppose he had nothing much to offer the Americans. . . ." He put away the plastic white bullet. "Not like you, comrade. If you were ever in a position to take such foolish action."

The song had left his lips. Replaced by the voice of secret authority that served czars and other dictators and the party with unswerving treachery; the voice of those who chose murder and intrigue as others choose dairy farming or quantity surveying.

And here was the voice in a coffee shop on Forty-second

24

Street, New York City. Zhukov's reactions chilled: Grigorenko was the underling, Mikhail Brodsky the boss. Perhaps *the* boss, with an ambassador, a minister counselor, counselors, secretaries, attachés under him.

"If you think I am the sort of person who would take such an action then I should never have been sent here," Zhukov said.

"I didn't make the choice." Brodsky lit a mentholated American cigarette. "But it was very foolish of you to go wandering around in New York on your first day here."

"Apparently I was not alone."

"You could have been mugged."

"Mugged?"

"Robbed, beaten up. I don't know how the word came to be. Perhaps because only mugs allow themselves to be robbed."

"In broad daylight?"

"Certainly in broad daylight. This is a dangerous and decadent society, comrade. A man will knife you in a cinema queue for the money to buy drugs." He leaned forward, blinking behind his gold-rimmed spectacles. "Like myself you are a sensitive man. You write poetry, I believe?"

"How did you know that? It's never been published."

Brodsky slipped the question. "I too write poetry. Some of it has been published in *Novy Mir*. And once I wrote an amusing little poem about Russian women wearing shorts. Calling them *shortiki*—an American-derived term—instead of *trusiki*. It was quite well received."

"I'm happy for you," Zhukov said.

"I'm trying to illustrate that people like ourselves should be both sensitive *and* realistic. It's not wise to let sensitivity get the upper hand in this country. Values can become unbalanced in a sensitive mind. You can be dazzled by the abundance of food and drink and clothes and apparent freedom and forget the misery and oppression and violence."

"Thanks for the warning," Zhukov said. "I had many like it before I left Moscow."

25

"Nevertheless these first impressions can be quite traumatic." He sang a couple of bars and relaxed. "Now it seems to me that we should go."

The woman behind the bar called out, "Good-bye, folks. Have a good day." And confided to her senile suitor in the Stetson, "English tourists—I can always tell 'em."

But Mikhail Brodsky was not quite finished. "The safest place to talk," he confided, "is in a crowded street."

They cut up Madison Avenue, turning right down Fifty-third. Zhukov looked with pleasure at the legs of the mini-skirted girls and surmised that they must have very cold asses.

Brodsky walked very carefully, despite his rubber overshoes, leaping like a ballet dancer over the street-corner swamps.

After a while Zhukov asked him what was on his mind.

"I believe certain approaches were made to you in Moscow."

"Such as?"

"About your responsibilities in Washington. Above and beyond the call of duty."

"They told me to keep my eyes and ears open for any information that might be useful to the Soviet Union."

"A delightfully euphemistic way of putting it." Brodsky leaped a small lake on the corner of Lexington. "Mr. Hoover has estimated that eighty percent of all personnel at the Soviet Embassy in Washington are spies." His gold glasses slipped and he pushed them back with his woolly mittened hand. "Who would have thought that the great Mr. Hoover would have indulged in such understatement?"

While he was waiting for Valentina to powder her nose Zhukov flipped through the Manhattan phone book. One number printed prominently at the beginning startled him. U.S. Secret Service 264-7204. It didn't seem to Vladimir Zhukov to be very secret.

26

Chapter 3

THE RED HOUSE in Washington is a grayish building on Sixteenth Street a few blocks—two-fifths of a mile maybe —from the White House. It is fairly ornate having been built for a good capitalist, Mrs. George M. Pullman, whose husband designed and built Pullman cars for America's railroads; and one of its first tenants was the Embassy of czarist Russia. But the building, four stories high including the ground floor, is a poor place compared with the great mansions of other countries ranged along Embassy Row, Massachusetts Avenue, where many expansive architectural styles vie with each other. (Here Britain seems to score with a statue of Sir Winston Churchill, who looks as if he might be hailing a bus, outside its elegant manor.) The Russians are perpetually aggrieved at the faded modesty of their home, but the Americans decline to do anything about it until they are given a better embassy in Moscow. Likewise the Russians refuse the Americans more resplendent accommodation until they are given more prestigious premises in Washington; this childish intractability is often said to be symbolic of the two powers' attitudes toward settling larger issues such as wars.

A small driveway leads up to the door, only twenty feet from the sidewalk. The windows have balconies; there is an undistinguished tree, pleading to be struck by lightning, in the small front garden, wire netting around the hedge, some interesting aerials on the roof arranged in the sort of art forms that normally outrage the Kremlin. Outside a West German Volkswagen or two, with diplomatic plates, which seem to indicate that ideological differences need not stand in the way of commercial economy.

27

Among the embassy's neighbors are the *National Geographic* magazine and the University Club. The Washington *Post* lies around the corner.

A little way down Sixteenth from the embassy CIA agent Joseph Costello sat at the wheel of his Thunderbird chewing on a dead cigar butt and privately expressing his opinion on what Mother Russia could do to herself. Snow mixed with freezing rain bounded along the street encasing the car in ice. And what's more he wouldn't put it past the stupid bastard to walk: he wouldn't put it past a Russian to break the ice on the Potomac and go for a swim.

But I know my limitations, Joe Costello, Vietnam veteran and hero, acknowledged. Not for me the cocktail parties with the Beautiful People. I am strictly for surveillance and I am eternally grateful for the opportunities afforded me by my heroism (refusing to act stupid in front of my buddies) under enemy fire. Costello, hairy, squat and honest, further confided to himself: I wish to hell I'd made the grade as a professional football player for the Redskins. Still, I'm lucky to have a job like this, a cut above the FBI, two cuts above the precinct.

But surveillance on a shitty night like this! And for what? All he knew was that he had to follow the Russian and make sure that the meet with the State Department clerk took place as scheduled and that the Soviets didn't try and hijack the clerk or anything. As far as he, Joe Costello, was concerned, he would be very happy if they put a bullet in the State Department guy's guts if he was a traitor. But who was he to express an opinion? Just surveillance.

Tardovsky, tall and thin and unmistakable, emerged from the embassy. Please get in your nice comfy little Volks, old buddy. But the Russian bent his thin neck into the rain and snow and walked quickly down Sixteenth.

You son of a bitch! Costello got out of the car quietly and spat the cigar butt onto the sidewalk.

The meet was supposed to be in a bar on Fourteenth,

where pornography and bar flesh prospered alongside the palatial seats of national and world power. Very dark, probably, with a dirty movie grunting along in the background.

Tardovsky was heading in the right direction. But hadn't anyone told him that Washington was the worst city in the States for getting mugged? And what the hell did he do if the Russian *was* jumped? On Fourteenth anything could happen.

On this sad street the orifice-filled bookshops and the girlie clip joints were doing fair trade. A few bums, junkies and sharply dressed blacks hung around the doorways. Jesus, Costello thought, right on the President's doorstep.

Then he became aware that he was maybe not the only tail on Tardovsky. Behind the two of them he sensed another shadow. They were about to play games. But who the hell was the playmate?

Tardovsky entered the bar just off Fourteenth and sat down at a table. On the screen a long way down the tunnel of the bar a couple stripped and simulated copulation; the girl showed her genitals with abandoment, her lover was more coy—maybe he was ashamed of them, Costello thought.

Tardovsky ordered a beer and took his hat off. Right, Costello thought—you should take off your hat in the presence of a lady. He sat way behind Tardovsky and glanced at his wach; five minutes till the meet. He ordered a scotch from the girl in the crotch-high black skirt.

The second shadow sat down to the left of Costello, three tables away. Costello took a look at him. Very wet, like himself, very cold. Powerful looking, impossible to distinguish his features behind the turned-up collar of his bulky topcoat.

Why hadn't they told him more? "Just keep your eye on them to make sure nothing goes wrong. Keep in touch." But they hadn't mentioned a third party who could be Russian, American, British, Czech (they ware pretty high in the espionage stakes these days). Three minutes to go.

Tardovsky, who looked bored with the repetitive sex,

29

looked at his watch and went to the toilet. The man in the bulky topcoat followed. Which means I have to follow too, Costello decided.

But the toilet wasn't designed for espionage or the prevention thereof. With two big men bulging in the confined space behind him, Tardovsky didn't bother to finish what he was doing at the stall. He zipped, ducked between them with giraffe agility and was gone.

"Shit," said Costello. He turned to follow.

"Not so fast," said the other man, his face blond and fierce behind the collar.

"Who the hell are you?"

"Who the hell are *you* buddy?"

"It doesn't matter now." Costello heaved toward the door.

"Oh, yes, it does. Sure it does." The stranger chopped at Costello's neck but hit his elbow on the wall. Costello got him in the stomach with two karate fingers, although the topcoat blunted the impact.

They fought savagely for a couple of minutes. But the toilet wasn't designed for pugilism either. So they identified themselves and, while the faucet over the stall urinated noisily, silently contemplated their plight.

On the screen in the bar corner the young man indicated facially that orgasm was near, while the girl sighed with what could have been ecstasy or frustration.

The personality of Wallace J. Walden was split down the middle on the subject of his capital city. He reveled in its dignified masonry, smooth lawns, stern statues, its libraries and museums and broad avenues, the stately homes of President and government, the Washington Monument poised like a stone rocket set for launching. He loved to see tourists patrolling beneath Japanese cherry trees and expressing admiration at such a grateful seat of power. Sometimes he interrupted—"I couldn't help overhearing" —and set them straight on historic facts: Washington offered five hundred dollars for a design for the Capitol and Dr. William Thorton from Tortola in the West Indies won (Italian Renaissance, you understand), the city was originally conceived by Pierre Charles L'Enfant, a protégé of Lafayette, as "a capital magnificent enough to grace a great nation. And did you know that Washington who chose the site here in Maryland and Virginia was a surveyor himself? Few people seem to know that. . . ." Then he gave them the Visitors Information Service number (347-4554) before moving on to survey the Reflecting Pool, pillared palaces of bureaucracy, the spruce, beech and magnolia, with an awe and pride that had survived twenty-five years' acquaintanceship.

The split occurred because Wallace J. Walden detested Washington's principal industry—politics. Or, more particularly, he disliked intriguing politicians. Which was ironic because Walden's own job was intrigue.

He admired ambition but abhorred its crude application; if there was one person he disliked more than a Senator peddling a cause with votes in mind, rather than humanity, it was a Senator's wife pursuing the same objective over tea or martinis. Jesus, he thought this glacial morning as he walked beside the whispering ice on the Tidal Basin, God save us from the women of Washington. (He was both a blasphemous and God-fearing man.) But, like it or not, Washington was a women's city, every secretary trying to do a Jackie Kennedy. Only last night he had read in the *Evening Star* that the president of the Democratic Congressional Wives' Forum was advising freshmen lawmakers to employ professional comedians to spike their speeches with gags. If they had their way, Walden ruminated without humor, Bob Hope would become President. Or Bill Cosby.

The wind blew eddies of snow across the ice separating Walden from Thomas Jefferson standing on pink Tennessee marble behind the white portico of his dome. *"I have sworn upon the altar of God eternal hostility against every form of tyranny over the mind of man."* So had Walden. He regretted that the means to his end involved intrigue, subterfuge and murder. But he had no doubts that the means justified the end.

He gulped down the iced air hungrily, felt the cold polish his cheeks. A lonely figure with heavy pipe gurgling,

31

welted shoes marching firmly on the crusty ground, hat never too firm on the springs of his graying cropped hair.

Here every morning, after leaving his wife and enigmatic teen-age children in Bethesda, Walden assembled his day. Today he was thankful for the ache in the air because, to an extent, it numbed his anger at the stupidity that had once again spoiled an inspired maneuver.

Tardovsky had been a prospective defector. One of the intellectuals who had smelled liberty, nibbled at abundant living, appreciated the ripe fruits of democracy. A patriot, sick of doctrinaire Socialism, hesitating on the portals of freedom. Now he was lost forever.

Walden had decided that Tardovsky was not the man to be courted with gifts, sleek-limbed girls on Delaware beaches, visits to perfect American homes with gentle and obvious persuasion over blueberry pie. So his honest, devious mind had considered other ploys. A doubter from the Soviet Embassy meeting a doubter from the State Department. Together they would renounce the duplicity of both great powers and seek refuge in some snowbound haven in Canada—where all the American trash found bolt-holes. But even if Tardovsky had ended up in Toronto or Montreal the defection would have occurred in the capital of the United States. A highly prestigious landmark on the road to The Final Solution: universal understanding of the Communist (and atheist) myth.

The FBI had been pursuing the scheme energetically. A phony State Department traitor had been established. Then apparently the CIA had got wind of the stool pigeon's double-dealing and, never for one second allowing for the possibility of double double-dealing, had arranged its own surveillance without confiding its plans.

Result: A fishfight in a men's room in a dirty movie bar.

Thus, through the offices of bumbling incompetents did tyranny survive. Thank God the KGB was also served by incompetents who did everything by the book. If only I had the Mafia on my side . . .

Walden left the gaze of Jefferson, entered the spectrum of Lincoln and watched the children skating on the Reflecting Pool; it was their future he was fighting for. A jet rose heavily from the National Airport, keeping ominously low to restrict its noise, laboring over Lincoln's Colorado marble shrine of freedom, justice, immortality, fraternity and charity. The qualities he had to preserve.

The grumbling line of traffic on Constitution Avenue opened at a red light and Walden crossed, heading for the State Department where he coordinated the various intelligence organizations behind a vague political title. That bum Costello! The heating in the lobby of this throbbing modern building, the laboratory of American influence, escalated his anger—a menacing, inexorable quantity not unlike the lurking hatreds of the intriguing church dignitaries of history.

Walden summoned to his office that morning the heads of Security and Consular Affairs, Intelligence and Research, and Politico-Military Affairs. Also the deputy heads of the FBI and the CIA.

"Gentlemen," said Walden, handing around cigars, "a fiasco was perpetrated in our city last night. It is probably not necessary for me to say that, to an extent, we are all responsible."

The ensuing silence did not imply unqualified agreement.

"It *is* our joint responsibility, goddamnit!" He picked up his pipe. "I'm sorry, gentlemen, but I'm disgusted at the way this operation has been handled."

Jack Godwin from the CIA, a shifty egghead in Walden's opinion, with an irritating habit of detaching morsels of tobacco from the tip of his tongue like a conjuror, ventured an opinion that, as the operation had been Walden's brainchild, the failure was his responsibility. "Just like you would have accepted the plaudits if it'd been a success."

Walden turned on him. "If you had kept me informed of your suspicions this foul-up would never have happened. Surely to Christ the CIA is aware by now that its primary function is overseas intelligence?"

"Sure we realize that," Godwin said. "But with practically every foreign country represented in Washington our job begins at home."

"You could coordinate with the Federal men. You could perhaps trust them to pass on to you any information they think you need."

Godwin shrugged. "How do they know what we need?"

Arnold Hardin from the FBI said, "It's not outside our capabilities." A neat, late-middle-aged man, sarcastic and ingenious, as tidy as Godwin was unkempt.

The other three participants from the State Department kept their counsel. A secretary bearing coffee came into the aseptically chic office with its multiple telephones, maps of Moscow indicating the limits within which Americans could move, its photographs of the President, Vice President and Secretary of State, its small battery of reference books which included the Bible.

The five of them stirred and sipped and waited.

Finally Gale Blair from Security and Consular Affairs said, "You shouldn't take it so hard, Mr. Walden. Think of all the successes." She was a smart, kindly woman.

They all thought hard.

Crawford from Politico-Military said, "The FBI didn't do too badly when they caught the Czechs trying to bug the office of Eastern European Affairs."

"Thank you," said Hardin, crossing elegant legs, flicking dust from a polished toe cap. "But don't forget to thank Frank Mrkua, the passport courier who made it possible by cooperating with us."

"And we should also be thankful to the FBI," said Godwin, spilling coffee on his lived-in jacket, "for tapping the German Embassy and finding evidence of the Nazi-Soviet pact. In 1939," he added, timing it nicely.

Crawford, a diligent and enthusiastic man, said, "The FBI also nailed Wennerstrom. They've got a whole bevy of defectors in the past couple of years. And what about this guy they caught making a drop under the railway bridge in Queens—he's helped bust the Soviet network wide open. And the Soviets still think he's working for them," Crawford supplied in case anyone present didn't know.

"Maybe he is," Godwin grunted.

Hardin sharpened his voice. "I sometimes wonder when

34

they come to write the definitive history of the CIA whether they'll record the occasion when bugs were found inside the eagle the Soviets presented to the American Embassy in Moscow."

Intelligence and Research spoke for the first time. "At least they were found." William Bruno, recognized as a shrewd nut; a reputation enhanced by his deep and golden silences. What went on in his Machiavellian mind during those contemplative periods? Bruno, thirty-fiveish with ambassadorial ambitions, was too shrewd a nut to tell anyone.

"Jesus Christ . . . ," Godwin began.

Walden cut him short. "Let's get back to the goddamn point before we start on Penkovsky or the U-2." He stuck his pipe in his mouth. "We have to find a substitute for Tardovsky. He's so scared now he won't ask an American the way to the john. Any ideas?" He turned to Hardin. "How are the infiltration stakes on Sixteenth?"

Hardin made neat replies. "Pretty much the same as usual. A few bugs installed, most of them discovered. It's tricky when all the manual work is done by Russians and even the cleaning's done by the wives. But as you know or should know"—he looked at Godwin—"most of our approaches are made these days through other embassies. They work through the Cubans or Czechs, we use the Canadians and the British."

Walden said, "But we could do with a good defector with all the inside dope. A name to make a splash like Dotsenko. Another Krotkov. And we need him in the United States, right here in Washington. We need something good and powerful to counter some of the lousy publicity our country has been getting lately. Don't forget"—he stared at them individually—"that it's a war we're fighting here. A war in which nearly the whole world's involved—one hundred and fourteen ambassadors, twenty-five hundred diplomats. It's a war more important even than World War Two because the enemy is more powerful. It's a war democracy has to win." His fingers reached out and touched the Bible.

Gale Blair said she understood perfectly and she was sure she spoke for everyone.

Walden swept on, massaging the graying stubble of his hair, pouring himself a cardboard cup of ice water. "The Communists have determined on an all-out bid to penetrate our intelligence agencies, our departments of State and Defense, our technological organizations, Congress itself —and I'm quoting from the forthcoming FBI report *Subversion from Abroad*. It's essential that we find a way of penetrating their headquarters in Washington—the goddamn embassy itself. It's my job to coordinate this operation. So please," he said, holding up his hands, "no more internecine feuding. For Christ's sake let's not have any more foul-ups like last night. That wasn't just any old foul-up, gentlemen, that was a military defeat." He tossed back the water as if it were neat vodka. "Now, any ideas?" He picked up a folder on his desk. "What about this new man, for instance? What's his name?" He opened the folder. "Vladimir Zhukov. What do we know about him?"

Hardin extinguished his cigar with a quick stab. "I guess that's your department, Godwin. How much did your guys in Moscow get on him?"

Godwin pulled a folder identical to the one on Walden's desk from a bulging briefcase that looked as if it might contain sandwiches. "As a matter of fact," he said in his loose voice, "Comrade Zhukov *is* a possibility. No more than that. A faint, faint possibility."

"If he's any *kind* of a possibility," Walden said, "then it's up to us to make him into a probability."

"It's very vague," Godwin mumbled.

Hardin said, "Don't play games. If you've got something tell us what it is."

"It's just that he writes poetry," Godwin said.

Godwin and Hardin stopped to talk in the hallway a few yards from Walden's office, beside a sign bearing the words FALLOUT SHELTER IN THIS CORRIDOR.

"Jesus," Godwin said. "What a pompous bastard he is."

Hardin nodded impatiently. "Maybe. A ruthless one,

36

too. But he comes up with some good ideas. Like the little scheme we goofed on last night."

"We?"

"Oh, come on, Godwin. Forget your worldwide network just this once. You're here in Washington—the capital of the little old United States. Sure, *we* goofed. And you know it. And Walden's right—we've got to come up with something. So let's you and I go and have coffee and work on it *together*."

Godwin regarded him with massive, rumpled suspicion. "Okay, let's go." He was still holding his thin dossier on Vladimir Zhukov.

Hardin opened his expensive black and silver attaché case. "By the way, I've got one of those too." He took out another folder marked Vladimir Zhukov.

"I know," Godwin said, "we circulated it to you."

Chapter 4

IN A STUDENT'S living room in Alma-Ata near the Kazakh State University a girl of eighteen with braided hair—now loosened—and wide eyes, just a little Mongolian, surrendered her virginity with enthusiasm.

She anticipated the textbook possibility of pain and absence of sensual feeling—"the pleasure will come later, my dear." But it was there the first time. Insistent pressure from his hard muscle, then, oh! like a finger through parchment. And as he filled her the pleasure was instant, mounting, so that she clawed and bit and cried out, "I love you, Georgi. Oh, I love you."

Not that Natasha Zhukova did love Georgi Makarov. But, she decided, I am certainly going to enjoy sex. With a few selected and privileged men who were clean and strong, handsome and intelligent; particularly intelligent. Like Georgi with his muscled belly, arrogant features—a little petulant sometimes—and his defiantly shaggy hair. A few such selected affairs before marriage and children and fidelity. I hope I'm not pregnant, she thought in alarm as his fluid escaped; but still, abortion was a mere formality.

"I'm sorry, Natasha Zhukova," Georgi said, lying back and lighting a cigarette and not looking sorry at all.

"Don't be so bourgeois," she said irritably. Beneath the coarse blanket she explored the expended muscle, limp and sad. Such was the transcience of masculinity; she would have liked to try it again.

Her thoughts wandered from the satisfied body beside her and wondered what sex would be like with the man she loved. If mere physical attraction could produce such earthy pleasure what delight lay ahead when love partnered consummation?

Another alarming thought: What if the man she loved and wished to marry despised her because she wasn't a virgin? Wasn't it Lenin himself who had said, "Does a normal man under normal circumstances, drink from a glass from which others have drunk?" But, Natasha reassured herself, the alarm was academic: She would never love a man so narrow-minded. And it was certainly too late—by about five minutes—to worry.

The trouble with Soviet morals was that they were so confused. The party denounced promiscuity but made abortion easier than a visit to the dentist, and divorce not much harder. And only fifty or so years ago, before the glorious Revolution, a red cloth used to be flown over a bride's house if she turned out to be a virgin, a white cloth if she didn't. And when she was eight, only ten years ago, Natasha had read in *Komsomolka* about a girl, suspected of adultery with a married man, who had been solemnly advised to visit a clinic and get a certificate of virginity to display to her accusers.

Nowadays the party was more concerned with general liberalism, with suppressing free expression. Natasha agreed with most Kremlin edicts. Its foreign policy

38

(vaguely), its calls for collective effort to farm and weld and research, it severity with drunks and those who were not sufficiently energetic in building Socialism. Although she became quickly bored with the dreariness of their pronouncements.

What Natasha Zhukova could not countenance was the Kremlin's treatment of intellectuals. Georgi Makarov was an intellectual. And a rebel, too. Every girl was attracted by a rebel. She slid her fingers through his thick brown hair, cut and combed with a suspicion of decadence.

"You're a strange girl, Natasha Zhukova," Georgie said. "The others have always cried."

She knew he expected her to whine, "Others? Have there been others?" Instead she said, "What's there to cry about? It happens to most girls at some time or another." She also knew that he resented such practical reactions; they were the property of men.

"Have you no romance in your soul?"

"Of course—I am Russian. I have the soul of the taiga. And I am almost a Kazakh so I have the soul of the mountains. Or"—she turned on her side and grinned at him— "a ripe Oporto apple waiting to be plucked."

He shifted petulantly on the bed and lit another cigarette; his fingers were tobacco-stained like those of all true revolutionaries. Except that his revolution was confined to a few secret essays, a signature on a petition seeking the release of Daniel and Sinyavsky, a few progressive jazz records. Outwardly it was all virile protest; inwardly bewilderment at the conflicting calls of patriotism and enlightenment.

Georgi said, "You sound like one of those American women with their demands for equality and free love. By love they mean sex. Conveyor belt sex. A woman should love from the heart."

"And not a man?"

The rebel shrugged.

"It seems to me," Natasha suggested, "that the Americans and British are a long way behind us in many ways. We had the revolution of the sexes after the great Revolution. 'Down with bourgeois morality.' Wasn't that the cry?

39

Didn't Alexandra Kollontay preach that we women should free ourselves from the enslavement of love to one man? Don't the older women still talk rapturously of those days when virginity was held up to mockery?"

"Attitudes have changed again," Georgi told her. "Extremes always follow revolution. We have come to our senses again. Only the West pursues self-indulgence. Like the Romans—and the Romanovs—the people of the West are pursuing their own self-destruction." He sat up self-importantly.

Natasha stood up and walked to the window. Naked, enjoying his gaze. She looked across her father's city, blurred with gentle snow that belied the dagger of winter. The City of Apples, *karagachs,* Lombardy poplars and birch trees, of wooden cathedrals floating with gold husks, of apartment blocks as standard as dogma, of ditches that sang with melting snow in the spring. And, of course, V. I. Lenin in the central square: a reminder, stern but gentle, of the dangers of too much frivolous appreciation.

And beyond Alma-Ata . . . the cuff of crumpled mountains, burnished wheat in the virgin lands, the gold of Ust-Kamenogorsk, the grapes of Chimkent, the sounds of stars above the launching pad at Baikonur. All helping to confuse allegiances: to the Republic of Kazakhstan ("We occupy one-eighth of the Soviet Union and we are still regarded as peasants"), to Russia, to the party, to young private doubt.

"Georgi," she said, turning her back on him, proud of her smooth arching back, "why do we only read criticism about the West? Drugs, racism, exploitation." *Pravda's* dictionary opened up in her mind. "There must be a lot of benefits from life in America and Britain." She knew she was being naïve.

"Because impressionable young language students like you might get ideas."

"And you . . . don't you get ideas? About music, about art, about self-expression? Isn't that what your protest is all about? That writers here can't write the truth as they can in the West?"

40

"We do what we do for ourselves and for our country—even if our country doesn't appreciate it. We don't imitate what they do in the West."

"Why are copies of that magazine you read smuggled out to the West then?"

"So that they don't believe all they read about Russia." He wrapped a sheet around his waist, more shy after love than this formidable girl at the window, and stood beside her.

"That's what's so sad," she said. She felt the warmth of his body behind her, smelled his sweat. "We don't know the truth about America and I'm sure few Americans know the truth about us."

About our gaiety most of all. Sad that the Americans never heard guitars strumming in the parks, smelled stews cooking in communal apartment blocks, ate cheese and sausage sandwiches and drank *kvas* at student parties, sang and cried (drunk even on mineral water), camped on river beaches, kissed on steamers. To Americans, Natasha suspected, Russia was a prison camp. And the smuggled literature of Georgi and his dangerous friends only encouraged that belief; it was ironic that all this free thought only made the picture of Russia blacker.

"The West must know the truth," Georgi, who was studying political science, had explained.

"But they already know everything bad about Russia."

"Only from their own propagandists."

"And what about our propagandists?"

"Their work is so crude that no one in the West bothers to print it."

"So no one in America ever reads anything good about the country?"

"I suppose not. And no one here ever reads anything good about America because their own propaganda is just as crude and no one bothers to reprint it here."

"It's very bewildering," Natasha pronounced. "No one seems to make the effort to tell the truth. Either about themselves or the——" She had hesitated then.

"Or the enemy?"

41

"I was searching for a more suitable word. But what chance have any of us if no one tries to explain?"

He had kissed her fondly, patronizingly. "I am glad you're studying languages and not philosophy or logic or politics." Stick to your English and your sweet singing, his tone indicated.

But that was before they'd made love. Now the arrogance had receded, a dog's bark lost in a blizzard. Paradoxically her loss had given her strength, and the spirit of Alexandra Kollontay stirred within her. She giggled and led her confused lover back to the bed. The snow had stopped and the late sun cast dying light on the City of Apples. A snowplow prowled, a branch of silver birch, ice-sheathed and glittering with diamanté, scratched the window.

"How much longer do we have?" Natasha asked.

"About half an hour. Yuri and Boris are very tactful."

"Since when?" asked Natasha, thinking of Georgi's two boisterous roommates.

"They understand."

"You mean you made a pact with them to stay away while you deflowered a poor virgin?"

Georgi denied it—so indignantly that Natasha knew he was lying. She was pleased with this new insight into the behavior of men. She told him not to be so dramatic; *someone* had to deflower her.

"Is that all it meant to you?"

Instinctively she knew that it was the woman who usually said that. "You were a wonderful lover," she said, taking up the script.

"How would you know about that?"

"Certainly I can't make any comparisons. But you were wonderful." She combed his hair with her fingers so that it fell in a thick fringe across his forehead. How many more scripts? She was not even sure what sort of man she would love. Big and strong and brainy was all very well, but she knew that such statutory requirements were discarded when love (not infatuation—she was prepared for that treacherous experience) finally surfaced.

She looked down at Georgi the rebel with affection. He

42

is an attractive boy and at least we share bewilderment. And now, I think, a little honesty. She brushed a nipple across his face, felt his sharp ribs, hips, the awakening phallus—more arrogant now than its owner.

Then he made love to her again. Or was it the other way around? Anyway, it was even better than the first time.

"Georgi," she said, pulling in her gray skirt and black sweater, "don't you think you should get your hair cut just a little?"

"You sound like a wife already," he grumbled. He lingered on the bed, probably hoping to be caught in the middle of dressing—the conquering lover disturbed. How shallow, how presumptuous, how conceited. Perhaps she should say, "There he is, gentlemen, I have just seduced him. He's all yours."

She said, "I was only thinking of your own safety. The other night a Komsomol patrol grabbed a student off the street and forcibly cut his hair. They also read his notebooks."

Georgi shrugged. "It's a cheap way to get a haircut."

"But your notebooks, Georgi. . . ."

"I'm not stupid enough to write anything incriminating in them." He lit another cigarette. "Anyway they probably only did it for a little fun. It's their job to stop hooliganism. There's nothing wrong with that, is there?"

Natasha agreed that there wasn't and began to braid her long shiny hair. She searched herself for the irreparable sense of loss that was supposed to accompany the loss of the maidenhead. She felt only satisfaction and a little soreness.

Georgi continued to lecture. "Although there are still changes to be made we're lucky to be young now, in 1968. No Stalin, no Beria, no two A.M. knocks on the door. And also we're just young enough not to have been too badly affected by Khrushchev's denunciation of Stalin. In 1956," he added in case she wasn't too good on contemporary history. "Can you imagine what it must have meant to those kids? Why, once upon a time they used to sing a hymn to

43

Stalin." He sung a few bars. *"Leader, scattering darkness like sun, Conscience of the world, Luminary of the ages, Glory to him."*

They heard footsteps outside and a tentative knock. Georgi leaped out of bed, pulling on undershirt and pants. "Answer the door, Natasha. That'll be Boris and Yuri."

She smiled at him with maternal indulgence and went to the door.

The two plainclothes policemen pushed past her. "Georgi Makarov," one of them said, "please finish dressing and come with us."

Chapter 5

IT WAS two weeks before Vladimir Zhukov staged his first unspectacular revolt. But the desire to buy was drooling in him. More than thirty years' preparation for the impact of bloated capitalism and I am like a kid with five rubles to spend in a toy store.

Valentina observed his craving with contempt. "Don't forget, Vladimir, that it has nothing to do with their system. It's all a question of natural resources. And the fact that the settlers in America were the toughest and bravest people from Europe. And, of course, they avoided the devastation of the last war. . . ."

"I know," Vladimir said, "I attended that lecture, too."

In any case her nagging was unnecessary. He despised the gluttony of living. But when in Rome. . . . Would it do any harm to taste a little of the plunder? A single orgy couldn't corrupt. A practical experience of decadent extravagance.

He began gently. At a drugstore on Du Pont Circle called the People's Drug—the name soothed his guilt. But even in this humble American mart the horn of plenty sounded loud in Zhukov's ears. Stationery, perfume, magazines, paperbacks, ice cream, pills and potions to ease the punishments of gluttony.

But it's difficult to spend money after a lifetime of frugality, Zhukov discovered. He bought a comb and a tube of pink transparent toothpaste which Valentina might prefer to her tin of powder. So hard to spend and so easy to pay: no abacus, no hour-long queues, no trips from counter to cashier and back.

Shyly he ordered a cream soda from a daydreaming black girl. Slyly added a dollop of ice cream. Then furtively treated himself to a hot dog, squirting it thick with mustard, burying the punchy-skinned sausage in green relish; swallowing some paper napkin with his first bite.

The waitress said, "You go on eatin' like that and you're goin' to be a plenty sick man."

The schoolboy Zhukov apologized. "I didn't have any breakfast." But his accent defeated and bored her. She moved indolently away, gawky-limbed and graceful.

But why feel shame, Comrade Zhukov? Aren't Muscovites the greatest eaters in the world? Stuffing themselves with creamy borsch, fat meats, black bread, cucumbers, potatoes, the *gurievskaya* kasha that Valentina cooked so well, the salted pig fat on thick bread that peasants still ate, the finest and creamiest ice cream in the world. I shouldn't feel shame at eating these synthetic snacks. He prodded the floating ice cream with disdain. And coffee, perhaps, to complete the culinary adventure. The girl who wore a blue-black wig slid him a cup and he experimented with the cushion of sugar and tiny pot of cream as if he were in a laboratory.

As he paid at the cash desk he belched.

He urged himself on past stockades of root beer and Coke, hesitated at cosmetics. Juices of conceit, long corked, spurted. He remembered women at May Day and Revolution anniversary parties paying him compliments capsuled in bubbles of Russian champagne. "You are an attractive man, Vladimir Zhukov. Not handsome, perhaps, but you have strong features and a commanding presence.

45

That is what women like." The flirtatious heritage of czarist sophistry still giggling beneath stern Socialist surfaces.

Zhukov bought some hair dressing said to be enriched with protein and headed back to the apartment with his guilty purchases in a brown paper bag under his arm.

So ended the first unspectacular revolt.

The second followed a few days later. Because the lust had not been sated, the experience of decadence not fully assimilated.

In his West German bug Zhukov drove first to Hecht's on Seventh and F where he had been told by colleagues that there was many a bargain to be had and no Russian need feel too badly about distributing his puny allowance there because didn't the underprivileged and victimized blacks shop there? They certainly did, Zhukov discovered; and so did many whites who had once shopped at Garfinckel's before glimpsing the dark waters of recession beneath the tissue ice of prosperity.

Again he was intoxicated by the profusion of merchandise. Broad silk ties, corduroy and soft suede jackets, fragments of lingerie, shirts which only homosexuals outside the Bolshoi in Moscow would have worn, novelties, Valentine cards already, drapes, perfumes. . . . The disinclination to spend was still strong in him, but his arms were growing longer, his pockets shorter.

In Hecht's Vladimir Zhukov, uncomfortably aware of his styleless clothes, bought a wide silver tie lined with blue satin and a broad leather belt with a peace buckle, designed to hold up nothing (except, perhaps, a slumping belly) but which might come in handy for beating a wife. Or vice versa.

The young man who served him confided that the belt might be the basis of a new image for Zhukov. "We don't want to draw attention to the approach of middle age, do we, sir?" He withdrew his hand from Zhukov's sweating nylon shirt with alacrity.

Outside Zhukov observed the droppings of soiled snow —and heard the scrape of old women's shovels on the sidewalks of Moscow.

He climbed into his stone-colored Volkswagen and drove

to a supermarket. Its cornucopia was the biggest shock of all. Not just the frozen, packaged, price-cut, sliced, chopped, condensed, fortified, concentrated, dehydrated, evaporated, regimented abundance of it all. No, it was the permutations; the calculating ingenuity of choice: simple selection grated hopefully into shreds that might appeal to different ages, sexes, races, colors, types. An indulgent carve-up of what had once been ordinary shared hunger.

Take olives, for instance. Not particularly favored by Vladimir Zhukov; nevertheless the pure stony fruit of history, to be eaten with goat cheese beside a hill where shepherds rested under the olive trees' undistinguished branches. Here, in an avenue of cartons and deep-freeze troughs, they rested in specimen bottles: black salad olives, manzanilla olives stuffed with sweet peppers, water, salt and lactic acid, pitted olives, Spanish olives stuffed with pimentos, giant California olives . . .

Influenced as always by old movies, Vladimir Zhukov had always fancied orange juice with his breakfast—prior to coffee and toast and kidneys served from a silver platter. But perhaps he was old-fashioned. Frozen concentrates of lemonade, pink lemonade(!), grape, apple, iced tea, Hawaiian Punch, peach and orange. And there at the end of the surgical trough the cold cylinders of pure frozen orange juice.

He walked away with nothing, selectivity battered senseless.

But I will buy some sausage, he thought. The sausage that as a student I used to wolf between dry bread while the vodka bottle circulated. Bologna, liverwurst, salami, turkey salami, blood and tongue, corned beef, chicken loaf, olive loaf, hot Italian loaf . . .

"Some sausage, please," he said to the scrubbed young man in the chef's hat.

"What kind of sausage?"

"Any kind."

"You got to make the choice, buddy. It's you that's eating it, not me."

Zhukov pointed wildly at a gnarled pink forearm of meat.

47

"How much do you want?"

Zhukov indicated with his hands—"About that much" —popped the sausage into his still-empty shopping cart and hurried away to rally his powers of choice beside the mixes —whiskey sour, pussycat, diaquiri, gimlet, Bloody Mary and Tom Collins—stacked beside root beer, birch beer, spruce beer, grape soda, black cherry soda . . .

He rested there, drunk with choice, as Nicolai Grigorenko hove past, his basket on wheels stacked high with decadence.

"Greetings, comrade," Zhukov said, sanctimonious about his single tube of sausage.

Grigorenko turned as quickly as a man going for a gun. Alarm, suspicion, menace; then a blush of guilt on his drooping face. But he attacked just the same. "What are you doing here, Comrade Zhukov?"

"Observing the fleshpots of capitalist degeneracy. And you, comrade?"

The Growler faltered. "Just doing a little shopping for one of the counselors." Inspiration assembled slowly. "He's giving a party for some French diplomats. You know how they like to eat," he added hopefully.

"I do indeed, comrade." He appraised Grigorenko's basket of loot. "How will the counselor serve aerosol shaving cream?"

"That is for the counselor himself. It is his only weakness."

"If American shaving cream is his only weakness then he is a very fortunate man."

Grigorenko nodded heavily, already planning further explanations and revenge. But for the time being I've got you on the defensive, Zhukov thought with satisfaction. It was quite an achievement to score over an officer of the KGB, however slight the indictment.

He picked up a small cardboard can from Grigorenko's pile. "Lemonade, eh? Another Gallic specialty?" He read the label and smiled. "I'm pleased to observe that it is pink lemonade, Comrade Grigorenko."

Grigorenko growled and departed. With an easier conscience Zhukov began piling many permutations of decadence into his own basket. Starting with chunky blue cheese dressing.

The embassy was jumping, but the ambassador didn't jump with it. He had survived too many international crises in his Sixteenth Street kremlin to be overexcited by the seizure by the North Koreans of the American spy ship *Pueblo;* besides he had a heart condition.

The trick was to smooth each crisis into the day's working routine that began at his desk at 8 A.M. and finished at midnight. Never agitate yourself—particularly in public —like Khrushchev or a Senator exposing corruption; composure was one of the essences of diplomacy, even if it wasn't always appreciated by the hawks of Moscow. But Soviet diplomats were at last learning the sophisticated approach, and he, Valentin Zuvorin, considered that he had overtaken the Americans in the delicate art. A smile, a half-truth, a witticism: a swift rapier thrust of assertion through lowered defenses. Thus one President had been moved to call him a liar, another had told him to "quit horsing around." Small victories of behavior—even if policies had been defeated.

Zuvorin picked up the phone in his high-ceilinged, somewhat czarist office, and called the press counselor. "What's Moscow putting out on the *Pueblo* affair?"

The counselor began to read a Tass report of an article in *Izvestia.* There was the usual line on American aggressive intent and expansionism, plus a suggestion that the American President was using the incident as a pretext to call up reserves for Vietnam.

"Thank you," Zuvorin said, as the predictable tirade continued.

"But . . ."

Zuvorin hung up. Competent of its kind and ineffectual. The language of protest blunted by repetition. Even the outrage over Vietnam had lost its impact, like the lingering atrocity of the war. If only the propagandists would seek some diplomatic style.

He sipped his lemon tea and scanned the dispatches from Moscow. Aid pouring in to the Arabs who would squander at least half of it; such waste because of political necessity. During the Six-Day War Zuvorin had privately enjoyed some of the jokes. "Come to Israel and see the pyramids." He smiled again now; you had to admire the flyweight prizefighter felling the heavyweight. The rapier over the machete. Not that Valentin Zuvorin doubted the Kremlin policy in the Middle East, because ultimately it would be a victory for Socialism. And he believed steadfastly in socialism.

And now Czechoslovakia. Antonin Novotny had been ousted from his post as first secretary of the party—a job he had held for fifteen years. *Soon I shall have to lie again and eventually my lies will be exposed. Because the Czechs will try to break away and they will have to be taught a lesson.* Zuvorin admired their spirit; but, sadly, blood had to be spilled, tissue destroyed, in the ultimate surgery on mankind.

Although, in the camouflaged recesses of his soul, Valentin Zuvorin loathed and feared aggression, as anyone who had lived through the siege of Leningrad well might. He endured the humiliation of the Cuban missile crisis because a world war had been averted; he secretly rejoiced when the Arabs capitulated to the Jews, when the Koreans came to terms; he grieved before sleep at the plodding tragedy of Vietnam. He envisaged a time—not in his day—when the world solved its problems through diplomacy. Provided the settlement favored Socialism.

The ambassador's philosophies were complicated by one particular factor: He had come to regard Washington as more of a home than Moscow. He enjoyed the company of many of its inmates and considered John F. Kennedy to have been the finest man he had ever known. Such was his easy absorption into the Washington scene that he had been summoned to the Kremlin to explain his attitudes. How had he arrived at the conclusion that the President did not want to escalate—even the new phraseology of war was ugly—the Vietnam hostilities into an all-out attack on Socialism? "Because, gentlemen, I know the President and, with respect, you don't." So Soviet and American leaders had subsequently met and now the

50

Kremlin was willing to talk about missile disarmament.

A small aching protest behind the sternum. Zuvorin took a white tablet (American) with his last sip of tepid tea.

How much longer before his recall? Until they found another man as fluent and deceptively amiable in his conversations with the Americans as Valentin Zuvorin. A difficult task, the ambassador flattered himself.

Within limits he enjoyed the socializing. The guarded banter, the outrageous flattery. "You are so suave, Mr. Ambassador. So witty—so unlike so many other Russians. . . ." Hand to the mouth at the martini indiscretion. Himself—he only took two drinks, no more. But, of course, flattery, however flagrant, always worked. He cherished his reputation for cultivated conversation; his laugh, he had been told, was a pleasure to hear.

How dreary, by comparison, were the parties given by his Socialist allies. Valentin Zuvorin ducked the gaze of V. I. Lenin high on the wall.

Black ties and banquets and cocktails. Such dismay when he declined vodka—"I bought it especially for you" —and took whiskey. World affairs and American politics bundled together into a hub of parochialism in which treaties and pacts were as casually treated as village-green boundaries. Lovely girls with haughty faces offering their bodies, young men their souls. And the official spies with medals jingling, as subtle as tanks. And the spies spying on the spies; always a little obsequious, just as blatant with their trained ears and stilled tongues. And others less obvious.

Such a magnificent, incongruous phenomenon, this Washington. All its palaces of power, its burrows of bureaucracy, archives of history, vaults of intrigue, all clustered within a few blocks of celebrated architecture; squalor halted around the edges of the village green. The White House and the Capitol, the thrones of Western power, overlooking the garbage cans of domesticity.

Often Valentin Zuvorin felt sad about the American people. An emotion dangerously akin to sympathy. Their patriotism, their naïve disgust at corruption in their midst, their bright scalpels of sincerity slashing ineffectually at their cancers, their decent inability to crush dissidence as we crushed the Hungarians.

Most of all Zuvorin admired their unequivocal belief that they were right. That was their weakness. The crusaders had lost and they would lose.

The ambassador sighed. He picked up his agenda for the day. While his aides digested official anger over the *Pueblo* incident—the Americans' crime, Zuvorin privately thought, was getting caught—he would interview a newcomer to the flock. Vladimir Zhukov.

He replaced his diplomatic mask and looked Lenin straight in the eye.

The ballroom at the top of the marble stairs was empty except for a grand piano and a couple of chairs, the gloom heavy behind the half-closed drapes on the tall windows.

Zuvorin explained, "I sometimes have informal chats here because it's cooler. Did you know," he asked chattily, "that our embassy is said to be the hottest building in Washington during the winter? About eighty degrees, I believe. It's too hot. But, of course, we Russians are used to heat indoors in winter."

The ambassador appraised Zhukov. A good servant of the party, he judged. Perhaps a little too honest with himself; a mouth that betrayed a poetic soul. Although what the hell was wrong with a poetic soul from a country that had produced Tolstoy, Tchaikovsky and Pushkin, Zuvorin couldn't imagine. He was pleased that they were now sending him people instead of puppets.

Two men who had survived war and purges; one senior because of circumstance and ambition. To me he is still young, Zuvorin thought. To himself he is hopefully young. To the young themselves he is an old man—and I am senile. "And how are you enjoying Washington?"

"It's interesting," Zhukov said carefully. "Much as I imagined it."

"But still a shock to the system . . . not quite as it is painted to us before we leave the Soviet Union?"

"Not quite."

52

"You are a good diplomat, Vladimir Zhukov."

"Thank you, sir."

Not quite as it is painted! Such ludicrous understatement. Why couldn't the two of them share the truth? The oppressed masses smoking cigars and running two cars. That's what hits you. We both know it, so why not be honest with me? But he was being naïve to expect such candor between a second secretary and an ambassador. He put the two chairs in front of the grand piano because it was an unlikely nest for a microphone. Not necessarily an American microphone; there were plenty of Soviet bugs around the place. It was part of the system. Why not, if you had nothing to hide? On the other hand you could hardly expect junior members of the staff to be expansive within such a system. "What," Zuvorin asked, "has impressed you most about America?" The puppets usually denounced the exploitation—before he stopped them.

"Their houses, I think," Zhukov said.

"The houses? In what way?"

"The way they live in units. Isolated, if you like from each other." Zhukov felt his way with caution. "I just don't see how they can ever understand us. The communal soul of Russia, I mean. Their characters are so different, so self-sufficient. . . ."

Together they saw the hibernating family and friends around a stove in a wooden village hut; the city apartments with their communal kitchens and bathrooms; the old and the new settings of shared gaiety, love and strife.

"An unusual first impression, Comrade Zhukov. But I don't think for one second that they want to understand us. It is we who should try and understand them—it is we, after all, who are trying to spread Marxist-Leninism throughout the world."

"You are right, of course," Zhukov said. "But it seems a shame. . . ."

"I believe," said Zuvorin, skirting the tortuous alleys that might lie ahead, "that you speak excellent English. That is how you came to be given this post. Where did you learn the language? I must confess I am a little jealous." He waited.

53

"Your English is perfect," Zhukov said.

Zuvorin nodded happily. He *did* enjoy flattery. But at his age was it not forgivable?

"I studied languages at the university," Zhukov said. "Then I became an interpreter in the Army. I improved my English when we met the British and Americans in Berlin."

"Ah so. Our allies. They should have followed Patton's advice. Where would we be then, comrade?"

Zhukov said he didn't know where they would be.

"So that is all that has impressed you about Washington —the houses?"

"I have, of course, been struck by the standard of living."

"Of course you have," Zuvorin murmured. He offered Zhukov a cigarette. Sometimes he was surprised that more of his staff didn't defect, because he knew perfectly well that many of them contemplated it when they first tasted the milk and honey. But they were deterred by family hostages "held" in Russia, by language difficulties, by the knowledge that after the headline glamor of defection they would be misfits. Also loyalty was encouraged by promises of promotion to other Western fleshpots; and when they visited the Soviet Union they were big men, regarded with as much awe as football players or movie stars. But, the ambassador sensed, Zhukov's temptations would be different: He would taste and savor freedom of expression. And he spoke excellent English. A man to watch; but, of course, he was already being watched . . . as, perhaps, was Valentin Zuvorin himself.

"I have formed the impression," Zhukov continued, "that they are a nation bent on suicide. Too much food, too much smoking, too much alcohol, no exercise. And," he added, "I have been very impressed by the fact that they never walk anywhere. Then they wonder why so many die from heart attacks."

Zuvorin massaged his chest with two fingers and stubbed out his cigarette. Officially he was supposed to suffer from asthma. He managed a deep melodious laugh. "You are an original man, Comrade Zhukov. A dangerous thing to be a few years ago. But now many things have changed.

54

Your originality—and your excellent English—has been recognized. You are to be promoted. Although you will have to wait some time before you officially become a first secretary."

Zhukov expressed surprise. "I am honored. But I have only been here three weeks. . . ."

"You have been fortunate," the ambassador said. He stood up and paced the gracious room. "A first secretary called Tardovsky has been recalled to Moscow at very short notice. A question of health. . . ." He glanced at Zhukov to see whether he had heard rumors; Zhukov remained impassive. "Tardovsky spoke excellent English also. You seem to be the man to take his place."

The ambassador wondered whether to confide in Zhukov. Such a confidence might be interpreted as weakness in himself; perhaps even Zhukov himself was a senior member of the KGB—second secretary at forty-four did not seem to be much of an achievement for such an intelligent man. You could never tell; nor could you equate seniority in the KGB with diplomatic seniority. Although Valentin Zuvorin was fairly sure of his authority.

To hell with such furtive considerations; he, Valentin Zuvorin, occupied the most important post in the Soviet overseas diplomatic service. He sat down again near the piano. "Tardovsky," he said, "was on the point of persuading a neurotic American from the State Department to hand over secret documents about American intent in Vietnam and the Middle East. The Americans thought Tardovsky might defect—he had no such intention, of course. Anyway the CIA and FBI got wind of it. There was a squalid scene in a bar on Fourteenth Street"—no need to elaborate—"with the result that Tardovsky has lost all credibility and therefore all usefulness to us in Washington either as an agent or a diplomat. So he has been recalled through no fault of his own." Although, Zuvorin thought, his future has not been enhanced.

"I see." Zhukov pondered the fortuitous factors of success.

"Is that all you have to say, comrade?"

"I am deeply honored, of course. But. . . ."

"But what?"

"Does this mean that I will have to carry out similar subversive duties?"

Zuvorin almost patted him on the head. "Don't worry yourself about such matters. It is sufficient that you have been chosen to fill an important diplomatic post. That is all that matters for the moment."

For who am I, the ambassador asked himself, to say whether or not you are to become a spy?

Zhukov found that his new office duties were really an extension of his old ones. Only now the emphasis was more political. He still translated American newspapers, magazines, government reports, but his reading was more selective and he was expected to be more interpretive—hooking nuances of meaning lost in flat translation. He was also asked to translate government directives that somehow reached the embassy before publication, and some that were never published at all. These were given to him by Mikhail Brodsky, and Zhukov only typed two copies of his translation, one for the ambassador, one for Brodsky. More deference from the rest of the staff, an office of his own, the satisfaction of responsibility: These were the perquisites of the new job, and they were balanced by the demands for industry and punctuality of Ambassador Zuvorin who answered similar demands from Moscow.

Most of the day Zhukov sat at his desk in his high-ceilinged Pullman office where perhaps once a nanny had put the children of rich parents to bed. He drank gallons of tea made with lemon and Narzan mineral water imported from Russia. At night he took his work home and slept with dreams dominated by United States policies, and sometimes in his waking moments wondered what other duties might lie ahead.

* * *

One Saturday shortly after his promotion Vladimir Zhukov, on the advice of several well-wishers from within the

56

embassy, took Valentina for a drive into the ghetto. Time, they said, to see the other side of the coin.

First he buzzed over the Potomac, a humble bug among all the limousine dragonflies, to take a look at the Pentagon. From the parking lot he gazed at one of the five sides of the complex, built in classic penitentiary style, with qualified admiration.

"There you are," he said to Valentina, "the United States Department of Defense. Or war," he added.

Unsolicited statistics lit up in his brain like figures on a computer. "The world's second largest building," he recited. "Did you know that they take one hundred and ninety thousand phone calls a day in there? And that they have forty-two hundred clocks and six hundred and eighty-five water fountains?"

"Really?" The sarcasm was gentle. "And how many cups of coffee do they drink a day?"

"Thirty thousand," Zhukov said promptly, grinning apologetically.

"It's strange to think they could be speaking to the Kremlin right now."

Zhukov looked at his watch. 3 P.M. "They probably are. Every hour on the hour they test the teletype machines. The messages are very reassuring. I read, for instance, that one test message from the Americans on the hot line was a four-stanza poem by Robert Frost—'Desert Places.'"

"And what did the Kremlin reply with?"

"Excerpts in Russian from a Chekhov short story about birch trees. I understand twenty message passed between Washington and Moscow during the Arab-Israeli war. They probably averted a world war on those teletypes."

"Who sent the first message?"

He patted her knee. "Premier Kosygin." He was pleased about that, too. "And the President keeps the messages in a green leather album as a memento." Statistics and trivia forever accumulating in the filing cabinet of his brain; substitutes for the sonnets he once planned to deposit there.

He pointed the Volkswagen toward the ghetto. Losing himself a couple of times in the graceful geometry, finding

57

Fourteenth and following its route, its lament, to the black quarter.

In the Saturday afternoon quiet it was an abandoned place. A pool scummy with neglect. Tenements leaning, small shop windows rheumy. A few blacks strolling to nowhere; not a white face in sight.

Valentina said, "Can we get out and walk?"

Zhukov shook his head. "They advised me not to."

"We wouldn't come to any harm."

"Why not? Because we're Russians? Red Panthers? How would they know? You can't explain after you've been knocked unconscious."

"I think it's exaggerated. They don't look very dangerous."

Like many women she had the knack of converting discretion into cowardice. "The ambassador's wife in New York thought the dangers of Central Park were exaggerated and she was mugged there."

"Mugged? You sound very American, Vladimir."

"I try to speak their language—it's my job."

They stopped at a red light, the stubby car vulnerable in the listlessly hostile street. An old Pontiac slid up beside them; the black driver grinning at them without friendliness. A snap-brimmed hat was tilted on the back of his head; one elbow rested outside the window with self-conscious nonchalance. But you couldn't see his eyes; only your own reflection in the mirrors of his glasses. Chewing, grinning, he spat toward the Volkswagen as the lights changed and took off fast, tires screaming, briefly victorious over white trash.

This flaking road, Zhukov thought, led to the Deep South. There were still mounds of soiled snow on the sidewalk, but the disease of the place was tropical, leprosy, sleeping sickness, the wasting of cholera.

He turned into a residential street where pride was resurrected. Terraces of clean red brick with portals and verandas for summertime courting and grizzled remembering. And cars slumbering outside.

He drove on, rounded a block, returning to Fourteenth.

58

Waiting for the lights to change, a girl of sixteen or so danced to the beat of distant rhythms. Dressed to kill in a black leather micro-skirt with tassels swing and a red breasty sweater; no coat on this cold and dead day. She may not have known she was dancing—as conscious of her rhythm as she was of her heartbeat. Words unwritten—"I don't give a damn, I don't give a damn." Breasts bobbing, buttocks taut under black leather. Fingers flicking, orange baubles of earrings bouncing. She felt them staring; the rhythms froze, the smile, a snarl. She said something, but they couldn't hear. An obscenity, no doubt, in this hopeless place.

Valentina sat tensely. "It was like this," she said, "before the Revolution. Streets like this are deceptive. This is where it's happening." She pointed behind shutters, behind walls. "And why not? Compare these streets with the streets of Bethesda, Georgetown, Alexandria."

"At least the government it trying to do something about it."

"*They*. Trying? It's not even *their* city, Vladimir. Where are those statistics of yours? How many blacks and how many whites in Washington?"

"Five hundred thousand blacks," Zhukov admitted. "And three hundred thousand whites. Something like that. But they *are* trying, Valentina. Schools, housing, black mayors, black politicians. What more can they do?"

"Get out of Vietnam and use the money to help their own people."

For God's sake, he wanted to cry out. Stop strangling yourself with politics. To hell with bloody politics. Wasn't Russia doing the same as America? Grabbing millions of rubles for armaments and the race into space while its people stood in line for shabby overcoats, steel teeth, sprouting potatoes, shoes like polished cardboard. What's more, if Russia had been faced with a crucial problem none of the black dissident meetings behind closed shutters would have been allowed. The rebels would have been chopping wood and sinking mines in the lost camps of Siberia. (He was surprised that he permitted such thoughts.)

59

He wanted to hurry away from the ghetto where all sympathy was spurned. "Maybe," he said, "you would like an apartment here among the blacks."

She didn't reply; his Valentina, companion for twenty years, mother of their only child, Natasha. Valentina—the soul of Mother Russia, her wild song confined to a monotone by rules. So that she hardly recognized her own small hypocrisies anymore.

"Would you like that?" he persisted. "Would you like an apartment here? You could do a lot of good work among these people." He rubbed her cheek lightly with the back of his hand.

"Don't be foolish, Vladimir. You know it would be impracticable." But she smiled at him and held his hand to her cheek for a moment. "How could a diplomat live in a black ghetto?"

Another red light stopped them. Vladimir noticed a group of black teen-agers lounging in the doorway of a dead-eyed shop. Apprehension stirred. He peered to the left and right to see if he could jump the light. Indisputably with more cowardice than discretion. The spirit of Leningrad, Vladimir Zhukov! He wound down the window of the bug with bravado.

The young men were gathered on the opposite side of the intersection. One of them, hair combed out in black wings around his ears, held up a clenched fist. "Hello, whitey," he shouted.

Too much to hope that they would recognize the diplomatic plates. Vladimir Zhukov, soldier and diplomat, called back, "Hallo there."

"Why," said the leader in a brown leather jacket, "this chalk wants to be friendly. A friendly whitey! Ain't that something. What do you want, whitey—a nigger chick to screw?"

Zhukov implored the lights to change, but they remained steadfastly red.

"Please drive on," Valentina urged him.

"I thought you wanted to get out and walk. Meet the people."

60

"Don't be stupid, Vladimir. Drive on before they attack us."

Zhukov wound up the window. But he refused to drive on against the lights. Why, he couldn't determine. Some gritty Soviet, Kazakh perversity. Had the lights jammed?

From the pocket of his pink satin jeans the leader took a slingshot, sighted with deliberation and pulled back the lethal rubber.

The lights changed. Zhukov jammed his foot on the gas pedal, the stone smacked the windshield drilling a small hole and frosting the glass.

But they were away. As he drove Zhukov punched out the glass. His hands were shaking and his foot on the gas was wobbly.

In the driving mirror he saw them in the middle of the road, fists raised in Panther salutes, faces triumphant.

"Do you still want to live here?"

"Please, Vladimir."

He noticed a trickle of blood on her cheekbone.

"I'm sorry," he said. "Is it serious?"

"It's nothing. The stone just grazed me."

"Shall I take you to a hospital?"

"I told you . . . it's nothing.". She reached back and picked up the stone lying on the back seat. A small sharp flint.

On the sidewalk Zhukov saw a drunken old man with a folded black face and a jockey cap picking up a cigarette butt from the gutter. Through a vista ahead he briefly saw the tip of the noble white dome of the Capitol.

Chapter 6

IT WAS A perfect night for spying, socializing, intriguing and electioneering in Washington, D.C.—activities which blended easily into an entity in the capital city. A fine frosty night; the sky filled with calculating stars, the sidewalks glittering with jewels.

At the black-tie affairs in the mansions and palaces around Massachusetts Avenue—held simultaneously with clandestine meetings in the ghetto where they were plotting to overthrow the whole elegant caboosh—the organization was as smooth as a butler's voice. Although this evening there was some unfortunate coincidence because there were affairs at both the French *and* Spanish embassies *and* a select dinner at the White House garnished with rumors that, over liqueurs, there might be an important leak about the President's intentions in the election. (During the day, Richard Nixon, vying for the Republican nomination, had promised in a speech in New Hampshire to finish the war in Vietnam with these words, "I pledge to you that the new leadership the Republicans offer will end the war and win the peace in the Pacific.")

God knows how the clash occurred. The French and the Spaniards were both highly desirable invitations for palate and prestige, and it was surely a prima facie case for establishing a clearinghouse for such occasions. Even the current *in* hostess (wife of a Midwest crusading Senator), whose blunt wit had made her some sort of reputation, was in a quandary. She had planned first a few pithy but serious words of advice for Franco which would be relayed to the Generalissimo; then the French invitation had arrived and she had composed some saucy directives for De Gaulle;

then deciding to visit both and fearing that she might confuse her messages, she had resolved to crystallize her words into two well-timed cracks that *could* apply to either leader. Thank heavens, she thought under the dryer at Jean-Paul's, that through some bureaucratic oversight they had forgotten to invite her to the White House dinner.

Elsewhere in Pierre L'Enfant's dream city the beautiful, the ambitious, the dedicated, the sycophantic, the established and the insecure pondered the invitations. Democrats and Republicans, the Chief Justice, the Secretary of State (thankfully committed to the White House), the Attorney General, several ministers, umpteen advisers, Congressmen, journalists, a pet author, a vivacious pop singer, some aristocracy from Britain, a couple of Italian diplomats of impeccable lechery, all the ambassadors and many of their henchmen, innumerable spies, innumerable courtesans, a general or two, lawyers seeking slander, some widows still game at sixty, a couple of Mafia junior officers disgusted by so much overt intrigue, the FBI, the CIA and the KGB, a blackmailer, one virgin, half a dozen TV producers, their sons and daughters, and there among them all a future President or two.

Almost everyone omitted from the White House invitation list elected to attend both receptions. Thus the problem became simply one of strategy: Which to attend first? Because the implied insult of visiting one's host second was worse than declining the invitation altogether. The *in* hostess decided to grace the Spanish reception first and explain to the French that she had been asked to deliver an urgent message to Prince Juan Carlos, heir apparent to the Spanish throne.

At the Russian Embassy the debate was less refined. It was merely a question of who was to be let out on a leash for the night. Among the few given a pass was Vladimir Zhukov because his new duties entailed mixing with the Beautiful People.

With his paranoid conviction that, like himself, everyone was a potential eavesdropper, Mikhail Brodsky chose

63

an open-air venue for the briefing. They met on the steps of the Capitol.

"Greetings, comrade," Brodsky said in his imprisoned voice.

Zhukov nodded, almost a first secretary now.

"Shall we walk? It's such a fine morning and Washington is a beautiful place on a day like this."

As indeed it was, Zhukov thought. Velvet buds enticed by the thaw, trees straining for summer, the Roman dome of the Capitol gleaming in the sunlight, Stars and Stripes rippling against the winter-blue sky, frost melting on the city's recuperating carpets. Over all this nobility an airliner lingered like a spent match. He remembered Leningrad, another noble city, on mornings like this.

"Why all this secrecy?" Zhukov demanded. "I nearly didn't come."

"You are perhaps feeling your authority now that you are nearly a first secretary?"

Zhukov shrugged. "You, after all, are only a third secretary."

They turned into the Botanic Gardens. (Ninety varieties of azaleas, five hundred kinds of orchids, Zhukov's computer reminded him.)

Brodsky was silent for a while. Smarter than usual in a light-gray overcoat and plaid scarf. His hat and his poor shoes and, somehow, his gold-rimmed spectacles the giveaway. Finally he said, "You are doing very well, Comrade Zhukov. But you mustn't get drunk with power." He giggled.

"A first secretary can hardly do that."

"But you mustn't forget that position is nothing in the Soviet system. We do not recognize the cult of personality on any level." He tucked a lock of girlish hair under his hat. "And you mustn't forget that some of the least significant members of the party have certain other authorities." His voice iced up. "You could be demoted just as easily as you have been promoted. In fact, in certain circumstances, you could be put on a plane back to Moscow within a few hours. Tonight, for instance."

"I doubt it," Zhukov said without conviction.

They walked slowly down Capitol Hill, and Brodsky assured him that no such move was anticipated because it was well known that Zhukov was a loyal servant of the party and the Soviet Union. And he reverted to the tentative approaches made in Moscow about extensions of his official duties in Washington.

Zhukov remembered the approaches: "You may be asked to mix a little. To make friends in the right places. To socialize just a little more than some of your colleagues. After all, we have to keep contact with our hosts and you are an excellent linguist. . . ."

Brodsky danced over a fallen branch. "They no doubt put it very vaguely. And, of course, at that time you were only going to be our second-string socialite. Until the Tardovsky fiasco. Now you have taken his place. You have because you have a certain charm, because you are a man of sensitivity and comparative sophistication. In short, Comrade Zhukov, you are an attractive and articulate man."

"You are very kind." Perhaps Brodsky had some homosexual inclinations? "Do you mean you want me to become a spy?"

"Nothing so dramatic. If we—they—had wanted you to become a spy your training in Moscow would have been far more rigorous. No, we do not want you to arrange any drops on the Bronx subway or under the railway bridge at Queens." He paused, conscious of vague indiscretion. "Those two drops, incidentally, have been abandoned." He stopped to light a cigarette. "No, it will merely be a matter of mixing. Becoming known as an unusually extrovert Russian, a valuable catch for the hostesses." He grinned sideways at Zhukov. "You may even recite some of your poetry."

They arrived at the Monument reaching for a fragment of cloud. "The tallest masonry structure in the world," Zhukov supplied. "And for what purpose am I to do all this socializing?" Although, of course, he knew.

"You are not such a naïve man, Comrade Zhukov. However, I will elaborate."

A line of school children accompanied by a pretty and

enthusiastic young teacher passed them, headed for the Monument fringed at its base with a circle of Old Glories. Brodsky regarded children and teacher with distaste.

Zhukov said, "I presume you want me to assess opinion and trends."

"Exactly so," Brodsky said. "To take the pulse of Washington, as it were. You will find many Americans and other diplomats anxious to make friends with you because a socializing Russian is something of a rarity in Washington." He squeezed Zhukov's bicep for no particular reason that Zhukov could determine. "Most of us have to go straight home. In any case"——an explosion of mirth like suppressed laughter escaping in a classroom—"can you imagine Comrade Grigorenko at a cocktail party?"

Zhukov said he couldn't.

Brodsky continued, "Many of your new friends will, of course, be trying to take the pulse of the Soviet Embassy through you. You will naturally supply their wants—after we have decided what they should be told."

"Is that all?"

"Not quite." The saliva froze again. "In Washington there are always weak men in low places with access to valuable information. However diligently they are screened they manage to hide their weaknesses." He stared at Zhukov from behind his scholarly glasses. "We screened you very carefully but we could not reach your soul." He lit another cigarette—American, Zhukov noted. "Such people seem to flourish on the party circuit. Men and women. It will be your responsibility to listen for indiscretions, because these people respond to sympathy, particularly on the third martini. You will make friends with them," Brodsky ordered.

"So I *am* to be a spy?"

"Far from it. Merely a specialist in judicious fraternizing. The social bear of the Soviet Embassy."

"An *agent provocateur?*"

"A theatrical term and out-of-date. You're hardly the type to be a masculine Mata Hari. In any case most of the spying is carried out by the lesser embassies these days.

66

You will primarily remain a diplomat with an extension of duties which is not, after all, confined to Soviet diplomats. You will merely be our representative—or one of our representatives—in this field. You see," he explained, "we leave the heavyweight operations to the military attachés —every country does. The more devious work to our friends in other embassies. We carry out duties of a more dignified nature."

A women's club passed by on their way to the Monument. Brodsky's distaste deepened to disgust.

"Supposing I am not fitted to these duties?" Zhukov asked.

"We—they—feel that you are. Or rather you're the best candidate there is in the embassy."

Zhukov said he was, searching for supporting words like a supposed to do about these . . . these weaklings, when I meet them?"

"Report their weaknesses to us. Determine how they can be blackmailed. Men, women, alcohol, money . . . every American with two cars wants three, every American with a co-op wants a town house. But," he added, "I use the term 'weak' loosely. You may meet strong men seeking only an outlet to contribute to the glorious cause of Socialism." His glasses glinted in the sunlight. "Their strength may be their determination to supply us with information despite the risks involved."

"Traitors, you mean?"

The grip on Zhukov's bicep was reapplied, unexpected strength in the delicate fingers. "Sometimes I am surprised by your reactions, Comrade Zhukov."

Zhukov shrugged—it wasn't in his character to apologize. Then inspiration came to him on this inspired morning. "I have a daughter in the Soviet Union, Comrade Brodsky."

Brodsky looked surprised. "I am aware of that. As a matter of fact I was going to mention her. . . ."

"Mention Natasha? Why?" Alarm curdled into nausea.

"It doesn't matter for the moment. What were you going to say?"

"Tell me why you were going to mention Natasha?" Sweet, innocent Natasha with her mother's loveliness and her father's questing spirit.

"No, comrade, you first."

Zhukov's voice faltered. "I was merely going to ask if you thought it would be possible for her to visit us here this year."

"You mean as a reward for your social activities?"

"I thought it would be a wonderful experience for her. . . ."

"Anything is possible," Brodsky said thoughtfully. "It could be arranged."

"And now, why were you going to mention her?"

"It seems that she has been keeping bad company in Alma-Ata. . . ." And with relish Mikhail Brodsky recounted the arrest of Natasha's lover with the true narrator's delight in detail. Down to the shirt and underpants.

* * *

Vladimir Zhukov sweated with self-consciousness and the effort to be suave, like a teen-ager dancing with a haughty girl. All the subjects in the universe available for discussion and all original comment—any comment for that matter—eluded him. He hated the setting, hated the people. He suspected that they regarded him as a curiosity, a peasant: he, the representative of the most powerful nation on earth; he, an intellectual and a man of cultivated habits; he, a man of forty-four staring at his drink and digging his nails into the palms of his hands like a kid of eighteen.

The diplomat sent from the cultural section presumably to keep an eye on Zhukov was getting drunk and belligerent at the bar at the end of the ballroom. He didn't seem to be a very cultured man despite his job, and when Zhukov noticed him through the heads and drinks and diamonds he was prodding a Czech in the chest with a karate forefinger.

A baptism by fire, Brodsky had said. And it certainly was. Champagne among the Matisse still lifes, the Sèvres nymphs and the Gobelin tapestries on French territory in

68

Washington, followed by more drinks and dancing at the after-dinner reception on Iberian soil. He stroked the wattered silk on the lapel of his tuxedo; very decadent, soft—like stroking a seal.

"What do you think?" The earnest and boring Rumanian with the crinkled forehead waited with anticipation.

"I'm sure you're right," Zhukov said.

"Really? That is very surprising. Very surprising indeed."

Zhukov wondered if he'd contradicted Soviet policy on Rumania which had become a little recalcitrant of late. Tomorrow the contradiction would be relayed and worried over all day at the Rumanian Embassy. Had Zhukov made a deliberate leak? they would ponder. Was the Kremlin going soft on Rumania—fearful of the Chinese menace, perhaps?

At that moment Zhukov didn't care what interpretation they decided on. In the first place, he had no idea what the question had been; in the second, his job was to fraternize with Westerners, not Kremlin lackeys; and in the third, his mind was slurred with the champagne and vodka he had drunk in abundance to oil his conversation. And he was desperately worried about Natasha. The message hadn't been subtle: Cooperate and produce results and Natasha can visit you; behave obstinately and she'll be arrested like her lover.

Zhukov looked down miserably at his intense companion. How did you circulate at these functions? If you managed to dispatch a bore than you stood the risk of being isolated—an inarticulate peasant stranded among the sophisticated and effete. So he endured the Rumanian's pleas for enlightenment a little longer, hardly listening, checking on the clip behind his black tie, wishing he'd brought patent-leather shoes.

Across the room Zhukov's watchdog, whose name was Dmitri Kalmykov, was becoming louder in his attack on the Czech; but the Czech, sustained by the new liberalism flowering like spring blossom in his country, was not cowering. He prodded back, answered with quiet contempt and infuriated the bulging, pudding-faced Russian. Interests and tension shivered in the air. A fine watchdog and instructor, Zhukov sighed to himself.

To the Rumanian he said, "Get me another drink." He was not normally a curt man but such grinding platitudes could not be endured for too long. He thrust his empty glass at the Rumanian who crinkled a little more at the injustice of it.

In the ballroom, with its walls draped with red silk and its splendid tapestries, Peter Duchin and his orchestra swung sibilantly into "Strangers in the Night." Above the music Zhukov heard Kalmykov's voice, like an angry vocalist singing a different song.

He gazed into the crevice of two plump breasts and revived somewhat. Their owner said, "You're Russian, aren't you?"

Zhukov said he was, searching for supporting words like a badly rehearsed actor.

She was in her mid-thirties, English, faded, but still fruity—like a pear just beginning to go soft, Zhukov decided, taking the vodka from the Rumanian and dismissing him. He tried to typecast her, but, unlike the wives of most British diplomats, she didn't fit into any preconceived slot. The usual stifling sense of decorum and protocol hadn't affected her, unless it had accelerated the premature bruising of vitality, removed some of the bloom from the skin.

"I could tell," she said, her voice blurred by drink.

"Is it so obvious?"

She leaned forward as if pulled by her breasts. They were firm but traced with delicate veins. "Of course," she said, "you are so masculine."

Vladimir wished valiantly for the presence of Valentina; but he had been told to operate alone as much as possible —"you appear more attractive and more vulnerable that way."

The woman had fashionably pink lips—Zhukov preferred a scarlet cupid mouth—and dyed, straw-colored hair, its lacquered height collapsing. Zhukov had seen photographs of the Duchess of Kent and this woman reminded him of the duchess as she would be in a decade or so.

"And you," he said, "you are English?"

"How clever of you." She was drunker than he had supposed. "My husband is over there somewhere trying to be an arrogant aristocrat and a sycophant at the same time. It's very difficult for him, poor darling, because at heart he is a pure sycophant. I thought you should know," she confided, "that my husband is present, because it's always best that people should be absolutely honest with each other at this stage."

"What stage?" There was no difficulty in making conversation with this one, Zhukov thought.

"Where is your wife?" she demanded.

"At home. She doesn't like parties very much."

"A sensible woman. Is she a sensible woman? A sensible Russian woman?"

Zhukov didn't want to talk too much about Valentina. She *was* a sensible woman, and he loved her. He smiled. It was strange that, by chatting with this middle-aged bedworthy flirt, he was carrying out the orders issued him that morning.

Peter Duchin slid into "More." Kalmykov and the Czech shouted frenziedly above the music. Anticipation gathered joyfully around them.

Zhukov asked curiously, "What made you come and talk to me?" With this woman you could ask anything; you could even confess insecurity or fear because, with all the hypocrisy around, confession would emerge as a strength.

"You're not very sure of yourself, are you, comrade?"

He shrugged.

"I don't mean in your life, your work. I mean here—among all these performers. . . . I don't blame you, Mister—"

"Zhukov. Vladimir Zhukov."

"I don't blame you, Vladimir. But don't forget—they're all just as unsure of themselves as you. In fact they're pretty scared of you. They don't know what to make of

71

someone like you. The Russian bear in their midst. They try to kid themselves that you're boorish because of your blunt manners and your clip-on tie"—she reached out and touched the black propeller—"but they're really worried. For one thing you represent Russia . . . missiles, strength, the Iron Curtain, all that. For another you challenge all their standards."

Zhukov began to relax. "What standards, Mrs.—"

"Massingham. Mrs. Massingham. But you can call me Helen."

"What standards, Mrs. Massingham?"

She spread her arms. "All this talk, all this posturing, all this rehearsed wit. You make a mockery of it, Mr. Zhukov, and they know it. Have you ever paused to think how much insecurity a wisecrack covers up? Probably not. And, of course, you even challenge their attitudes, the whole premise of their society, and this they do not like at all."

He nodded appreciatively. "Do you know something, Mrs. Massingham?"

"What's that, Mr. Zhukov?"

"You are a very competent person. You know how to give a man strength when he most needs it. In that respect you are the complete—" He searched for the right word.

"The complete bitch?"

"Far from it." He put down his glass on a passing tray.

"Vladimir," she said, "would you like to dance?"

"I would be charmed," said Vladimir Zhukov, soldier, diplomat, *agent provocateur,* spy, gentleman.

Wallace Walden, accompanied by his patient wife, Sophie, looked around him with contempt. He disliked career diplomats and opportunist politicians because he believed that all their conniving was directed toward personal rather than patriotic ends; this, he had long ago decided, was the cardinal difference between himself and the other Washington players.

The dinner jacket made his body look very squat and powerful. He was drinking scotch on the rocks and smoking a thick cigar—from Tampa not Havana, he explained. He jerked the cigar toward a group of laughing men in their thirties accompanied by healthy shiny-haired girls with Florida tans carefully maintained. "Some one important's made a joke," he said. "A dirty one, most likely." He dismissed them with his cigar. "Court sycophants."

Henry Massingham from the British Embassy said, "Don't be too hard on them, Wallace. After all it *is* election year."

"They make me sick," Walden said.

"I don't see why. It's all part of democracy, merely human nature applied to politics. No better, no worse than business or commerce or sport. Out of it all emerges one of the best governmental systems in the world."

"Maybe," Walden conceded. "But that doesn't mean I have to like them." Or you, he thought, squashing out his cigar in the Waterford glass ashtray.

Massingham's business was political assessment. An elegant and professional eavesdropper. Almost a caricature of the British diplomat because he had discovered that American ridicule of *the typical Englishman* disguises considerable reverence. At first he had been self-conscious about his deep and decent voice; then he had found that his American companions (and antagonists) were just as self-conscious about their accents in his presence; so he ladled it on with the result that he was often complimented by Washington women on his divine diction. Massingham also worked on the accompaniments to his accent: suits of striped and slightly crumpled elegance, regimental tie askew, wavy hair a little too long. When he overheard a White House aide describe him as "that limey pansy" he managed to interpret the insult as an inverted compliment.

Henry Massingham had also established a reputation for erudition and artistic appreciation and it was rumored that he wrote poetry. "A real culture vulture," the Americans said, unaware of his rather mediocre degree at Trinity College, Dublin. Which was one of the reasons that Henry Massingham, in his late forties and beginning to accept that he would never become an ambassador, or even a minister,

73

adored the Washington scene; unlike his own kind they hadn't unmasked him.

Walden took another cigar from a leather case and said, "Henry, I wonder if you and I could have a little talk. And you, Jack . . ." to Godwin.

They were sitting at a table within sight of the ballroom. Massingham looked inquiringly at Walden's wife. But, attuned to implied orders, Mrs. Walden was already snapping her evening bag, stubbing out her half-finished cigarette. "I must go and have a chat with Maggie Hardin," she said. "If you gentlemen will excuse me."

Massingham stood up and bowed.

After she had gone Massingham said, "You're a very lucky man, Walden."

"Why's that?"

"Your wife. A wonderful woman."

"Yeah," Walden said impatiently, "she's great. Massingham, we've got a favor to ask you."

"How very intriguing."

Shit, thought Walden, any minute now he's going to call me *my dear fellow*. He glanced around. No one seemed to be listening but just in case. . . . "Let's walk down the passage."

"Very well."

"I'll be frank, Massingham. We've got to get closer to the Soviets in Washington and you can help us."

"I'm very flattered. But how on earth can I help American intelligence?"

"By making friends with a Russian."

"Just any Russian?"

"One in particular. Vladimir Zhukov. He's now here. He's taking Tardovsky's place. You didn't hear about the Tardovsky affair?" Walden probed without much hope because, after all, Massingham was in the same business.

"Yes, I heard. In a toilet in some clip joint on Fourteenth Street, wasn't it?"

Walden said it was.

Massingham asked how Walden thought he was going to make friends with this Russian. A newcomer at that.

74

Hardly any of their people—except the ambassador, the minister counselor, a counselor or two and a few spies—were allowed to mix with the degenerates of Washington. "I'm told they even have to ask permission to go to the cinema. What do you want me to do? Play footsie with him in Loew's Palace?"

"I understand he's something of an egghead. Like yourself, Henry."

Massingham nervously poked a handkerchief up the sleeve of his dinner jacket. "It's very daring of them to let an intellectual out of Moscow."

"I guess they must be pretty sure of him. But he's all we've got. It shouldn't be too difficult to arrange a chance meeting. He speaks fluent English and they might get him to help the cultural attaché's staff. He might even come around and see some of our Soviet and East European Exchange guys on the fourth floor. And if not, I'm pretty sure he'll go to the National Gallery of Art and other places like that. Godwin's boys will keep an eye on him and call you when he moves."

"And then what am I supposed to do?" Massingham asked. "Solicit him in front of some suggestive sculpture?"

Godwin who looked as if he'd obtained forced entry into his tuxedo said, "I understood you were pretty experienced in operations like this, Mr. Massingham."

Walden said, "Sure he is. Come on, Henry, don't bullshit us. You know how to play the game as well as anyone. When it comes to screwing someone in these kind of stakes, you limeys have the edge on the world."

"It's very decent of you to say so, Walden. But why me?"

"Like I said, you and Zhukov have the same interests. You write poetry, don't you?"

"The occasional stanza when the mood takes me. Nothing for publication, though."

You're damn right they're not for publication, Walden thought. Difficult to publish the nonexistent. "Also," he went on, "you have the great advantage in this instance of not being American. Any overture we made would be doomed—especially after Tardovsky. They use other embassies for this kind of maneuver and we'll do the same. It's a long shot at the moment. But think it over, while we see what we can dig up on Zhukov."

Massingham shrugged elegantly. "I shall have to consult, of course."

Walden blew out a jet of smoke. "Is that really necessary?"

"Of course it is," Massingham snapped.

"For Chris' sake don't get insulted, Henry. I was only querying the wisdom of sharing this thing with too many people." He gazed speculatively at Massingham's handsome, has-been features. "By the way, Henry, what was that degree you got in Dublin? You never did tell me."

"Very well," Massingham said in his melodious and resigned voice, "I'll see what I can do for you *without* consulting anyone."

Back at their table Walden looked around for his wife. Scanning the dancers, he snapped his fingers and pointed again with his cigar. "Jack," he said to Godwin, "do you see what I see?"

"Where?"

"There, dancing with Helen Massingham."

"Well, I'll be damned," Godwin said.

Walden took Massingham's arm. "Do you see that guy dancing with your wife?"

Massingham nodded. "Who is it?"

"That's Vladimir Zhukov," Walden said.

On the other side of the room the confrontation between Kalmykov and the Czech was becoming vicious. Kalmykov's face was flushed and he had spilled vodka down his jacket. And the Czech had lost his discipline. Willowy, with hairless cheeks and surprisingly powerful fists, he was shouting at the Russian. "The dictatorship will soon be over. Dubcek and Černik are our leaders. To hell with the Kremlin." He gulped at his whiskey. "You'll see. Soon it will happen."

"Hooligan," Kalmykov shouted. "Son of a bitch. You will come to hell just like the traitors in Hungary did."

The Czech, searching for the choicest Russian invective, suggested a relationship between Kalmykov and his mother.

The sophisticated and the cultivated guests edged closer.

Kalmykov tossed his vodka into the Czech's face, the Czech swung. Zhukov intercepted his fist and put a lock on the arm. "Comrade," he said, "remember where you are."

The Czech struggled a little but Zhukov was too strong for him. He relaxed, breath sobbing.

In front of them Kalmykov sneered. "Thank you, comrade. But I did not need your help." And to the Czech he said, "See what happens to you when you get impertinent? That is what will happen to your country and your fool-hardy leaders."

Zhukov took Kalmykov's arm. "Come," he said, "it's time to go." Ironic, he thought, that he was supposed to be in Kalmykov's charge.

"Who the hell do you think you're talking to?"

Old military authority returned to Zhukov. "Don't argue—just come with me."

Kalmykov glanced around, noticed the audience. He became sulky. "You can't order me around."

"Come," Zhukov said. "As it is you'll have a lot to answer for in the morning." He took Kalmykov's arm.

Fear quivered in Kalmykov's voice. Zhukov was glad that, in the secret hierarchy of authority, seniority was never clearly defined.

Kalmykov nodded uncertainly. "But I did right, didn't I—putting that treacherous pig in his place?"

"Others will judge you," Zhukov said ominously, not completely sober himself. "Now we must go."

They threaded their way through the delighted crowd while in the background Peter Duchin glided into "Lara's Theme" from *Dr. Zhivago*.

Chapter 7

AFTER THE Germans had been beaten Vladimir Zhukov retired sick to Alma-Ata. He was twenty-one: a veteran. But the siege of Leningrad had sucked at the juices of his youth; his body needed more than rotten potatoes, horse and dogmeat and moldy bread.

He was born a Muscovite but his father, a trusted officer in the party, was posted to Kazakhstan to guide the peasants whose loyalties sometimes became confused. After all, until the glorious victory of the Bolsheviks, they had been nomads traversing the steppes and salt marshes, sleeping in their felt tents.

Vladimir suffered from long debilitating fevers that were never confidently diagnosed. "Malnutrition, his very soul has been poisoned by the Nazi atrocities—let him rest and he will recover," said the doctors, always elaborately sympathetic toward a Zhukov ailment because Zhukov, Senior, was now a secretary and respected party elder.

So Vladimir rested all summer in his parents' home, his body skeletal, the poetry that had been numbed by warfare released by fever—pollinated by the distant bee-buzzing of tractors, the flaky whispering of poplar and silver birch, the scent of apple blossom and rose.

And, as his body gained strength, so did his stunted idealism. He heard vaguely of purges and prison camps and presumed that all victims were guilty. His God was still the heavily mustached little marshal from Georgia who had chased the invading Nazis from the land.

He read with pride of the collective farming that was making the wilderness blossom; heard the music of collective toil purring across the wheatfields. And he saw factories and apartment blocks piling up in the city, acetylene sparks spilling like soft words into the night.

He read most of the permitted foreign authors, giving precedence to the French because they were more available. Hugo, Balzac, De Maupassant, Zola. And Dickens (contemporary England still much the same, he understood), Kipling, Shakespeare, Hardy; Shelley, Burns and Byron. Mark Twain and Dreiser from America.

But despite the languor of the southern summer, when Vladimir Zhukov wrote verse on coarse grainy paper, his words were about war.

In the late summer he took to wandering into the city, once called Verny, drinking tea at one of the *chaikhanas* and watching young workers taking time off from the assembly lines to play. Komsomols and Young Pioneers, they all seemed very gay and sunburned this summer of salvation as they paraded, Turk, Mongol and occasional Chinese, beneath the *karagachs*.

Zhukov also loved the market because it seemed to him to be the gaudy southern symbol of communal effort —"production and distribution for the benefit of all, instead of profits for a few." For the benefit of all a dozen races, pigments, minorities—even a few Chinese ancients with mandarin mustaches—cheerfully sold spices, stubby brooms, kabab, fruit, elixirs for hiccups and bad breath.

The Fascist enemy had been decimated (with the help of the Americans and British) and now only poetic industry with sunny, carousing rewards lay ahead.

It came as something of a shock to Vladimir Zhukov, then, to realize that a new enemy—or rather a very old one—had replaced the Nazis: the entire capital West.

And, as the fever receded, it came as an unpleasant surprise to him to discover that not everyone reveled in the workers' paradise that shone from the pages of *Pravda* and *Izvestia*.

On a bench in Gorky Recreation Park, fondly observing lovers' trysts, he got to talking with a factory worker munching a goat cheese sandwich and an Alma-Ata apple for his lunch; one of the twenty-eight heroes of Ivan Panfilov's Kazakh division which helped throw back the German tanks from the outskirts of Moscow.

"Where do you work, comrade?" the man asked. He was built like a general with pearly scars on his brown southern face.

"I'm not working right now," Vladimir replied, feeling shame for the first time.

"You are very lucky—or very privileged."

"Not privileged. I was at Leiningrad and I picked up some sort of fever."

"Then I salute you," said the man. "You had it worse than us. You're lucky to be alive, comrade. But"—he looked at Zhukov suspiciously—"you don't look very sick."

"I'm almost fit again, and I'm looking forward to starting work."

"Then you're a fool," said the worker, chewing up the core of the apple.

"Why do you say that?"

"Never work until you have to. And that will be soon enough. To work you must be given a decent incentive. . . ."

Vladimir was astounded. "Incentive? Surely we have the greatest incentives of any nation in the world?" He was becoming angry and he had been told to avoid excitement.

"It's no incentive to see work wasted. Did you know that a million acres of grain will remain unharvested this year because the combines haven't been repaired?"

Zhukov said he didn't know that. But was it surprising when a country had suffered as Russia had suffered? When factories had been making guns, and women had been doing the work of the men?

"The combines could have been repaired. But the peasants have no interest in work when their spirit's crushed by taxes. Do you know that even trees are taxed here? That many peasants have cut down their own fruit trees to avoid the tax?"

"Then they're fools," Vladimir Zhukov said. "The taxes

are for the benefit of Russia and Socialism—and ultimately for the peasants themselves."

Suspicion was crystallizing in the mind of the hero with the big chest and bigger stomach. "May I ask, comrade, what your father does for a living?"

Zhukov told him proudly.

"That explains everything." The man stood up, closed his cardboard sandwich box and was gone, hurrying across the sunlit park which, to Vladimir Zhukov, suddenly seemed like a mirage.

Above all he was mortified that he'd been considered naïve. He was of age, a Leningrad veteran, world traveler (well, Berlin), man of letters, patriot, potential party stalwart. Who the hell did that guy think he was? It was as if noble aspiration had suddenly been ridiculed as maudlin. *I should report him: Men who sabotage everything Lenin and now Stalin have fought for should be thrown in prison camps.*

That night he told his father about the rebel as they ate Uzbek-*plov,* the rice thick with mutton and carrots and raisins. His father, soft now at fifty-five with obedience and conformity, didn't seem surprised. "Who was this man?" he asked, shoveling the buttery food into his mouth, steel teeth catching the light.

"I don't know his name."

"Then there isn't much we can do."

Vladimir found he was glad. *After all the man was a hero. And I don't want to punish his wife and children.* No, what he wanted was reassurance, doubts dispelled. "Doesn't it shock you?" he asked.

His father, who looked sixty-five, shrugged. His mother, silent and lost elsewhere as always, disappeared into the kitchen, unmoved by rebels or politics.

"Well, doesn't it?"

"Not really. There are others like him. Ungrateful dogs," he added without emotion.

"Are there so many, Father?"

His father assumed his official voice. "There will always be capitalist lackeys who seek to further their own selfish ends."

"But this man was a worker, not a capitalist lackey."

"More shame on him then." Zhukov's father wiped his mouth thoroughly with his handkerchief. "And now, my son, I have some things to say to you." He went to the varnished sideboard dominated by a photograph of Stalin tousling a child's hair in front of an adoring crowd, among them Zhukov's father smirking fervently. "Just what are these?" He held up Vladimir's folder of poems.

Vladimir flushed. Now he understood why his mother had retired to the kitchen. "You have no right to read those."

"I have every right," said his father mildly.

"You are not the secret police."

"I'm not." He permitted a smile. "But never presume too much, my son."

Again Vladimir felt that he was being indicted for naïveté. "It's only scribbling. I wrote down a lot of incoherent words when I had the fever."

"Not so incoherent. Unfortunately." He read a poem to himself. "Why war? Why do you always write about war?"

"Because it's all I lived with for a long time. . . ."

"I understand that. You were one of the heroes of Leningrad and we're very proud of you. But it's the *way* you've portrayed the war. The suffering, the lack of supplies and reinforcements. Soldiers of the Red Army wondering if they'd been forgotten."

"That's how it was," Vladimir said. "And in any case it's only poetry."

"It implies inefficiency," his father said. "It implies"— he whispered the words as if afraid of being overheard— "it implies that our glorious leader may have been at fault." *God doesn't make mistakes.*

"I didn't mean to imply that. But does it matter? A few verses on a dozen or so sheets of paper?"

"If they got into an enemy's hands they could matter a great deal," his father said sadly. "In your own interests, my son, I suggest we destroy these verses."

"Why the hell should we? They're private—no one else's business."

"It's better that we get rid of them. Please believe me. I

82

know." And swiftly he ripped the sheets of paper in half, then in half again.

Vladimir pushed away his plate. "That wasn't necessary, Father."

In Leningrad he had vaguely heard soldiers, and some officers, talk about the human automatons manufactured by the state. Staring at the corpses preserved in ice, wincing at the explosions of shells, nursing the burn of his hunger, he had ignored them. Soldiers always grumbled. If they were so discontented with Stalinist Russia then they certainly wouldn't be resisting the Germans so stubbornly. Likewise he heard about anti-Semitism. But, again, that was the crime of the Nazis: You didn't fight an enemy if you shared his sins.

His father tore the paper into confetti. A trace of old emotions animated his bony, conformist face. "Our country has enormous tasks ahead of it. Mistakes will be made, directives misunderstood. It's all part of the healing process. It's not the hour for poetry or intellectuals. It's the time for common endeavor. I suggest, my son, that you keep your poetry in your head."

Vladimir gazed out at the honeyed day dying on the skyline of communal cubist endeavor. Like my ideals, he thought melodramatically. "But I want to work," he said. Ridiculous that he should feel like a boy. "I want to be part of it all. . . ."

His mother returned with green tea, served in cups without handles, Uzbek style. "Have you had your little chat?" she asked. Vladimir regarded her more as a grandmother, a *babushka;* she was only fifty-three, but she had retreated, prematurely, into the limbo of memory.

His father said they had. "And now me must think of the future. What you are to do with yourself. As a matter of fact," he added quietly, "I've made some plans for you."

"What plans?"

"You have too good a brain to waste working with your hands. And in any case the rewards are small." It was a confession more than a statement. "You also speak excellent English——a great asset in the fight against the enemies of Socialism. I still have influence in certain quarters in

Moscow. Nothing very powerful because a party secretary in Alma-Ata doesn't rate very high in the hierarchy. But I've arranged for you to study at Moscow University."

But did he want to go to Moscow? To leave the tractors' music, the south, the workers. The land of the novelist Auezov, Djabeyev the akyn poet, Kunanbayev, the father of Kazakh literature.

"I expected more gratitude," said his father; but he had lapsed into his official voice again, a voice that really expected a little. "I have also tentatively arranged for you to take up a junior post at the Foreign Ministry—if, of course, you pass your exams. If you concentrate on facts instead of poetry."

"It's very good of you, Father. Let me think it over."

A few days later his confusion was compounded by the arrival of a girl named Valentina. She was on holiday from Moscow with a study group of Komsomols and, with a couple of other group leaders, had been invited to dine at the Zhukovs'.

She was eighteen, hair worn in bangs, reminding him of the Brontë sisters whom he'd read, face city pale, cool and informed in debate—the sort of girl who made young men hot and stupid through trying too hard. She was excessively neat, black skirt and white blouse with breasts demurely contained, shoes a little decadent with raised heels, single pearls on her ears. Despite her pallor Vladimir noted dark pigment alien to the Muscovite; also a slight Mongol set to cheekbones and eyes.

Her conversation was assured. But the talk over the rough brandy and red wine bored him. So he made few contributions, pondering tactics to upset her aplomb for reasons which he didn't yet understand.

He found his chance during a debate on productivity in which yawns inflated in his throat like balloons. A sudden inspiration about her coloring, the surprisingly blue eyes.

"The Soviet Union will never prosper until the peasants of Siberia are cured of their laziness," he announced grandly and incongruously. Like a trade union leader exhorting renewed labor.

It worked astonishingly well. "What do you know about work?" she demanded, color rising. "You people of the south are notorious for your idleness."

He grinned nervously. "You're a Sibiryak?"

"My parents came from Irkutsk. A wonderful city. Moscow may be our capital but it isn't the true Russia. Nor is the south." She paused seeking ammunition. "You produce apples and we produce diamonds."

The brandy, Vladimir suspected, was contributing to her passion. And to her disrespect for her hosts. (His father looked decidedly disgruntled.)

"We also produce good manners," Vladimir said, proud of his nonchalance.

The girl glanced at his parents, at the other two startled Komsomols. "I'm sorry. But I get tired of hearing people dismiss Siberia as if it were some medieval wilderness. Siberia," she recited, "is the prosperity and the treasure chest of the Soviet Union."

"I'm sure it is," Vladimir goaded. "If you don't mind your feet frozen off by permafrost in the winter and being blinded by dust storms in the summer. If they *have* any summer, that is."

She regarded him with distilled contempt. "Siberia has the finest climate in the world. Actually your ignorance appalls me. The cold in the winter is dry and bright— none of the foggy November mush of Moscow. And we have twice as much sunshine as Moscow. Did you know that, hidden away among your apple trees?"

Vladimir said he didn't and he was surprised because wasn't Siberia where all the enemies of Socialism were dispatched? If what she said was true then it was just like sending prisoners to sunbathe at a Black Sea resort.

The other two guests, earnest young men with red triangles of sunburn glowing between the open necks of their white shirts, tried to divert the conversation. Vladimir's father said, "We shouldn't compare the republics of our country. We must regard ourselves as a single great nation." Vladimir's mother retired to the kitchen to make green tea.

Valentina spoke with exaggerated patience. "Of course

85

prisoners are sent to Siberia. Because it's so vast they can't escape. It's the biggest forest in the world—bigger than the whole of the United States of America put together. Even Krasnoyarsk is three times the size of Texas."

"You've convinced me," Vladimir said, "that Siberia is very big."

"You are a fool," said Valentina.

"And you sound like a travel brochure."

She tossed back half an inch of brandy and gasped. "I believe you fought at Leningrad?"

"I was in the siege, yes."

"Then you have suffered and Russia is grateful."

"You are very kind."

"And you will know, of course, who were the bravest and toughest fighters during the war?"

"Let me guess," Vladimir said. "The Sibiryaks?"

She nodded. "The Nazis called them polar bears because not even the iciest blizzard could stop them. And whenever they fired a gun they hit the target."

"They were good fighters," Vladimir acknowledged.

Smoldering peace ensued. The guests drank their tea quickly. Excused themselves with alacrity—they had a full day ahead. Departed. And Vladimir went to his room to escape retribution.

But not before he had made a date to continue the debate next day. An invitation accepted with sulky bad grace.

The hostility soon faded as it does in the courtship of many animals. And the Komsomol did not receive quite the dedication it expected from Valentina.

Also her severity softened. Especially in the foothills of the mountains where birch and poplar conceded to conifer, loam to granite—mauve at sunset—drunken cidery perfumes to scents of pine needles and eternal snow far above.

They found a basin in this stern terrain, scooped there for lovers, jungled with rich grass and yellow flowers of the meadow. There he unloosened her earphones of glossy hair, embraced her and the future, kissed her and respected her although he was not sure about the wisdom of that.

86

Russia seemed to them then to be the finest country on the globe for young people. To help in the resurrection after war; to unfurl the red flag of equality wherever the poor were exploited. In their insect-buzzing arbor they saw noble warriors of peace, muscled athletes carrying torches. Although occasionally it seemed to Vladimir Zhukov that Valentina saw the future a little more seriously than necessary. The heritage of the Young Pioneers, the Komsomol. The wood-smoked evenings, the violet crags, the lights of the city below switching on: This wasn't the setting for Marx and Lenin and the class struggle.

So he kissed her and quieted her. And momentary unease was forgotten.

In the evenings they went to a café where a dreamy young man in a black cotton jacket and a sleepy bow tie played folk music on his guitar and, when the tea had been laced with sufficient brandy smuggled past the bearlike doorman, a few Glen Miller numbers including "In the Mood" and "Moonlight Serenade." Although the guitar didn't quite string along the Miller way. Afterward, to silence critics, he played a string instrument called a *dombra*. "Once upon a time," Vladimir explained, "the folk poets used to meet in a felt tent and hold contests of song and poetry." Which led to a guided tour by Valentina through Siberia including—encouraged by the brandy —a verse of "Glorious Baikal, Sacred Baikal" all about the deepest and coldest lake in the world. And a few snippets of lore from the taiga including the information that the horn of a particular deer was said to be an aphrodisiac. Which made Vladimir regret his chivalry in the mountains; these Sibiryaks were wild and passionate people. Maybe she thought he was impotent! Bitterly Vladimir regretted the girl in Berlin, the first and only time . . . Ridiculous for a man of twenty-one. He felt ashamed of the one time, ashamed of his purity; but in Leningrad a hunk of moldy bread had been more desirable than a woman's body.

They danced a little and she told him that he looked melancholy.

"You're leaving tomorrow," he said. They hadn't mentioned it all day. "Can't you stay a little longer?"

87

She shook her head, hair still loose and brushing his face. "I have to return to my work with the Komsomol. I've already neglected my duty here."

To hell with the Komsomol, he thought.

She kissed his ear. "But you will be coming to Moscow soon to study at the university?"

He hadn't made up his mind; but he made it up then. The city of Alma-Ata was suddenly an arid and provincial place. The harvest gathered, tractors stilled in the snow, his father's stifling obedience disguised as crusading endeavor. He was, after all, a Muscovite. There he would meet intellectuals, the Kremlin leaders, make his contribution to the cause through the arts of diplomacy. Become an ambassador of their faith in Paris, London, Washington. Peking, perhaps. Why had he hesitated? The confusions of his fevers, probably. Her breasts pressed against his chest. Warmth and tumescence. The sharing.

"Of course," he said. "Soon we'll be skiing together down the Lenin Hills."

And ski down the gentle slopes they did. Gazing with smug wonder at the sprawl of Moscow, its spires and fragile gold baubles belying its history: its purges and pogroms, its invasion by two dictators whose megalomania had perished in flames and frostbite. City of gilded aristocrats— and peasants goaded to mutiny when their misery was patronized. A poet's city, a musician's city; city of one God, mustached and smiling, inviolate in his bulwarked cathedral. All its cruelty, all its ponderous authority so alien to its graceful heart, softened now by snow and the low smoke of evening, the domes as delicate as soap bubbles.

Vladimir was studying, poetry banished—except for an occasional midnight scrawl—to make way for languages, economics, history and, inevitably, sociology which seemed to be a pseudonym for socialism. But he was content, with party membership almost attained, with this city of plodding aspiration and occasional ballet graces, with Valentina and the sharing.

And tonight he was going to make love to her.

When the polish on their cheeks began to glow. When

the tea was drunk. When the curtains in the wooden rooming house off Gorky Street where he lived were drawn and his room was as snug as a *babushka* in a shawl. Then he would undress her on the sighing bed and show her how to make love. With gentleness and caution because, for a girl, the first time was painful and could cause frigidity if mishandled. (In Berlin he had read an American textbook on the subject.) But with immense authority to illustrate, now and forever, that the horn of the Siberian deer would never be needed.

He undressed her rapidly and looked with great excitement at her flesh and fur. Wondering if he should confess to the incident in Berlin, because that's all it had been—an incident. A thrust from a starving soldier seeking the rewards of victory. At least the girl, as thin and frightened and inexperienced as himself, had been willing, not like some of the girls raped by the conquerors. Valentina, hair still in bangs, held out her arms to him and he decided not to confess just yet.

"I won't hurt you," he promised; the German girl had pleaded with him not to hurt her.

"My love," she said.

Such a mingling of affection, respect and lust. And marriage ahead.

With brief chagrin, he found that the need for textbook delicacy was unnecessary. Valentina had been shared before. But for the moment there was no place in his hunger for recrimination. And only very much later did he wonder who had possessed whom.

"I know," she said carefully—her words like cats' paws feeling the snow—"I know what you are thinking."

"I didn't realize," he said miserably.

"It was only once."

"An official of the Komsomol, I suppose."

"No," she said. "A student."

Desire sated, prim disgust and jealousy took over. "Did you love him?"

"Not really. I suppose you could call it infatuation."

But she wasn't the girl for infatuation. Nor, with her common sense and practical ways, was she the sort of girl to sleep around. Or was she? Again the indictment of his naïveté. "Just the one?"

"Yes," she said, "just the one. I'm not all that old, Vladimir. And is it so important? I love you and it has meaning now."

"So it had no meaning the other time?"

"Not much. He wanted to. I was curious. Girls are just as anxious for experience as men."

"Supposing there'd been a child?" Perhaps there had been! Disgust at himself for questioning and doubting.

"No," she said, anticipating the next question, "I didn't become pregnant."

Triumphantly Vladimir tossed some of his new knowledge at her. "You know, of course, that under the law of July 1944, you would have had no claim on the father. You couldn't sue him for a single kopeck."

"I know," she said. "The law for men."

"Not such a bad law. It's meant to encourage men and women to get married instead of living together. To end the old Bolshevik immorality."

She covered herself with a blanket, fear beginning to assemble. "Aren't you being a little hypocritical, Vladimir Zhukov? After all, you've just made love to me. What would happen if I became pregnant? Wouldn't you support me and the child?"

"Of course." He knew she was inviting a marriage proposal, but the moment had been spoiled.

"And am I the first girl you've made love to?"

"No."

"There you are then."

He felt she should have been disappointed, but she didn't seem to mind. "There have been several others," he lied.

"Then why should you be so disgusted because I have slept with one other man?"

"I suppose I should have anticipated it," he said. "What more should I expect from a Sibiryak?"

She turned and clawed him, getting in one good scratch on his cheek before he grabbed her wrists.

To hell with you, he thought. To think I treated you with such respect up there in the mountains. When all you wanted . . . He pushed her arms down on the pillow, spread her legs. She fought, then called his name.

Afterward she cried. And it seemed to him as if it had been the first time for both of them.

A year later they were married.

Vladimir Zhukov's patriotism and idealism remained fairly steadfast despite many onslaughts.

It was sustained by the war he'd fought and by the privations and shortages that lingered in Moscow. Crude sugar, no soap, endless queues in the frostbiting cold for bread and potatoes and crude cuts of meat. The blood war had been won but the battles of peace still had to be fought. Vladimir observed with fierce pride the head-scarved women waiting outside eyeless, nameless shops for food. They as much as the soldiers of Leningrad and Stalingrad had beaten the Fascists. And if the capital was truly *kupecheskaya Moscva*—the Moscow of merchants—then the *kupecheskaya* were having a thin time of it right now.

Just the same the onslaughts on belief were insidious. Particularly when you were a student. Surely it was the birthright of youth to question everything. But often the ones who asked questions vanished overnight. And for a few days the rumors about Beria the Butcher and his orgies with girls taken off the streets at night, about the massacres of Jews, about the imprisonment of Russians for sins of ancestry were hushed by fear.

And indeed none of them wanted to believe that the Nazi monster they had defeated had a blood brother in the Soviet Union. Vladimir Zhukov concluded that, even if any of the rumors had substance, they were the hangover of war; a necessary evil like the purges after the Bolsheviks seized power.

More accurately Vladimir didn't *want* to know. There was nothing he could do. An ideology based on equality was the only possible solution to the world's torment and to this he applied himself in his unspectacular way.

Once in Red Square he saw two *stilyagy* in American-styled beach shirts obtained from God knows where picked up by plainclothes police. Very frail they looked with their bright shirts flapping over their belts; the children of war. They were kicked and rabbit punched and thrown into the back of an ancient black sedan. It sickened him; but there was nothing he could do. Hadn't the Nazis been worse? Weren't the American cops just as bad? Violence and suppression were instruments of evolution; Vladimir Zhukov wasn't born to interfere with evolution.

Occasionally he questioned the Soviet acquisition of great tracts of Europe. In the loneliness before sleep it didn't seem much different from imperialist expansionism. And he listened gratefully to the university lectures explaining that it was no such thing; it was Socialism reaching out to embrace the world.

Gradually a small attic in Vladimir's mind began to fill with questions not wholly answered and sentiments not fashionable in the postwar motherland. In this attic he also stored fragments of poetry which might be considered subversive. Although he didn't open its trapdoor very often; it contained only diversions and obstacles to purpose. Soon the hinges became rusty.

Marriage. A junior post at the Foreign Ministry. Admission to the party. The birth of Natasha. A car after a two-year wait. A small but new apartment with bathroom not far from the American Embassy which looked like an old hospital in need of treatment.

Vladimir became a bureaucrat. But he still managed to rejoice. At the spring exuberance of his people after hibernation in the igloo of Moscow. And he argued vehemently with the Westerners he met through his job when they attacked the pattern of life: the alleged rule of the secret police, the dreary regimen.

Most of the Westerners were diplomats and businessmen seething at delays in negotiation. "You criticize," Vladimir snarled, after tilting the vodka bottle over lunch, "because you can't make money here as quickly as you can in America or Britain. You criticize because you come here with preconceived ideas. You look for faults and you find them. You don't consider the miracles that have been achieved in the thirty years since the Revolution—despite a war in between in which we lost a generation. You don't look for the music and laughter. Instead of coming to the beaches you stay in your hotels drinking and bitching. . . ."

And it was on the sandy river beaches of the Moscva, and the Volga that Vladimir liked most to enjoy the country he'd defended. Watching the long-distance pleasure boats throb past. Bottles of beer cooling in the lapping shallows. Tents in the birch glades, volleyball and ping-pong. Pale Muscovites, emerging from winter like the first thawed insects of spring, tanning every decent inch of skin, except their noses which they covered with protectors made from *Pravda* or *Izvestia*.

There, while Valentina nursed the baby, while guitars strummed in the matchstick woods, while massive women in pink and white brassieres laid out their flesh for burning, while children guzzled fizzy fruit drinks and rich ice cream, while a breeze smelling of boats and pine frilled the water at a fat turn in the river, there while all this happened and Russia discarded the uniform by which the West recognized it, there on that sandy display case Vladimir Zhukov saw the world as it might one day be.

Promotion at the Foreign Ministry came slowly. It was as if word had gone around that in his student days Zhukov had mildly questioned policy. (He'd shared a room in the wooden rooming house with an Armenian student whose hero was William Saroyan, an American-Armenian; the Armenian had incited argument on arctic evenings until their heated breath sent the frost patterns sliding on the inside of the windows. At lectures they had to accept dialectical materialism or be ostracized, but not in their timbered room designed for conspiracy. Except that they hatched no plots, just growled and scoffed, always solving the equations in favor of Russia.) But questioning was akin to accusing in the ears of snoopers. Perhaps, also, they'd found snatches of his amateurish poetry while he was at classes, the poetry that in spite of his father he'd gone on writing. You could never tell how long spite could be stored; certainly it never decomposed.

Then in February, 1956, God fell. And, although dead,

was duly crucified. At the 20th Party Congress Nikita Khrushchev denounced Stalin as a tyrant. A Hitler. The young could hardly absorb it. Their elders withdrew in bewilderment to examine the long knives in the corpse.

Vladimir and Valentina heard the news at a dacha in the forest forty miles from Moscow that a friend had lent them for the weekend. A neighbor, minding seven-year-old Natasha for the afternoon, told them about the denunciation, read at a local party meeting, as they buckled on their cross-country skis.

"Well?" Vladimir asked as they pushed themselves along a trail gleaming through the ice-sheathed silver birches.

"It's difficult to believe." She looked at home in the forest, he thought, face framed by a fur bonnet frosted by her breath.

"But it's true. I know that. So do you. All those rumors we heard and discarded because they were heresy—they were true, too."

He cursed the dead dictator who'd intruded into their afternoon because all week he'd anticipated the interlude in the cocoon of winter, alone in the silence. A break in routine; an escape from party matters which occupied more and more of Valentina's time until sometimes, in nocturnal moments of fear, he wondered if they weren't becoming more important to her than her family.

"I suppose so," she said.

"Anyway let's forget about him for now."

"Forget? How can we do that? Stalin molded our lives."

"Just for this afternoon."

The silence beckoned them, the stillness disturbed only by the occasional clatter of glacial twigs.

The trail tilted and they accelerated.

Vladimir said, " It reminds me of the days when we used to ski down the Lenin Hills."

She remembered too. "They were good times." Her voice was tender.

The hill straightened out and they slowed down, sliding along beside each other.

"It hasn't really changed so much, has it?" he said.

"No, Vladimir. Except that we have more responsibilities. Your job, Natasha. . . ."

"And the party." Now it was he who was disrupting the idyll.

"That's as it should be. We have each other. And we both have the party."

They skied down another gentle slope, stopping beside a frozen river, the ice deep below the snow. A mile away, on a curve of the river beside snow-bonneted cottages, they could see men fishing in round wounds in the ice.

Vladimir pulled back the hood of his blue parka and breathed deeply, feeling the air prickle in his nostrils. But his mind wouldn't stop worrying. "Tell me," he said, "if one day you had to make the decision, who would come first—family or party?"

She shook her head impatiently. "That's a stupid question. Sometimes you don't seem to have grown up at all since the day we met."

"That's good. It means you still love me."

"You mean you doubted that?"

"Not really. But the party means so much to you."

"Only because it's my work—like foreign service is yours."

"I don't think that's quite true, Valentina."

She thought about it. "No, perhaps not. It does mean more to me than it does to you. I've always known that, I suppose. Maybe it's because I'm a little younger than you. While you were fighting for Socialism during the war I was just a girl. When you left the Army, a little disillusioned perhaps, I was just beginning the work of rebuilding. Then it was the women who pulled Russia through. The women backed by the party. Young women like me. You know how it was, Vladimir, with so many men dead and wounded. . . ."

"Yes," he said, "I know how it was."

"The Fascists were beaten leaving the ruins behind. It was then that I knew that everything I'd learned in the Komsomol was true. Socialism was the only answer. Yes," she told herself, "it means everything to me."

95

"Everything?" A mouth of fear opened inside him, and the white afternoon that had welcomed them was suddenly hostile. A flurry of snow blew up the river hiding the crouching fishermen.

She looked at him in alarm. "You mean everything to me, Vladimir. You and Natasha."

"In what order?"

"No order," she said. "Why are you making us fight like this? We've been happy, haven't we? Wonderfully happy. . . . Why do you suddenly ask me to choose between you and what we both believe in. A woman wouldn't ask a man in time of war to choose between her and his country."

"We're not at war."

"Not with guns, maybe. But the West is always at war with us."

The sweat was growing cold on them and the breeze following the course of the river was strengthening. Sunlight briefly found the matchstick forests across the ice and touched the old wooden cottages before being extinguished for the day. Time to move on.

But the happiness was frozen.

Vladimir said, "You didn't answer my question."

"What question?"

"The stupid one. Which comes first—family or party?"

"I don't have to answer such questions. Why, Vladimir? Why are you talking like this?"

"Because a ghost has appeared from its grave. Because I remember what we all believed in. Blindly, without questioning. If we were wrong then can't we be wrong now?"

"We weren't wrong," she said. "We were wrong about one man, not about Socialism."

"And you won't answer my question?"

"To hell with your question," shouted his Sibiryak, tears glistening in her eyes. "To hell with you." She turned and began to ski back into the still forest.

A few flakes of snow fluttered from the sky.

"Long live the party," Vladimir yelled after her.

He gave her a couple of moments, then followed. But she

didn't take the trail. He could see her ahead, a flickering shadow among the trees crowding in on her. "Valentina," he shouted. "Get back on the trail."

The shadow vanished.

The mouth of fear yawned. *I should never have asked such questions. The trust and love of their marriage severed: a precipice, broken skis, blood dark on snow.* He felt the cruelty of the thickening dusk as he propelled himself through the thin trees, following her trail over the crust of the snow.

In front of him the forest angled away steeply, a few young pines like arrows among the birch. Faster, faster, skis whispering on the snow. Falling snow blurring his vision.

Steeper went the hillside. Then there she was lying at the foot of a tree, one ski snapped, her outline blurred in the fading light.

"I'm all right, Vladimir," she said.

"Are you sure, my love?"

"I've twisted my ankle. That's all."

He unbuckled her skis. "Are you sure?"

"There's nothing serious, anyway."

He felt her injured ankle. No bones broken as far as he could tell. "Does it hurt very much?"

"Not too much. Don't worry, Vladimir, I'm all right."

Blobs of snow. Aching cold. He bent and picked her up. "Valentina, I'm sorry."

She said, "It seemed to me you were questioning our marriage. Our love. I couldn't bear that."

"There's never been another love like it," he said.

He picked her up and took her back to the trail. Then helped her limp back in the snow-scurrying darkness to the dacha. And that night, with the pain eased, they made love that crystallized all they had known together. All that might lie ahead.

Nine months later a novel called *The Difficult March* was published in *Novy Mir*. In it a character asked, "What shall I believe now?"

But still the fall of one man could not destroy a faith. The virgin lands burgeoned, the factories thundered, the new leader made contact with the West—if a little tipsily on occasions—the good word continued to be disseminated, the dissemination occasionally accompanied by tanks.

Vladimir Zhukov rose laboriously in the ranks of the Foreign Ministry. A trustworthy if less than fanatical party member. An incomparable English speaker borrowed from time to time by the Kremlin leaders when they parleyed with the West at times when Churchill's "balance of terror" had to be observed in an atomic age. Valentina was promoted within the party to the point where friends speculated that, *if* Vladimir were given a foreign posting, it would be his wife they were dispatching as an emissary.

Natasha became a Young Pioneer.

A world war was averted.

Khrushchev fell and the tempo of change slackened.

Despite the traumatic changes, Vladimir Zhukov rarely opened the trapdoor to his attic of doubt and sensibility. Until he went to Washington.

PART II

Chapter 1

NATASHA VLADIMIROVNA ZHUKOVA was picked up with a mixture of professional expertise and blatant sexual maneuver.

The professionalism was the man's—the doggy-faced Russian, not unlike Brezhnev, who was determinedly following her.

He was defying the red DON'T-WALK traffic lights at an intersection down Connecticut Avenue from Du Pont Circle, hurrying in front of three hooting cabs, when two cops wearing guns and sideburns stopped him.

They told him he was jaywalking and thereby breaking the laws and regulations of the District of Columbia and one of them began to write a warning ticket. Nicolai Grigorenko shouted in his inadequate English that he was a Russian diplomat and had immunity. But the cops didn't seem to understand him at all and when he tried to reach for his identification papers they restrained him as if he were going for a gun.

Grigorenko, seeing Natasha Zhukova fading in the shopping crowds, kicked at a police shin. The cop helped Grigorenko's foot on its way and Grigorenko fell, supported by big hands on his biceps. "You bastards," he shouted.

One of the cops said, "Knock it off, fella."

It was only when Natasha Zhukova was well clear that the misunderstanding was sorted out. Quite easily, with Grigorenko's hand free to reach his wallet.

Apologies and oaths. "You will be sacked for this," Grigorenko told them.

"Maybe," said one of the cops combing a sideburn with his fingernails. "Maybe not."

"Everybody makes mistakes," said his colleague.

"Have a good day," said the first cop, as Grigorenko plunged through the crowds like an aging bloodhound after a bitch in heat.

The other patrolman tore up the ticket with the words "Courtesy Notice" printed in red letters on the bottom.

The maneuver, about as subtle as a girl dropping a handkerchief, was enacted in the Discount Book Shop on Connecticut about a half block below Du Pont Circle. Piles of newly minted hardbacks, batteries of paperbacks and two dozen or so members of the public jay-reading among the covers.

Natasha Zhukova, dazed, awed and frightened, wandered in and put out a hand to pick up a book called *Russians as People*. She was overcome by the luxury of possession around her, by the clothes and cars, by the birthright of elegance of some and the assumed scruffiness of others. Most of all by the actuality of what she'd read about; by her very presence here.

Another hand reached the book in synchronized movement. The young man removed his hand and said, "*Pazhalista*." The word fell and lingered, a friendly autumn leaf on a winter day.

She picked up the book.

The young man continued in modest Russian. "At least the author acknowledges that Russians are people."

She went on thumbing the pages, reading nothing, fear pulsing.

"You're Russian?"

She nodded.

"I thought so. Your clothes and your features."

She spoke in university English. "I didn't know it was so obvious."

"I didn't mean to offend you." He returned gratefully to English. "I think your clothes are just great. Ours are so damned affected."

"I don't think so—they are very beautiful."

Her shyness infuriated her. Where was the liberated Natasha Zhukova whose rebel lover was currently serving two years in prison?

100

"And our women are so brash," he added.

"Brash? What is brash?"

"Like that," he said, pointing at a girl with white-blond hair and pink dueling fingernails leafing through a cookbook.

"She is very attractive." With her braided hair and brown fur-collared coat Natasha felt like a schoolgirl wearing her mother's clothes. She put down the book, balling her hands into embarrassed fists. "It has been very nice meeting you. Now I must go."

But when she reached the sunlit square he was still with her. "I wonder," he said, "if you'd like to join me for a cup of coffee."

She shook her head emphatically. "I cannot do that. I am sorry."

She quickened her stride among the alien, indifferent crowds. Spring breathed around them, the scent of blossoms not entirely defeated by car exhaust.

"Please," he said. "Just coffee. You see I'm going to Russia soon and I'd like some advice."

They reached Lafayette Square. The White House behind its fountain glistening with sunshine as if it had been painted overnight; porticoed and colonial, majestically snug behind Kensington railings. The baronial hall of the big bad baron himself. It was too much for Natasha Zhukova just at that moment. She gazed instead at the church on the corner, St. John's, the "Church of the Presidents." Sunlight imprisoned in its gold domes above its clean cream walls. Plucked, she thought, from the Kremlin, or a clearing in the taiga where, in such churches, moths of old women still worshiped with fragile defiance. The house of a rejected faith glowing now with familiarity.

He spoke again in Russian, expanding the aura of familiarity and stepping deftly inside beside her. "Perhaps you'd like to see the church. It's a pretty little place."

She glanced at him curiously, timidly. Until now she'd been aware only of his camel's hair coat, bright-tan shoes and button-down shirt; aware of his neatness. Now she appraised the man. About twenty-four, a bit like an actor with his hair longish by Russian standards (unless you were a rebel). On the skinny side which helped him to wear his clothes well, she supposed. A trace of a suntan from last summer, or a winter resort maybe—there was no telling where a man like this wintered. Hard gray eyes set with gentleness, ears a little flappy. Certainly the most elegant man she'd ever spoken to. And the most courteous, especially when she had previously consigned American males into seven brackets—the principals of *The Magnificent Seven* which she'd seen in Moscow; especially when the whole race was always dismissed as hooligan. Certainly someone to describe to envious girlfriends back at university—if she were ever readmitted.

The little church rejoiced in the sunshine and she said, yes, she would like to see inside.

Red pews. And tremulous watercolor patterns from the stained-glass window above the altar.

"The Last Supper," said her guide, pointing at the window. "Beautiful, isn't it?"

Natasha Zhukova agreed. The whole church so self-composed and clean and golden.

The young man said, "The original church was built like a Greek cross. The architect was a guy named Latrobe. He helped to build the Capitol and the White House. And he wrote to his son, 'I have completed a church that has made many Washingtonians religious who had not been religious before.' "

Natasha Zhukova smiled for the first time that day; for the first time for many days. "It seems to me they're not very religious today."

"Not today maybe. It's too nice outside. I don't think God—our God—would object to that." He led her down the aisle to Pew 54. "That's where the President worships. Every President since Madison has worshiped here."

"Let's go now," she said. Because she had a sudden frivolous desire to sit where the President's backside had been. I am eighteen; I must curb such immature irresponsibility. But the church had done its job: tranquilized her heathen mind; the fear—or most of it—had been lapped up by the melting watercolors beneath the Stars and Stripes on the wall.

Beside the railings of the White House a Sikh wearing long leather boots and turban displayed a placard bearing the words: MY FAMILY IS THE LARGEST. THE HUMAN RACE. BE A WORLD CITIZEN. The guard on the gate regarded him with indifference.

"He will surely be arrested," Natasha said.

"Why? He isn't doing anything wrong."

"I don't know. . . ."

A panting silver bus unloaded a posse of sightseers who headed, cameras joggling on their chests, for the Executive Mansion.

"Would you like to go inside?"

"No, please. I must go home."

"You don't have to worry about anything. Everyone who comes to Washington goes to the White House."

"Everyone who goes to Moscow goes around the Kremlin."

"But can they go around the home of President Podgorny? Or Brezhnev or Kosygin?" he asked cautiously.

"I don't know. But the Kremlin isn't the sort of prison that you Americans seem to think it is. Moscow's a beautiful city. And Leningrad—that's even more beautiful. It is not unlike Washington, I think."

"I'm glad you like Washington." He hesitated. "I'd like to show some of it to you. There have been some great architects involved. . . ."

"You seem to be very interested in these buildings of yours."

"I am," he said. "I'm an architect. I've just passed my exams. And you—what do you do? What brings you to Washington?"

"It doesn't matter." She had once decided never to lie; particularly not to herself. But wasn't silence the easiest lie of all? She noticed that his attention had wandered to a girl in a mini-skirt airing her thighs in the new sunshine. "Do you work here? And do you make a point of talking to strange girls in bookshops? That would never happen in Moscow." Or at least it had never happened to her.

"Yes," he said. "And now, please, won't you come and have coffee with me?"

103

"Just one," she replied, surprising herself. "Just five minutes and then I must go home."

"Where is home?"

"Not far away." No lies.

One coffee and, because he insisted, a hot dog. Which she ate very quickly because she was suddenly hungry; gurgling catsup and mustard onto it. Pouring cream and crystals of colored sugar into her coffee. Vague guilt surfacing at the memory of rectangles of sugar that rested like stones at the bottom of thick cups.

Here, among the jeans and the girls discussing last night's boyfriends or lack of, among the clerks and tourists and worried men fingering the Help Wanted sections, he looked too smart. Bars, she thought, beckoned him; bars with dim lights and olives floating in cocktails and girls of ravenous sexual appetite and impossible elegance. She would, she decided, ask her father for some money for a few clothes and to have her hair styled. And a mini-skirt! But I would have to change into it far away from the embassy. In a toilet, perhaps. To emerge with bare thighs rubbing, exciting the boys. Except that my thighs are so white, and in any case my legs are not my best feature. Russian men like plump women. I am not yet plump but I could easily become so. (She discarded the insistent desire for another hot dog.) Am I so decadent then? Guilt and excitement. Poor Georgi.

He put his hand on her arm. "May I see you again?"

"Why me?" she asked.

"Because I like your company."

But not, she thought, because of my allure. With my braids and this old coat with a winter collar like a rat clutching my neck. But at least she wasn't a degenerate trollop like the girl in the bookshop with the cruel fingernails. If I had a pair of shears I'd hack my braids off.

"May I see you again?"

The mini-skirted fantasies faded. Cinderella in the daylight. The warnings, her guilt, the faces of the plainclothes police, her father's position which she had already imperiled—all these ganged up on her. She shook her head,

104

tasting crystals of blue and red sugar on the tip of her tongue.

"Why not?"

"It is just impossible. And now I really must go. You have been really kind."

"Very well," he said, courteous in defeat. "May I ask your name?"

She told him and asked him his.

"Charles," he replied. "Charlie to most people."

"Charlie," she repeated. "I like that very much. I am glad you are not called Genry."

"Genry?"

"Yes," she said. "We Russians have much difficulty in pronouncing 'haitch.' " She had difficulty with that, too. "And would you be so kind as to tell me your other name?"

"Sure," he said. "It's Hardin. Charlie Hardin."

He called her a cab and she went back through the wide, free-breathing, fast-flowing streets to the apartment building near Du Pont Circle.

She could have been back in Russia: the small apartment provided for the Zhukovs in the middle-aged block which predecessors had made as Soviet as a bowl of borsch. Except for the electric cooker with cockpit dials and rotating spit, the humming refrigerator in which there was always a slippery heap of steak for communal stews—and a small decadence of Hawaiian Punch and blue cheese dressing bought by her father, and a washing machine with a built-in spin-dryer. The rest was Russia: plastic flowers, furniture with slivers of veneer rising like cockroach tails, a bowl of red currants coated with icing sugar, a faint aroma of brilliantine, a bottle of vodka and a bottle of brandy bought at the embassy commissariat, the table with its cloth the color of fog laid for dinner with elegant glasses and a plate of poppy seed rolls and black bread. An old Motorola TV set on which her father missed nightly soccer and a record player on which the Red Army choir, their militancy a little scratched, could still be counted on to inflict defeat on the TV commercials.

Here in the evenings Natasha joined other Russian guests for soup and stew and tax-free liquor; moist reminiscences, throaty songs and television, the most popular shows being variety, *Get Smart,* Ed Sullivan, Lucille Ball and *I Spy*; and loud comments about America which, unlike the normal symptoms of tipsyness, became more sibilant and furtive with intoxication—when, in fact, a little praise was being bestowed, when only trusted friends were present. Sometimes the Zhukovs went to other Russians' homes, sometimes to Czechs' or Hungarians' apartments; rarely elsewhere. Except for her father who these days dressed better than his colleagues and went out two or three times a week, leaving early and returning late and noisily.

Everything, of course, was shared by V. I. Lenin in reproduced oils and the three top Kremlin leaders enigmatic in glossy black and white.

This afternoon Natasha hurried to her sparse room and gazed at herself in the mirror. The plain white blouse, clerical skirt, those braids, soap-clean face with a touch of powder on the high cheekbones, unplucked eyebrows. The only crudity missing, she thought, was a set of steel teeth.

What had he seen in her?

So elegant, sophisticated, assured. In a city teeming with attractive women, a city whose only shortage was men. (Like Moscow.) Perhaps he had wearied of all the cultivated sexuality; perhaps he saw her as a quaint alternative whose gaucheries could be recounted to smirking friends.

You, Mr. Hardin, she accused angrily, would be the quaint oddity in Russia, the greatest power in the world, where values have not been depraved by excess.

Could he have been honestly attracted, though?

My hair is thick and glossy and men seem to enjoy loosening the braids, as if they're loosing faucets of water. My face is not beautiful, but the touch of Mongol makes it interesting—so I've been told. I'm not unintelligent; although certainly not brilliant, emphatically nonintellectual, as my studies proved. I enjoy sex with a wholesome appetite; perhaps this shows . . . And my body . . .

She took off her blouse and brassiere, smoothing her big

breasts in front of the mirror. Took off the rest of her clothes to see what men saw. Felt between her thighs with curiosity. Untwined her braids, but in doing so noticed the hair at her armpits. Intuitively she knew that Washington women would remove it. In Russia I was desirable; in America I am a peasant.

Natasha Zhukova lay down on the bed and considered her appetites, summoning the honesty that she insisted on. Honestly she saw no wrong in them. Civilization had made hypocrites of women. Dearly she wished to fuse sex with love.

Unsolicited, Charles—Charlie—Hardin presented himself in her imagination. Even as Georgi had deflowered her—Georgi the instrument for the inevitable experience —she had wondered what shape and form love would take.

But not Charlie Hardin. Instant attraction occurred, not instant love. That was for bourgeois magazines. And in any case this attraction—it might be nothing more than curiosity—was doomed. East and West. Taboo.

She dismissed Charlie Hardin, but he stayed.

I know, she thought, that he did not approach me merely because he wanted advice about Russia. "A woman knows," she told herself, quoting some novelist or other.

But why?

In one month there had been so much that had been inexplicable. Why, for instance, had the Soviet authorities suddenly allowed her to visit America although she'd been suspended from the university because of her association with undesirable dissident elements? Poor Georgi.

She went first to Garfinckel's. But, like the White House, it was too much. A superabundance of elegance where phantom czarinas looked down at her through lorgnettes; hushed halls chiming faintly with golden sovereigns. She picked up an ornamental egg of polished stone, sea-green and cool, feeling its weight while she sought escape.

A few counters away an elegant male assistant warned the house detective about Nicolai Grigorenko lingering incongruously among the Christian Dior ties and frilled shirts.

107

Then she was away into the street looking for a drugstore more suited for a muzhik with thirty rubles to spend. Behind her, on an invisible leash, came her bloodhound, tail between his legs, shaggy face desperate after the abuse from that little shit Brodsky.

At the cosmetics counter of the drugstore shyness mastered her. So humiliating in the society she'd been taught to despise. Milky cleansers, skin lotions, moisture lotions, lipsticks in shell pink and even white (for the blacks? she wondered), eyeshadows in green and mauve and blue—some glittering with stardust—powders, mascara, lacquers, pictures of girls bathing orgiastically in rainbow soapsuds . . .

Beside her a busy girl applied lipstick samples to the back of her hand like warpaint. Nerving herself, like a child trying to slip into an adult movie, Natasha Zhukova copied her. Together they crayoned. Finally Natasha chose "Show Pink" because pink seemed to be fashionable. The slithery texture and the perfume reminded her of the wild flowers that peasants sell in Moscow—lilac, lily of the valley and cowslips—intoxicated her and she embarked on a tiny orgy of cosmetic spending. Lotions, cleansers and conditioners, whose uses she only vaguely understood. And a pair of eyebrow tweezers with which to barber those two thick question marks. But how did you pay? No abacus. She joined a queue of Washington girls, elegant, laughing, gossiping girls; all industriously absorbed with the trivia of the day.

Natasha handed the saleslady her purchases.

"Nine dollars thirty-five," intoned the saleslady, a middle-aged woman with bubbly blond hair and rhinestoned glasses.

Natasha fiddled with her bills which all looked the same, panicked and handed the saleslady five dollars.

"There's only five here, honey," she accused, with the monotone assurance that American women seemed to have.

"I'm sorry. . . . How much more do you want?"

"Another four thirty-five, honey." She stopped chewing

108

her gum. "Gee, honey, where you from? Alaska or some-place? Soon you'll be telling me all them bills look the same."

Natasha sensed the implication that she was trying to cheat. The blood of Siberia and Moscow boiled angrily. "Are you accusing me of anything?"

All around the gossip stopped.

The saleslady fielded the indignation—and the probability that she had made a mistake. "No, honey," she said. And then, "Are you from around here?"

The audience listened delightedly.

"I am from Russia." As if she were announcing herself at a chandelier-hung ball.

"Gee," said the saleslady. "Ain't that something. Or," she asked doubtfully, "are you just putting me on?"

"I beg your pardon?"

"Are you kidding me?"

"I am from the Soviet Union." The silence was solidify-ing: even more dramatic now—as if she'd swung into the store like Tarzan. She found another five-dollar bill. "Here is the rest of the money. Kindly give me my change."

The woman nodded like a basking lizard. "Well, I'll be darned." She took the rest of the money. "But come to think of it you do look a bit Ruski. I guess it's them braids. How long you been in the States? I mean how many years has it taken you to pick up the language?"

Despite the embarrassment of it all, pride raised its smug head. "I've only been here a week. I learned all my English in Russia. We have very good education in the Soviet Union."

"One week!" She looked around like a talk-show moderator. "How about that?"

The audience was receptive. The squaw with the lip-sticked hand said, "Have you ever met that Khrushchev? What a wild guy he was."

The faces formed a circle. She remembered her braids, her virginal blouse, her untended eyebrows, her father, the embassy, the police. "Please," she pleaded, "my change."

"Don't you want your purchases, honey?"

109

"Please." Bravado cringing close to cowardice.

"It's been a pleasure serving you, honey."

The faces parted as if she had musclemen guarding her. And the saleslady's voice followed her: "Have a good day. Have a good time in the States. . . ."

Such a hooligan approach, such formality and politeness, such innate kindness snuggled like the kernel of a winter-hard nut . . .

Later she cried, inexplicably. But not before she had asked her father for a few more dollars to get herself a hairdo and a new coat and a tiny skirt to be donned in some secret place in Washington.

Two days later, when she emerged from the apartment building, Nicolai Grigorenko, sulking in his Volkswagen, didn't recognize her from the back: long hair flowing glossily around her shoulders, hand brushing it from her forehead, shaved legs, round-toed shoes with tallish heels, yellow spring coat from Hecht's, walking with the arrogant spring stride of an attractive girl. So Grigorenko sulked on, waiting for a braided girl with stubby shoes and uncertainty in her gait.

She walked down Connecticut with the intention of reaching the ceremonial mansions and spring-blooming gardens of the capital. It was the most direct route; it also took her past the bookstore where she'd met Charlie Hardin.

But of the elegant Mr. Hardin there was no sign. Although, if she had studied the traffic closely, she might have seen him hunched in the back of a dawdling cab.

From Farragut to Lafayette and the desirable residence of the Chief Executive at 1600 Pennsylvania Avenue, NW 20500 (Phone 456-1414).

But it was toward the little gold-capped church, looking jaunty today beneath high sailing clouds, that she looked.

Excitement, fear, guilt, embarrassment at her schoolgirl expectations. If I don't see him then I am suitably reprimanded and in a few days' time such absurd and unpatriotic emotion will expire.

He turned the corner of the church still managing to look elegant in a suede jacket with a cream shirt beneath, gray slacks and moccasins.

Do you wave? Shout across the broad avenue of traffic outside the President's home?

Somehow he noticed her, waved hesitantly, charged the traffic rashly.

"Hi," he said. "Say, you look great. Different somehow."

"Hallo," she said.

They grabbed desperately at receding words.

"What a fantastic coincidence. I mean it's unbelievable."

"It is," she agreed, "a surprising coincidence."

"Where are you going?"

Where was she going? "Nowhere in particular. Just looking around. And you—what brings you back to this place?"

"This place?" He grinned. "This place *is* the home of the President of the United States. And I do work just around the corner."

"Ah."

"Do you know," he said, "I almost didn't recognize you."

"Didn't you?" she said, already pleased at what he was going to say. "Why was that?"

"You really do look different. Wow," he added, "you look terrific."

"Thank you." She realized that she hadn't yet learned how to accept a compliment.

"Were you about to sneak inside the President's home?"

"I was thinking about it. But I was too scared. It is very difficult to comprehend that I can go into such a place."

"Come on." He took her arm and she allowed herself to be escorted through the portals of the big bad baron.

A confusion of impressions. The East Room where Lincoln and Kennedy had lain in state; heavyweight chandeliers and a piano mounted on eagles. A shirt-sleeved guard with a military stripe down his trousers. Green Room, Blue Room, lustrous drapes and noble features

111

frozen by the brush of portrait painters in the midst of their deeds and misdeeds.

Beside them two hippies sneered their way as far as the East Room, then cowered beneath the weight of history—faltered in this inhabited museum.

"Is he here now?" Natasha asked.

"Who?"

"The President."

"Maybe."

She imagined him upstairs, dashing off a cable to the Kremlin, stuffing himself with Texas steak and french fries.

Cautiously he permitted himself a small joke. "This is your room."

"Why?"

"The Red Room." And in case she should take offense he rushed on, "This is where the President's wife receives guests. And those guys up there are Presidents McKinley, Cleveland, Coolidge and Wilson."

"But anyone could wander around here—even plant a bomb."

"I guess they could. Although these gentlemen here" —he pointed at military-striped trousers—"can smell a nut a mile away."

"Please?"

He explained as they reached the State Dining Room. Golds and creams and eagles and candelabra and Lincoln considering his responsibilities.

Outside again, he led her, unprotesting, to the lawns around the Tidal Basin where the fringe of Japanese cherry would soon bloom and die as swiftly as butterflies.

He sat down on the grass and she sat beside him.

"This is very bad," she announced, permitting the badness to stay.

"Why's that? We're not doing anything wrong."

He took a pack of cigarettes from his breast pocket—they always carried them here—and lit one. The smoke broke into lace.

"It's difficult to explain." She examined the strolling office workers and determined tourists.

"And why do you keep looking behind you?"

112

"I don't know." A habit, she supposed.

"Tell me about yourself. What are you doing over here? On some sort of exchange program, I guess. What part of Russia do you come from?" He lapsed into Russian again, the persuasive Russian. "Come on, tell me about yourself."

She sighed deeply, nibbled the sheathed stem of a blade of grass. "There isn't much to tell." Evasion and trivia. "I'm the daughter of a diplomat at the Soviet Embassy."

He choked, lungs full of smoke. "Well, a girl from the Red House. . . ."

"Please?"

"The Red House—the opposite of the White House. What does your father do? And what are you doing over here? I thought they only allowed the kids to stay in the States."

"You seem to know a lot about it?"

"I read my newspapers. Haven't you got a place out on the Chesapeake someplace?"

"Yes," she said. "Black Walnut Point, I believe." She wondered if the grass would stain her teeth green. "You're right about the children. They go to our own school here. Then just before they reach their teens they're sent back to the Soviet Union to continue their studies. Just like American children in Moscow, I believe," she added defensively.

"You're very pretty," he said.

"Thank you." Perhaps she should stand up and curtsy.

"But what are you doing here in Washington?" He returned to English.

"It's a complicated story." Compromising with honesty.

"Will you be here long?"

"I don't know. . . ." She longed for access to the all-American girl's phrasebook. A perplexing volume. Especially the language of flirtation which puzzled her because its purpose seemed mainly to antagonize.

In a drugstore downtown/uptown (she had no idea which was which) she'd been unable to resist the temptation to eavesdrop on four teen-agers. One boy in blue jeans and combat jacket covering a ricket-thin body had made some remark about a baseball team called the Chicago

113

White Sox. Worship of values that birth had denied him quivering in his voice. Natasha guessed that he had to make smart remarks to survive.

The girl opposite him (his girl surely not) with long dull hair, baby breasts nippling her thin sweater, said, "Jesus, Brad, there you go again, man. What a load of crap. With supporters like you the White Sox don't need no enemies. They must have been tickled pink when your ma and pa came to this dump."

"Ah, screw you," replied the thin boy affectionately.

The other girl, sucking Coke through a straw and tapping monotonously at a cigarette, said, "Show us your muscles, tiger."

The second boy, stocky and brutal with thick-curled hair, stretched and belched. "Knock it off, will ya?" he remarked amiably.

The first girl regarded the thin boy balefully. "Jesus, what a jerk." Then suddenly she leaned across the table and kissed him with passion.

Natasha decided that they were children of the underprivildeged proletariat. Although even capitalists' daughters seemed to beckon their lovers with insults.

Charlie Hardin stubbed out his cigarette and lay on his back, hands behind his neck. Boyish and more approachable than he was in his city clothes. Fair hair curled at the V of his shirt and his Adam's apple looked vulnerable. Of his character, she thought, I know nothing. He has shown me nothing.

He said, "Can you come here tomorrow?"

"I expect so."

"And the next day?"

"I expect so."

"Then we have the present. The future can take care of itself."

"I suppose so," she said, wishing that he didn't try so hard. "Do you mean you really want to see me again?"

"I would like that," he said carefully. "Very much. But, hell, today's only just beginning."

"I have to get back."

"Why? You're not working for the Reds—I mean the Russians."

"So we are the Reds to you?"

"Just a word. Like we're Yankee imperialists or something to you."

"We don't care what you call us. It is quite immaterial. Always the Americans have been great ones for talking."

He held up his hand, freckled and strong with a gold ring on the little finger. "Please, let's not get involved in the cold war. Look at the sky—it's warm and deep."

She examined his gray eyes; although you couldn't tell character that way. There was a young crease on his forehead, a little hair on his cheekbones too high to shave.

He smiled uncertainly. She wondered if he was a dominant lover like Georgi had pretended to be. She didn't think so, though perhaps he too acted the part.

She said, "I don't understand you, Charlie."

"Why not? There's not much to understand."

"Because you talk without sincerity. And yet you are not a shallow man."

He searched for a cigarette, a diversionary and delaying tactic. "Maybe I am. Which proves I'm honest, which is maybe better than being deep and interesting?"

"It seems to me that you are not shallow."

"You sound as if you're accusing. As if intellect is a crime."

"Sometimes," she said, "it is."

An antique propeller-driven airliner lumbered over the snowcap of Jefferson's rotunda hedged by cherry trees.

Natasha said she had to go and reluctantly Charlie said okay as long as she promised to see him tomorrow. They hadn't talked about anything yet, he added, and he could become the biggest damn bore alive when it came to talking about architecture. Also he would like to take her into the country—Hagerstown way maybe—in his green MG (explaining what that was). Natasha agreed to meet him, caution overcome with an ease that surprised her, but said, no, she couldn't go into the country because the embassy staff and their relatives were confined to a thirty-mile

115

radius of Washington and she might stray over the boundary by mistake. Already I have brought enough trouble to my father, she thought. He said fair enough, maybe they could do the Capitol tomorrow, and then see a movie.

She looked into his eyes, through the sun-touched iris, through the sun-contracted pupil into the dark cranial depths where the life and times of Charlie Hardin were filed.

"Why?" she asked. "Why me?"

He squinted in the sunlight. Hand searching for a cigarette. "Why not?"

"Because there are so many other beautiful American girls who would love to ride in your green BG."

"MG."

"Why me, Charlie?"

"Because you're more beautiful than any American girl I know." But he wasn't looking at her when he spoke.

"I'm going now," she said.

"I'll walk you to a taxi."

"No," she said. "Please. I think I'll walk part of the way." To analyze his dishonesty and decide whether she wanted to see him again because lies she could not accept in a man. Not a man who might matter to her. And her own dishonesty implicit in her silences, her evasiveness.

"Okay," he said. "But be careful, Natasha. This is a dangerous city. Stick to the main streets. Only yesterday I saw a middle-aged woman robbed in broad daylight."

"Didn't anyone stop the thief?"

"I guess he ran too fast. In any case people aren't in any hurry to go to your rescue. They tend to look the other way. In this and any other country," he added defensively.

"But you saw him," she accused.

"I was on the other side of the street. In my car."

"I see," she said. "Good-bye, Charlie."

"Till tomorrow?"

But she was walking away from him, full of her betrayal of Georgi here in this city of violence and deception.

Ten trees away the mugger leaped. One arm encircled her throat, and with his free fist he hit her arm just behind

116

the elbow, stunning it. But she managed to hold onto her purse.

She screamed.

"Drop that purse or you get this knife right through your sweet ribs."

She smelled his breath, sweet and pungent like liquorice. Smelled his sweat flowing with his own fear.

She kicked backward with her new shoes, whimpering. Broad daylight. Jefferson. The Monument spiring the clouds nearby.

"I warned you. . . ."

She felt the blow through the mugger's body. His grip slackened and she tore herself loose.

She saw Charlie Hardin's fist swinging toward the man's throat and shouted, "Look out, Charlie, he's got a knife."

Fist and knife missed. The mugger, unkempt and starved-looking, lunged again. Hardin sidestepped, catching the arm, breaking it with a snap, hurling the man forward in a crumpled half-somersault. He yelped and ran.

Hardin said, "You okay?"

"Yes."

He began to chase, gave it up after fifty yards or so. There were two or three other people around; no one paid much attention.

They learned against a tree together. Comprehension of their plight assembled between them. Comprehension, not yet totally identified, of man's infinite capacity of creating suffering and then immersing himself in it. The bears of the taiga growled, the prairie buffalo bellowed. Sunlight finding its way through the curls and wafers of emerging leaves played at their feet.

He reached out and touched her cheek.

Next day Nicolai Grigorenko was put on the first plane back to Moscow.

Chapter 2

THERE WAS ANGER in the neat house in Alexandria that night. Anger young and guilty.

The house was one of half a dozen styles dispersed along the avenues of a subdivision within earshot of Highway 95. Mostly cozy red, some white-pillared in suburban-colonial, others a little squashed, they seemed to be parked outside their cars. Garden lamps burned all day, squirrels darted and nibbled among the open-plan trees. Comfortable and secure. Except that, on Sunday afternoons, many an overweight car polisher who had spotted the first two letters of RECESSION edging into the headlines wondered how many more working Monday mornings there would be.

In one such house—the most expensive style but by no means extravagant—Charlie Hardin argued futilely with his father. His father, he thought, should be planted on the lawn, a garden gnome unperturbed by summer storms or winter blizzards.

Also present were Wallace Walden and Jack Godwin from the CIA pulling a shred of tobacco through his teeth like dental floss.

"To hell with it," Charlie stormed. "I'm not going through with it. She's a nice kid. She doesn't have to be involved in some crummy conspiracy that you've cooked up. And I don't either."

His father who had always shaved recently smoothed his hair—whitening healthily and smartly—and said, "Don't talk like that, Charlie. Remember your promise. . . ."

"I didn't expect the job to be quite as immoral as this."

"Listen," said his father, lighting a cigarillo, "you

wouldn't have given a damn if you hadn't been attracted to this girl. I know . . . I'm your father and I know at least a part of your mind because it's mine. If this had been someone else's girl and you'd been immersed in some other courtship you wouldn't have had any scruples about what you did to her. You've got to think of it that way, Charlie. It changes nothing because you've gone soft on her. You know where your loyalties lie. I don't have to remind you."

"Bullshit," said his son, unhappily aware of elements of truth in his father's words. *Go and get your hooks into this young Russian broad; then we'll have an "in."* "Okay, so I agreed to do it because you asked me. Because there was no one in the FBI who could take the part. But I was wrong. We're committing a crime. An obscenity. Supposing," he suggested, "that this girl was your daughter?"

But he should have known better: He was the son.

Walden took over the paternal duties; one hand on the color TV, the other holding his pipe like a pistol. A stratum of tobacco smoke lay like a tablecloth over the expensive simulated antiques in the room.

Certainly, he told Charlie Hardin, he understood his scruples—and admired them. "They're rare commodities in the circles I move in, son." And it was a crying shame that he should have become the instrument of this particular intrigue. But had it occurred to Charlie that the Soviets might be playing a dirty game—that they might be dangling the girl as bait? Why had they brought her over?

"To get at her old man," Godwin said, scraping at a scab of unidentified food on his fly.

Hardin, Senior, handed him an ashtray for the tottering ash of his cigar—too late. Hardin said, "Why would they do that, Jack? Surely they had a bigger hold over Zhukov when the girl was in Russia?"

Godwin shambled across the room and poured himself more whiskey from a glass decanter. "You've got me there"—as if this were rare—"but my guess is that they haven't quite got Zhukov where they want him yet. He hadn't been groomed sufficiently when they shunted Tardovsky back to Moscow. Incidentally, I wonder which cobalt mine *he's* down right now? Anyway, so they've got to soften Zhukov up. Playing the old hot and cold game. Starve the prisoner, then give him a meal, then starve him again. I figure they're letting him have a good look at his one and only daughter. Then, in a couple of months they'll whip her back to the Soviet Union as quick as shit through a goose." He turned to Charlie. "I don't want to be too brutal. But she is the daughter of a Soviet spy and you have agreed to help out your father and the bureau. Forget the architect and peasant girl crap. And just remember"—he pointed a nail-chewed finger—"just remember that this little broad of yours might come from the virgin lands but she isn't a virgin. We know what happened that night in Alma-Ata. Right?"

Charlie's hand tightened on his crystal whiskey glass. "I know. There's no need to bring it up."

Hardin, Senior, said, "Anyway, how's the CIA master plan coming along?"

"No master plan," Godwin said. "Just feelers. We're making contact. The darnedest thing is that Zhukov seems to be trying to contact us. Just as we're about to arrange meetings between him and Henry Massingham from the British Embassy up he pops, as smooth and fishy as caviar, with Massingham's wife. Which also makes you wonder if the British are trying to get at Zhukov on their own."

"I think," Hardin, Senior, said carefully, "that you and the British have a common denominator."

"And what would that be?" Godwin didn't like being maneuvered so that he had to ask questions.

"Mrs. Massingham."

Charlie said, "What my father means is that maybe both you and the British want Zhukov to screw her." He tried sometimes to shock his father, but it never worked.

"Cool it, son," Walden remarked.

"Well, isn't that what *you* want? My guess is that if anyone wants to compromise anyone from the Communist bloc they arrange for Mrs. Massingham to lay them. Or if they want the guy strictly to themselves they get some dame to pick him up in a bar in Columbia Road in the closed season for Soviet wives when they've gone back to Russia

120

with their kids. Or get some doll in a bikini to throw sand on him when he's sneaked away to a Delaware beach."

Hardin, Senior, said, "Mrs. Massingham never seems to object." He squashed his little cigar, flicking the ash from his fingernails which looked as if they should have been manicured but weren't.

"The whole thing," Charlie announced, "disgusts me."

Walden swirled brandy in a glass almost as big as a goldfish bowl. There were disgusting aspects of every profession, he reminded Charlie. In banking, real estate, brokerage, law . . .

"Not in lumberjacking," Charlie said.

"I suggest," said his father, "that you lay off the scotch."

Walden continued. The maggots of corruption were at their most disgusting in the apples of politics because so often personal ambition was the driving force. In Washington they were surrounded by intrigues rooted in selfishness and greed. Not that he was saying that all politicians were corrupt; the United States of America had the best government setup in the world. But the politicians' motives were sometimes confused. This wasn't the case with Intelligence. They had only one aim: the protection of America and its people. "It's a war we're fighting, son. Make no mistake about that. It's another arm of the war against Communism being fought right here in Washington. Not for nothing have the Soviets got nearly one hundred diplomats here plus wives and staff. And they're waging war just as sure as they're gunrunning to Hanoi and Cairo. War, as someone said, is hell. And its weapons are filthy —no one can deny that. Napalm, gas, missiles. . . . In our war we have our own weapons. Don't think for one goddamn second that I enjoy our methods. But we have to beat these bastards at their own game." He downed the last of his brandy. "You're one of our weapons, son. You with this girl. And we sure as hell have to use you."

Charlie sat down wearily in a red-quilted Regency chair and watched the cold flames of the plastic logs in the fireplace.

Hardin, Senior, said, "I'm sorry, Charlie."

Charlie didn't reply because he didn't believe him.

121

Hardin, Senior, said, "And don't forget that the Soviets might be using her."

He spoke, thought his son, as if there was nothing the Soviets wouldn't stoop to. "I don't understand. How could *they* be using *her* when *I* picked her up?"

"Maybe she was waiting to be picked up."

"Bullshit."

"Your father's right in examining every avenue," Walden observed. "She seems to have been very easy to get on the same wavelength with."

"She was just bewildered by Washington. It relaxed her to hear a friendly voice. Speaking Russian," he added.

"Sure she was bewildered," Godwin said. "So bewildered that she had a tail on her. She must have known she had a tail. She isn't that stupid."

"Jesus," said Charlie, "you guys suspect everyone. Everything. Of course she had a tail on her. Every new Russian is followed. Especially an eighteen-year-old girl. For Chris' sake, she's already been caught consorting"—he chose the word with care—"with some guy who was smuggling anti-Soviet propaganda out of Russia. Do you expect them to let her go walking in Rock Creek Park by herself?"

Walden sat down. "Let's forget it. It's only speculation. The point is we have to work fast. All our other leaks from the embassy are closing up. Almost as if someone's been tipping them off." He stared briefly at Charlie, but within that moment Charlie glimpsed the ultimate penalties of betrayal. "And we need to get something on their attitude to the North Vietnamese peace talks. The President's not standing for reelection and he's halted the bombing. But how serious are the Russians?"

Godwin said, "And how serious are the Chinese?"

Walden said, "I'm glad you mentioned them. Maybe Comrade Zhukov can enlighten us on how much provocation the Soviets are prepared to take from Chairman Mao."

Godwin watched a measure of ash fall off his cigar on to the carpet, rubbed it absently into the deep, green-and-red pile with the toe of his unpolished shoe. He was said to possess a beautiful wife and a brilliant degree. He could have fooled me, Charlie thought.

His father sat motionless, a waxwork figure with human hair implanted. His hinged jaws moved. "I hope the CIA will get questions like that licked by their men in Moscow."

Godwin sought a reply in the glowing tip of his cigar butt which he would smoke to the last tongue-burning puff. "From what I hear you FBI guys in Washington soon won't have much time for the international scene. The word from the ghetto is that things are coming to the boil."

"Okay," Walden said. "Let's wind it up now." He looked at his frogman's watch. "Mrs. Hardin will be home from the movies any minute now. We'll have a last drink. But before we do I want to make myself plain." He aimed his words at Charlie. "The atmosphere's been relaxed. Like it should be when a father and son are together in a private house. We've had a few drinks and the atmosphere hasn't been as formal as it would have been over at the department. But please don't think that I wasn't giving orders. . . ."

Charlie said, "Okay. I'll talk it over with my father. But tell me one thing."

"What's that?" asked Walden, warming the goldfish bowl in his large, competent hands.

"Why me? Why did it have to be me?"

"Who else, Charlie boy? To begin with, you speak Russian."

"And what else?"

"You're the right age. You're tough. You're single. You're Arnold Hardin's son." A note of menace there. "It had to be you, Charlie."

Godwin, holding the wet cigar butt between his fingers, added, "And you're also sexy."

Across the room the dummy moved, trouser creases staying put. "May I make a suggestion?"

"By all means, Arnold," Walden said.

"Why don't we persuade the girl to defect?"

Charlie regarded him with distaste. You despised your father but you did what he had asked—pleaded, rather—because he had sired you, nurtured you, forked out the money to give you the chance to become another Le Corbusier or Walter Gropius. But at the time the whole assignment had seemed like a lot of patriotic fun: sinister intrigue with bugles offstage. Not anymore.

Walden said, "You might have something there, Arnold. Talk it over with Charlie. But don't forget that the main objective is getting intelligence out of the Soviet Embassy," he added without conviction.

The discussion was terminated by the sound of Mrs. Hardin's key in the lock.

Charlie lingered amid the cigar smoke while his father saw Walden and Godwin to their cars and his mother, who had lost at bridge, emptied the ashtrays. With dismay he saw himself as the all-American boy suddenly grown up; dismay because he hadn't admitted that such a transition was necessary. Behind him lay college, his graduate work in architecture, a few easy girls and one romance of applied sincerity until, with relief, he found her shacked up with one of his buddies. Now, with the liquor burning a protest in his stomach, he saw it all like a series of episodes in the locker room after a game. Also he observed the vagueness of his ambition which was a glass shaft sliding with soap-bubble rainbows, an obelisk owing much to the Lever Brothers building on New York's Park Avenue, the neighboring House of Seagram and the icicle of the Inland Steel Building on the corner of Dearborn and Monroe streets in Chicago. One day, he had thought; but for the time being had contented himself by frequently quoting Minoru Yamasaki: "The social function of the architect is to create a work of art" and feeling noble. Now all his aspirations seemed immature. All somehow exposed by the advent of Natasha Zhukova.

Steadfastly, resolutely, incorruptibly, he'd tried to assure himself that the girl with the Mongolian cheekbones and unsettling honesty was the enemy. Or, if she wasn't the enemy, an expendable pawn in a war being fought with guns in Vietnam and the Middle East, with intrigue in Washington. Even now Old Glory fluttered bravely in the background. Nothing has really changed except that I, Charlie Hardin, have fallen in love with the sacrificial lamb and grown up.

124

His mother took away the empty glasses and his father returned.

"Fancy a nightcap?"

"Just now you thought I was drinking too much."

"You were acting up a bit in front of Walden."

"I don't have to lick his boots."

His father poured drinks. "Nor do I, son."

"Then why can't you tell him you don't want your son to go through with this?"

"You know why. We've been through all this before. You did promise. . . ."

"I don't know why. You didn't really explain and it didn't seem to matter at the time."

"Walden could get me fired tomorrow." His father's neat clothes looked like a husk now. "Or retired, as they would call it."

"So you said. But how? He's in the State Department and you're in the FBI."

"Maybe so. But he is supposed to coordinate all American intelligence activities."

"Then it's he who should be fired." Charlie sipped at the whiskey which suddenly tasted like medicine. "And you don't mean to tell me that he should override Hoover."

"He could advise him."

"Advise him about what?"

"A couple of jobs I loused up. Nothing too serious but clear evidence of senility in this age-conscious country. Only Walden knows the exact details." He bowed his head over his scotch and murmured, "We blamed the CIA."

Charlie regarded his father with disappointment. A college flirtation with Communism or an experiment with homosexuality would have stirred his sympathy more. "And that's it, is it? That's why I have to betray a beautiful young kid?"

"There's a little more to it than that, Charlie." He paused. "You're making this very difficult for me. A father shouldn't have to plead with his own son. But I guess it's part of growing up, finding that your father's fallible."

"I always knew it," Charlie said. He waited.

"Okay," his father said, "I'll lay it on the line. Brief and to the point. The bottom's fallen out of my investments—and your sister's still at college. I need money badly, Charlie. And don't forget what it cost to make you an architect. . . ."

Charlie stood up and swallowed the last of his medicine. "Okay, I acknowledge the debt." Contempt grated his words. "I'll go through with it."

"Thank you, Charlie."

"Think nothing of it."

"It's also your patriotic duty, Charlie."

"Sure it is," Charlie said. Touching her cheek beneath a tree beside the Tidal Basin.

They had been out once more since the mugging attempt beside the Tidal Basin. To the movies. Paul Newman, Jackie Gleason and George C. Scott in a revival of *The Hustler* which surprisingly Natasha seemed to understand. "We have a game that is very much like that in Russia," she confided as Minnesota Fats cracked the balls into the pockets.

He bought her popcorn and a Coke and felt like a teenager on his first date. It was ridiculous and something would have to be done about it; he with his MG and bachelor apartment, his drawing board and stereo, his water skiing and his way with dry martinis. Now wondering whether he should put his arm around a girl at the movies; and if he did, whether he should fondle her breast.

Paul Newman sent the balls scurrying around the table and Natasha whispered, "He's very handsome."

He put his arm around her shoulders. Then felt her breast and she leaned toward him. Just like two kids, he thought. Tenderness stole around them in the flickering darkness, followed by a swelling need for her.

Then he remembered his role. The bastard he was. How much bigger a bastard he'd be if he tried to make love to her later. He kissed her cheek and took his hand away from her breast, leaving his arm around her shoulders. This couldn't go on; something would have to be done.

126

On the screen Paul Newman won his hollow victory and the lights came on.

"Your patriotic duty," repeated his father.
"I heard you the first time," Charlie said.

Chapter 3

BESIDE VLADIMIR ZHUKOV'S bed there stood a slovenly pile of newspapers. On his dressing table a mound of books of matches. The first grew untended and had to be decimated every two days; the second grew cunningly, like a sand dune, and was cherished.

To Vladimir Zhukov, who was beginning to embrace America with an affection which he conveyed to no one, the matches were a commentary. He collected them with the perseverance of a philatelist but was grateful to them for their message because, despite his courtship with the West his beliefs and creed were still anchored on the river beaches of Moscow. The matches reminded him: What peasant living in Appalachia could afford free matches extended with mint digestives and toothpicks at a downtown nighterie or a Howard Johnson's? And each flap with its fire warning, each phosphorescent wand, was a class distinction in itself: cardboard covers of crude commercialism, covers of shining gold and silver, crenellated miniatures—collector's items for the showcase; and the firesticks themselves: cardboard budded in red or white, little black arrows tipped with dormant gold fire, silver fire.

It was the other pile—the newspapers—that worried him.

The riches of America he could accept. For these he had

127

been prepared, the other side of poverty, racism, violence. It was the Americans' capacity to project their own troubles that bothered him. A disturbing symptom of muddled honesty.

It was part of his routine job—his front if you like—to read the papers every day. And every day he was bothered a little more.

From her bed, separated by the newspapers, in their Russian tableau of a bedroom, Valentina Zhukova, swallowing the porridge of *Pravda* and *Trud* with disciplined appetite, observed her husband with disappointment. "You seem to enjoy the bourgeois press."

"It's my job."

"I've never known you to carry out your duties so avidly."

"You should be pleased that I'm applying myself to my new job."

"And the nights when you're away—do you apply yourself then?"

Soon, Vladimir Zhukov thought sadly, a row would erupt. But how long had it been fermenting? "You know what I have to do. I do my best."

"And these women you meet. These high-class whores. Do they apply themselves?"

"Please," he said. "It's for the common cause. You know that. I have never been unfaithful to you." Wondering if he protested too much.

He picked up a Sunday newspaper, it weight bulging his muscles. Supplements and sections spilled on the bedclothes. Democrats and Republicans sparring in the early rounds of this Presidential year. Truth and lies bubbling in the test tube of the system.

The smell of the ink and newsprint answered restless appetites.

Columns about America's acceptance of the North Vietnam peace talks offer. Attacking, defending, questioning. Even the President cartooned, lampooned.

He turned the troubled pages. Race riots in the Deep South where, in his mind, bosomy belles still beckoned and Mississippi steamboat gamblers cheated. A gang murder

128

in Chicago. A rape near the Capitol, the girl assaulted three times, her boyfriend clubbed unconscious. A high school raided and drugs found. Pollution gathering above the cities, unchecked because big business would have it no other way.

The prosecution rested. But its printed presence presented a passionate defense. By its very existence.

Once Vladimir Zhukov had flown to Georgia where Stalin still lived in statues and portraits. He had seen an anti-Khrushchev riot harnessed by tear gas and rifle butts. But when he returned to Moscow he found that the event had gone unrecorded. Valentina claimed she knew nothing about it—although she must have heard through the party—and had belittled his eyewitness report.

I wonder, he thought, sitting in bed in striped flannel pajamas which belied his new romantic role, how many Russians ever suspect the truths of the world or truths of the motherland.

He lit a cigarette with a red-budded match from a restaurant called Le Provençal.

"Why do you hoard those matches?" his wife asked.

"It's a saving. We don't have to buy any." Fifty-eight books, his statistical department recorded.

He returned to the disquiet of his duty-reading. If the press so blithely chronicled America's sores then it was possible that their disclosures of injustice in Russia were true. Just possible.

Did I have to come to America to learn the truth of Russia?

This was the greatest disquiet of all. A proposition from which he shrank. He approached Prague down a long column of print. Then withdrew strategically to the color supplement. To Muhammad Ali, the motels of Miami and advertisements for patterned toilet paper so pretty that it could be pasted on the walls.

Valentina turned out her plastic-shaded lamp. "Good night, Vladimir. Please don't believe everything you read."

Nor you, he wanted to say; but didn't. He considered joining her in her bed. Love was not often given expression these days. Politics the adulterer?

She looked so gentle and desirable there, waiting for sleep. His Sibiryak. Their sharing, their journey, written on her calm believing face.

Her closed eyelids quivered, her mouth relaxed, she slept.

Vladimir Zhukov turned his troubled thoughts to his daughter, asleep, he hoped, in the room next door. Perhaps they were using her, too, for their plotting. Indisputably she was being used as a bait—as a reward if he did what he was told. (Already he had visited the Massingham home, avoided the ripe embrace of Helen Massingham, made contact with Americans and French, reported views which may or may not have been fed to him.) But the ferret brain of Mikhail Brodsky would never rest with a single accomplishment. If he could find a further use for Natasha he would. *I should never have brought her here. Better that I had betrayed my own values.*

The color supplement tore in his hand.

He swept the news from his bed, switched out the light and applied himself to the nightly equation that never equated. His one-party homeland, the comparative peace and endeavor that accompanied its obedience; twenty million dead and all the subsequent achievement; lilac around a village water pump and the knitting-needle rhythms of ping-pong balls on a Moscow beach. Against that freedom. Not prosperity or possessions; just freedom.

He half-opened the attic of poetry and doubt; then shut it again firmly.

To his daughter he said, "You're looking very attractive, my dear."

He was pleased she'd bloomed in the West, pleased that Vladimir Zhukov had a daughter who compared with the American beauties massed in Washington, every vista a fashion magazine background.

Valentina was not so pleased.

"You're wearing too much makeup," she pronounced. "You don't have to copy these American girls scavenging for husbands."

130

"I'm not wearing much makeup," Natasha said. But, her father noted, some of her spirit was missing. And there was a red blotch on her neck as if coarse material had been rubbed against the skin.

Surely, he thought, she hadn't acquired a lover—Russian, or American. He was an indulgent father and had forgiven Alma-Ata. He was not the kind who thought that *his* daughter, unlike anyone else's, had retained her virginity. Although she'd been young—too young. And a morsel of reaction applauded Georgi's two-year sentence. (He would emerge all the more mature for it!) During the formal recriminations he'd almost told her that it had been the same thing with Valentina and himself. Except that you couldn't reveal yourself . . . and perhaps chastity was more important than people seemed to think these days. Respect did shrivel, as it had done in that wooden room in Moscow many years ago. Irrationally.

Unsolicited, a fragile girl—now a mother or now dead —presented herself from the ruins of Berlin across the cheese and imported black bread and lemon tea and California orange juice.

Vladimir Zhukov asked, "You're not sick, Natasha?"

"Sick? No. Do I look sick?"

"You look a little pale."

She nodded, spreading the cream cheese thickly on the bread. You know how it is, her silence hinted.

"How are you spending your time here?" With the subtlety of an inquisitor.

"Just walking, looking at the city," she said.

"Are you sure you're all right?" There was a scratch, too, on her cheek.

"There's nothing wrong, Father."

He nodded without belief. And delivered his daily warning about the perils of existence in this tribal society. "And stay clear of the ghetto area. According to our information there may be trouble soon." More than information, he thought; you could smell it, feel it lurking on the intersection of Gentility Avenue and Shabby Street.

Today the paternal lecture was augmented by mysteri-

131

ous injunctions to report to him any approaches made to her by anyone.

She looked at him speculatively, rolling crumbs of bread into a pellet. "What sort of approaches?"

"Any approaches."

Valentina, already dressed—unlike husband and daughter—asked, "What are you driving at, Vladimir?"

"Just that we are in an alien land and the daughter of a Soviet diplomat must be particularly careful."

Valentina said she absolutely agreed, "But why were you so emphatic about approaches from *anyone?*"

"Anyone," Vladimir Zhukov repeated.

After which Valentina delivered her gentle dose of doctrine. The homily on focusing the Land of Plenty in its proper perspective. Of equating Garfinckel's against Skid Row (she illustrated this with a newspaper picture of winos holding up empty bottles like telescopes). Then mild recriminations about Natasha's treachery in Alma-Ata.

Odd, Vladimir Zhukov mused, washing away the taste of cheese with pink lemonade, that Valentina was more upset by social intercourse with a dissident than sexual intercourse, aged eighteen, with a man. Although, he supposed, eighteen was usual these days. Certainly in America.

Natasha, my baby, if anyone hurts you then I will kill them.

He contemplated playing "The Red Flag" on the record player. Instead he switched on the television. Still amazed at the number of newscasters competing with the munching of breakfast cereals, at the earnest debates at hours intended for yawning and scratching, at *Captain Kangaroo* whom he hadn't quite fathomed.

It was then that the Zhukovs learned that a good man had died. That Martin Luther King, Jr., had been killed by an assassin's bullet.

Martin Luther King was shot at 6:01 CST leaning from a second-floor railing outside a room in the Lorraine Motel in a predominantly black quarter of Memphis, Tennessee.

132

He was pronounced dead at 7:05. Police took possession of a small suitcase and a 30.06 Remington pump rifle with telescopic sight.

Zhukov read the newspaper reports in his office in the embassy where genuine shock and grief hovered, awaiting the official lead from Moscow.

The shooting, then the funeral. The body buried in Atlanta after a service at the Ebenezer Baptist Church. The Vice President of the United States present and a sermon taped by King himself anticipating "that day." *"I'd like for somebody to mention that day that Martin Luther King, Jr., tried to give his life serving others. . . . I'd like for somebody to say that day that Martin Luther King, Jr., tried to love somebody. . . . I want you to be able to say that day that I did try to feed the hungry . . . that I did try in my life to clothe the naked . . . that I did try in my life to visit those who were in prison . . . that I tried to love and serve humanity. Yes, if you want to, say that I was a drum major for peace . . . for righteousness."*

The President canceled his trip to Hawaii for a conference on Vietnam and on television said, "The spirit of America weeps for a tragedy that denies the very meaning of our land."

Zhukov grieved with the nation and read with dismay the plodding, insensitive Soviet reaction—like dandruff under a fingernail. *Izvestia* took the opportunity to recite that the United States was "a nation of violence and racism." *Pravda* intoned, "Terrorist murders have become as ordinary an aspect of the American way of life as road accidents. . . . Violence and terror roam American streets."

In the Soviet ambassador's office on the day after the shooting heads of departments gathered. Including Vladimir Zhukov whose immediate superior was visiting the mission in New York.

Also present was Mikhail Brodsky, a mere third secretary. But no one questioned his presence.

Tea was served.

The participants sipped guardedly awaiting a lead from

the ambassador, sophisticated and articulate (often described in the capitalist press as "wily") successor to unsmiling Georgi Zaroubin and Mikhail Menshikov who used to be called "Smiling Mike."

The ambassador swallowed a small white tablet—informing the gathering that it performed wonders for his asthmatic condition—and said, "Gentlemen, it is only a question of time, hours perhaps, before massive violence erupts. It may even be of the magnitude of a second civil war in this country. In light of this we must formulate plans and policy with some urgency. I suggest we adjourn."

Which meant, Zhukov knew, that they would move to the bug-proof chamber lined with thick steel. Its locks were changed regularly and it was intruder-proofed with an elaborate system of lights and buzzers.

Brodsky came up beside Zhukov, shaking his head so that curls fell over his ears. "Not you, Vladimir," he said.

"Who says so? You, a third secretary?" He appealed to the ambassador. The ambassador, reluctantly it seemed, confirmed that the deliberations were not for Zhukov's ears.

"Don't forget," Brodsky whispered, "that you have a meeting with Massingham."

"To hell with Massingham."

"Our work continues, comrade. In the long run ours is the most important work of all."

And on this day of historic tragedy Brodsky left Zhukov. Feeling like a gigolo.

The National Press Building stands on the corner of Fourteenth and F. Once the tallest building in Washington, it is only two blocks from the White House, and a short cab ride from the Capitol in one direction and the State Department in the other. It is surrounded by shops and is midway on Fourteenth between porno and poverty and governmental grandeur. A drugstore, the excellent Brentano's bookshop and a newsstand are within its environs; all that a newspaperman could want—plus, of course, bars—is there. Such is the abundance of provision, such is the welter of tape and press release, that the truth-seekers have to be careful that they are not waylaid by convenience, that in their deliberations they mentally spike much of this facility. Several such spikes are needed to accommodate the evasions and deviations, delivered with intense sincerity, at press conferences, and the incessant flow of esoteric outrage lobbying anything from lettuce growers to prohibitionists—the latter a forlorn cause in such company. Sometimes a newspaperman, frustrated by bureaucracy, will boot the heaps of handouts deposited unsolicited outside his office, down the corridor with relish.

The pressmen are accommodated in hundreds of offices on different floors. There, for the most part, in bouts of frenetic concentration, they arrive at truths which disgust those whose job it is to forestall such accomplishment.

Each office is a microcosm of elsewhere. Midwest, Deep South; Moscow, London, Paris, Bonn, Jerusalem, Cairo, Tokyo, Melbourne, Durban, Ottawa, Lima, Dublin, New Delhi. Their countries, creeds and pigments fight; but here they live together, as if the building were a luxurious penitentiary, and only occasionally do battle on the fourth Bloody Mary or across the chessboard. Time assists some of them, haunts others filing daytime news when the last edition is going to press in nighttime London or Brussels. The agencies have no such considerations; they file on remorselessly, rejoicing in the accolade of a few seconds beat.

From this building the affairs of the capital of the world's most powerful nation—or second most powerful, according to which way you look at it—are tossed around and hung out across the globe.

On this particular day, as editors in far-off citadels demanded reaction, the atmosphere in this tower of articulate babel was more intense than usual.

In the elevator taking Vladimir Zhukov to his appointment with Massingham, both guests of a German correspondent, the speculation was about the bloodletting that would follow the murder in Memphis. An Italian and a Swede contributed; an Australian dominated.

135

Zhukov had been in the building twice before to meet correspondents. Because these days, Brodsky had told him, a lot of contact between the White House and the Kremlin was established through the press.

Zhukov had also visited the Occidental restaurant around the corner where in 1962 the Cuban missile crisis was said to have been settled, the Soviet terms being presented to an American journalist, John Scali. There, still posted on the window, were the Russian terms, the Russian surrender. Kennedy's triumph. Vladimir Zhukov had regarded the proclamation with confusion.

The elevator took him up to the thirteenth floor, dispatching various nationalities to their cubicle capitals on the way. On the thirteenth, in the two bars and restaurant, the journalists—newspaper, magazine, radio and TV—enjoyed their work: debating, scoring, swopping, listening, evaluating, feeding, selling, buying, postulating, fencing, recalling, recounting.

Henry Massingham met him; Irish Guards tie, hair thick above his ears, sensitivity in his long hands getting a little veiny these days, complexion straight from the ski slopes, although his neck had wrinkled in the central heating and he had bloodied his Adam's apple shaving. Wherever he stood he appeared to be leaning. "My dear fellow," he said.

Not for the first time Vladimir Zhukov wondered: Who is subverting whom?

They went to the more dignified of the two bars. A clubby sort of place that you didn't expect to find at the top of a sawn-off skyscraper. The Stars and Stripes prominent, red-carpeted space, a log fire shifting and waving plumes of sparks. The sort of fire for a general or President to toast his buttocks in front of as, long-legged and infinitely just, he relaxed after battle on the field or in Congress.

In the background the AP and UPI tapes machine-gunned away, faster than ever, it seemed today.

They ordered Bloody Marys and Massingham introduced Zhukov to the German newsman named Helmut Richter. An intermediary, Zhukov presumed, for confidences which it would be improper for two diplomats to exchange. He presumed this with his new awareness.

136

"I am very pleased to meet you," Richter announced. A man of Zhukov's age; an adversary, perhaps, during the siege of Leningrad. No monocle, no boots, no *Heils;* even now Zhukov found it difficult to see a German any other way. He felt patronizing: the victor. Twenty-three years after the war it was still the Germans that the Russians really hated; not the Americans or British or assorted lackeys.

But Herr Richter was not interested in the atrocious past; his wounds were covered with the roseate skin of good living, the precise suiting of Berlin, the sheen of leisurely brushing on his graying hair. Comfort had a stranglehold on guilt. His handshake was strong, his smile immediate, his accent careful.

He apologized with style. "I shall have to dodge lunch. You understand how busy we are today. But please be my guests."

Massingham finished his drink long before his companions. He ordered another round and drank thirstily, ice clinking against his teeth. His hands which had been shaking lost their palsy. He apologized for them. "Bit of a thrash last night. Needed these," pointing at the vodka and tomato juice brewed lavishly by a muscly barman.

Zhukov's palate searched for the vodka in the juice. "You had a party despite the situation?"

"Why not? There was nothing I could do. I mean I don't cancel a party if someone is assassinated in Latin America. Why should I behave any differently if someone'e killed in the States? I mean it's all equally foreign as far as I'm concerned."

"I see," Zhukov said, divining why Massingham had failed to rise in the diplomatic ranks.

He gazed across the rooftops, stepping stones to the ghetto. Below the window the shocked streets were emptying; across the road a group of blacks clustered in a pattern of inchoate anger.

The bar was empty except for the three of them.

The German said, "And now I must be off. Duty calls." Massingham stopped him. "Lunch on Sunday," he said.

"Can the two of you make it? Provided the whole bloody place doesn't go up in flames, that is."

"Its most kind of you," Richter said. "If things are not too bad I should be delighted to come."

"And you, Vladimir?"

"Of course," Zhukov said bitterly.

Richter left without clicking his heels as Zhukov had expected.

"Charming fellow," Massingham observed. "And very useful, too."

They regarded each other with civilized duplicity.

Just what, Zhukov wondered, does he expect to get out of me? My own assignment is simple enough: Prepare the way for blackmail. A coup as spectacular as a French ambassador's disgrace in Moscow (in bed with a movie actress) disclosed in detail by the KGB traitor Yuri Krotkov. Brodsky had suggested there were distinct possibilities with Massingham. His wife; or Massingham himself if, perhaps, he were a repressed homosexual. Brodsky's mind worked along certain well-traveled sewers.

Massingham's assignment was difficult to analyze. He was British and therefore not all what he seemed. But surely he could appreciate that Vladimir Zhukov was not of the caliber to indulge in treason. Although, come to that, I would never have thought I was of the caliber to become a second-rate spy. An *agent provocateur*. Perhaps, Vladimir Zhukov, now is the time to rebel; to sluice the self-disgust through your bowels. Then he thought of Natasha and his parents—those senior citizens—vacationing from their Bolshevik lives away from Alma-Ata among the apple orchards of Kazakhstan.

He looked speculatively at Massingham who had grown a red pencil mustache of Bloody Mary. And thought for the first time: Perhaps the bastard wants me to defect.

Outside he tried to hail a cab. But there were none to be had. He headed for the embassy watching a stray petal of cherry blossom from the Tidal Basin fluttering along beside him. The Japanese had presented the trees (three thousand of them) in 1912. At the time of Pearl Harbor someone had suggested they be cut down in retribution. Vladimir Zhukov smiled. And at the outbreak of World War I sauerkraut had been renamed "liberty cabbage."

He laughed in the lynching-quiet street at the magnificent absurdities of this land. And grieved for what was to come.

All weekend the violence grew and the flowers on the Yoshino cherry trees blossomed. Stokely Carmichael, exchairman of the Student Nonviolent Coordinating Committee, led young people down Fourteenth urging stores to close; within an hour the window smashing began. At a press conference Carmichael said, "When white America killed Dr. King last night she declared war on black America. Black people have to survive, and the only way they will survive is by getting guns." The President signed a proclamation that "a condition of domestic violence and disorder" existed. A curfew was imposed, poilce and troops were ordered to avoid excessive violence.

Murder, pillage and arson in Baltimore, Chicago, Kansas City and Washington. And to a lesser extent in Cincinnati, Detroit, Nashville, Newark, Oakland, California, Pittsburgh and Trenton.

In three days in Washington 10 died, 1,191 were injured, 7,650 arrested. There were 1,130 fire alarms and 13,600 federal troops were called out.

Black was on the rampage; black was beautiful in the light of the flames it had started. Glossy and snarling. Civil war marched closer. Where are you, Ulysses S. Grant? Where are you, Abraham Lincoln?

In the household of Henry Massingham it was deemed correct to continue with plans for Sunday brunch. Only couples with kids were forgiven if they declined to brave the smoldering streets. Which was fine with the Massinghams because, in any case, they weren't over-fond of brats littered around their feet.

* * *

The house was rented off Massachusetts Avenue not far from the Naval Observatory. In an area considered "safe"—an adjective already infiltrating the real-estate

139

ads. Near the home of the Australian Ambassador, former residence of Patton—enough to frighten off any rioters, they said.

French windows were open for the perfume of spring bulbs unsheathing and, perhaps, tear gas. The sunlight found half-devoured logs burning in the open grate, negating their puny radiance. Insistent good taste permeated the place: its baby chandelier, deep golden carpet, some Chippendale, leather encyclopedias, Dickens and Scott and American history behind mullioned bookcase windows. From the wall the queen approved. All rented.

There were the Massinghams, the Richters—his wife glossy, almost waxen, and incongruously skittish—some assorted Englishmen with enthusiastic wives, two American couples patiently courteous while they planned early escape, a Frenchman playing Yves Montand, a hungry Italian and an even hungrier Belgian.

But I, Vladimir Zhukov thought, without satisfaction, am the star.

Tlhere was also a lot of food. Cold beef, pork, chicken, ham. Bowls of potato salad, tomatoes, folded fans of celery. And much booze.

The talk was of the rioting. And the adventure of braving it.

"What does a Russian think of all this?" an English lady with a blue rinse inquired.

He smiled, shrugged. What does a Mongolian think? What does a Martian think? He opened a can of Budweiser which hissed at him. "It's a tragedy," he said. "A tragedy for America."

She nodded, "I'm so pleased you think so. We never quite know what you Russians think. It's such a pleasant change to find someone like yourself attending our little do's."

Yves Montand moved in, layers of pork and ham stretching the roll in his hand. "You must not judge America by what is happening today."

Zhukov nodded. It was the only response to such a blinding insight into the obvious.

The English lady asked, "Do you have any trouble with the . . . er . . . blacks in your country?"

A new arrival from Pakistan interrupted. "Any such trouble would be instantly crushed. I am thinking perhaps that is the answer. What do you think, sir?"

"As we don't have the problem," Zhukov said, "I can't answer your question."

"But surely am I not right in believing that you have some citizens of Negro descent in the Caucasus? And that they are almost completely illiterate and poverty-stricken? Surely I am correct in believing such information?"

Vladimir Zhukov said that indeed there were black slave descendants in Abkhazia but he could not vouchsafe for their standards of living.

He was rescued by Helen Massingham, luscious in tight cream trousers that showed the line of her pants, and tight mauve sweater. She exuded ripeness and thwarted fertility. A bitch in heat, thought Zhukov. From a pedigree kennel.

"How marvelous," she said. "I didn't think you'd make it." She brought him beer and food and maneuvered him into a corner. "I hope we're going to see a lot more of you." She glanced around. "It's so different having some-one like you here. And you didn't bring your wife."

Her eyes were creased at the corners, a vain woman suffering from nearsightedness who refused to wear glasses. Her hair was short and slithery, her breasts nudged him. Her mouth was shiny pink, lipstick flaked a little, and the rest of her cosmetics seemed to Zhukov to be like the bloom on a plum.

Her husband joined them. Cavalry twill trousers, rough old sweater smelling vaguely of stables. He was accom-panied by another British diplomat; his senior, Zhukov gathered. A chunky man, balding prematurely, aggressively fit with chipped-ice eyes and a broken nose. Zhukov was pleased to find that not all British diplomats were like his host. Although you couldn't always tell; it was probably Massingham's sort that had led the Charge of the Light Brigade.

The newcomer said, "Name's Barnes. Pleased to meet you." He put a wrestling hold on Zhukov's hand. "I think a lot of us would have given this a miss if it hadn't been for you."

Massingham laughed uncertainly. "Thanks very much."

Zhukov said, "Am I so interesting then?" The role was becoming increasingly repugnant to him.

"You are interesting, yes. And I know what it must feel like to be exhibited in this way. But can't you persuade your ambassador to allow your people to mix more freely? There's no harm done, surely. Perhaps a lot of the problems of East and West could be sorted out this way. A bit ambitious, I know, but it would be a start."

Zhukov agreed and told Barnes so. He liked the belligerent little man with the coal-face accents from the north of England. They skirted the obvious—the assassination and the riots—and advanced on politics.

A tall, impeccably sincere American from the National Foundation of the Arts and the Humanities joined them because you at least had to speak to the Russian before departing. With him was a quiet, pleasant-looking young man named Charles Hardin to whom Helen Massingham, bored with politics, turned her attention.

The sincere American, anxious to make friends, said that American legislators were deeply influenced by whatever the Kremlin did. Unhappily, he found himself wading into the Communist coup in Czechoslovakia in 1948. But as he was now in it—up to his neck—he struggled on. "That's what really made the isolationists in Congress support the Marshall Plan."

"I can understand that," Zhukov said. "It would have been strange if it had worked otherwise, it seems to me."

The American was surprised and waded fatalistically on. "You're surely not admitting the error of the Soviet Union in that instance?"

Vladimir Zhukov smiled at such blundering safari after truth. He didn't think it would be such a good idea for Russians to mix more freely. All the antagonisms of the world powers were alerted within seconds of contact over a can of beer. All observed by her ladyship up there on the wall.

The history of dissension continued with an attack from the Belgian on Russia's one-party system. An attack veiled as a question.

Zhukov sighed. But he could give as well as he could receive. It was time to remind the assembly that he did not accept invitations to lunches just to be set up for target practice. It is time to remind them that, although I am here by myself and therefore vulnerable, I represent the Soviet Union and the dream of Socialism. "There is little difference in our electoral systems," he began. Ohs and ahs. "In the Soviet Union we choose our own candidate in much the same way as yourselves—Americans, that is." The protests found voice, but Zhukov held up his hand, standing there on the rostrum in Red Square. "You have two parties, true. But it seems to me that there is little difference in the Democrats and the Republicans. . . ."

The sincere young American, itching to speak, stammered with indignation.

Again Zhukov held up his hand, aware that all other conversations in the room had stopped. And, because he was not too sure of his facts on political parties—but it was good provocation—he swept on to a fresh attack. (Although he was far from sure that Mikhail Brodsky would have approved.)

"America is in fact a dictatorship. Your President has total power, unlike the leaders of the Soviet Union. As I understand it, if an act is passed by both your houses, he can do one of four things. He can sign it. He can hold it which means it becomes law in ten days. He can veto it and return it which means it must then be passed by a majority of two-thirds. Or he can take no action which means that Congress adjourns within ten days and he has effectively thrown it out. Those surely are the powers of a dictator."

"The point," said the young American eagerly, "is that he does not exercise this latter power."

"It seems to me," Zhukov said, "that the power is there whether he exercises it or not. And if people are aware of this ultimate power then they act accordingly. And," he added, "as is well known, the President is also your Commander in Chief. Also he is in charge of foreign affairs

143

assisted by your Secretary of State. No such overwhelming powers are held by our leaders."

He eased himself through the circle to get more food, not anxious to continue the one-sided debate. A devastating thrust, strategic withdrawal. In his dark suit and white shirt he felt more conspicuous than usual among the sweaters and slacks.

He moved to the French windows trailed by Helen Massingham. "You showed them," she said in her juicy voice. "You really showed them."

"They seem to think that because I am a Russian they can criticize me in any way they like. They wouldn't dream of attacking a Brazilian or an Italian that way."

"You are rather different, Vladimir. Rather special."

She shook his arm and they were in the small garden. A few trees fluttering with mating birds, crocuses piercing the lawn still pale and attenuated from winter. A flake of ash swung down from somewhere like a black autumn leaf. Behind them, faces hovered in the French windows uncertain whether to follow, as if Zhukov and Helen Massingham were ambassador and secretary intent on state matters.

Helen Massingham said, "This house is a bit too grand for Henry, really. But I subsidize him. My parents are disgustingly rich." She peered around at him as if there were a tree in between them. "Does that put you off me?" She fitted a cigarette into an ivory holder.

"Not at all. If you live in a capitalist society you might as well be one of the privileged."

"My father's got a lot of racehorses, too. They're always winning, bless them. I love horses. Do you like horses, Vladimir? I think you do. I can imagine you as a Cossack or something galloping along and bending down from your saddle to pick up a handkerchief with your teeth."

"Then you have a very vivid imagination."

Her fingers tightened on his arm. "Poor old Vladimir. You can't really adapt to the Western sense of humor, can you? It must be awful because I'm sure you've got a wonderful sense of humor really. Just different, that's all. That's the greatest barrier of all, isn't it?"

144

In the mouth of the French windows Zhukov spotted Massingham, face bobbing anxiously like a man bidding at an auction. Through the trees he saw other houses like the Massinghams'. Grand, uniform, competing. He didn't know if he envied their owners with their rebel children, their mortgages, their sons in Vietnam, their coronaries, their wary pushing days fading into after-dinner brandy and Johnny Carson, the desperate enjoyment of their tanning holidays. With all their materialistic benefits they were probably no more content than a peasant donning his *valenki* to bring wood for the earthen stove in the middle of his wooden cottage.

"What," Helen Massingham asked, "do you admire most about America?"

He answered instantly. "The Mafia."

She laughed, holding the cigarette holder hard between well-tended teeth. "I knew you had a sense of humor. Why the Mafia?"

"Because they get what they want. Because they are efficient. Because democracy, despite all its claims, cannot put them down."

"America has the Mafia and you have the KGB."

"We all have a KGB of some sort."

"Are you in the KGB, Vladimir?"

"Of course."

Carefully he avoided treading on the crocuses. Next door two youths were excavating the garage. A canoe, tent, skates, barbecue, skis, baseball bat . . . Such assumption of possessions. In Moscow he had bought a toy for a friend's son. A rifle with a butt insecurely screwed, crude piping barrel, wobbly sights; the boy had been delighted.

She flicked the cigarette end into the bushes. "And what do you dislike most about America?"

"Drugs," he said. "How can I admire a capitalist society when it allows this to happen to its children?"

"I know," she said. "It's awful."

"It's more than awful. We have no such problems in the Soviet Union. You see, there is much to be said for our way of life. Our repressions. . . ."

"I thought you would say racism."

"No, that is inevitable. It is part of the war of evolution. It will determine itself."

She laughed uncertainly. "We're getting dreadfully serious, aren't we? I'm not a very serious person really. And this wasn't the sort of thing I intended to talk about at all."

"What then?"

"It's rather difficult," she said. "You're so different. So self-contained. You're fearfully attractive, but it's very difficult to get at you."

"What are you trying to say, Mrs. Massingham?"

"There you go, you see. Mrs. Massingham. How can you flirt with a man who calls you Mrs. Massingham?"

"Then don't try, Mrs. Massingham."

"You know how to put me in my place, don't you? Not many men do." She considered this. "Not any that I can remember."

"Not even your husband?"

"Henry? You must be joking."

"No," he said, "I wasn't."

"You're so . . . I don't know. Self-possessed. No, that's not the right word. Impervious. That's better. Impervious to all our blandishments. You make me feel superfluous."

At the window Henry Massingham looked as if he might join them at any moment. Beside him stood the Italian waving a glass of red wine.

Helen Massingham rushed on. "I wish you would be more cooperative. You make me feel so unsure of myself."

Zhukov waited.

"I wondered perhaps if we could meet. You know, somewhere safe because I know you people are not supposed to get involved in anything like that. Who is?" She giggled. "But I thought perhaps we could meet by accident somewhere—in the Madison or the Mayflower or the Statler Hilton maybe. . . ."

"It doesn't sound very accidental," Zhukov said. The young scents of spring made him homesick. A breeze playing the parchments of silver birch. Celandine, violets, anemones all presenting themselves at once as if they had been pushing at the ice all winter. Cheryomukha cherry

146

trees instead of the Yoshino—so much more shy. Hand in hand in Sokolniki Park. *Kvas* wagons emerging, cars uncovered and stuttering in the fresh air.

She said, "I think I've lost you."

He returned. "I'm sorry. You were saying?"

"Somehow you manage to be extremely polite and bloody rude at the same time."

"We Russians are not great ones for the niceties of conversation. I'm sorry."

"You might at least listen to what I'm saying. I'm making myself cheap enough as it is."

"You were mentioning a meeting. . . ."

"I thought if we could meet by accident we could have a drink. And then a meal, perhaps." She looked at him speculatively. "Perhaps I could take a room in one of those hotels. . . ."

"I don't think that would be very discreet."

"It could be done very discreetly." A gentle puppy nudge. "Don't you find me attractive, Vladimir? Most men do. The trouble is I don't find them terribly attractive. Well, not many of them, anyway. I suppose it's because the're all trying so bloody hard. Men should never try too hard. You don't, do you, Vladimir?"

Zhukov grinned at her and agreed that he didn't. She was, he supposed, desirable. Like a whore on a street corner. Like a dessert. Afterward you discarded the empty plate and forgot it. He could not sleep with such a woman and then return to the trusting if unresponsive body of his wife. He didn't condemn other men who did. It just wasn't him.

But he thought again: This is what I am expected to do. This is my infiltration. This is the seal of my success. My first break-through. He saw Helen Massingham rifling her husband's briefcase and bringing him the contents. Turning her antennae to the unguarded comment of a counselor from Chancery and relaying it to Vladimir Zhukov, secret agent.

You will have to compromise, Zhukov. Make your play before the cool sheets are drawn back for the ritual of sex. Those girdled breasts drooping a little, belly not quite as flat as its owner would have wished, black welcome mat of hair belying a certain aristocracy of feature. Plum juices fast flowing.

"Can we then?" she asked, eager little girl. "If you think so, don't say another word. I'll arrange it all."

Should I? Mikhail Brodsky replied, "Of course." Valentina, Natasha, Vladimir . . .

"Very well," he said. "But please—be discreet."

Menry Massingham joined them, accompanied by the Italian, tongue and teeth mauve with wine.

On the landing, emerging from the bathroom, he found Helen Massingham waiting. Downstairs the insect noise of the brunching guests. On either side cream-painted doors, and through one, half open, the end of a bed covered with coats.

Her breasts brushing his chest. Her breath smelling faintly of gin. Lips against his, mouth open, lipstick that tasted of strawberries. Thighs moving, hand pulling at the hair on his neck.

He felt himself respond. Grabbed her arms theatrically, pulled them down and pushed her away.

She stood back. "What's the matter, Vladimir?"

"You disgust me."

"Do I?" Knowingly, with her bitch knowledge.

And I disgust myself, he thought.

"I suppose I should say something like, 'No one ever does that to me.' And vow vengeance."

He moved to the top of the stairs. "I'm leaving."

"And I shall go ahead with our little arrangement."

"Do what you please."

He ran down the stairs.

"Hallo, old man," said Henry Massingham at the bottom. "We were beginning to wonder what had happened to you."

Zhukov fought a desire to smash his fist into the decent, second-class face. Possibly Massingham was plotting the seduction. Would be there with his camera in a closet in the Statler Hilton. Such a man as Massingham would not hesitate to use his own wife. Most likely she'd been used

148

before—and had enjoyed it. Such were the people Vladimir Zhukov now mixed with. "I'm leaving now," he repeated.

"So soon? I was looking forward to having quite a chat. Everyone else will be disappointed."

"You'd better find another performer. I should imagine a Chinese would be quite an attraction. "

"Don't be like that," Massingham said.

Zhukov took his gray hat, FBI style. "Good-bye. Make my apologies to your wife."

"But when shall we meet again? I thought we might play a little chess. Although I realize I'm not in your class."

"No," Zhukov said. "You're not."

"But when?"

"I'll call you."

Chapter 4

WASHINGTON BURNED. And Vladimir Zhukov bled for it. He wanted to help, he wanted involvement—to exorcise the sickness of his own self-disgust.

He drove his little bug fast through the empty Sunday streets in the direction of the smoke clotting the skyline to the northeast of the city.

He wound down the window and smelled the fires, heard gunfire—puny at a distance. You couldn't believe distant gunfire until you saw the dead, the dying, and the wounded. In Leningrad they had shot those beyond help, those with the blood pumping energetically from the inner tubes of their guts, and he had turned away from the eyes of men imploring the executioners of mercy to permit them a few more moments of life.

Despite those memories he still couldn't believe the

distant gunfire crackling like the dripping red and green rockets that celebrated the Great October Socialist Revolution every year in Moscow.

His beetle skidded and rocked and he drove faster. He lost himself and found that he was among the first showcase buildings of Washington. A cop jumped from the sidewalk waving his gun.

Zhukov swerved and scurried on. He heard the cop shouting at him to stop and in his driving mirror saw him take aim. But no shot came; the CD plates, unexpected on such an undiplomatic automobile, chaining the cop's trigger finger.

Ahead were more cops. He still tried to reach the fires but stopped on Seventh attracted by the crowds and the sound of plate glass shattering.

At an intersection the lights changed imperturbably. And a dented Chevy, crammed with blacks and loot—a coffee table, a record player and a plaster display dummy roped to the roof—stopped at the red, its indicator winking left, very law-abiding amid the pillage.

Vladimir Zhukov laughed aloud.

Gunfire nearer. A few potshots followed by a crackle of machine-gun fire.

Through the streets of Moscow stormed the Bolsheviks seizing what had been denied them since the czars first wrote the history. Killing exploiters of the masses who stood in their way.

Excitement pulsed in Zhukov's breast. The beat of a war drum. Yet he wanted to grab the looters, the rioters, the vengeful and tell them, "This is not the way. This is the way to lose the dignity you've sought."

Martin Luther King, man of peace, had died and the funeral rites were war.

The Chevy, still winking conspiratorially, turned left crunching broken glass beneath its tires. No hand signals.

Down a side street three cops stood together watching the grinning looters make their exit. Still, they had observed the red lights.

Daggers of glass lay in the road ahead. Zhukov parked his bug and joined the fun.

One of the cops shouted, "Get the hell out of here. You crazy or something?"

Zhukov grinned, waved.

But the hatred came a poor second to pure avarice. It was a carnival of robbery. Grinning, laughing, they sacked the shops. All color televisions gone now, stocks of black-and-white dwindling fast.

Clothes, shoes, food, cosmetics, suitcases, boxes of candy and other assorted merchandise were placed in waiting transport. The cops stared in the opposite direction as if they were watching a baseball game.

Smoke eased its way down from the ghetto fires.

Two blacks wearing ladies' wigs, one blond, one brunette, combed with style, came toward him down the sidewalk, sidestepping the glass.

One of them struck Zhukov's shoulder, fingers digging in hard. "Why don't you grab yourself something, whitey?"

"Grab yourself a black wig, white man. Grab yourself an Afro."

"This is not the way," Zhukov shouted.

"Sure it's the way, whitey. We're as good as you, whitey."

"Not like this."

"Say, you German or somethin'?"

"Russian."

"Shit. Whoopee." They hesitated, not too sure what Black Panthers did about Red Russians, then swaggered on.

Afternoon settled into sulfurous evening.

Zhukov passed a store with eight enticing plate-glass windows still intact and the furniture behind it as inviolate as a room at Mount Vernon. Why? Because it was owned by blacks, he guessed.

In Red Square boots smeared the frost on the cobblestones. The rape of the privileged was under way in its first tumescent thrust.

Berlin. And the Fascist oppressors crawling helplessly in the debris. Oppressors such as rheumy old men and skinny girls.

Why do humans desecrate triumph?

151

Zhukov wended his way through the cheerful robbers toward his patient car. Volkswagens the thieves did not seem to want.

As he backed the car up and turned, a squad of troops arrived at the intersection in a jeep. They fired tear gas which was circulated by the spring breeze. The weeping crowds dispersed to find other bargains at rock-bottom prices.

Zhukov drove to Constitution and followed a silver tour bus, bearing the sign CHERRY BLOSSOM FESTIVAL, packed with women peering through cameras.

The bus turned up Fourteenth. Zhukov accelerated, overtook it and waved it down. The driver was small and phlegmatic, withered by gasoline and dust, potbelly permanently adjusted for driving.

Zhukov climbed out waving his arms like an usher. "Don't go up there. There's a lot of trouble."

"Sure there's a lot of trouble," said the driver. In his white cap was stuck a cardboard badge printed with a cluster of pink blossoms.

"You can't take these ladies up there."

"They wanna go." The driver stuck his thumb over his shoulder indicating the monolith of American womanhood to which, long ago, he had acknowledged defeat.

"They'll get hurt."

"You tell 'em, buddy."

The ladies from the Midwest directed outraged hostility Zhukov's way. Tier on tier of middle-aged self-determination, intent on emancipation, contemptuous of masculine frailty.

Zhukov shouted, "There's shooting up there."

One woman wearing baggy pants and a lumberjack shirt beneath a sweater came to the door. "You're not American," she accused beneath bright bouffant hair.

"I'm Russian."

"Ah." She turned. "He's a Russian, girls."

"The cherry blossom's that way." Zhukov pointed toward the Tidal Basin.

"Then you go see it."

The driver chewed with the rhythm of wheels. "See what I mean? I'd back this bunch against the blacks any day."

The door closed and the bus moved off. Zhukov accompanied as escort.

Up the street bus and car were stopped by police with guns, visors, walkie-talkies, gas masks, lights flashing on their cars.

The ladies from the Midwest poured out of their bus. Combat troops alighting.

A cop came over, stuffing his gun away in respect of their sex. "Better go home, ladies. Washington ain't no place for sightseeing today."

The ladies disagreed. They moved down F Street commanded by the woman in the red-and-black lumberjack shirt who had put on glasses saped like butterflies the better to see it all. The looting blacks paused. The cop shouted, "Hey!"

The advance was orderly at first. But within the ranks there lurked a brash spirit. In sensible shoes and sensible skirt, large backside pugnacious, face flushed and perhaps even distracting thirty years ago, she suddenly left the phalanx.

The leader bawled, "Florrie, come back here."

Florrie returned—carrying a Scrabble set. "Mine's worn out," she explained.

They broke ranks in orderly fashion. Each to her own.

"Girls!" The leader's authority cbbed like a hemorrhage. "Well, watch the glass anyway." And, if you can't beat 'em join 'em so she helped herself to a handbag.

The ladies took a prize apiece. No more. Getting aggravated with any blacks who resented their presence. Then formed up, about-faced and returned to the bus.

The cop, Irish face bunched beneath his cap, appealed to Zhukov. "What do you do, Mac?"

Zhukov said he didn't know.

The cop looked at the blacks and the women. "Jesus, I don't know who's going to take the world over. But it sure as hell ain't going to be us. And I don't reckon it's going to be them either"—pointing at the rioters.

Outside the Press Building Zhukov met the German, Helmut Richter. Still glossy despite it all, Slavonic features always assessing.

"Want to come up? You'll get a wonderful view from the club."

"Thank you," Zhukov said. He left the Volkswagen across the street.

In the elevator Richter said, "It's pretty bad. It's broken out all over the country. It's as near as damnit to civil war. They've even got a machine-gun post on Capitol Hill."

"I don't think it will come to civil war," Zhukov said. "This is America." The phrase hung naïvely in the car.

Richter looked surprised. "An odd remark for a Russian."

"Not really." If you couldn't explain it to yourself you certainly couldn't explain to a German intermediary.

"It is strange, is it not, that you and I were fighting each other nearly a quarter century ago? Now here we are together in an elevator for ring-side seats of Washington burning?"

From the windows of the elegant bar, the Stars and Stripes limp behind them, the world's newsmen watched the skyline across the assorted rooftops. Smoke black and white and thick above the ghetto cubes—like an old black's hair, Zhukov thought. And flames bursting high in digestive belches as the fire at the buildings, then subsided comfortably. Fatly and thickly, or gray and sparsely, according to the meal, the smoke rolled gently in the evening sky.

Beside them the agency machines punched out bulletins on what was happening a few blocks away.

Richter brought back a scroll of communiqués and gave it to Zhukov.

The report placed flexible borders around the rioting. Fourteenth and New York Avenue up as far as Randolph Street and east on H Street as far as Fifteenth.

And from the window the world watched. Oriental, Occidental, Democrat, Republican, Communist, capitalist, black, brown, white, Deep South, far North. All engrossed in the flames.

Who is the enemy?

Zhukov read on, his mind imprisoning facts and statistics.

These were the troops: Third Infantry Regiment, Fort Myer, Virginia, 700 men; Sixth Armored Cavalry, Fort Meade, Maryland, 2,200; District of Columbia National Guard, 1,300; Marine Corps Schools Battalion, Quantico, Virginia, 700; 91st Engineers Battalion, Fort Belvoir, Virginia, 700; First Brigade 82d Airborne Division, Fort Bragg, North Carolina, 2,000; 716th Transportation Battalion, Fort Eustis, Virginia, 600; 544th Support and Service Battalion, Fort Lee, Virginia, 700; 503rd Military Police Battalion, Fort Bragg, North Carolina, 500.

And the black mayor, Walter E. Washington—such a name—had pushed the curfew back from 5 P.M. to 4:30.

Also a soul singer called James Brown—such a name—had flown to Washington from Boston to make a radio-television appeal. "I'm fighting for the black man to have pride. From one brother to another—go home. I'm not a Tom. I'm a man. Nobody can buy me. This is America. A man can get ahead here. Don't burn. Give the kids a chance to learn. Don't terrorize. Organize."

Feeding the scroll through his hands, Zhukov nodded in agreement with James Brown. Don't destroy the dignity you are seeking. We are all seeking.

An Australian, looking curiously at Zhukov, asked, "What will your people make of this?"

"My people?"

"Yeah. *Tass, Pravda, Izvestia.*"

"They will report it," Zhukov replied.

"Sure," said the Australian. "Sure."

Richter took the communiqué from Zhukov. "Want to go up there and have a look? I've got a pass. You should get through all right. At your own risk, of course."

"I should like to go," Zhukov said politely.

On the skyline the convoluted smoke, the flames brighter in the thickening dust, had obscured the first stars.

It was war. A beleaguered city after the first onslaught awaiting the second wave of shock troops.

Armored cars lurked down side streets, snouting and

malicious. Troops and cops in white helmets and visors guarded the corners, stopping blacks, okaying Zhukov and Richter and telling them it was their own funeral.

Excitement and a desire to participate regrouped in Zhukov's breast.

"Let's take a look at the White House," Richter said. As sleekly imperturbable in his suede jacket and black turtleneck as a Luftwaffe ace; Leica slung around his neck. You had to admire him.

They turned down G, past the Treasury. There stood the White House—"like an English clubhouse," as Dickens had once described it. Inviolate and mellow amid its lawns; a lordly colonial sundowner.

"But if the blacks had mortars," Richter mused.

Troops surrounded their Commander in Chief's home; an armored car was parked outside a small church crowned with gold which Zhukov hadn't noticed before.

An officer shouted an order and the troops steadied their guns. Down the street came a gang of blacks whooping, hands clenched in Black Panther salutes. "Kill us," they cried. "Kill us like you killed Martin King."

They proceeded unkilled.

The troops relaxed.

"Better get outta here, you guys," a young officer said to Richter and Zhukov.

Richter showed his pass.

"Still better move."

The troops, Zhukov thought, looked as tough as hell. Any fear hidden behind their armor.

He and Richter struck back toward Fourteenth along New York Avenue. Passing a store called the Spy Shop selling electronic surveillance equipment (bugs), closed-circuit TV, self-defensive aerosol dispensers which could incapacitate an attacker for thirty minutes at twenty feet.

Back to the go-go and porno of Fourteenth. "A pity they didn't burn this," Zhukov said.

Richter nodded noncommittally; perhaps he liked pornography.

The smell of burning was strong now. A few sparks spiraled above them like fireflies. Dusk gave way to night.

Now they were in the portals of the ghetto. They saw a couple of cops kicking and punching a teen-ager—ignoring the order to use restraint.

Richter said, "Are you sure you want to go on?"

"Sure."

"I'll go another block. No farther."

"Okay," Zhukov said. "Another block." Pleased that it was Richter who had called a halt first.

Just off Fourteenth they came upon a liquor store almost drained of its juice. Booze ran on the sidewalk as dark as blood in the light of the fires. Propped against the wall were the bodies of those those who had passed out, stacked their like empties. Scotch, vodka, gin, vermouth, wine, brandy, mived on the road, a wild cocktail spiked with broken glass.

The blacks danced, hugged and wept, slicing their shoes on the bottoms of bottles (the tops picked up as weapons).

A hundred yards away firemen jetted water onto a blazing discount store.

Beyond the flames, beyond the fast-flowing booze, the Civil Disturbance Unit waited with lethal sobriety.

"Time," Richter said, "to go home."

A black brandishing a bottle of champagne caught them creeping away. "You there. Where you goin'?" He waved the bottle in their faces. "You know what this is? It's champagne. Champagne like you drink, whitey. I ain't never tasted champagne before. I like it, man. I think it's wild. You want a drink?"

Zhukov shook his head.

"Why's that, baby? 'Cos my big fat lips have been 'round the bottle?"

He shoved his face near Zhukov's. He wore a colored handkerchief knotted around his neck, hair brushed out at the sides, a pair of sunglasses missing one shade so that you imagined nothing but a socket behind the other. The unshaded, bloodshot eye gleamed.

"I don't like champagne," Zhukov said. Excitement and fear breathing together, but you never showed it. Never. His hands hung loosely at his sides; he took a step back.

"Here," Richter said. "Give me a drink. I like champagne."

"Guess you can afford it, whitey. Guess you can just fucking afford it. Who killed Martin Luther King, eh? Who killed that good honorable man?"

"I don't know," Richter said. "Can I have a drink or not?"

"Sure, man. You have yourself a drink." He spat on the top of the bottle. "Go on, baby. Drink up the good black man's spit at the same time."

A little more than a good gauleiter could take. Richter wiped away the spit and tilted the bottle.

"And now you, white trash."

Zhukov shook his head.

"I should drink it if I were you," Richter said. "Then we'll get the hell out of here."

Zhukov looked into the one eye regarding him from behind the deformed sunglasses. He thought: I want to help you. That's all I want to do. Who is the enemy?

"You goin' to drink?"

Zhukov shook his head again, shocked by his insane perversity.

"Fuck you." The black swung the bottle. Zhukov ducked and the bottle smashed against the wall, California champagne foaming down the paint-flaked bricks.

But the explosion of the bottle was drowned by a roar of flames from the blazing store.

The black fell forward, hitting his head on the wall, sliding to the ground where he stayed, his one visible eye closed.

"Okay," Richter said. "Enough is enough. We were crazy coming here."

They sought escape among the firemen. But the drunks had joined the fire fighters and were throwing bottles into the flames.

Somewhere above bricks grated.

A loudspeaker opened up, nasal voice calm. "Please clear the street. Please clear the street. The wall of this store is in danger of collapsing. Please clear the street immediately. I appeal to you for your own sakes—clear this street."

Again the crepitus of bricks.

The cops moved in to clear the happy looters away from the sacked liquor store. They dragged the living empties away but the livelier one didn't want help.

They fought with wild swings, blurred black punches, kicks as slow as they were vicious. The Civil Disturbance Unit, trained for riot duty, moved in. Truncheon against skull; slurry snarls.

Then from somewhere among the legs a small boy emerged. Eyes wild in the firelight, hands pushing aside the legs; a cut on his fuzz of hair.

The wall bulged.

The firemen retreated. The cops retreated and the drunks got the message through their retreat. The child ran on toward the building.

Zhukov went after him. Cops, firemen, rioters were shouting at him. But you didn't stop, did you?

He could see the wall leaning outward. A couple of bricks fell slowly like drops of molten metal.

He grabbed the boy and ran on hearing the groan and the sigh and the crumbling roar behind him. A brick clipped his shoulder—but they were clear.

The firemen moved back. One patted Zhukov on the shoulder. Zhukov leaned down to the boy and asked, "Where are you trying to get to?"

The boy started to cry, skinny fists knuckling his eyes in his skinny face.

"Where do you want to go to?'

A woman with a frightened-looking face grabbed the boy's arm. "What you doin' with my kid, white man?"

"I wasn't doing anything."

She pulled the boy away. "This ain't your night, white man. Get out of here. Get your hands off our kids. This is where the poor blacks live. Get back to your side of the town."

Two cops, blank-faced robots in their visors, came up. "Better do as she says. This is no place for a white man. You're only making our job tougher than it is."

159

Zhukov nodded. "All right."

Richter joined him. "As they say—there ain't no justice."

"I don't care," Zhukov said. And he thought: I have participated.

They walked briskly down Fourteenth toward the stately homes and the dirty bookshops. Soon they were back in the white ghetto.

Chapter 5

THE WHITE CHINA bowl of stew stood in the kitchen with a tidemark a quarter of an inch above the solidifying surface where Valentina Zhukova and Natasha had sampled it without appetite. A beautiful stew, enough for a dozen, with its cubes of cheap steak, stock, mushrooms, potatoes, carrots, and an archipelago of dumplings. Two bottles of scotch, and some Rhine wine bought extravagantly and—it seemed to Valentina—disloyally for guests developing Westernized tastes.

But the Russian guests plus two obedient Hungarians (a Czech and his wife had declined the invitation) hadn't come because of the disorders. Natasha had taken to her room where Valentina had recently found novels by Updike, Bellow and Malamud.

Valdimir was missing and Valentina was worried.

From their very first meeting—their youth was now a separate entity with middle and old age coalescing—she had discerned his weaknesses. Crystals of spurious gold in granite. And she had accepted her responsibility to guide him through the long loving conversation of marriage.

Hadn't *she* once confronted herself? The wild Sibiryak with the easy ways who had hurt Vladimir, his teen-age

160

romanticism unexpended because of the war. (Childhood was now a photograph of a little girl standing amid snow-heavy firs with a *laika* hunting dog. A schoolroom and a red Young Pioneer scarf.) Duty had prevailed over wild instincts. Implanted by parents sowing Socialism in the virgin lands; accepted unwittingly in the red-scarved Pioneer play camps; carried proudly aloft in the earnest, energetic endeavor of the postwar Komsomol. And finally the party.

In their Muscovite apartment in the heart of Washington Valentina Zhukova turned the dial of the old TV seeking distraction. Riots and fires interrupted by commercials for detergents and antiperspirants. (One commercial for insurance nicely following a blazing ghetto store.) Rival newscasters, each with the same voice. Then, with the last click of the dial, redskins instead of blacks rioting, with James Stewart shooting them off their horses while he waited for the cavalry. She let him wait there, rifle stuck through a crack in a fence, because she had to admit that she enjoyed a Western.

Where was Vladimir?

Since they'd arrived in America suspicions had begun to assemble about her husband, good man that he was. We will give him the Washington post, they had told her, because together you are strong. They must have had a lot of faith in their union to toss him into the embassy circuit of gossip and decadence.

Something akin to jealousy stirred. To be put down instantly. Duty, such duty. The familiar glow of self-sacrifice spread its halo.

An ad for a breath freshener appeared, forcing James Stewart to wait a little longer for the cavalry. Valentina went into the kitchen to make some tea with lemon. She called out to Natasha asking her if she wanted some; Natasha's voice, distant from reading or thought, said, no, she didn't.

Valentina cut a slice of lemon. It isn't as if I don't have temptations. The clothes and cosmetics, Vogue fashions and uplift bras, women driving the second car, the hairdressers, the houses with their drives, attendant gardeners

161

and smug composure. But it was the gadgets that tempted her most. Electric mixers, dishwashers, can openers, spits, floor polishers, air conditioners.

Yes, she would have dearly loved a good gadget as a toy. But gadgetry had to be put aside; symbolic of the Americans' ingenuity in cultivating idleness. While families in upstate New York (so she had read) existed without knives to ease the burden of the rich man tackling his Sunday roast.

Such were the bizarre inequalities which would one day be erased from the world. Not in her lifetime, perhaps. But the satisfaction of helping to found a new civilization of equality was there.

The cavalry arrived in the nick of time. Valentina switched back through riots and newscasters grim at their global desks.

Where was Vladimir?

In their bedroom she picked up an early portrait of him. Brilliantined hair brushed straight back, square strong face with the giveaway mouth. The face of a soldier composing sonnets in the trenches. How she had loved him, his weakness the catalyst, maybe, to attraction. Frozen there in studio lights on the dressing table, half-smiling into the hesitant future which she had helped stabilize. Her warrior, her child.

She switched on the radio. Riots. Alarm for his safety began to override fear for his soul. Surely he wasn't fool enough to go anywhere near the ghetto? She looked at her wristwatch. Eight o'clock. He had been gone eight hours. She switched off the radio and fed her worry.

You couldn't tell with a man like Vladimir. In everyone there is a chamber to which no stranger has access. You couldn't tell what he had kept locked away—even from himself. What key had been turned in this ruthless, window-dressed country.

A woman?

Perhaps she hadn't been such a good wife to him lately. But she had presumed that he understood her mature attitudes. And hadn't he agreed that the role of women had

162

changed since pre-Revolutionary days when they were either peasants with a load of brushwood on their backs or fragile playthings sighing their way from courtship to pampered motherhood? (In her early reading Valentina had searched for the heroic qualities of Russian women, finding them in the Olga of Oblomov, even in the pure souls of Turgenev whose courage dwarfed the frailty of their men.)

She had been fortunate enough to be born into an emancipated age when she could implement qualities corseted for so long. Article 122 of the Constitution: "Women in the Union of Soviet Socialist Republics are accorded equal rights with men in all spheres of economic, governmental, cultural, political and other public activities."

So sterner duties had to be set after the first passions of love had been spilled. Even if your own body sometimes urged you on to a surfeit of pleasure. (Such oiled depths, such tender cruelty in the wooden rooming house that first time; such sweet fulfillment in the dacha in the snow.) No, you had to curb self-indulgence, or so it had seemed as she peered into middle age.

She returned to the bedroom, stroked the dust from his posing face as if she were trying to erase mistakes.

Then she went to the window and saw the glow beneath the smoke beneath the stars. This time love vanquished duty, propelled by the worry of lost sharing. She sat at his hospital bedside, wept at his grave.

Unless he was at some party given by a red-taloned, swan-necked hostess . . .

From the drawer of the desk—the key of which she kept in a secret place—she drew the report she had begun to write that afternoon. She wrote a few words, but duty was a poor second this evening. She replaced the report, but, because of her worry, forgot to lock the drawer.

In the mirror she regarded her worried face. Hardly heroic. Hair, powder and white blouse a uniform. A few ski trails of gray in the hair thrust back dutifully into a tortoiseshell comb. Where was your wild Sibiryak now? Breasts spreading, relaxing, waist conceding; a servant's

163

figure. Daughter of the Revolution, mother of an ideology.

She thought with wretched clarity: You couldn't blame Vladimir if he were unfaithful.

But I can. Two decades of devotion. To what?

She pushed her hair forward at the ears, feeling it pull through the comb. Moistened her finger and smoothed her unplucked eyebrows. Undid the top button of her regulation bouse.

I love him and it is up to him to understand the nature of my love.

She heard a crack like a pistol shot and the clatter of breaking glass. But there was nothing to see outside the window except the empty lamplit street.

There were his newspapers filled with boasts. (Although they did seem to be remarkably honest about defeats in Vietnam.) There were his schoolboy piles of matches. She picked up one from a bar called the Black Rose. She wondered who her husband had met there in these new sacrificial duties that brought him home the worse for liquor twice, sometimes three times, a week.

The apartment looked very drab, even the sugar-coated red currant sweets had lost their whiteness. She saw him in a luxurious apartment with crystal cocktail shakers, hi-fi and the elegant hostess just changing into something simpler.

Craftily circumstance, worry and duty nudged a preposterous question: Was it possible that Vladimir Zhukov could ever defect? At this she smiled, touching his photograph again. No, not Vladimir Zhukov, hero of Leningrad, faithful servant of the party. Warrior, husband, child.

She knocked on the door of her daughter's room and said, "May I come in?"

Natasha lay fully dressed in her new clothes on the bed. Beside her lay a fashion magazine. It didn't look as if it had been opened. "Where's Father?" she asked.

"I don't know. I'm worried."

"You don't usually worry when he's out late. At least you don't seem to."

164

"Your father can be a headstrong man. He may have got himself involved in the troubles."

"He'll be all right. He's a big tough bear. And in any case we've all been told to keep away from the riots."

"Perhaps your father is not so obedient."

Natasha looked surprised. "He's always seemed obedient enough to me. That's why they sent him here, isn't it?"

"There may be rebellion underneath. But it's futile to be a rebel when we're all working for a common cause."

Natasha sat upright. "For God's sake, Mother, this common cause of yours is the result of a rebellion. Your mother and father were rebels. It's born in some men to be rebels."

"But only to rebel against injustice. . . ."

"And isn't there any injustice in Russia today?" Her liberalized hair veiled her face, making a secret of it.

Valentina sat in a protesting wicker chair beside the bed. "Don't talk like that or they'll send you back to Russia."

The veil parted. "You sound as if that would be a punishment. Are you becoming influenced by this bourgeois society?"

"I thought you might regard it as a punishment to be parted from your parents again. . . ."

Natasha nibbled at a chocolate bar. "I would. I'm sorry."

"I'm worried about you, Natasha."

"I'll be all right."

"There are many temptations in this country."

"I can resist them."

Valentina wanted to point out that Natasha hadn't taken long to succumb to a girl's biggest temptation. But nor had she for that matter. There was nothing wrong with experiments in sex—as long as Natasha kept them in their right perspective. But there was a lot of Vladimir in their daughter, his romanticism perhaps.

Natasha said, "Don't think I'm going to start smoking pot, or anything."

"Pot?"

"Yes, pot. Marijuana. Grass, I believe they call it. As

165

for sex . . . well, you know all about that. A very full report, I gather. They don't miss anything, do they, Mother?"

"I've forgiven you that. It had to happen sometime."

"No, you didn't mind that. What you minded was me sleeping with a dissident. A traitor. An enemy of the state. Poor Georgi—just a student behaving like a student and they lock him up for two years. That wouldn't happen here, Mother."

Valentina moved as if to put her hand over her daughter's mouth. "Please don't speak like that, Natasha. Please, I beg of you."

"But it wouldn't, would it?"

Valentina slumped in the chair, worry churning into nausea. "Perhaps not. But in this country a student can be shot down in a riot. He can become a drug addict. He can be posted to Vietnam and die there for a worthless cause. Or he can escape and be on the run for the rest of his life. Is any of that so much better?"

Natasha broke off a piece of chocolate. "But he can write what he pleases, read what he pleases. Choose his own destiny." She chewed thoughtfully. "What would you say if I were pregnant by Georgi?"

"Are you?"

She shook her head, hair moving glossily. "I thought I was but I'm not."

"Are you sorry?"

"You mean would I have liked to have *his* child? No, it's a nice martyred idea. But I wouldn't. I'm not that much of a fool." She swallowed the last of the chocolate. "You know," she said, "it's ironic what's happening to you. All of a sudden your daughter is exposed to everything you and all your kind have warned me about all my life. What all Soviet kids are warned about. And you think you can see it affecting me already. It doesn't say much for your system, does it, Mother, if you are frightened that I will run to capitalism and embrace it on sight?"

"You are still young," Valentina said. "You are impressionable. Your values have not formed yet."

"I can't see anything wrong with being impressionable.

166

I've been impressed all my life with one system. Now I'm seeing the other. The values should sort themselves out very neatly in my young impressionable mind. You shouldn't have brought me over here, Mother."

"Your father wanted it," Valentina said. She looked at her watch again. Nearly nine. If he didn't come soon, she would call the embassy, though she didn't want to get him into trouble.

"My father's wishes wouldn't influence anyone very much."

"Don't talk like that about your father."

"I didn't mean it like that. I love my father. I love you both—you know that. All I meant was that the opinion of one junior diplomat doesn't hold much sway with the Kremlin. Are you sure there's not some other reason for me being here?"

"Other reason? Not that I know of. What other reason could there be?"

"I don't know. I wondered. It seems odd to be rewarded for being suspended from the university." She swung her legs over the side of the bed and faced her mother. "And why am I followed every time I leave this place?" She searched her mother's face for dishonesty.

"If you are being followed it's just a precaution. To see that you don't get into any trouble. To see that you don't get attacked. . . ."

Natasha smiled.

"Is that so funny?"

"Not really. Except that I don't think that's the reason. Anyway"—she flung herself back on the bed triumphantly —"I usually manage to give him the slip. I wonder why he doesn't report it? I suppose he's afraid to get into trouble. Like that big doggy man Grigorenko."

Valentina held up her hand. "Please." She lowered her voice to a whisper. "If you want to stay here with us do not say these things. You do want to stay here, don't you, Natasha?"

Natasha's mood changed suddenly. "Yes. Yes, of course I want to stay." She stared at and beyond her mother.

Valentina's maternal reflexes reacted. "What is the real attraction here, Natasha?"

"It's a beautiful city. I'm educating myself."

"Nothing more?"

Valentina knew that her daughter tried never to lie.

Natasha said, "There are many attractions."

Valentina knew then that her intuition was right: A man was involved. Tomorrow they would go out together and talk. Under the cherry blossoms in Potomac Park. If the riots were over.

Natasha elaborated hastily about the educational advantages of Washington. "Do you know what their adopted flower is?"

Valentina said she didn't, wondering who he was.

"The American Beauty rose. Isn't that lovely?"

Valentina agreed.

"And their tree. Do you know what their tree is?"

No, Valentina admitted, she didn't.

"The scarlet oak." She laughed nervously. "That should please you, Mother."

They looked at each other through a curtain of dishonesty.

Natasha changed tactics. "How is the Soviet Union interpreting these riots? We never seem to say much about race riots. I wonder why."

"They are America's problem."

"I thought we made capital out of America's problems."

"Not this one. It has no place in our scheme of things."

"I should have thought it would," Natasha mused. "After all, it's class struggle, isn't it? And that's what Socialism is all about. Or perhaps," she pondered, "it's merely part of the development of democracy."

"It's the birth of a revolution," her mother said.

"It's very confusing." She'd regained her confidence. "And I think other Soviet citizens would find it a little confusing too. I wonder if we keep so quiet because we really. . . ."

Again her mother warned her, holding up her hand, anticipating the rash questions of immaturity. "I'm going to phone the embassy," she said. "He may be hurt."

Her daughter leaned forward and embaced her. "I'm sorry. . . ."

"I know," Valentina said, stroking her hair. "I know."

They heard a key in the lock and from the living room Vladimir's voice calling their names.

He ate his stew hungrily, mopping up the gravy with hunks of black bread. They might not have as much money as Western diplomats but, with wives like Valentina, they could make a meal last a week, like French peasant women with their stockpots. From the cornucopia of American food they preferred hamburgers, hot dogs, steaks and lamb chops; they disliked the cheese, sausage and bread—particularly the bread.

His two women watched him while he ate, waiting. Like the good Russian women they were—always make sure your man has a full belly. Stuff him with bread and potatoes before pleading for money, making love or launching an attack. Ah, the women of Russia, shoveling, bricklaying, breeding, feeding, shouldering the work of a nation which had lost a generation of men, with grace in their souls and eyes if you looked for it. Fighting their own sex war like the women of America: If man *and* wife went out to work why should only the wife cook and clean? Why should the wife wash and scrub on holidays while the husband paraded in the park? All they sought was chivalry; but the Kremlin was a man's club.

He mopped up the last shred of steak and Valentina said, "Well?" He had only told them that he had become involved in a riot.

"A little tea, perhaps?"

"Very well." She went to the kitchen, allowing one more small delay.

He felt content, a soldier returning. To his daughter he said, "And how is my little girl?"

"Why did you allow it to happen, Father?"

"First," he said, "my tea."

"Mother was nearly out of her mind. She was going to call the embassy."

169

He spread his hands, the errant youth, and sipped his tea, making a business of it.

Valentina said, "You were very stupid, Vladimir." Classically, he thought, anger would now replace concern.

"I wanted to be part of it."

"Part of it? Why? It's none of our business."

"It's everyone's business," Vladimir said vaguely.

"You are jeopardizing your position." She remembered the bugs which weren't confined to foreign premises. "But let's talk about it later. Tomorrow perhaps. . . ."

"Why not now?" He considered the tactic with surprise; then understood and was angry. "I'm free to do what I please. To say what I please." But was he? "If you must know I went to the ghetto with a German newspaperman." Surely they hadn't bugged his own home . . . but if they had they would record that with approval. "That's part of my job. Meeting foreigners," he added for the sake of his daughter. He found himself addressing the microphone which he was convinced didn't exist. Such is our upbringing, the heritage of Beria. "The German's name was Richter, Helmut Richter, and after what happened this evening I've established a strong link with him. The camaraderie of shared danger." A good phrase.

Natasha said, "You could have been killed. You didn't stop to think of Mother. Or me." Indicting the entire immature male sex.

He tore off the dark jacket that had made him seem like an undertaker among the lunchtime slacks and sweaters. The shoulders were sprinkled with ash and dust; also a crusty blob that might have been blood.

Natasha leaned across the table and touched his hair—which had grown a little more fashionable since his arrival, longer but rebellious at the neck here it had flourished free from a lifetime of clipping. "You're hurt," she said.

"A scratch."

Valentina examined the cut; a sliver of glass, probably, from the smashed champagne bottle. She bathed it and dabbed it with antiseptic. "It will be all right." Anger stepped briskly forward again. "Why, Vladimir? You are a diplomat, not a bloodthirsty hooligan."

"Ah," he said, "such hooligan behavior. Such a degenerate."

She shook her head vigorously and put her finger to her lips.

"I can speak in my own home!"

Natasha, the diplomat's daughter, said, "I think you should go to bed now, Father. Perhaps Mother is right. . . ."

"Neither of you understand, do you?"

"I don't know," his daughter replied. "Perhaps I do. . . ."

Valentina said, "Do you, Vladimir?"

He lit a cigarette—American and roasted. "It's difficult to explain." But she was right, of course, he didn't understand. Not really. Disgust. Involvement.

"I don't understand," Natasha said, "why the Soviet Union doesn't make more of these troubles. It's a weapon for them, surely. To show the world how the black man is treated by a democratic nation."

Guiltily, Vladimir wondered how a black population would fare in Moscow. Some black students had returned to Africa complaining bitterly of indignities allegedly suffered there. He sensed impending danger in the trend of Natasha's thoughts. He, too, held up his hand, put his fingers to his lips, feeling foolish. "Perhaps," he decided, "you are right. I should go to bed."

"Such foolishness," Valentina muttered.

Perhaps she was right.

At the dressing table, wearing flannel pajamas and a coarse dressing gown tied with a cord, Vladimir Zhukov brushed his hair energetically.

Valentina took the comb from her hair and, wearing a yellow cotton nightdress bought in a moment of weakness, climbed into her bed.

Vladimir brushed on.

"You need a haircut," she said. "You wouldn't have worn it like that in Moscow."

"I'm not in Moscow."

"You're becoming very Americanized, Vladimir."

"In this dressing gown? These pajamas?"

"No, in your ways. Your talk. Your mannerisms. The other day I heard you say five bucks instead of five dollars."

He laughed. "Stop nagging. If they want me to mix with Western diplomats then I'm bound to become a little Westernized. It's only on the surface," he assured her.

"Are you sure?"

"Of course I'm sure."

"But you're so impressionable. I worry about you, Vladimir. And about Natasha. . . ."

"Yes," he said, "I worry about her, too."

"We shouldn't have brought her here."

"What should we have done, then? Left her in disgrace in Alma-Ata with the newspapers ridiculing her?"

"I suppose not. But she's been telling me things today. Just before you came home."

"What sort of things?"

Valentina shook her head. "Not now."

Such prudence was ridiculous, Vladimir thought. If his superiors were eavesdropping they would pick up the implications. Implications more suspect than the truth.

As he put down the brush he noticed a drawer slightly open in the dressing table. "Hey," he said, "I thought we had lost the key to this." He opened it and took out a pad of lined paper, the top sheet half-filled with Valentina's writing. "What's this?"

She was beside him closing the drawer. "It's nothing. Just a letter I was writing. I found the key this afternoon." She moved a little closer. "Come to bed, Vladimir."

He felt her breasts through the yellow cotton. Heavy and luxurious, not like Helen Massingham's. Mother Russia. Her belly thick and warm. Battle-scarred and baffled, the warrior allowed himself to be comforted.

Chapter 6

IT HAD BEEN a bad day for lady spies, the ambassador thought, knotting his silver tie and taking a sip from the glass of J & B on top of the bathroom cabinet beside his tablets and throat spray. (The scotch he needed because the reception was being given by the Czechs and at this deteriorating stage of relations he would need a nip to his charm.)

First of all the FBI had photographed an Australian girl handing over documents to a Cuban in a bar in Yonkers or Queens or somewhere. (Which means they would have reached us eventually via Havana.) The girl's loyalties were confused, her competence suspect—her bedworthiness vouchsafed by forty-three diplomats, agents, government staff, politicians and one cabdriver whom she hadn't been able to pay.

She was a dark, freckled girl; you imagined her striding through the surf on Bondi Beach, hollow-bellied and athletic, a strong swimmer who still had to be rescued by lifeguards. She had a beautiful expressionless face and a discordant voice.

Ambassador Zuvorin who had met her on the cocktail circuit had never quite fathomed her and speculated that this was because her depths were so shallow that they were unfathomable.

Perhaps she even thought she *was* working for the Cubans with whom America had no diplomatic relations. Had considered that the poor little offshore island which seemed to suffer from a chronic shortage of razor blades was getting a raw deal. Although why an Australian should take such an interest in Fidel Castro's sugar plantation was beyond analysis.

Unless she imagined she was collecting information about Cuba—and every other nationality that she had bedded—for the Australians acting, perhaps, on behalf of the British.

It was very complex. And, like many apparent complexities of espionage, Zuvorin suspected that the key was the naïveté of the girl, as pure—not pure perhaps—and as simple as the driven surf.

Certainly all the information she had passed to the green-jacketed comrades in Havana had been worthless. This the ambassador knew. Likewise he believed that the men who claimed to have slept with her hadn't imparted any secrets; otherwise they wouldn't have boasted about it. It was said on the martini rounds that one Congressman, assisted by a surfeit of alcohol, had successfully accomplished an all-night filibuster with her.

In my youth, thought Zuvorin . . .

His wife called from the living room of their home in the embassy. "What country are we visiting tonight, darling?"

"Czechoslovakia," he said, returning to the middle-aged present.

"Oh." She paused. "How are we to conduct ourselves?"

"With charm as always. But a little more sternly than usual. A little ice in the caviar."

"Is there going to be trouble in Prague?"

"It looks very much like it." Which meant more double-talking in the American capital which had warmed to him —and he to it.

"A pity," she said. "I like the Czechs."

"I'm afraid that is beside the point," said her husband.

He adjusted his charm in front of the cabinet mirror. Always a Russian, almost a Westerner. If only the enemy were still the Germans.

He took his drink into the living room. His wife was there, adjusting her necklace of Baltic amber. Plump but infinitely gracious: his strength, his love.

"Are you drinking already? I hope that doesn't mean

174

you are going to have your usual two drinks on top of that. You know what the doctor said."

"Only one drink with the Czechs. I don't want to stay there too long anyway. It might be a little embarrassing."

"You've had a hard day," she said. "I can feel it."

"No more than usual."

"I suppose these terrible riots have made it difficult for you."

"Not really." Riots there had been before; in many countries. He assimilated them with ease; they occupied a small place in diplomatic negotiation—except, perhaps, when they were organized and financed at embassy level with flags and transport. Instant riots, the Americans called them; presented like amateur theatricals for the press and TV cameras. Or when they threatened to get out of hand as these had done. But now the immediate danger had passed; there would be no civil war yet. Of far greater moment were the burgeoning Vietnam peace talks in Paris. And Czechoslovakia.

She didn't inquire any further: she had learned when to stop.

He swirled the smooth pebbles of ice in his glass, thirsting for another scotch. Instead he poured himself a ginger ale, taking the precaution of identifying it to his wife.

But it had been a trying day. Because the other lady spy in the limelight was a Russian.

She worked as a secretary. In her thirties, attractive in a Russian sort of way. Comely but indifferent to the sophisticated techniques of the Washington beauty parlors which made fortunes from the society hostesses. She knew her powers: She knew that the weak men of the West liked to boast that they had seduced a Russian.

But today a magazine had printed an article with pictures speculating about her activities. "The Red Mata Hari." And Zuvorin had summoned Mikhail Brodsky to his office to inquire why the girl's activities had been allowed to get so blatant. To expend some of his accumulated dislike of the other powers who existed alongside him.

Also to ascertain more clearly just who was the boss at the embassy.

First point to Brodsky. He had suggested that they adjourn to the bug-proof chamber and Zuvorin had gone along with him.

Within the steel wallpaper Zuvorin lit a cigarette—one of the six permitted per day—and said, "Why could you not have been a little more subtle about it, Brodsky?"

Behind the gold-rimmed glasses the pale eyes stared, assessed. I am the KGB resident; you are the ambassador. But just who in the Kremlin are your latest friends?

Brodsky's hesitance encouraged Zuvorin. He wondered what the hell he was doing treating a third secretary almost as an equal. He who held the most diplomatic post in the world outside Moscow. It was ludicrous. But the shadow of a police tyranny lingered beyond the deaths of its leaders. "Well?" he prompted.

Brodsky shrugged without apology, but warily. His whole existence was wariness. "I can't control the speculation of the sensational capitalist press."

"Of course you can't. But on this occasion they seem to have been pretty near the truth."

Brodsky said, "So you knew she was a spy?"

"Don't be insolent, Brodsky. I'm the ambassador and you are a very junior diplomat."

Brodsky pondered this, thin fingers coiling and uncoiling a lock of soft hair above one ear. Zuvorin wondered if he were a homosexual. Probably not: Brodsky's satisfaction was intrigue and furtive power.

Brodsky said, "I didn't mean to be insolent. I merely wondered how you knew that this girl was engaged in such activities. Such matters are surely outside your responsibilities. . . ."

Wearily Zuvorin realized that Brodsky was speculating whether he had his own contacts in the hierarchy of the KGB—possibly at the summit of the security organization.

"Comrade Brodsky," Zuvorin said. "It is not for you to decide what my responsibilities are."

Brodsky crossed his legs, examined a pointed black toe cap. "I was merely wondering. . . ."

"Then please don't." Zuvorin decided to press home the attack. "In the future I suggest that you exercise a little more restraint when issuing your instructions"—not orders, *that* acknowledged too much authority—"to members of *my* staff. Also I suggest that you be more discreet in the reports that you send back to Moscow." A suggestion, the product of a lifetime of verbal jousting, that he knew the contents of Brodsky's reports. I don't, thought the ambassador, but I've got a very good idea.

"I have my work to do," Brodsky said, sulking.

"So have we all, Comrade Brodsky. It is my task to see that each of us carries it out competently. It is my view that your competence of late is open to question."

Brodsky staged a small rebellion. "I take my orders from Moscow. You know that."

"You also take your orders from me. And if you continue in this vein I shall make it my business to see that very shortly you will be back in Moscow to accept those orders firsthand."

Brodsky sulked some more. Uncertain. Trained to suspect everyone.

The ambassador stubbed out his cigarette with regret. Five more to go and a Czech reception to cope with in the evening. But he could not let up now. "For instance," he said, "how are the new duties of Comrade Zhukov working out?"

Brodsky looked perturbed. "Comrade Zhukov is a worthy member of the party. He carries out his duties admirably. What more can I say?"

It was not difficult, Zuvorin thought, to alarm Brodsky. After all, if Hoover were right and 80 percent of all Soviet personnel *were* spies, the odds against successfully naming Zhukov as one of Brodsky's cohorts were small. "Tell me about his duties, Comrade Brodsky."

Brodsky's sinus seemed to fill as he concentrated. He fished out his white plastic inhaler and plugged each nostril with it. Time to think. Finally he said, "He is expected to meet people. To make contacts, to socialize. We are not very strong in that department. With the exception of yourself, that is."

"Is that all he has to do—meet people?"

"Uh-huh." Brodsky tuned in. "Just the same as the

diplomats from other countries. We have to mix and we have to listen. More and more is being achieved these days away from the bargaining table. Through junior diplomats, through journalists. . . ."

"Comrade Brodsky," Zuvorin interrupted, "you don't have to lecture me on the current trends of diplomatic procedure. What concerns me is the fact that your own peculiar responsibilities seem to be affecting the normal running of the embassy."

Brodsky squeezed the bridge of his nose where it was dented by his professor spectacles. "I think perhaps that my responsibilities and your responsibilities have the same end in mind."

"I am fully aware of our joint responsibilities," Zuvorin replied. "I was present at the last Party Congress in Moscow," he deliberately reminded Brodsky. "What alarms me is the way in which subversion and infiltration and diplomacy are becoming one." Which was not quite true; they always had been one. It was Brodsky who concerned him, his furtive authority and his pollution of good Russians. Men like Zhukov. "Why is Comrade Zhukov's daughter over here?"

"Because Zhukov wanted it. It is an encouragement to him to work even harder for the cause."

"For your cause."

"For our cause."

All this, Zuvorin knew, would be transmitted to Moscow where it would be digested and used according to Zuvorin's latest rating assessment at the Kremlin. He wouldn't be surprised to discover that Brodsky himself had bugged the FBI-proof room. "And how much progress has Comrade Zhukov made in cultivating Western contacts?"

"He has done surprisingly well. Our capitalist friends seem to like him."

"Does that surprise you, Comrade Brodsky? Is there any reason why a Russian should not be liked?"

Brodsky blocked a nostril. "*Uh-huh.* No reason at all. It was merely that we socialize so little that it is difficult to assess our popularity."

Zuvorin chuckled. "That is very simple to assess: We are unpopular. Comrade Zhukov is accepted because he has a likable personality. Also because he is a novelty—a performing seal, as it were. Also because our Western friends see him as a possible entrée to our affairs. You are, I presume, aware of that aspect of Comrade Zhukov's socializing?"

"Of course." Brodsky's confidence rose and fell like the capitalist stock market. At this moment it was in the ascendant. "I'm very well aware of that. In fact it's interesting to observe the identities of those who have been detailed to approach Comrade Zhukov."

"Such as?"

Brodsky frowned and polished his spectacles, deliberating whether such information was for release. Zuvorin watched him polishing, searching for some snotty little compromise. I am very fortunate, he thought, that I was retained for majestic dishonesties at four-power level. Better to exchange lies with a President than to feed on human weakness. The firm, knowing handshake of falsehood! He doubted whether Brodsky trusted himself; one day he would pick his own pockets.

Brodsky said, "Henry Massingham of the British Embassy has gone out of his way to cultivate Zhukov."

"Which surprises no one," Zuvorin said. "And Mrs. Massingham. What part does she play in this?"

"The usual," Brodsky said, replacing his gold-rimmed armor.

"You realize, of course, that Zhukov is a happily married man?"

"So?"

No, Brodsky wouldn't have taken such a point. Not for Brodsky the great Russian tradition of family life with the *babushka* nodding gummily in the corner and the cherished children dotingly stuffed with candy. The ambassador admired Zhukov, sensed much of himself in the man. A patriot not equipped for this complex role. Zuvorin also feared for him: A man of such sensibility was ill-fitted to evaluate the reports of Kremlin policy that reached the American press.

Zuvorin said, "So it doesn't bother you that you may break up a marriage, a family?"

"There must always be sacrifices. You yourself know that. But, in any case, his wife is well aware of the complications that may accompany her husband's new duties."

A tiny pain wandered across the ambassador's chest. Mikhail Brodsky, with all your furtive knowledge of motive and weakness, how little you know women. That is *your* weakness: the weakness of a sexual neutral. "I am glad to hear it." Skepticism lost on Brodsky. "Have you ever considered what other effects this sort of life might have in such a man as Zhukov?" Immediately he sensed that this was a mistake.

"You are surely not suggesting that Vladimir Zhukov is the sort of man who could be influenced favorably by Western decadence?"

"On the contrary I am wondering what sort of effect your intrigues might have on a man of principle."

But Brodsky didn't believe him. "You need have no worries in that direction. His parents are still in the Soviet Union. We have his daughter under constant surveillance. And we have great faith in his wife, a devout patriot and servant of the party."

"Nicolai Grigorenko didn't seem to have his daughter under constant surveillance. Can you be sure that his successor is more competent?"

"I have assigned a good man. He reports back daily."

Zuvorin inserted the doubt which men like Brodsky always accept. Rat poison, he thought. "I'm sure he reports daily. He doesn't want to be sent back to the Soviet Union in disgrace like Grigorenko."

"Uh-huh." And again: *"Uh-huh."*

Zuvorin decided to end the meeting while Brodsky's stock was in decline. He stood up. "And now, Comrade Brodsky, I have more important matters to attend to."

Brodsky replaced the cap on his inhaler. "I have noted your remarks."

"And I trust you have noted my remarks about this magazine article. Please make sure that in future this woman operates with a little more discretion, otherwise the

180

Americans will be demanding her return to Moscow. And then we shall have to demand the removal of some wretched woman in the American Embassy in Moscow. It is a tedious process, harmful to diplomatic relations. And"— he tossed in a last grenade—"please see to it that the next attempt to infiltrate a man across the Canadian-American border at Niagara is executed with a little more professionalism. Last week the United States Immigration stopped one of your men although he had Canadian license plates and said he was Canadian. He had to pretend he had left his Canadian passport behind and had to go back to collect it. It could have been highly embarrassing."

"That is not my responsibility," Brodsky said.

Which indeed it wasn't. But it illustrated the extent of the ambassador's knowledge. A small triumph of diplomatic technique over pedestrian cunning.

They closed the doors and the locks were sealed with wax.

But, sipping his ginger ale, the ambassador still debated within himself the reception that would be accorded the interview when Brodsky transmitted it to Moscow (which he probably had already done). Although, he told himself, I have no cause to worry: I am the ambassador. Then he thought: But Khrushchev presumed he had no cause to worry . . .

"Don't look so worried," his wife said.

Three years to go before honorable retirement. And you could never tell what was happening in the hierarchy of the secret police—an essential arm, he conceded dubiously, of a state only fifty years old.

When he had been a boy it had been the Cheka—the All-Russian Extraordinary Commission for Repression of the Counter-revolution and Sabotage. And then the GPU —the State Political Administration. Then the OGPU. Then almost immediately the OGPU became part of the NKVD—the People's Commissariat of Internal Affairs. And, such are the essences of intrigue and blackmail, the most competent exponents of the black arts surfaced at the top. Yezhov, followed after his execution, by Lavrenti

181

Beria—Russia's Himmler. Joyfully Beria isolated his secret police machine from the NKVD and it was called the NKGB. After the war, in which the rival Gestapo of Nazi Germany was exterminated, Beria's thugs operated under an organization nicely called the MGB—Ministry of State Security.

Stalin died, Beria was executed. Terror was diluted in the form of the present KGB. Diluted but not dissolved. Beria left behind him many heirs. Men like Mikhail Brodsky flexing their talents of intrigue and blackmail in case one day circumstances went their way: the same way that had enabled Beria to reach the summit of tyranny.

But I *am* the ambassador.

"Come, my dear," he said to his wife, "we must go."

He took a pill and swallowed the last of his ginger ale.

Zuvorin was on his third scotch of the day and his seventh cigarette. One too many of each. The day had been unsatisfactory and the reception was in keeping with it.

Three more years of these, Zuvorin thought. With luck! Usually he extracted modest enjoyment from the various reactions to his presence—acknowledging that it was the Kremlin and not his personality that made them react. (In many American minds the Kremlin was still an Alcatraz in which the criminals had seized power.) The Eastern European diplomats excessively polite, unctuous even, nationalism camouflaged by diplomatic manners and fear; the American Communists for whom the ambassador had the least respect because most of them were failures within their own system seeking salvation and vicarious importance through the true revolutionary Socialism of the Soviet Union; the begging emissaries of jungle states seeking Russian arms, Chinese labor and American money; the jocular American statesmen—all foreigners tried jocularity for openers when dealing with sinister Russians—who insulted your beliefs with an isolationist guffaw; the duty CIA agent using someone else's invitation; the Washington wives acting on husbands' instructions and sometimes coy motives of their own.

But tonight the escapist pleasures of observing human

182

endeavor given voice by alcohol were marred by the atmosphere. In Czechoslovakia the mood was rebellious and the mood had reached this outpost of Czech soil.

At the moment Zuvorin was being accosted with jocularity that was icing up a bit by two Senators whose sons were on an exchange visit to Czechoslovakia. Zuvorin welcomed them because he wanted to avoid unpleasantness with any cocky Czechs who in six months' time would be totally subservient once again.

They talked in Senate voices treating all the world's problems like Chicago graft. Currently the Chinese problem.

One, a crusading white-haired cherub from the Midwest said, "Chairman Mao's really got you guys by the balls. What the hell's going on in the Kremlin? Mao tells you what a load of punks he thinks you are and all you do is fire off a note or two. Even his soldiers bare their asses to your comrades across the river. And what do the Soviets do? Nothin'. Then Mao's Red Guards make a rumpus in Red Square. Red Square of all places—right under the windows of the goddamn Kremlin. And still nothing happens. But when it comes to putting Czechoslovakia in its place I guess you won't be so cautious, eh, Mr. Ambassador?" He chuckled to indicate that this was bluff, locker-room stuff.

The other Senator, a sad man with a buttery Southern voice, said, "I don't think you should be quite so facetious about it, Joe. There's one helluva war brewing up between Russia and China while we're all breakin' our necks over Vietnam and Israel. The biggest war I guess the world has ever known if they ever get at each other's throats."

The cherubic Senator who had demanded neat scotch in preference to the "gnat's piss" being served on trays observed that it might not be such a bad thing for the West if the Soviets and the Chinese knocked each other cold. So anyway, what was the Kremlin going to do about it?

Zuvorin, who had considerable respect for the strident liberties of Congress, asked, "What would you have us do, gentlemen? Start a war that might make the whole globe radioactive? Or maintain our responsibility to mankind

183

just as we did in the Middle East last year. If we had responded to the pleas for armed intervention when Israel attacked Egypt then we would now be engaged in World War Three." He left Vietnam alone; just this time. "In any case, perhaps it would not be such an ideal situation for the West if the Socialist powers were to negate each other. After all, it is always argued that the foundation of justice in a democracy is the system of parliamentary opposition. Perhaps the same applies to the world."

The Senator with the mint-julep voice said, okay, but the way things were going Peking was just biding time while it developed sophisticated nuclear weapons.

"Son of a gun," said the slightly tipsy cherubim. "The way things are going the Soviet Union and the United States will be allies fighting the yellow peril. What would you say to that, Mr. Ambassador?" His shrewdly pouched eyes hazarded a guess that Zuvorin had formed quite an attachment for the enemy capital.

Mikhail Brodsky, Zuvorin thought, would give his gold-rimmed eyeglasses to hear my answer. "An interesting speculation." The melodious laugh reached at least a couple of women. "But, as you Americans say, strictly for the birds."

"Jeezus," said the cherubim. "How's about that?"

The ambassador, skilled in the art of cocktail-party movement, excused himself from the Senators with regret. Diplomatic exchange was a formula: Congress was a language. Equally he enjoyed talking to New York cabdrivers.

Wearily he promised consideration—the euphemism for shelving—for more aid to Tanzania. The fund-seeker respectfully drew his attention to American imperialist intentions in other parts of Africa. But what he really meant was: Give us some more rubles or we'll strike another bargain with the Chinese. The black blackmail.

He moved on from Africa to the inevitable confrontation with Czechoslovakia.

The other participants were a first and second secretary from the Czech Embassy, a Canadian from the Cultural section, Vladimir Zhukov and his new playmate Henry Massingham.

184

The Canadian was saying, "No free people has ever voted for Communism." He stared challengingly at Zuvorin. But the ambassador was curious to hear how Zhukov handled himself.

Zhukov took the cue. "In the first place you are quite wrong. In the second place you should never generalize. Every day Socialism is gathering strength in your free countries. In France, Italy, all over South America, Africa. Even in Iceland. It is the inevitable outcome of the class struggle. It can be restrained for only so long. Your Senator McCarthy knew that. As is well known he acted through fear. As is well known that was a blatant suppression of freedom."

The Canadian, chunky with lumberjack muscle sagging with culture, switched his offensive. "Svetlana Stalin didn't seem to agree with you. What do you think of her, by the way?"

"She is a traitor," Zhukov said simply.

Not bad, the ambassador thought. A bit Tass-like, but not bad.

The Czechs, who looked like twins, downy and blinking, came in from the far corner. "Socialism and freedom can live together," one of them said. "Side by side," echoed the other. After that their voices seemed inseparable. "We in Czechoslovakia are proving this very truth. There is a new liberalism abroad encouraged by the enlightened leaders of our own party. The principles of Marxism-Leninism will survive." Then they went too far for the ambassador. "But we will exist as a nation and not merely as a lackey of the Kremlin."

The ambassador led them out of earshot of the Canadian and Massingham who was reticently anxious not to offend any of his new contacts.

The twins looked at him, blinking.

"You will do," said the ambassador quietly, "as you are told."

Zuvorin put down his empty glass. Glanced at his watch. Signaled to his wife. Ducked the Canadian's next offensive.

Exchanged coldly cordial farewells with the Czech ambassador.

To Vladimir Zhukov, he said, "Enjoy yourself." And squeezed his arm to indicate approval.

By the time he had reached the door he had declined two invitations from eager hostesses. Let Zhukov accept them, he thought.

At the door he took a last glance around. Vladimir Zhukov had been disengaged from the group by Helen Massingham. She was standing very close to him, making wandlike motions with her cigarette holder, flirting with her breasts.

She looked very confident, Zuvorin thought. Very proprietorial. The implications depressed him.

Chapter 7

ONE STORM finished the cherry blossoms. Now they lay thick and wet on the ground, afloat on the flat waters of the Tidal Basin, a butterfly season dead.

But central Washington, its riots spent, bloomed in the manner for which it had been designed. The fertile scents of rain on dust were followed by the classy perfumery of spoiled botanic flowers. The cathedrals and museums of administration opened their windows and breathed with relief; summer cumulus began to assemble grandly overhead.

On Capitol Hill the elected rulers who had been in session for sixteen throat-relaxing months smelled the spring and applied themselves, like restless students on the last class before vacation, to a tax on corporations and individuals aimed at raising ten billion dollars. On the lawns outside couples courted with historic elegance and consummated with contemporary haste in apartment buildings across the Potomac.

But for Natasha Zhukova and her American young man there was no fashionable scurry into bed. Between them there existed barriers of dictates as delicate as gauze, as tough as plate glass. So they kept company with unworldly Bronte hesitancies: a droplet of lavender water on the big bedding handkerchief around them.

Natasha Zhukova eluded her tail with slippery ease in the foyer of the Mayflower Hotel. She shrank like an anemone into the hotel bookshop and watched him blunder past, desperation sweating his face.

Then she caught a cab to a pub called the Hawk 'n' Dove near the Capitol and glowed when she saw the MG hunched outside.

But why hasn't he tried to make love to me? In a way sexual reticence was a form of dishonesty, if you felt the way she did. Because Natasha Zhukova knew now that this was the face and the boy she had wondered about in the past. The one that fitted. You didn't mock his weaknesses; you nursed them; that was love.

He was sitting at a table pouring a beer. "Hi," he said rising. She saw the happiness on his face before the mask was replaced.

"Hi," she said, very American.

"Like a beer?"

"Please. That would be good."

They sat for a while watching the bubbles spiral. Sharing.

"What about a drive out into the country?"

"I don't think that would be so good."

"Why not? They don't confine you to Foggy Bottom."

"Foggy Bottom?"

He explained that it was a part of bureaucratic Washington that collected fog, and added that perhaps they could compromise and drive to Mount Vernon, the home of George Washington.

All right, she said. But no farther.

Outside Charlie reverted for a moment to Washington

guide, explaining the architectural history of the Capitol. Thornton's prize-winning design; subsequently Latrobe, Bulfinch and Thomas Ustick Walter who raised the great dome and built the two outlying wings. Natasha enjoyed his enthusiasm and his knowledge, but not his facts. "Would you like to design a building like that?" she asked, hoping for more of his sap to flow.

Charlie shook his head. "Perhaps a monument one day to our age. Glass and gray stone and shining metal reaching for the stars through the clouds." He looked embarrassed. "But first of all I'd like to design good houses for people who can't afford good houses."

Natasha thought he sounded surprised at discovering his ambitions.

In the car they shared the imprisoned spring warmth like a pillow. It smelled of leather and speed. Stumpy gearshift, wooden wheel. The car a terrier rather than a greyhound. And that was how he drove it, nipping and charging and boasting. A weakness; but all for her benefit.

"One day," she said, as they wandered the lawns of Mount Vernon, "I would like to show you the Kremlin. It is very beautiful."

He didn't reply.

They visited the smokehouse, the barn, the coachhouse, the schoolhouse, the museum and the "slave" quarters where sixty of the two hundred servants once lived.

"I guess both our countries went to war because of slavery," he said. He took her hand: such intimacy! A courtship fueled by American history.

They sat on the lawn near the house which looked very composed in the sunlight, as secure as Sunday lunch, white-walled, red-roofed, colonial. Sparrows sprung on the turf and a voyeur squirrel came down from the trees behind them.

Charlie Hardin, casual in striped slacks and blue terry-cloth shirt, rolled on his stomach and examined the grass with concentration. "I guess," he said after a while, "that you might think we overdo the patriotism a bit."

She shook her head. "No, I admire it." The flags in

188

suburban gardens and light switches with metal eagles above them. "It's the same with us Russians."

"It's a pity we can't somehow manufacture a combined patriotism."

"Then it wouldn't be patriotism."

"No, I guess you're right." He burrowed in the grass with a twig. "You know a lot of the guys that you meet in Washington probably seem ridiculous with their intrigues, their electioneering, their swaggering."

"I don't meet people like that."

"I suppose not. But I do. And they're good people, you know, Natasha. Well, most of them, anyway. They can get a little pompous and they have a lot of complexes, but their motives are good. The hell of it is that so much of their effort is channeled into futility. They don't understand your country and you don't understand ours. And no one tells the truth."

Who, Natasha wondered, were these people? They didn't sound like an architect's contacts. "I know," she said. "We only read about the decadence of capitalism. You only read about the gray colors of Socialism. Neither are accurate. Why does it have to be so?"

"Because of a few men," Hardin said.

"It is very sad. Both countries, it seems to me, want to have friendship. And yet both work against it. They use up all their energy making bad propaganda about each other when they could be trying to understand each other. I suppose I sound naïve. . . ."

"Sure you do—thank God. We could do with a little more naïveté. Too many people dismiss honesty as naïveté. The half-smart guys."

"And you, Charlie . . . are you naïve?"

The mask which had been slipping was adjusted. "I try to be."

"Is it so hard?"

"It's just about the hardest thing in this world. Have you ever tried telling the truth all day? About every little thing? It's impossible."

"You mean you lie to me?"

189

He resumed his examination of the grass and the sparrows hopped nearer. Behind them in the trees a red cardinal swooped through the branches, a whistle of scarlet. "I try not to," he said.

She adjusted the pink mini-skirt she'd put on in the lavatory of the Hawk 'n' Dove. (Why did they call lavatories rest rooms?) Her legs were still sun-starved. "You shouldn't have to try, Charlie." He wanted to explain; she could feel it.

"I know. It's like you're sitting in the Kremlin and I'm in the Pentagon. . . ."

"An architect in the Pentagon?"

"Figuratively speaking, I mean." He searched the turf for an escape route. "That's a wild skirt you've got on. You're getting downright degenerate, Natasha Zhukova."

"Do you like it, Charlie?"

He whistled. "Sure I like it. So would any other red-blooded American. But you're supposed to wear tights or something with it, you know."

But she didn't want to wear tights or anything. She wanted the sun on her legs. The freedom. The admiration. She moved closer to him so that she could feel the warmth of his body. In her mind he no longer inhabited cocktail bars with scarlet-taloned women. He was just Charlie. The hair on top of his scalp was thinner than the rest; at forty he would be balding and that would be nice. She was pleased that he wasn't too handsome; that there was character there—and toughness, too. She wanted to see his face in passion. His hands on her body.

"What has impressed you most about us Yanks?" he asked, still swerving away from intimacy.

"You're very polite and you smile a lot. In a shop the other day a saleslady said to me, 'You're welcome.' And I said, 'Thank you.' And she said, 'You're welcome.' I wondered how long we could have gone on for."

He grinned and she noted that his ears moved slightly. "Is that all?"

"No. I've never known people so 'Right' so often. Right?"

190

"Right," he said. "All right. But what about their character?"

"It seems to me that they try just a little too hard. Always they try to be clever when there's no need. Also I think a lot of people don't know whether they're more proud of being Italians or Germans or just Americans. Also they seem too interested in sex." (Except you, Charlie Hardin.) "As if they've just discovered it. The permissive society they call it, I believe. With freedom to make love, I suppose. And yet they still treat sex in the films and magazines as if it were something dirty. It's such a contradiction."

"I guess you're right. Right? But it'll pass. In many ways we're a backward nation. What's the attitude in Russia"—very tentative here—"to sex?"

"The natural attitude," Natasha replied promptly. "They like it."

Charlie skirted that one, too. "But our society. What do you think of that?"

"You're in the middle of a revolution," she said. "It seems to me that you're trying to shake off all the old fixed ideas. Even in war—no one seems to want to have American soldiers in Vietnam and yet they're still there. I think your politicians find it hard to keep up with the changes. When you first arrive in America it seems as if the young people are a different nationality; they are quite separate from Washington and your government. And the young people themselves—they are divided about what they want. Either to do something which has social value or to do nothing at all. I think," she added carefully, "that they all seek a new leadership that will guide them away from the tired old ideas—war and meaningless wealth."

"Maybe," Charlie said. "Maybe."

"You never commit yourself, Charlie."

"I was listening to your views. They're interesting. How do the young people compare with the kids in Russia?"

"In Russia they have more sense of purpose. For instance, our young people built a whole city. It was called Komsomolsk in the far east of the Soviet Union. In America they would do the same if they thought there was any

191

point. But they don't think one group, one individual, can achieve anything. They need this new leadership. Something new and exciting, not like the promises of elections. Because from what I read, Charlie, the young people are looking for good causes all the time. So much idealism squandered"—she was speaking in Russian now—"by your industrialists and politicians. It is shameful. I think perhaps you should have a movement like the Komsomol. . . ."

Hardin lit a cigarette. "You're right, of course," he answered in Russian. "Up to a point. These kids are missionaries in their own country. When they haven't got a mission, they turn to drugs."

"That," Natasha said firmly, "is the very worst aspect of your society. It should never have been allowed to happen. And it would never have happened in Russia. . . ."

"Sure," Charlie said, irritation grating his voice a bit. "I guess they just get drunk on vodka instead."

She stopped preaching. "I'm sorry. There is so much that is good about America."

"Like what?"

"Like freedom," she whispered.

A garden laid out with petal precision. Iris unfurling, tulips drooping, daffodil bugles already crisping, cultivated bluebells sweetening the air. Bees with furry rumps protruding from suckling flowers.

His hand was dry and strong. She wanted emancipated, liberated love that would last forever; finding me the woman, the Sibiryak; deep and carnal and spiritual. Her breasts ached with it.

With this man. (Poor Georgi.) The man who had reached for a book in a Washington shop. Born for her and waiting here in an alien land. What happened if you married and then, by civilized mistake, met him? Natasha Zhukova considered predestination. I was sent here from a town called Alma-Ata in the republic of Kazakhstan to meet a man possessing vulnerable sophistication, a pleasant face and a secret mask. Inevitable? Ridiculous. Imagine all other circumstances that could have arisen, Natasha Zhukova. But they didn't. This was the one that arose, here in a green corner of the ground of the late George Washington and his wife Martha. Ludicrous.

Involuntarily she tightened her grip on his hand; and he turned and faced her; and kissed her as gently as the flowers around them. And then with the intensity that she knew existed behind the mask. So that it was a consummation within the circumstances.

"Charlie."

"Yes?"

"Nothing. Just Charlie."

But he didn't tell her that he loved her, although she knew that he did.

One May day when the heat was swelling in the capital city he met her at the Hawk 'n' Dove and told her with un-American hesitancy that he had found a place where they might spend a few hours together.

"Where, Charlie?"

"It'll sound ridiculous, I guess."

"Where, Charlie?"

"Out at the National Airport. You can take a place there for a few hours. While you're waiting for a plane. Will you come?"

Of course she would come.

They didn't speak much as they drove in the green MG across the Potomac toward the diesel-smelling, jet-roaring runways.

"It isn't the most romantic rendezvous in the world," he said as they let themselves into the aseptic motel room overlooking the serpent faces trundling along the runways for takeoff.

"It's the most romantic place in the world," she said.

Even then he was shy. Although she knew that the shyness was not natural. It hadn't been this way with other women. She was different: a quaint peasant. Or was there some other reason for the anachronism of his courting? To this fearful proposition she blindfolded herself.

In Russia, she thought, we do this on the glib white river steamers. Without the dishonesty of manners.

"Charlie."

"Yes?"

"I love you."

He nodded.

She began to take her clothes off, showing him her breasts, a little heavy the way Russian men liked them.

He went into the bathroom and reemerged, towel around his waist. Slim and better muscled that she had imagined; the athlete's ripples at the sides of his ribs, skin paling just beneath the navel, hair on his belly growing into a reverse parting.

She climbed into the bed and waited. He joined her, still wearing the towel.

And the eternity, the perpetuity, the seal of indefinable feeling that, with waiting, had advanced way beyond attraction, was achieved with frantic speed.

Afterward she thought: He didn't ask. He didn't wonder. Why?

She said, "Charlie, I wish you had been the first." Which was a lie, or a half-truth, or something.

He stroked her. "It doesn't matter."

Immediately she wished that he had wanted to be the first. Such stupidity about sex when hitherto it had been unconnected with love. Now in reverse.

"Would you have preferred it if I had been a virgin?" she asked.

"It doesn't matter. It just doesn't matter." American-like, he reached for his pack of cigarettes on the bedside table.

"I think it does, Charlie." A nerve-gas suspicion poisoned her thoughts. "It's almost as if you *knew* that I wasn't."

He inhaled deeply, making a meal of smoking. "I told you—it doesn't matter." The blindfold again.

"I'm glad, Charlie. Because it never mattered before. And it was only once."

He turned and regarded her. "Only once?" His words approaching hatred.

Sickness inside her . . . and she said, "Yes, Charlie, only once."

He crushed the cigarette, breaking it in half. "I believe you. But, as I said, it doesn't matter."

And he made love again, with an initial cruelty that spent itself in tender pain.

Chapter 8

CHARLIE HARDIN awoke in his apartment in Georgetown in a state of euphoria born of satisfying dreams. It deflated almost immediately into guilty depression.

He lay for a while in his bachelor bed, occasionally shared, listening to the circulation of the city getting under way after the night. Then he went into the kitchen—more electric machinery than food—and made coffee. And sat at the window watching the traffic, like beads on a thread, being pulled into the capital of the United States.

He smiled without realizing it. Her honesty extended to her lovemaking. Intuitive responses substituting for experience. Nothing like the textbooks which made sex like a driving lesson.

He poured himself more coffee and remembered their second visit to the National Airport, fancying that he could smell the fumes of burning jet oil in his apartment.

* * *

They had the whole day yet within five minutes of arriving they made love. Now they lay beneath a sheet, hands clasped, the taste of passion still lingering. A stem of cigarette smoke from the ashtray swayed and eddied beside them; outside the big nosing jets chased each other in the sky.

"A whole day together," she said.

"What do you want to do?"

"Just stay here with you, Charlie. Be close to you. Make love again later."

"Twice more, maybe," he said, boasting a little.

"That would be good," she said, enfeebling the boast.

His hand moved to the moisture at her loins, his moisture, and she held it there. He wanted to talk deeply and tenderly of his love, but the wisecracks of the past strangled him—the wisecracks themselves camouflaging shyness.

After a while he remembered, "I bought you a present." He reached for his briefcase which contained a copy of the British *Architectural Review,* a toothbrush and some after-shave, and took out a pocket chess set, the pieces allegedly ivory, the leather case embossed in gold with her initials. "I thought we might have a game. Lying here. East versus West."

She kissed him. "You are very sweet, Charlie. I love you so very much."

Charlie who considered himself moderately astute at chess pegged in the pieces and let her be white. Pawn to king four, pawn to queen's bishop four; knight to bishop three, pawn to king's knight three; knight takes pawn, bishop to knight two. The Sicilian opening proceeded with orthodoxy; but within his concentration certain promises fidgeted.

On the eighth move he castled and asked, "Just what does your father do at the embassy, Natasha?" With such theatrical nonchalance; such glaring deceit.

Pawn to knight five. "He is just a diplomat."

"I see." Knight to king one. "I see." Staring hard at the little board between them, wondering how plausible he might have been if he hadn't loved her. "Does he do consular work?" His voice so softly offhand now that the treachery shrieked above it.

Pawn to king's rook four. "Most of the time he reads newspapers, I think. He has to find out what America thinks about Soviet actions."

196

"I see."

She stroked his chest, his belly, his groin. "It's your move, Charlie."

I can't do it, he thought. I can't. But the promises nudged him again. Your family, your country. Oh. Christ! Knight to bishop two. Miraculously the right reply. With grotesque levity, "And what *does* America think of Soviet intentions?"

She looked at him with surprise. "I don't know, Charlie. You should know that."

"I mean what is your father's assessment?"

"I've no idea. I don't ask him about his work." She moved a pawn to bishop four. "You seem very interested in my father, Charlie."

"Not really."

"Then why do you ask so many questions?"

"It's your move."

"No, Charlie, it's yours."

"So it is." Pawn to king four. A good move, you treacherous bastard.

"Why are you so interested in my father?"

"I'm not." A little impatience to disguise the dishonesty. "Just making small talk, I guess."

"Talk for the sake of talk? We don't have to behave like that, Charlie."

"I suppose not."

"It seems to me that you are only truthful when we are making love. Perhaps I should ask you questions then." The sheet fell to her waist but she didn't bother to pull it up—nipples puckered after their passion. "Why aren't you honest with me, Charlie?"

He nearly said, "I want to be." Instead he said, "I am. There's nothing to be dishonest about. I'm not the world's greatest talker, Natasha. Perhaps that's the trouble. Perhaps you're used to brilliant fiery talkers." (Like Georgi Makarov maybe.)

The smell of burned jet fuel trickled into the air-conditioned room. She moved a knight to king two. "There's no chance for us if we start off with lies."

197

"There aren't any lies," he lied. "For God's sake, Natasha, there aren't any." The luxury of the day receded; fear of losing her whimpered inside him. But you couldn't tell such a girl that you have picked her up to make her into a spy. Not yet. Not now. Later—in the fall, maybe, when they were engaged, when she was able to understand that he had to do it. . . . But not now because he would lose her. He saw her then with other men, observed their intimacies with terrible clarity, forcing upon himself evasive anger with took root. "This is the way I am," he shouted. "Charlie Hardin. Mister Ordinary American, never a great orator. Not given to passionate speeches, not a great seeker of the truth like your other lovers. . . ."

"There was only one," Natasha said.

"I believe you," Charlie said, implying that he didn't, shocked at the ugliness he'd created.

She made a Russian gesture, throwing a handful of nothing at him. "You disappoint me," she said. And when he didn't reply she added, "It's your move."

He moved a pawn.

"That was a bad move," she said. "Check."

"To hell with it," Charlie Hardin said.

"You resign?"

"Yeah, I resign."

"Very well. And now we must go." She began to dress as if she were alone in the room.

"I thought we were going to spend the day here."

"There's no point. We will only hurt each other more."

"Okay. If that's the way you want it."

Outside the young summer heat wavered from the assembly lines of parked cars, and the jets, arriving and leaving as if there were half a dozen in circuit, flashed mirrors of light. The MG's top was down, the seats hot. They left with a squeal of tires. They said nothing for half a mile, the wind pulling at their hair. Ahead the bridge and across it the nest of Washington, D.C. Abruptly the anger spent itself and the road unfurling in front of them was the desolate future. He stopped the car.

"Natasha."

"Yes, Charlie?"

"I love you." He spoke in Russian.

"I love you, Charlie."

"I always will."

Her hand on his thigh, nodding, smiling, crying.

Behind them cars hooted and swung into another lane as the drivers gave their views on young love.

He looked at his watch. "There's a lot of the day left. Shall we go back?"

She nodded again, brushing the wind-blown hair from her eyes. He leaned over and kissed her. "And maybe we'll have another game of chess."

He showered, shaved and dressed, the guilt heavy on his back. I can't go on with it any longer. Not for my family, not for any creed. What sort of democracy is it that expects it?

He knotted a knitted silk tie between a striped button-down collar. But even if I told Walden I was pulling out what future do we have, Natasha and I? One day she'll return to Russia and I'll stay here; a small, lost affair that accidentally wandered outside the thirty-mile limit.

But could he quit? His mother, his sister who deserved the same advantages as him, his country . . . for their country men shot a gook, became murderers. For freedom, goddamnit, and all the decent clichés into which he had been born.

"*. . . to form a more perfect Union, establish Justice, insure domestic Tranquility, provide for the common defence, promote the general Welfare, and secure the Blessings of Liberty to ourselves and our Posterity. . . .*"

And for the next lesson Winston Churchill . . .

He polished his shoes with aerosol shoeblack. Gazed at the group photographs and the baseball bat on the wall. A kid's bedroom. The past written in campus slang. But you're a man now, Charles Hardin. The smell of jet fuel burning.

I can't go through with it.

"I can't go through with it," he told Walden.

"I know how you feel, boy," Walden said, pouring

bottled spring water into a paper cup. "I know just how you feel. I often feel the same way myself."

"You do?"

"Sure I do. I look out at this beautiful city of ours and I think, Jesus! Do we have to protect it *this* way? But we have to beat them at their own game, son, otherwise we're dead ducks." He gulped his water and leaped back in his chair behind his desk in the State Department. His voice, Hardin thought, was almost kindly. Almost. He went on, "I guess this is just about the first time you've been faced with any decisions like this."

Hardin said yes, it was.

"Getting the peach fuzz off your cheeks at last, eh? Well, give it a little thought before you start making any rash decisions."

"I've thought about it," Hardin said. "I think the assignment stinks."

"I agree." Walden took himself to the window overlooking his city. "Tossing a grenade into a tank stinks. Bombing a city with women and kids in it stinks. But we're fighting. . . ."

"I know. We're fighting a war."

"If we relax, the Commies will take immediate advantage. Here in the capital of the United States of America. The aims of the Communists are very simple, Charlie: They want the world. If we let up here, then one day they might get it. How would you like that? A world ruled by the Kremlin. Not being able to write a letter or a poem or design a new building without glancing over your shoulder. Not knowing if the guy next door is reporting you. The purges are over for the time being, but believe you me, Charlie, they still rule by fear over there. It's only the Chinese keeping them in check now. Look around you." Walden gestured vaguely over the marbled history of Washington. "We enjoy a land of plenty."

"Not if we lived in the ghetto."

Walden ignored him. "A heritage, Charlie. Shops and cars and fine houses. The rewards of enterprise. And the freedom we take for granted. The kids demonstrating on the campus, for instance. What do you think would happen to them in the Soviet Union? What happened to your girlfriend's Georgi? Just for publishing some student magazine—the sort of screwball rag that students all over the world turn out. Why, they put him inside. You don't go to Sing Sing for speaking your mind here, Charlie. Think about these things."

"I have," Charlie replied. "I've also thought about the drugs, the riots, the violence and the corruption in our country."

"Hmmmm." Walden filled his big burned pipe, pressing the tobacco home with his thumb. "I don't go for that sort of bullshit, son. It makes me wonder who's been brainwashing who."

"For Christ's sake," Hardin exclaimed. "I'm only pointing out things that *are* wrong with this country. Everyone knows about them."

"I got the distinct impression, Charlie, that you were comparing the United States of America with the Union of Soviet Socialist Republics. And that the United States was coming out second best."

Hardin shook his head. He got up and poured himself a cup of water. "Look, Mr. Walden. I think the United States of America is the finest country in the world. Let's make no mistake about that. It's only that I think we should try and equate the advantages and disadvantages of both countries."

"That's better, Charlie. I don't like to hear that other kind of talk. Okay, so we make your equation. What the hell good does that do? They'll still be against us and we'll have to go on fighting them."

"I'm only trying to say that we should try and understand each other a little more." The words floated naïvely around them like soap bubbles.

"Sure," Walden said, inhaling the smoke that smelled of autumn leaves burning. "I understand." He paused. "By the way, have you told your father that you aren't going through with this?"

"Not yet," Hardin said. "I thought I'd speak to you first."

"Why?" A steel tip to his tongue.

201

"Because you're the boss of the whole operation."

"I coordinate it, that's all."

"It's the same thing. You're the warlord."

"Mr. Hoover wouldn't like to hear you say that."

"Well, I understand you're the boss in an operation like this when the CIA and the FBI overlap. When defections and subversion in Washington are involved."

"That still doesn't explain why you came to see me first."

"I came to see you," Hardin said, "to let you know that my father has done everything in his power to persuade me to go through with it."

"I see." Steel tip snaking back. "He told you I had threatened him?"

Hardin recoiled from this bluntness so abruptly bared. "He said you were very insistent that I do the job."

Walden crushed the cardboard cup in his hand. No sign of Bible thumper or jingoist. "Is that all he said?"

"He suggested you could make things tough for him."

"I could." Walden released the cup like a squashed insect. "And I would." He tossed the remains of the cup into the wastepaper basket and relaxed. "But I don't want to, Charlie. I really don't. I have to make these sort of threats to get things done. Our duty comes first. Yours and mine, Charlie."

Hardin remembered what his father had said: that what Walden thirsted for most was defections. Big fat defections. Fugitives proclaiming the horrors of life in the Soviet Union and the delights of life in the States. Another Svetlana. Or, perhaps, a defection with romantic appeal. . . . He decided to sound out Walden. "What exactly do you want from the girl?"

"Information," Walden said. "You know that. Access to documents that Zhukov may bring home. And if that's asking too much we want her as an eavesdropper. Any chance remark by her parents or any of the embassy staff which will give us an idea what they're up to. Currently we're very interested in the proposed Vietnam peace talks. Czechoslovakia, of course, and their real feeling about Red China. Just how tough are the Soviets prepared

202

to get with China? Anything she can pick up."

"And you really expect me to make love to her and then ask questions like that? You must be crazy."

"You'd be surprised," Walden said. "It won't be the first time. A woman in love will do almost anything. Steal, cheat, walk out on her husband and kids, betray her country."

"Not Natasha. I'm telling you, Walden. I know." Intuitively he added, "And I think you know it."

"I don't know the girl."

Hardin sensed that they were converging on compromise. Bartering for her soul. "She won't do it, Walden."

"I think you're wrong, Charlie. But. . . ." He paused to load his pipe. "Let me put it this way. In the first instance we were after a defector who could get up on the platform and counter some of this lousy propaganda we've been getting lately. We had this guy Tardovsky lined up but that fell through. So we had to look around again and who better than his successor, Vladimir Zhukov? But by this time all our leaks within the Soviet Embassy had closed and we needed information more urgently than defections. So we got to work on Zhukov. Then, like manna from heaven, his daughter turned up."

"Aren't you forgetting one thing? Aren't you forgetting that Natasha will be going back to Russia soon?" He could smell the compromise now.

"Maybe she will, maybe she won't. That doesn't stop us getting what information we can while she's here. We need it badly, Charlie."

"I told you she won't do it."

Walden nodded, holding a match until it almost burned his fingers. Then he leaned across the desk, paternal once more. "Are you really in love with this girl, Charlie?"

"I guess so."

"And you'd like to marry her?"

Which wasn't any of his goddamn business. "Maybe."

"Then if she stayed in America everything would work out just fine for the two of you."

"You mean you want me to try and persuade her to defect?"

"If all else fails."

"You know damn well all else is going to fail."

Walden shrugged. "We want information. If we can't get it. . . ."

"Then you want Natasha."

"I'm sure she'd make a wonderful wife, Charlie."

A bubble of possibility expanded inside Hardin. Life in the States with Natasha. He saw them sitting together on the veranda of a white house surrounded by autumn woods. But first he would have to confess his duplicity, and he knew how she would react.

He said, "What about her family? It would knock hell out of them. I met her father briefly at a party the other day. He seemed like a nice guy."

"I know what you mean," Walden agreed. "I'm a family man myself. But Jesus, Charlie, there are more important considerations."

"I guess you're right," Hardin said doubtfully.

"Play it by ear. Inside information is top priority." (Like hell, Hardin thought.) "If that fails, well, you can't say you haven't tried. Then try to get her to stay. And maybe"—he spoke carefully—"maybe the CIA will bring Zhukov around to the same way of thinking."

"You're getting a little ambitious, aren't you?"

"It might seem over optimistic. But there are possibilities." His voice gloated with the possibilities.

"You mean with this Massingham woman?"

"Right. That and other things."

"What other things?"

"CIA business," Walden said.

"I think I'm entitled to know when I'm trying to make a traitor out of the guy's daughter."

"I guess you're right. The truth is that we figure Zhukov's wife is pretty high in the KGB. Think what an impact a discovery like that might have on a man like Zhukov."

"It would be pretty rough on him, I guess."

"Maybe it wouldn't be such a bad idea to get a girl like Natasha out of a setup like that," Walden suggested.

"No," Hardin said. "Maybe it wouldn't."

PART III

Chapter 1

DID YOU ADMIRE or condemn? There on this soupy June day, smelling of churned mud and exotic blossom, there before the portals of administration lay the shanty-town of impoverished frustration. The grapes of wrath spilled between Lincoln and the Monument. Resurrection City.

Warily, Vladimir Zhukov walked beside the reflecting Pool where naked hippies bathed with bravado.

The temptation was to condemn. An indictment as easy as swallowing. Nearly three thousand representatives of deprivation who had marched from all over this democracy to protest. And had built a plywood slum in the trench mud a mile or so from the contented mansions of capitalism.

Warily, Vladimir Zhukov peered into the shanties of Georgia, Carolina, Alabama, Mississippi, and into the ghettos within the black slum: Appalachian mountain poor, North Dakota Indian poor, hippies psychedelically poor, the Steinbeck poor. So much for the rotten system.

But could it have happened in Red Square?

Niet.

And in ten years—bearing in mind the boundaries of political promise—the President had promised to build six million homes for the poor. Plus proposals to find jobs for five hundred thousand unemployed; plus food programs for two hundred and fifty-six emergency areas.

For this particular appraisal of the democracy Vladimir Zhukov wore old trousers put together in East Germany and a frayed nylon shirt that collected sweat like a sponge. Also he hadn't shaved because, on an earlier occasion, his neat appearance hadn't been appreciated by the shanty-town inhabitants protesting outside the Supreme Court about the conviction of twenty-four Indians for breaking the fishing laws of Washington State.

Zhukov had been observing an Indian chief named George Crow Flies High in buckskin jacket and head-dress leading his team up the Roman steps, when a very black black astride a very white statue flung a paper bag bomb filled with mud at him. Zhukov moved to grab his sandaled foot but the mob closed in protectively, rubbing the mud into the suit bought with extravagance on F Street.

Zhukov shouted at the black in Russian, the language momentarily quelling the mob. Then left with muddy dignity as the Indian women whooped while their men-folk smashed windows and hauled down the American flag.

Now there were feuds within the ramshackle community steaming in the sun. Different pigments indicting: brown, red, and white accusing black of pushing them around. From creeds to colors to nations to communities to foot-ball supporters to villages to neighbors, Zhukov thought.

Who is the enemy?

He turned away and headed down Seventeenth, his shirt wet against his skin, the air damp after the rain. The Saturday streets were lazy, the open doors of shops ad-vertising their coolness. WALK and DON'T WALK—it didn't seem to matter with the cabs sauntering, Congress adjourn-ing, nubile secretaries off to the beaches, only the tourists inspecting their rulers' courts determinedly posing each other, in bright shirts and damp blouses.

But I'm not seeing America, Zhukov grieved. He wanted to visit the molasses South, the gangster Chicago, the Midwest of dusty endeavor, Florida dripping with suntan oil and orange juice, San Francisco's little cable cars, the smoking factories of Detroit, Los Angeles where film stars—now dead or autumn-wrinkled—once took baths of ass' milk.

So far permission to tour had been refused—by his own people.

Vladimir Zhukov, undergoing a menopause of valuation, also sought in unguarded moments the ordinariness of relaxation in the Soviet Union. Even its suburban drabness had, after six months of the permutations of luxury, a certain allure; almost nobility, he thought, gazing into a store selling garden furniture made of white iron scrollwork where "all major credit cards" were welcomed. Purity, too. Gorky Park: guitars strumming, fruit drinks and plump courtship beside a mossy lake, a row of chess players slapping down their pieces flamboyantly to disguise defeat, the evening sunshine that always involved autumn.

Not that he rejected Washington. He was honored to be there; even if he no longer bought out the local drugstore. You had to discipline regret—otherwise you could spend the hot summer mourning for the white embrace of winter and vice versa. But sometimes Vladimir Zhukov wondered if, for him, the transition had come a little too late.

Back in his apartment he poured himself pink lemonade and, in the American papers, followed the Soviet military maneuvers warning the Czechs.

* * *

A few days later he was reading in the newspapers about the murder of Senator Robert Kennedy, age forty-two, who had just won the California primary. Reading in detail: the shooting at 12:16 A.M. PDT on June 5, the assassin five feet away firing eight shots from a snub-nosed Iver Johnson Cadet pistol. Kennedy's last words were "Oh, no, no, don't" or "Don't lift me, don't lift me." Robert Kennedy, whose brother, President John F. Kennedy, had been assassinated less than five years earlier, died on the sixth at 1:44 A.M.

The President said of Robert Kennedy's murder that it would be wrong to conclude from this act that the country was sick and had lost its common decency. "Let us, for God's sake, resolve to live under the law. . . . Let us begin in the aftermath of this great tragedy to find a way to reverence life, to protect it, to extend its promise to all of our people, this nation and the people who have suffered grievously from violence and assassination. . . ."

Reading his papers and watching his television, Zhukov wondered how the Soviet press would react.

The body lay in state in St. Patrick's Cathedral, New York, from June 7 to June 8 and in twenty-three and one-half hours one hundred and fifty-one thousand people filed past the bier. The burial under floodlights took place at Arlington National Cemetery and a service at the White House was conducted by the Reverend Billy Graham. June 9 was declared a national day of mourning.

Amid the stunned grief there were touches of nobility—such as the mourning figure of Mrs. Martin Luther King.

Izvestia said: "A cancer of violence is eating away at the organism of capitalist society. Violence is innate to imperialism. . . . For Washington, international law has been transformed into freedom to murder anyone with different opinions. American society, acting abroad like an international gendarme, is degenerating more and more into a gangster within its own borders."

* * *

Down came Resurrection City, its City Hall and Freedom General Store, its chicken-hut homes. Plop in the mud before the hammers of the orange-helmeted General Services crewmen. Leaving behind a small swamp as testimony to the labors of the Reverend Ralph Abernathy and the underprivileged as the privileged euphemistically called them.

At the Red House reactions to the events of this traumatic Presidential summer were predictable. Shock at the violence and death contained within balloons of outrage to conform with Kremlin comment. What did you expect in a bandit society where guns were as available as umbrellas? Where seven hundred and fifty thousand had been killed by firearms since the turn of the century.

But soon a lot of the outrage was quelled by awareness of events across the Atlantic. Inside the Socialist bloc there was a rebel rashly launching democratic reform. And the stalwarts of the KGB intensified their surveillance of their weaker brethren inside the embassy in Washington; in particular those following for the first time defiance of the Kremlin in the Western press.

Lying in bed beside his pile of newspapers, or watching the Czech leaders on his Motorola, Vladimir Zhukov wondered how much the Russian people knew about these reforms. Not much from what he had read in *Pravda* and *Izvestia*. Soon they might read about an imperialist plot with the CIA indicted as always. A few might pick up the BBC.

Carefully Zhukov sifted American interpretation, tempering it with the party line. And it seemed to him that the Kremlin was right to take precautions to curb outrageous defiance, if it threatened the Socialist dream. I understand that, he informed himself, and I must not pay too much heed to an alien press seeking to undermine the dream through the actions of a few misguided Czechs.

But there on televsion were Dubcek and Černik speaking with decent moderation.

No Western exaggeration there.

And gradually and tentatively Vladimir Zhukov became more equivocal, forming the secret opinion that perhaps there was no great harm in Socialism individually styled, provided it stayed within the bloc, within the expanding dream. But would I have formed such an opinion in Moscow fed a strict diet of Soviet journalism?

Once when they were viewing the Czech leaders Valentina angrily extinguished them with a flick of the dial. "That," she announced, "is enough of that"—speaking for both of them.

"There's no harm in hearing their viewpoint."

"The viewpoint of traitors?"

Vladimir poured himself a scotch. (Just recently he had been taking a glass or two extra, finding that it helped him rationalize.) "They are good party members. They talk about the party all the time."

"They are poor fools who have been duped by agents of imperialism. The sooner we send in tanks to protect them the better."

Vladimir regarded Valentina with apprehension. "That

won't be necessary." The whiskey encouraged confidence in statesmanship. "A compromise will be reached."

"Compromise! Such a feeble word."

"Compromise means common sense. It's the language of diplomacy."

"I pray," Valentina said, "that you're not fooled by what you read in that trash"—she pointed toward the bedroom—"that you read every night."

"I am not fooled by anything." He was cosseting his words. "But I don't believe that we will invade Czechoslovakia."

"Invade? You don't invade your own kind."

"They're Czechs and we are Russians."

"And we're all Socialists."

"You were once very proud of being a Sibiryak."

"I still am. But there are stronger loyalties than the call of your birthplace." She began to set the table for supper—stew again. "I'm worried about you, Vladimir. I am worried that you're in danger of losing all your values."

"You needn't be. But tell me, Valentina, can you see nothing good outside the Soviet Union?"

She clattered the plates around on the table. "Of course. The rebellion of the young people for one thing. But progress is a ruthless process, Vladimir. If you start appreciating such merits then your course becomes deflected. And we both agree, don't we, that the ultimate purpose of everything is a world based on equality?"

Vladimir said they did, which was true.

Valentina said, "Nothing has ever been achieved without singleness of purpose."

Vladimir reasserted himself by switching on the television again.

Valentina said, "Very little has been achieved without bloodshed. It's always been so, it always will be so." She took his empty glass from him. "You're drinking too much, Vladimir. And now I see that you always take ice with your drinks—it used not to be so."

"Because we didn't have a refrigerator," Vladimir pointed out. "And for God's sake, leave me alone."

210

"You've already had three drinks tonight."

"So I'm a drunk."

"It's all those parties you go to. I imagine the drinking at them is disgusting."

"It's all for the sake of the party," Vladimir said with satisfaction. "Like bloodshed."

Dubcek and Černik were replaced by a commercial for detergents.

"Also," Valentina said, "I'm worried about Natasha. She's away far too often and she seems very distracted when she comes home. I think we should stop her going out so much."

Vladimir shook his head, fishing deeply in the milky iced soup that preceded the stew. "That would be a mistake with a girl like Natasha."

"A mistake? Why do you say that, Vladimir? She's a Russian girl, not an American. She understands obediency."

"Like going to bed with an intellectual? An enemy of the state?"

"We weren't there to control her. Your parents are too old. In any case I suppose it was time that she knew a man. . . ."

"But not an intellectual?"

Valentina took the cold plates to the kitchen where she usually regrouped her forces; just as his mother used to seek refuge from polemics. She returned with the stew.

"It's too hot for stew," Vladimir grumbled.

"You never complained in Moscow when the temperature was in the eighties. What would you like instead? Escargots, smoked salmon, Dover sole washed down with a bottle of hock? I never thought I would live to see Vladimir Zhukov fussing about his food like some Parisian bourgeois. In any case," she added with Soviet practicality, "you should eat hot food in the hot weather—it cools you down."

Vladimir sniffed the savory steam. Perhaps she was right. It was your palate that became corrupted first. Yes, a bottle of hock would have been pleasant. And a saunter

211

around a cold buffet, spearing shrimp and sardines, cracking lobsters' claws and wheedling out the sweet white meat. How soon after the palate did the mind corrupt?

He remembered her budget and was contrite. "I'm sorry. It's the heat and the humidity—suicide weather. It's a beautiful stew." He ladled it into his mouth.

Food appreciated always soothed her. She said in kindlier, maternal tones, "I didn't mean to imply weakness, Vladimir, but you mustn't be so easily influenced. You must surely appreciate that. Your beautiful people, as I believe they are called, thinking they're starving if they are reduced to one automobile. Compare them with those poor souls in Resurrection City. Can that be right, Vladimir?"

No, he agreed, it couldn't be right. Solzhenitsyn could have done just as good a job with postwar America as he had with Russia.

Valentina served coffee, thick and black. She said, "When do you think Natasha will return to the Soviet Union?"

When Brodsky has dangled the carrot long enough, Vladimir thought. When he estimates that my gratitude is at its zenith. When he wants some particularly reprehensible act committed for the cause, then he will send her back, reminding me daily of what might happen to her in Alma-Ata if her father doesn't cooperate.

He switched up the air conditioner, brought the bottle of Georgian brandy from the warped, bargain-basement sideboard and swung the Red Army into action on the record player to distract Valentina from the liquor.

"Vladimir, I asked you a question."

"I don't know when she'll return. I think her time here is good for her. She's becoming worldly."

"Is that so good?"

"It's good to see both sides of the coin."

"I think she's too young. Too impressionable."

"Then you admit there's a lot to be impressed with here?"

"I'm merely saying that she's too young."

"But not too young for sex?"

212

"No," Valentina said emphatically. "Not too young for sex. In her body she is a woman. It's her mind that's still immature."

"Perhaps," Vladimir suggested, "she's out with some nice American boy." The brandy burned in his belly amid the stew.

Valentina put a finger to her lips. As if the microphones, if they existed, were selective in their eavesdropping. "She said she was going to the National Gallery of Art. I'm sure that's where she is."

"Then there's no need to worry. Shall we watch television?"

"It's all such trash."

"But we're not intellectuals."

"If you watch television than I shall go to bed."

"Very well," said Vladimir and the brandy. He switched the set on again.

She hesitated. "Vladimir, can't we talk anymore?"

"Of course we can talk." A little explosion of stew and brandy up his throat. "If only we could *just* talk. Instead of quarreling."

She sat down again at the table opposite him. "Vladimir."

"Yes?"

"You haven't met another woman, have you?"

He felt suddenly sorry for her. Her middle-aged waist, her trust in a faith that excluded all debate, their years together that had transformed the once-wild face. They said that, together, you didn't notice each other aging. But now he did because in this middle period she was growing away from him. He saw her as he might see another middle-aged woman and it startled him. We should grow old together, he thought. My wife: the mistress of the party.

He touched her hand. "No, I haven't met another woman."

"I'd hate that," she said.

"You need never worry."

"Have I been a good wife to you, Vladimir?"

"The best," he said. "The very best."

"I think maybe you need a more affectionate woman. But just because I don't show it as much as you might wish, it doesn't mean to say I don't feel it. And I worry about you. I don't want anything to happen to you."

"I understand," he said, squeezing the hand of his proud Sibiryak.

Across the room the television flickered with soundless life. A talk show—faces clowning and grimacing, posturing heightened by the silence. Then, with scant respect for so much wisdom, the commercials for dish-washing liquid and feminine hygiene. Then the news. Race riots followed by Czechoslovakia. Vladimir turned the volume control.

The newscaster was saying: ". . . and the Czechoslovakian government has again openly defied the Kremlin. Dubcek has announced that, despite mounting pressure from the Soviet leaders, the reforms will continue. . . ."

Valentina said, "I think I'll go to bed, Vladimir."

"I'll join you in a minute," he said quickly, not wanting to miss developments.

Across the screen trundled a Russian tank, gun questing like an antenna. The newscaster recalled Hungary.

No, Vladimir assured himself, it will not happen again. You did not crush a show of nationalist pride, which was within the Soviet framework, with guns. All that had changed.

From his seat at the table Vladimir was then privileged to witness some of the fighting in Budapest a decade ago. Followed by a still of an improvised execution, young faces snarling with disbelief as they died. He didn't remember seeing any of this on the television in their Moscow apartment.

The newscaster said, "In Washington there are profound fears that the Kremlin may be contemplating similarly drastic measures if the Czech rebels do not come to heel."

Washington! What the hell did the pundits know about Kremlin intent in Washington? Only what they gleaned from the cocktail contacts—who certainly weren't putting out any such theories because he, Vladimir Zhukov, was one of those contacts. The *fears* were pure speculation based dangerously on historic behavior. Contemptuously he poured himself another small brandy. Valentina was perfectly justified in condemning such irresponsibility.

Then another thought occurred: He had been given to understand that armed intervention was out, and dutifully he had conveyed this across to Massingham, Richter and the other cocktail ears. But here was Valentina, much closer to the party than himself, calling for the intervention of the tanks as if she were urging the implementation of the inevitable.

Vladimir wondered if he were being duped to dupe others. And that the others, quite accustomed to duping, were presuming the opposite of what he told them. After all there, for God's sake, were the tanks on exercises.

No. You don't send an army to subdue student patriotism. Moscow should be grateful for such fervor within the party.

He went into the bedroom, stumbled over the pile of newspapers as he searched for his flannel pajamas under the pillow.

One day in late July the ambassador invited Zhukov to his home at the embassy for a drink.

"You may be wondering why I have asked you," Zuvorin said, pouring them both scotch.

Zhukov said he had, a little.

"Because I want your advice. Although most probably I shan't take it."

Zhukov waited. The ambassador had four counselors and one minister counselor to advise him.

They sat in easy chairs in high-ceilinged Pullman elegance—the fittings not too elegant—the drinks on a small table beside the window.

The ambassador put some Tchaikovsky, *The 1812 Overture,* on the record player and Zhukov wondered if the intention were to drown the conversation in case of bugs. Surely not. He dismissed the possibility, angry with himself for having considered it.

The ambassador said, "Sometimes I like the opinions

of ordinary men." He laughed, face alive with professional charm. "And that, I assure you, is a compliment." He lit a cigarette, smoking it with care, a puff a minute. "It seems to me, Zhukov, that you are an honest man." Sixty seconds elapsed and he inhaled, letting the smoke linger in his lungs. "That is a dangerous thing to be and you should be careful about so much honesty. However it is most refreshing. An honest diplomat," he mused.

Not so honest, Zhukov thought. Silence as great a dishonesty as a lie.

Zuvorin asked, "How are you liking your new duties?"

If he were so honest he would say he didn't like them one bit. Compromise. Blessed compromise. "It's a job."

"Mmmmmm."

A summer storm blew up outside, rain bouncing furiously on hot concrete and metal. The ambassador opened the window.

After a while—both mesmerized by the sound, and the smell of rain on dust—the ambassador spoke again. "Relations between the Soviet Union and America are at last progressing. It is a considerable achievement for the leaders of both countries."

Zhukov said what was expected of him. "And for you, sir."

The ambassador accepted the flattery with a gesture of his cigarette. "It would be agreeable if I were to leave Washington with a sense of achievement."

Disappointment assailed Zhukov. Like discovering the frailties of a family doctor, or overtaking the intellect of a teacher. Nothing wrong with seeking achievement: the retrospect and slave for the last accelerating phase of life. Perhaps, Zhukov thought, I am jealous. For what consummative retrospect will there be for me? A first secretary (by accident), nothing more. Young aspiration locked in the attic. "It would be very agreeable," he said.

"You are surprised by such vainglorious sentiments, Zhukov? By the cult of the personality here in the Soviet Embassy?"

Compromise, Zhukov. "It would be admirable, sir, if you manage to bring East and West closer together."

"Ah so." Zuvorin felt his chest with the tips of his fingers. His wary, pudgy face, distinguished by laugh lines and a noble nose, was weary—lines taking advantage of the tired skin. He took a rejuvenating swallow of whisky. "But would that really be admirable, Zhukov?"

"I'm afraid I don't quite understand."

"It is surely not the aim of Marxism-Leninism to make friends with the West. I sometimes wonder if I correctly interpret the wishes of the Kremlin. Maybe, Comrade Zhukov, the attainment of good relations with the United States of America would be regarded as a failure. It is ironic, is it not?"

The rain sluiced down the window blurring the skyscraper stumps of the city. "I don't think so," Zhukov said. "Surely the aims of Marxism-Leninism can be more easily won in an atmosphere of peace."

"Perhaps you're right." Zuvorin smiled. "I think maybe the President of the United States and myself have similar problems. We both want to leave the stage having made a final contribution to the good of mankind. So he stops the bombing in Vietnam and prays that good sense will prevail in Paris. I wish I shared his optimism." He poured more scotch. "I saw the President this morning."

Zhukov nodded, unsure of his role.

"I like the man. He is as honest as a President can be. Now the hawks are accusing him of showing weakness merely to achieve a last political triumph before his retirement. So, what is so wrong with that? Every politician in Washington—in the world—is motivated by ambition. It merely comes in different guises. Some holy, some blatant. If peace is achieved, even approached, then who the hell cares about personal motive? Or," he acknowledged with a grimace, "perhaps I am only making my own excuses."

"Was your meeting a success?"

"We understood each other. But he's the leader of his country, I'm merely the representative of mine. What he says is law, what I say can be contradicted."

The ambassador's wife came in. "How many whiskies is that?" she asked her husband.

"Two," he said.

"No more," she said. She addressed Zhukov. "See that he drinks no more than two whiskies, Comrade Zhukov."

"It upsets my digestion," Zuvorin explained.

Zhukov didn't believe him.

Zuvorin's wife smiled conspiratorially at Zhukov giving the impression that she was pleased to see her husband with a friend instead of a colleague.

When she had gone Zuvorin said, "We discussed plans for a summit meeting with Kosygin." He paused "This is highly confidential, you understand."

"Of course. But I don't quite understand. . . ."

"Why I am confiding in a first secretary recently promoted?"

"Yes," Zhukov said. "Just that."

From the record player there came the boom of 1812 cannons: thunder for the summer storm.

"Because I am interested in your reactions as an honest man. Not as a politician or diplomat. Not pausing to consider whether you are saying what is expected of you. Not glancing over your shoulder at Moscow."

"You make it very difficult for me," Zhukov said. "You may not like my reactions."

"I respect honesty," Zuvorin said. "I don't see too much of it." He took a cigarette from a box on the table, paused and put it back. "You needn't worry. There will be no recriminations. The summit will be called to consider further ways of limiting the arms race. Work is to stop on the antimissile defenses around Moscow and on the Tallinn defense arc. At least, so I am assured," he added carefully.

"That at least is good," Zhukov said, aware that there was more to come.

"The President also asked me about Soviet intentions toward Czechoslovakia." Zuvorin laughed, but without the usual melody. "He said he didn't want any bullshit. A good American word—a nice Texas ring to it. I don't think we have an equivalent in Russian, do we, Comrade Zhukov?"

Zhukov said he didn't think they did. Offhand he couldn't think of one.

"I told him that the Soviet Union merely wanted to ensure that the principles of Marxism-Leninism were adhered to. He said, 'You mean you want the poor sons of bitches to come to heel.' I reiterated what I had said. He said, 'Can I believe you, Zuvorin?' And said it wasn't the first time I had evaded the truth. They're still inordinately proud of the way Kennedy handled the Cuba crisis, these Americans." He took a cigarette, holding it unlighted between his lips. "With some justification, Comrade Zhukov. With some justificatiion. Although they tend to make too much of my *lies*. It was diplomacy, tightrope diplomacy. And we Russians played our part in averting another world war. It takes a lot of courage and good sense to accept humiliation."

"I don't quite understand," Zhukov said, "what it is you want me to judge."

"Not judgment . . . just reaction."

"So far my reaction can only be favorable."

"The President is a very forthright man. Another Khrushchev in some respects. He asked me outright if the Soviet Union planned armed intervention in Czechoslovakia. Did we intend to invade, was the way he put it."

"And you told him no?"

Zuvorin nodded, lighting the cigarette, sipping the melted ice at the bottom of his glass.

"Then everything is fine."

"Can I truthfully say that Russia has no intention of invading Czechoslovakia?"

A nausea of comprehension. "We would only send in troops, surely, in the event of an armed uprising. Not just to subdue a little patriotic liberalism."

"Who knows?"

"You mean that armed intervention is being seriously considered?"

"Actively considered might be a more accurate definition. And if the tanks do move in, then the Summit will collapse and once again I shall be accused of being a liar. Hardly an auspicious climax to my career. What would you have done, Comrade Zhukov?"

"I'm glad I'm not a Soviet ambassador," Zhukov said.

The storm spent itself and the sun began to coax steam from the sidewalks. And on the record player the battle ended.

The American press and television spared Zhukov nothing. Still he hoped; but foreboding lodged as firmly as guilt.

If the Russians did invade was there any extentuating factor?

Not that he could see. Not on the television screen. Just jubilation at the prospects of freedom budding. Student intensity of happiness—bespectacled and bearded and triumphant; older peasant faces smiling warily, more cynical of the ability of an occupying power to condone. They had, after all, experience of two master races in occupation.

What hurt Zhukov most, witnessing the renaissance of hope in the streets of Prague, was the conviction that they were defying a tyranny. That his people were the tyrants; that these blithely vulnerable liberals regarded the Russians as he had once regarded the Germans. That it was no minority band of gangsters "infiltrated by the agents of imperialism" or "financially supported from the coffers of a decadent society making a last pathetic bid to disrupt the glorious unity of Socialism."

No, these people hate us.

And no one—or almost no one—inside Russia would ever realize it. No one in Russia would ever see these films. The camera didn't lie. Wenceslaus Square was no movie lot.

If I still lived in Moscow I would never know.

Inexorably the crisis gathered momentum. As did Vladimir Zhukov's own.

On July 29 the Soviet Politburo and the Czech Presidium met in the village of Cierna, a railway junction on the Tisza River on the Slovakian-Soviet border, while extensive troop movements were taking place. At night Brezhnev, Kosygin and Podgorny recrossed the border into Russia in a green Soviet train to sleep.

On August 1 Dubcek said, "We have not taken a single step back."

On August 3 the Russians, Czechs and four East European countries most loyal to Moscow met at Bratislava and ratified the Cierna agreement.

To no avail.

The placid, voluble feature of Dubcek became a symbol to Zhukov of what was to be. The sincerity and naïveté of an unworldly priest: a weak face posed for a kick in the teeth from a jackboot.

In the Zhukov household the television became the catalyst of strife. On, off. And as the inevitable came nearer Valentina dispatched Natasha to the Russian camp at Black Walnut Point on Tilghman Island where children could spend the summer vacation for sixty-five dollars a month.

At about the same time Vladimir Zhukov realized that he was under close surveillance. It was as if they listened to his thoughts. Or anticipated the impact of unfettered information on ideals.

As if they expected Vladimir Zhukov, party stalwart, patriot and defender of Leningrad, to defect.

He switched from whisky to vodka to get drunk patriotically.

And one humid day, after a Bloody Mary lunch with Richter, he met Helen Massingham outside the Madison Hotel. She had a Delaware coast tan and smelled expensive. He got the impression that she had planned the meeting. "Vladimir," she said, "how marvelous." And then: "Perhaps we could have coffee in the hotel." Much more than coffee, she implied. To his surprise Zhukov almost accepted and found himself thinking: "She would make love better than anyone I've known." He dragged his thoughts from the bedroom and told her that he had an urgent appointment. But perhaps some other time. Soon. She was frowning as he left. One more Bloody Mary and what might have happened? No, not Vladimir Zhukov. But that was how it happened: men rejected, humiliated, betrayed. Stop feeling sorry for yourself, comrade. He

221

wouldn't be a man if he didn't feel Helen Massingham's attraction; but he had resisted it; that was what mattered.

He also wrote his first poem for years, for decades. About Prague and the Soviet Army threatening. And, with drunken cunning, substituted Leningrad and the German Army. He left it on the table and watched Valentina read it; but she knew, he could see that.

At the embassy, conversation about the crisis was guarded; conversation about most controversies was guarded, Zhukov thought.

Brodsky was less guarded than most. "What do you think will happen, Comrade Zhukov?" he asked.

"I have no idea."

"But you have the ambassador's ear."

"I told you . . . I have no idea what will happen."

"Then what do you think should happen?"

"I think right should prevail."

"We are becoming very diplomatic, are we not?"

"What do you thing should happen, Comrade Brodsky?"

"Obviously we must stamp out the subversive elements threatening the unity of our system. Would you not agree with that?"

"A lot of foreign party organizations faithful to the doctrines of Marxism-Leninism do not seem to agree with you, Comrade Brodsky."

"So you have been listening to the lies of the American press, radio and television."

Zhukov grinned despite it all. "It is my job," he pointed out.

"*Uh-huh.*" Triumph down a chord. "But it is not your duty to believe them."

"I didn't say I believed them. But not even the bourgeois press would invent party statements urging nonintervention."

"What would your reaction be if the Kremlin decided that the only way to control this outrageous provocation was to send the Army into Czechoslovakia . . . to go to the aid of the masses whose lives are being threatened by the meddling agents of imperialism?"

"I would say," Zhukov said, "that judging by that question, you stand a good chance of getting a job as an editorial writer for *Pravda*."

After drinking about half a bottle of Stolichnaya one lunchtime on a nonworking day Zhukov decided to lead his tail a merry dance.

He walked briskly down the hot sidewalks of Connecticut, skirted the White House and turned down Pennsylvania, heady with perverse exuberance.

Outside the headquarters of the Federal Bureau of Investigation he stopped and joined a cluster of tourists waiting for a tour.

On the opposite side of Pennsylvania, on the corner of Thirteenth, he could just see his pursuer, a young man with home-barbered hair and pale skin scorched pink on nose and forehead by the sun. Zhukov felt for him. Did you follow your quarry into the FBI? A unique predicament, he congratulated himself, in the history of professional pursuit.

The waiting tourists moved into a waiting room, unchecked, unquestioned. But surely observed.

A middle-aged straw-hatted tourist in shorts, white socks and polished brown shoes, stooping with the weight of his cameras, said, "Ain't this something! Here we all are right inside the FBI. That's democracy for you. Guess it couldn't happen in Russia, eh?"

No, Zhukov said, it couldn't happen in Russia.

"What part you from, mister?"

"Russia," Zhukov said.

The tourist laughed hugely, cracking his Pentax against his Yashica.

Zhukov walked back to the gates looking for his shadow. He spotted him hovering on the pavement unsure whether to follow or report that Comrade Zhukov had defected to J. Edgar Hoover. Poor bastard.

Their guide was thirtyish, compact, jacket tight on his gang-busting frame; textbook FBI except for the boyish grin at his own gentle jokes.

They saw pictures of the ten most-wanted criminals in

223

the days of Prohibition and the ten most-wanted criminals today. The guide pointed them out as if they were butter-flies pinned in a showcase in a natural history museum.

There, too, were Dillinger's guns and the straw hat he was wearing the day the FBI terminated his career as he emerged from the movies "with a genuine femme fatale." (Laughter)

Zhukov's tourist friend took off his own straw hat with a tartan band. "Makes me feel kinda vulnerable," he said, giving Zhukov a chummy dig in the ribs.

At each exhibit the guide asked, "Any questions?"

No one had any.

What, Zhukov wondered, would he say if I asked, "Yes—can I seek political asylum, please?"

He looked behind. No sign of the tail. Zhukov guessed he would be waiting somewhere near the gates, praying that Vladimir Zhukov would emerge. Because if he lost him forever inside the FBI he might as well defect, too.

The guide didn't make any jokes in front of the Fuchs exhibits. The Communist menace was not the subject for humor. Zhukov sought admiration for the traitor and found none. Nor for the Soviet consul, Yakovlev, in New York, who had fled after the exposure.

"Any questions?"

No questions.

Except that Zhukov wanted to say, "I am a Russian spy. And I am being followed through the FBI by another Russian spy. What do you say to that, mister?"

They passed by the windows of the laboratories where earnest men and women found criminals' mistakes in wafers of paint, drops of blood, the sweat stains and ex-crement of fear; in forged signatures, bruised bullets and the errant whorl of a thumbprint. Murderers, rapists, bank robbers, kidnappers were convicted in these meticulous chambers of detection by the thread of a jacket bought in San Francisco and caught on the fender of a car in Buffalo, by a single thread of hair grasped in the hand of a woman in her death throes.

"Jesus," said Zhukov's companion, "you wonder how anyone gets away with anything."

"But they do," Zhukov said.

"You have to be pretty darn clever to fool the FBI. I guess they could teach that KBG or whatever they call it a thing or two."

"I hope so," Zhukov said.

"Say, fella, you aren't much of a talker, are you?"

Zhukov pointed at the wall. "What do you think of that?"

The words COMMUNISM—FREEDOM'S ENEMY were printed in very bold letters. Beside a Hammer and Sickle set in a giant splash of catsup-blood.

"It's the truth, ain't it?"

Zhukov shrugged. His head was beginning to ache, the exuberance evaporating.

In the basement shooting range a marksman fired a submachine gun and a pistol for them.

Then they were out in the steamy outdoors once more. Across the road Zhukov spotted his tail, pink face desperate in the heat.

"Say," said Zhukov's friend. "You sure keep yourself to yourself." He replaced his straw hat on his crew cut. "Say"—cameras clattering excitedly—"you aren't *really* a Russian, are you?"

"What do you think?"

"I don't know. You've gotta kind of funny accent. . . ."

"I'll tell you this," Zhukov told him. "I'm certainly not a Czech."

A few days later Zhukov sought audience with Zuvorin in his office and formally complained that he was being kept under surveillance by agents of the secret police.

Zuvorin nodded, his concentration elsewhere. "If you are merely carrying out your duties as prescribed then you have no worries." His eyes were slits between cushions of fatigue.

"It is an insult to my dignity as a diplomatic representative of the Soviet Union."

Zuvorin who was still listening to the growling queries of the President of the United States held up one authoritive hand. "There are other greater dignities to be considered at this moment." He tapped a tune with the blade of a paper knife. "I could send you on a mission."

With similar phrases they dispatched out-of-line members of the Politburo to take charge of rural power stations.

Zuvorin said, "How would you like to go to New York for a few days?"

Zhukov wasn't sure how he would like it, and if it would solve anything. "For what reason?"

Zuvorin gave a shrug which meant: for no particular reason other than to disrupt your surveillance. "I should like firsthand reports of the forthcoming meeting of the Security Council of the United Nations. I am not altogether satisfied with the speed with which information reaches me from New York. Also," he added, humor briefly combating the scars of fatigue, "I find the Tass communiqués a little turgid. May I take it that you would be willing to go? Certain formalities will have to be completed first."

"I didn't know there was going to be a meeting of the Security Council," Zhukov said.

"A slip of the tongue. But, take my word for it, there will be one."

"Very well," Zhukov agreed. "It will be an enlightening experience."

"Without a doubt," the ambassador said. "And perhaps it might be a good idea not to discuss your mission too freely."

It was while he was packing that Vladimir Zhukov heard that six hundred thousand Soviet troops had invaded and occupied Czechoslovakia.

Chapter 2

PRAGUE WAS SEIZED in an advance operation in which military aircraft supported by MIG fighters were used. Almost immediately KGB units were installed.

Dubcek was reported to have said, "How could they do this to me? I have served the cause of the Soviet Union and Communism all my life."

Premier Černik was reported to have cried, "Treason! Betrayal!"

Crowds roamed the streets of Prague, Bratislava and Košice shouting insults at the invaders and scrawling Nazi swastikas on their tanks.

In Prague barricades were thrown up around the radio station and free broadcasts continued until 11 A.M. on the day of the invasion; then secret broadcasts began as the Czechs switched frequencies.

Stones and garbage were hurled at the Russians, Molotov cocktails were thrown at their tanks. A munition truck was blown up.

Demonstrators pranced in front of a line of Soviet tanks carrying banners RUSSIAN MURDERERS GO HOME. Numbers of the cars used by the KGB were circulated; a general strike was called.

Three young men distributing leaflets were killed.

All this Natasha Zhukova, trained from the nursery to accept the brotherly intent of all Soviet action, watched on the television at Black Walnut Point.

Black Walnut Point lies two hours' drive from Washington on an island called Tilghman in Chesapeake Bay.

Visitors are confronted by a notice, PRIVATE PROPERTY, NO TRESPASSING.

Not that there is anything formidable or particularly secretive about the Russian Camp, as locals call it. It occupies thirty-five acres and is inhabited in the salty steamy summer by forty or so Russian children aged between five and twelve—older kids having been returned to the Soviet Union away from the contamination of the West.

The Russians have another such residence at Glen Cove on Long Island for the use of their United Nations staff. It is an ominous forty-nine-room Tudor mansion which looks as if it might be haunted by the deported ghost of Beria. Since the Russians bought it some twenty years ago it has been the subject of tax disputes, the Russians claiming tax exemption because it is a full-time residence of a foreign government, the Glen Cove city taxmen claiming dues because they reckon it is only used as a retreat. But the taxmen have never been allowed to inspect this Kremlin in their midst.

Black Walnut Point is a joyous place by comparison. It contains an old white frame house with fine sea views. Children dance in its grounds and there is a flag-raising ceremony in which Old Glory and the Hammer and Sickle fly together. There are 8 A.M. gymnastics, a swimming coach who also acts as chauffeur, movies, television and Tom Sawyer hunks of watermelon to be eaten with meals.

On these hot seaside days a green MG was often to be seen parked nearby on the shore.

Natasha Zhukova thankfully accepted her removal from Washington, regarding Black Walnut Point as her private retreat for deliberation and reassessment.

She helped organize activities for the kids, swam faster than the chauffeur and got herself a tan. She was embraced with sweaty fervor by a wide-framed Ukranian on the staff, deflecting him with an easy tolerance of desire which he found disconcerting.

In the evenings, when she wasn't abroad in the green MG, she watched television—reconnecting the wires which had been disconnected by the staff during these difficult days of anti-Soviet feeling.

If Black Walnut Point was intended to redeem her from the corrupt freedoms of Washington, D. C., then it had the opposite effect. For one thing, the camp had its own childlike freedoms which accentuated memories of oppression barely realized at the time. The two flags fluttering contempt for adult intransigence; the saline drafts from the Atlantic breathing liberty. And the television recording nightly the suppression of green endeavor in Czechoslovakia.

Natasha was there in the streets of Prague with the students. You couldn't help it; youth was a crusade, youth was the future.

Whoever decided to send me to America, she thought, switching on the box of truth, dispatched me at the wrong time. All those young energies were being directed nicely into the cause; the industrious, commendable, self-righteous cause. Now they had been diverted.

But I am not a traitor, she assured herself, watching the end of a situation domestic comedy which she found childish. I believe in equality, in Socialism, which is not as dreary as they would have you believe in the West.

Building camps in the woods outside Moscow and kissing a timid boy beneath dripping lilac. Reciting Pushkin and Lermontov, and reading Marganita Aliger and Andrei Voznesensky. Feeling his timid, searching hands. (She could smell the mauve scent dripping from the sponges of blossom.)

Meeting artists in a park, taking a boat ride with one and feeling your first burn of vodka which you swore you would never touch again. Folk songs and guitars and copies of jazz records cut by decadent (always decadent) artists of vice-ridden capitals. Listening to Rostropovich and Shostakovich and feigning appreciation because the tickets had cost your companion a lot of rubles.

But always directed. Although you didn't pause to consider this. There was no time; you spent the pulse of youth wherever it was channeled. Painting a picture (conformist), plucking a flower, enjoying sex, building a town.

I am immoral, she thought. Already the lessons of my childhood are forgotten; the Fascist beast who did service for the wicked witch has fled. Fickle? Perhaps. If only her instructors hadn't tried so hard . . .

If only she hadn't seen the American homes with their unfenced lawns from which a power mower could go churning unleashed across the land to the sea . . .

(Although, it must be said, these nebulous sentiments were privately expressed by Natasha Zhukova without any thought that she might stay in America. So they had about them an element of a child's jubilation at his first visit to the seaside. And none of the guilt of a parent who leaves his children.)

The faces of Wenceslaus Square appeared on the screen. Grinning, winking, thrusting victory fingers into the camera lens with puny triumph.

Natasha Zhukova, child of the Soviet Union, triumphed with them. The voice of rebellion, whatever the cause. Only one cause—the voice of youth. (Even if many of the demonstrators were well over twenty-five.)

She glanced at her wristwatch, a present from Charlie, and a modicum of adult doubt disturbed the cause. She loved him, but she felt she hadn't really met him yet.

She switched off the television, unplugged the wire and made her way through the scented, insect-flying dusk to take a dinghy to meet her lover.

But Charlie Hardin wasn't himself this evening. He drove erratically, crashed his gears a couple of times and talked disjointedly like a man with a hangover listening to himself.

"Charlie," she said, "what's the matter?"

His face was tanned, the V between his shirt collar peeling slightly. She pulled a little parchment away—like stripping a paper birch. The muscles of his strong forearms were taut from his grip on the racy wooden wheel his hair looked damp with a glister of sweat on his brow which she wanted to wipe away with one finger.

A dark sandbank of cloud moved on the horizon and

the sun glowed, deep and final, a molten hump behind the flickering stems of pine trees. There was woodsmoke in the air, and a bat scything the descending night.

"Charlie," she said, "please be careful where you drive. You know I mustn't go outside the limit."

"You're outside the limit at Black Walnut Point anyway."

"I know . . . but that's permitted." There was a quality to his voice that frightened her.

"Don't worry. I'll look after you."

"Charlie—have you been drinking?"

He glanced at her in surprise. "No, ma'am. I don't drink too much. A little pot now and then, maybe. . . . I'm joking, of course."

With a sickening certainty she knew that he was going to leave her. Knew it. "What's the matter, Charlie?"

"A lot of things."

"Tell me, Charlie." My Charlie.

"I guess maybe we should find a place to park."

"And make love?" Because she didn't believe that any man could make love immediately before he abandoned a girl.

Charlie didn't reply. But the muscles on his forearms twitched as he took it out on the steering wheel.

A few miles later he said, "I suppose you'll be going back to Russia soon."

"I suppose so."

"We haven't talked much about the future, have we?"

No, Natasha said, they hadn't. She wanted nothing of the future, just the existing moment.

"What do you want, Natasha?"

She thought: I want you. The dry warmth of your body beside me. In waking moments. In suffering and in anger. Because you are the one, and there can only ever be one even though you may find substitutes and some forgetfulness. Those who had never loved would diagnose infatuation. But Natasha Zhukova knew that, even in the throes of infatuation, a part of you was able to identify it as such; you knew it would end with an unsolicited moment of perception—a laugh at cruelty, insensitivity behind handsome sensual features. But there were other weaknesses which you nursed; that was love.

She said, "To be with you."

He drove faster, speedometer quivering at ninety.

"We haven't made it easy for ourselves, Natasha."

"What do you mean, Charlie?"

"We didn't make it easy for ourselves by meeting."

"You mean you wish we hadn't?"

"No, baby. Nothing like that."

"Baby," she repeated. "I like that." Just an ellipsis of the sun now, animated by the speeding, telegraph-pole pines. And, diving beneath the fast road, a stream combed with boulders. Soon he will tell me, she thought.

"If I drove north to Baltimore," he said, "we would come to Friendship Airport. If I continued south we would come to Petersburg. How's that for homeliness?"

"You will be going to Russia soon, Charlie. Perhaps we shall go together."

"Perhaps," he said. And she could feel the lie.

"Where are we going, Charlie?"

"Anywhere."

Carefully she said, "That wasn't just chance—that meeting in the bookstore, was it, Charlie?"

"There are some things I have to tell you. I never thought I would have to. And I know that I shouldn't tell you now. Whatever I do I'm betraying someone. I guess to put it at its lowest, that it's a question of priorities. Although," he said to himself, "they've given me a sort of escape hatch." The car slowed to eighty, then advanced again to ninety.

Natasha said, "Please, Charlie. We shouldn't go any farther. I will get into trouble and my parents will suffer."

"Don't worry," he assured her. "I've got American license plates. No one would think to stop us."

They passed a couple of motels, swimming pools adjoining the road, illuminated arrows, chefs and old Dixie gentlemen soliciting.

"Shit," said Charlie Hardin.

"What's the matter?"

"The law."

The headlight of the pursuing patrol car flashed angrily in the driving mirror. Hardin pulled to the side of the highway beside a motel.

The cop was big and sour and conscientious. "These limey cars sure travel," he said. "You wouldn't think it to look at them."

Hardin said, "I'm sorry, officer. I wasn't thinking—and this little lady has to get home or else she will be in big trouble."

A second cop hovered menacingly in the background.

"Buddy," said the first cop, "you're in big trouble right now. You were doing a sporty ninety miles an hour just now."

He walked around the MG kicking the tires like a prospective buyer. "These kind of cars were made to break the law. Myself, I like a nice comfy limousine. I guess you think speeding's some sort of sport, fella."

Vehemently Hardin said he thought no such thing.

"Speeding ain't no joke. Not if you've seen the smashes I've seen. The kids crippled for life. I figure every driver like you should be shown a few smashes. They might slow you down a little. We had one today—a young couple in an American sports car thinking they were at Indianapolis or Daytona or someplace. Full of life, I guess, just out of the woods after a session most like. Now dead as dodoes. Took a left-hand turn relying on their acceleration. But the truck coming the other way was accelerating, too. Just went over them like crushing a beetle." He took out a pad. "The guy I feel real sorry for is the truck driver."

"But you said he was accelerating, too."

"Let's not make a fight out of it," the cop said. "He was driving legal. But, sure as hell, he'll remember that smash for the rest of his life. Now could I see your license, please?"

Hardin showed his license.

"And some identification from the little lady?"

"You don't need that," Hardin snapped.

"Now, look here, fella, you don't tell me what I need

233

and what I don't need. I want to know who that little lady is. Because the way you drive you'll mebbe get into a smash and then we'll need the identification."

"Jesus," Hardin said. "You sure have a morbid turn of mind."

The cop stuck out a hand. "Could I see some identification, please, ma'am?"

Natasha looked at Hardin. "Do I have to?"

The cop looked more interested. "Why, is there any reason why you shouldn't."

"No reason at all, officer," Hardin said. "But please, be a good guy and forget it. She wasn't doing the speeding and I'll pay my fine like a good American."

"Sure you will. Trouble is I'm getting intrigued. Why is this lady so shy? I ain't gonna put her in front of a grand jury. Unless she's on the wanted list or something."

"She's somebody else's wife," Hardin said.

"She sure looks young to be adulterating. And I don't see no ring. Maybe's she's got that in her smart little pastic purse there." He pointed at the shoulder bag Natasha had bought to match her mini-skirt. "In there with her identification papers."

"Look," Hardin said, anger lurking in his voice. "She doesn't have to show you anything and you know it. You're exceeding your rights and if you persist I'll make it my business to see you answer for it."

"Well, now," said the cop, widening the angle of his legs comfortably. "It's threats, is it? I might just have to slap a few other charges on you in addition to speeding and dangerous driving."

"Who said anything about dangerous driving?"

"I did. Ninety miles an hour is dangerous driving. Especially changing lanes at that speed without giving any indication."

Natasha put her hand on Hardin's arm. "Charlie, don't get yourself into any trouble. I'll give him some indentification."

"Say," said the cop, that's a mighty fancy accent the little lady's got."

234

Natasha dug in her purse. A report to the Soviet Ambassador, flown back to Moscow. Her parents disgraced.

"Hold on," Hardin said.

"Now wait a minute," said the cop, hand straying toward his gun as Hardin climbed out of the car. "If she identifies herself without any more trouble that's okay by me."

Hardin stood in front of him, lithe beside the cop's crashproof bulk. "We have to make a phone call."

"Now see here," said the cop.

"Please. It's important."

Natasha waited, shivering in the warm wet air. They returned in a few minutes.

The cop said, "I'll still have to charge you with speeding."

"Okay," Hardin said. "I'm sorry it happened."

He let in the clutch and they swooped away, leaving the cop with his hand raised in salute.

"Who did you phone, Charlie?"

"Someone in Washington."

"Who, Charlie? Tell me about it." She paused. "Tell me about everything."

"I was going to anyway. I'd like you to believe that."

"I believe you," she said. "You're some sort of policeman, aren't you, Charlie?"

He touched her knee. "I'll take the next exit and tell you all about it."

It was quite dark now with a lick of lemon moon high over the straight black trees.

It took a long time to explain on the grass behind the car beneath the slithering leaves and the assembling stars. A blanket, a cigarette, a blazer with fanciful buttons over his blue denim shirt.

Nor was the quiet wide night appropriate for shameful explanation, or even suggestions for living happily ever after. How his father had needed him to do it . . . how it had been his duty to his parents and his country. And hell—self-defensively—weren't the Soviets playing ex-

235

actly the same game? Who started this kind of intrigue? he wanted to know.

"I don't know, Charlie," she said. "Who did?"

Hardin confessed that he didn't know either, stubbing out his cigarette in the turf. Explaining how he'd never dreamed he would fall in love.

She talked, too, but the words were formalities—exhaled, like cigarette smoke, without thought. Like asking people how they are when you don't care.

The true Charlie Hardin. She thought: I expected weakness but not deceit. In the climax of love, even. Inside her. Still plotting. Disbelief and disgust shouted dumbly inside her.

She thought: So I was the poor little peasant girl. Naïve and quaint in my unfashionable clothes. Easy prey for a plausible Russian-speaking seducer. She saw herself in her awkward clothes munching a hot dog and came as near to crying as she would that night.

Hardin lit another cigarette, smoke melting in the darkness. Natasha Zhukova lay on her back and gazed beyond the stars until motives became grotesque and meaningless. And youth was suicide.

Vaguely she heard Charlie delving deeper into explanation. She explored infinity; looked down and saw the ball of the earth fuzzed with cloud. She saw beaches with shining waves. The snow-covered taiga waxed with loneliness, listening upon itself. Mountains riding high above clouds. Icebergs and pyramids.

"Are you listening to me?"

"Of course I'm listening, Charlie." With the tranquillity of icing fever.

"You know I love you."

"I know that, Charlie."

The silhouette of his head drooped. "If only everything I said didn't sound so empty. . . . But I have come clean, haven't I? I couldn't keep up the lie."

"Are you telling the whole truth now, Charlie?" she asked dreamily.

"Sure I'm telling the truth."

"You suggested just now that we stay here together.

236

That we get married. That would make me a defector, wouldn't it?"

"In a way it would, I suppose."

"Never to go back to Russia again."

"Never, I guess."

The smell of lilac and timid searching hands. The golden apples of Alma-Ata. The vodka on a student's breath. A guitar and a red scarf around your neck. Or a power mower that churned a free swathe through the grasslands of America.

She raised herself on one elbow and said, "It seems to me that perhaps you were given two alternatives. One to enlist me as a spy, sneaking secrets from my own father and mother. Or, if that failed, to persuade me to defect. Am I right?"

"None of it matters. I love you and want to marry you."

"Am I right? For God's sake try and be honest for once."

"Okay, so you're right. I'm not doing very well, am I?"

"It doesn't matter. Yours must have been a very difficult position, Charlie. After a while dishonesty must come quite naturally."

"Maybe. But I'm trying to do something about it." He drew on his cigarette and his face was illumined, all except his eyes which remained hollows.

"Are you? I don't think so. You knew me well enough to presume that I would never spy on my own parents. Or anyone from my own country for that matter. In any case quaint peasant girls aren't clever enough for that sort of thing." She paused, annoyed by the self-pity. "So you decided to do the next best thing . . . you decided to persuade me to defect."

"Okay," he said. "So maybe they did want me to enlist you as a spy. And maybe I did realize it wouldn't work. But I don't have to marry you to persuade you to defect, do I? And that's what I want to do. I want to marry you and have you live with me here in the States and for us to have kids. Is there anything so wrong with that?"

At least he hadn't tried to make love to her before the confession, she thought. Or maybe he would have if that policeman hadn't spoiled it for him. No—he had said there were some things to talk about. And he was the one, the only one: only substitutes ahead.

The moon climbed a little, losing its yellow glow. And its light found a chink of silver in the closed ranks of trees. "Look, Charlie," she said. "A lake."

"So?"

But she was on her feet escaping; brambles scratching her small skirt, twigs fingering her face. She could smell pine and mud. The lake was small—a pond if you wished to humiliate it.

"Hey," Charlie shouted. "Look out or you'll sprain your ankle."

She took off her shoes. Muddy sand beneath her feet. She experimented with it, picking up footfuls with her toes.

"Hey," he said, "wait for me," catching up with her.

The water was as calm as the deep sky. It needed to be broken. A shark fin knifing it was what it really wanted.

She took off her blouse and skirt.

Hardin said, "For Chris' sake, Natasha, this isn't the time or place to go swimming. There might be weed in there."

"There's no weed," she said calmly, knowing that she made him feel stuffy; not a very heroic figure at that moment.

First the night air bathed her body. And she smoothed her breasts, intuitively not coquettishly. It was a pagan night now, prancing with fawns, intoned with heathen rites.

Then she ran into the water which was almost tepid, as if it had been distilled from the heavy air. And struck out with her masculine crawl, feeling the fishtail of hair training behind her.

He followed, stripped down to his underpants. More heroic now, although still trailing the maiden.

When he was ten yards away from her she dived. Why she didn't know. Feeling fear as the moonlight receded, a phosphorescent ceiling above her. Seeking the serpents of dishonesty, the worms of untruth. A slipperiness touched

238

her legs and she screamed a bubble of water that made a capsule of her fear floating to the shining surface.

Down till I touch the bottom. Wanting to breathe lungfuls of dark fishy water and fighting the temptation. Down searching with one leg and finding only cold caverns of immersion.

Charlie Hardin and all worldly phenomena lost in the serpentine depths. Escape.

One foot touched slime. Prodded a few inches lower and found the bottom.

From that single toe she kicked off. An instinct, a primeval achievement achieved. And now the return. Kicking with a vacuum in her chest which her lungs labored to fill. Shooting towards the stars. Surfacing like a dolphin.

Hardin's arms were around her. "I thought you'd drowned. I've been down there looking for you. What happened?"

Through the water she could feel his warmth and she stayed there for a moment, shrugging herself into the fetal position so that he was carrying her in the water.

"I just dived," she said.

"Why, for God's sake?"

"I don't know. Because I wanted to."

"That was a helluva stupid thing to do." He held her tighter.

"It was just a dive."

She broke loose and swam to shore, watching her ripples preceding her along the surface of the dark disturbed water.

They smelled of mud and their bodies were cold. They didn't speak for a while, watching the oncoming headlights rush at them and duck away into the night.

Natasha heard adult voices in the future. "You'll get over it, my dear."

But you never did. She had always known that there was only one and pitied the women who met him after marriage, after children.

239

"Would you like some music?" he asked.

"I don't mind."

He switched on the radio at their knees. A brief out-burst of pop, a commercial for malted milk and a news bulletin about the defiant Czechs.

"That's what it's all about," Hardin said enigmatically.

"I feel for them very much," Natasha said.

"It must be very difficult for you," Hardin said gently. "They're defying your country."

"So it seems."

"But your feelings are with the Czechs, aren't they?"

She sensed the way it was going. "I admire their spirit but I'm still a Russian. I'm still a Komsomol."

"Would it be so unpatriotic if you decided to live in America? To marry an American? It's not regarded by other countries as an act of treachery to marry a foreigner and to live in his land."

"And is that how your father and his friends would de-scribe it? Or would they perhaps announce that I had sought political asylum? That I had defected? It seems to me, Charlie, that both our countries would say that. Al-though my people would qualify it by saying I was mentally unstable. And," she added, "I believe you know that, Charlie. And I'm sure that the people you're working for don't want a quiet marriage with the Hardins living happily ever after. That isn't what they've asked you to accomplish, is it, Charlie?"

Hardin said it wasn't.

They were nearing the Russian Camp.

Hardin said, "Is there any hope?"

The dark sharky waters of the pool closed in. "You can't take a girl out and ask her to defect just like that." The flippancy unfelt.

"I asked if there was any hope."

"Could you not have been honest from the beginning?"

He shook his head.

"I suppose not," she said. "And you're not coming to Russia?"

He shook his head.

"Couldn't you have told me that day at the airport?"

240

"I wanted to," he said.

"Yes," she said, "it must have been very difficult for you."

"So, what are you going to do?"

"I don't know, Charlie."

He parked the car and helped her out. They kissed like two old people going to bed after the clock has been wound and the cat put out.

When she opened the door of ther room the Ukrainian was waiting for her. Grinning with amateurish lust.

"Get out," Natasha said. "I don't know what you're doing here but get out."

He held up a fat hand. "You have been a bad girl," he said fatuously.

Her hair hung wetly over her shoulders. She looked in the mirror; her face, washed of its makeup, was a schoolgirl's.

The Ukrainian, whose name was Dmitri Sokolov, said, "I have been observing you, Comrade Zhukova. You have been breaking the regulations of this establishment. You have been playing truant, shall we say. And, I believe, consorting with an American in a green sports car."

"So?" Because she didn't care.

"So, that is very bad. If I make a report it will go very badly for you— and for your parents." Despite his white bulk his voice was soft and wary, as if he were accustomed to rejection.

"Do what you like," Natasha said. "Now get out."

He stood up, one button of his shirt pulled open by the drum of his belly. "Also I have observed you plugging in the television in order to watch the antics of the hooligans in Czechoslovakia. I got the impression that you admired very much what they were doing."

"You want to sleep with me?"

His thoughts slavered. "There would be no harm in it, comrade. Just a lonely man and a beautiful girl finding escape. . . . Perhaps"—his thoughts accelerated into perverted practice—"perhaps you have already been making love this evening?"

241

"And you would like that, comrade?" the schoolgirl asked.

He shrugged. Some of the hair on his chest, she noted, was gray. And there was a steel tooth among his tobacco-stained fangs.

"Where is your wife, Comrade Sokolov?" She was surprised by her authority.

"She is in the Soviet Union with the children. Other members of the embassy staff find relief in some of the bars of Washington and on the beaches of Delaware, so I am told. I am stuck out here. . . ."

"Get out," she said. She picked up a pair of scissors and advanced on all human deceit. "If you don't get out I'll stick these in your belly right up to the handle. Even now I can hear the noise of the puncture."

"But you seemed so understanding just now. . . ."

She jerked the scissors toward the frightened fat man's gut. "Out."

He left without dignity, throwing words over his shoulder about Russian women who preferred American lovers to Soviet manhood.

Natasha took off her damp clothes and climbed into bed. She slept in dark deep waters surfacing occasionally beside Georgi, beside Charlie Hardin, beside Dmitri Sokolov, beside a substitute husband with substitute children calling to her from a bed across the room.

Chapter 3

CENTRAL WASHINGTON and its white ghettos took the heat with colonial grace. A tinkle of ice on the terrace and, over the centuries, the slap of slavish feet on polished

242

floors. It had officer status and its humidity was perspiration, not sweat.

New York was noncommissioned. And it took its heat badly, vulgarly—pouring sweat. Heat bounced off the yellow cabs, cannonaded around the haunches of the high-rise office buildings and fell back exhausted in the streets.

It's airports shimmered with heat, its gasping skyscrapers stretched and nosed around for air, finding only pollution. Its bars were ice-cold, dark and dispensing pneumonia; its heavy newspapers smudged by moist thumbs. Talking taxi drivers talked less; the silent bitter ones, hunched over bruised fenders, opened up the dictionary of their bitterness.

In Central Park, where the grass was growing bald, the muggers went onto summer schedules with shorter hours. Hippies seeking repose there from the immorality of existence pulled back their wild hair with headbands and took off their battle blouses, stripping away a lot of swagger and sometimes disclosing poor thin ribs like Venetian blinds.

The unrelieved heat trapped beneath the smog brought out noise and smell. Florists smelled like jungles, hamburgers like Sunday roasts, garbage like disease; car horns signaled the troops to charge, and the blacks around Times Square slapped and chortled like pop groups.

Street trade in Italian ices, pretzels, giant balloons and soft drinks was thriving. And, of course, hot dogs, because they would still be eating hot dogs on the day the earth dried up.

To Vladimir Zhukov New York seemed like a bricklayer. He wasn't sure why. Something in its baked busyness. The old brownstone work in the suburbs falling apart and being stuck together again with a few professional smears of cement; the high-rise of Manhattan climbing away from the heat—each floor a brick.

He enjoyed his return. Even New York's corruption was red-blooded meat after the sinister white veal of Washington. You could hear pistons grinding, hearts beating. The sidewalk cafés selling bargain breakfasts were the bricklayer's sandwiches; the cocktail restaurants the foreman's lunch.

Walking down Forty-second Street, past Tudor City, watching emergent old ladies with ballerina poodles tanning their pink tongues, Zhukov bought a newspaper black with Czechoslovakia. He looked for the Soviet explanation and found little of satisfaction except that, under treaty, they had the right to station troops there. He stuffed the paper into a wire basket on the sidewalk.

From across the broad street, waving with water mirages, the United Nations looked cool and pure, like its charter. Its thirty-nine-story Secretariat, modeled like a carton of playing cards (with the world's poker hands inside), the Dag Hammarskjöld Library, the glacial motel of the General Assembly, the fountain and the herbaceous border of flags, each according to its style—defiant red, green and yellow shields of African emergence, celestial blues and whites of historic impotence, stars of bravado, crosses and stripes of wilting arrogance; every cotton anthem limp now in the city heat.

Behind this oasis of altruistic assumption—not without a few jobs for the boys—tugs plied the East River separating the UN from smoking acres of suburban ambition.

On the chessboard floor of the General Assembly lobby, near the model of Sputnik I, Zhukov met his resentful guide from the Soviet Mission, a stubby and hirsute linguist called Muratov, aflame with indignation over world reaction to the Soviet response to a cry for help. Muratov was an excellent linguist but, when excited, he tended to switch from one language to another. "We should hurry," Muratov said in Russian. "The debate is about to begin." He looked at his watch and exclaimed in French, "My God, any minute now we shall be late." And as they walked across the squares he said in English, "We do not quite understand what you are doing here. There have been no complaints before—from Washington or the Kremlin." A shade of emphasis on the last word. "You must be very well thought of at the embassy."

Zhukov said, "Not particularly. We are all equal there."

"Indeed," Muratov agreed hastily. (A very nervous one

this, Zhukov decided.) "Although one or two of our comrades here seem to have been influenced by the gutter press. It is shameful, is it not?" His face, dark and downy on the cheekbones, peered anxiously at Zhukov. "A very special watch is being kept on such weaklings in case. . . ."

"In case what?"

Muratov exclaimed in German, "We must go in now."

Brazil was in the chair surrounded at the horseshoe table by the permanent Big Five—America, Britain, France, Nationalist China and Russia—and the other nine countries there for two years: Algeria, Canada, Denmark, Ethiopia, Hungary, India, Pakistan, Paraguay and Senegal.

Zhukov and Muratov sat at the back of the chamber facing the horseshoe and the huge confused mural, painted by a Norwegian. A very cool place for heated debate with its starry lights in the ceiling, gray carpets and careful air conditioning. As anonymous as its delegates and visitors were nationalistic and fervent. Zhukov kept his interpretive earphones ready; Muratov pointedly spurned them.

Zhukov waited for justification but expected none as the meeting of the Security Council got under way. Or rather the Russian delegate, an avuncular man like all the best Soviet diplomats, tried to stop it from getting under way. He said, "There is no basis for the discussion of this matter by the Security Council. The armed units of the Socialist countries, as is well known, entered the territory of the Czechoslovak Socialist Republic on the basis of the request of the government of that state. . . . It goes without saying that the above-mentioned armed units will be immediately withdrawn from the territory of the Czechoslovak Socialist Republic as soon as the existing threat to the security is eliminated. . . . Upon the instructions of the Soviet government I inform you, Mr. President, that the Soviet Union resolutely opposes the consideration of this question in the Security Council because this would be in the interests of certain external circles, the forces of aggression."

Zhukov made a few notes, photographed by Muratov's eyes, and saw the faces in Wenceslaus Square.

The American delegate, tough with gray wavy hair, took up arms. "The situation the world faces tonight is an affront to all civilized sensibilities. Foreign armies have without warning invaded a member state of the United Nations. If the Security Council does not seize itself of this gross violation of the Charter and deal with it promptly and incisively, its vitality and integrity, its very seriousness of purpose, will be subject to serious question. . . ."

The American pressed home the attack, accusing the Russians of inventing the request from the Czechs for military help. "We all know that this claim is a fraud, an inept and obvious fraud." And he pointed out that when the Soviet Politburo met the Czechs at Bratislava it was those Czechs who were recognized as their country's leaders.

Hungary interrupted on a point of order. Overruled.

Zhukov thought: *If only we can produce evidence of a cry for help from the Czechs.*

Russia stopped America, supporting Hungary's point of order. And tossed in Vietnam and the Middle East.

The United States representative swept on, fueled by outrage. He charged that most, if not all, of the Czech leaders who shared in the Bratislava communiqué affirming "unbreakable friendship" were now under detention. "Did those leaders request that their country be attacked and overrun by foreign troops?"

He read a statement issued by Radio Prague, the official government station, that Zhukov had not heard. "This (the invasion) happened without the knowledge of the President of the Republic, the Chairman of the National Assembly, the Premier or the First Secretary of the Czechoslovak Communist Party Central Committee." Also a demand from the Czech Foreign Ministry to the Soviet Embassy there that all troops be withdrawn.

The demand, said the United States representative, was "a brave act which all free men must applaud."

But did anyone applaud or condemn on the river beaches of Moscow? Or on the shores of Lake Baikal?

246

Or among the ripening orchards of Alma-Ata? Not if they neither read nor heard it, Zhukov thought. Would I have known in my unenlightened post at the Foreign Ministry? Or in the cosseted cubicles of my home?

The American delegate read a declaration from the Czech Mission calling for the release of Svoboda, Cěrnik, Dubcek and the others, and the withdrawal of troops. "Working people, citizens. Remain at your working places and protect your enterprises. For further development of Socialism in Czechoslovakia make use of all democratic means. If necessary you will be able to defend yourself also by a general strike. We are confident that we will overcome these serious moments with pride and character."

Zhukov nodded. Yes, all that mattered was the cause of Socialism. The calls of the Czechs had some of the tone of the Bolsheviks; although already they were touched with brave hopelessness. A general strike against tanks. A dimpled baby's fist against a bruiser's knuckles.

Muratov, his fingers stroking the black down on his cheeks, said, "Such feeble accusations. Such blatant falsehoods."

Zhukov wondered if Muratov really believed that. Believed that the appointed representatives and leaders of Czechoslovakia were making it all up.

"I noticed you nodding, Comrade Zhukov," Muratov said. "I suppose you were amused at the American's nonsense."

Zhukov didn't reply. If only the Russian delegate could produce some evidence of any request for help. If he failed then Soviet integrity was humiliated.

Said the American, "In Czechoslovakia tonight the dark and ugly visage of the Soviet intention has been sharply revealed. It is the intention to destroy, to sap, to deter free debate, to prevent mankind from uttering or facing the truth. I know that the responsible governments represented around this council table will never be a party to such a shoddy business."

Then Canada has its say. And Britain, whose representative, a peer of the realm, an articulate country squire

247

of a man, read his government's statement. "This is a tragedy not only for Czechoslovakia but for Europe and for the whole world. It is a serious blow to the efforts which so many countries have been making to improve relations between East and West."

Then the peer turned on the Russian delegate. "All of us must have felt a sense of compassion for the man who has today endeavored to carry out such an unworthy task. We can picture his distaste, indeed his disgust, at having to defend such a disgraceful act. No wonder that in doing so he carried so little conviction."

You couldn't beat the British, Zhukov thought, when it came to the stiletto. A caress on the underbelly with refined Westminster steel, leaving a widening slit of blood.

Zhukov felt sorry for his compatriot. What could he say? What would I say? How much did he believe? How many lies are justified in the cause of Socialism? He noted, with pleasure, that the Russian delegate at the horseshoe table smiled at the Englishman's proffered sympathy.

Then Denmark had a say.

Then Russia again, still warding off the debate. "Attempting to deny the right of the Socialist countries to give assistance to fraternal Socialist states, or their friends, to the peoples of Socialist countries, is an old method of the imperialists, the goal of which is to shatter the unity and cohesion of the Socialist countries and to look for cracks in order to do so."

A whiff of *Pravda, Izvestia* and *Tass.*

The Soviet uncle talked on, and on.

Sentence by sentence, it came to Vladimir Zhukov that, whatever the outcome on this point, nothing would be achieved by the Security Council of the United Nations. Just words, angry words, demands, notes, protests, damnations. But they would do nothing; there was nothing they could do. Once again the people of Czechoslovakia would be sacrificed while their protectors snapped and protested with futile eloquence.

The Russian announced that he wouldn't insist on a vote. The President ruled that a vote there should be. Thirteen for, two against—Russia and Hungary.

Then the President invited a Czech representative to the table. Vladimir Zhukov, the Russian, the enemy, listened, hunched forward, fists balled and sweating. The Czech read a message from the Presidium of the Central Committee of the Communist Party of Czechoslovakia:

"On 20 August, around 11 P.M., the troops of the Union of Soviet Socialist Republics, Polish People's Republic, Hungarian People's Republic, Bulgarian People's Republic and German Democratic Republic crossed the state borders of the Czechoslovak Socialist Republic. This happened without the knowledge of the President of the Republic, the Chairman of the National Assembly, the Prime Minister, the First Secretary of the Central Committee of the Communist Party of Czechoslovakia or those organs."

Zhukov touched Muratov's arm. "I must go and telephone the ambassador in Washington."

"Very well, although I'm sure that the mission. . . ."

"I have my orders," Zhukov said. "Please make notes for me."

"Are you calling the ambassador direct?"

"What other way?"

Muratov expressed awe in some Scandinavian tongue.

But Zhukov didn't go straight to the phone. He walked into the hot street, dust like baking powder on the sidewalks, and brought another paper. The Soviets had dropped leaflets on Prague, set up a puppet newspaper.

He dropped the paper in the road and a shuffling old man, his face creased in all the wrong places, said, "You dropped somethin', mister."

"I don't want it."

The old man picked it up to resell for a nickel.

Zhukov returned to the international gardens of the United Nations and watched the tugs. They hate us. Sparrows at his feet. We who spent our youth fighting the tyrant Nazi. (There, in those spilled years of young manhood, was the foundation stone of his naïveté.) A helicopter buzzing the East River, looking cockeyed at a couple of junior skyscrapers, symbolized tyranny. But just the same a red-scarved ideal hung in the background of

249

his youth—maybe a little tattered—but fluttering just the same, like the wings of a scorched insect.

Blood must always be spilled, the lecturer had said, in the surgery of mankind.

Behind the hedge of flags they wrangled on. Czechoslovakia still on his feet probably. What would happen to the poor bastard when the Russians put their men back in power in the interests of unity? He could always defect, Zhukov mused. Unless, like Vladimir Zhukov, he considered defection to be an act of cowardice.

Then again you had to analyze cowardice. Only brave men could be public cowards.

And sitting there, between the isolationist tugs and automobiles, Vladimir Zhukov actually considered defection.

Considered it as a possibility, nothing more. An improbability, perhaps. But, by its very improbability, conceding possibility.

But not for any of the reasons that patronizing capitalists speculated that poor Communists standing in line for ball-point pens might seek the paradise of political asylum. Not for the Fifth Avenues of plenty, not for the vacuums emptied for free enterprise, not even for the free speech that allowed you to call the President a shit without having the tongue of your soul cut out.

No, you contemplated—contemplated was too strong —you considered, explored, nudged, the possibility of defection because of what you suddenly perceived about your own country, about your own system, from a distance.

Because you saw yourself as the enemy you had once fought.

He left the sparrows and the tugs, the helicopter wheeling exhibitionistically, and went into the bar of the United Nations where they dispensed international drinks. He ordered a Stolichnaya and drank it in one gulp, followed by a glass of ice water, beside a group of somber East Europeans and an Arab being coaxed, not for the first time, into having a scotch. A few journalists with distant deadlines stood at the bar waiting for the story to develop.

Zhukov considered another vodka, then rejected it. The barman who enjoyed dispensing patriotic drinks looked disappointed. But with the Russians you never could tell . . .

Zhukov went to the phone and called Washington.

"Yes?" said the ambassador.

"The debate is going ahead," Zhukov said. "By thirteen votes to two."

"No surprises there," said the ambassador.

"Had you already heard?"

"Yes," said the ambassador. "But don't let that worry you."

A good, avuncular man.

"The Czechoslovakian representative is talking," Zhukov said. "He has read a statement from the Presidium of the Central Committee of the party in Czechoslovakia claiming that we crossed his country's borders without the knowledge of the President, the Chairman, the Prime Minister, the First Secretary. . . ."

"Again, no surprises."

"No surprises?"

"No surprises," the melodious voice advised him.

"Then I will return to the Security Council and prepare further reports."

"Very well," Zuvorin said. And, a little more hesitantly, "Is everything else in order, Comrade Zhukov?"

"Yes, thank you, sir." As far as he knew because he hadn't been looking for pursuit.

Back at the bar he ordered one more Stolichnaya and stood, hands on the bar, contemplating it.

An Australian journalist moved in. "Excuse me, but you're with the Russian team, aren't you?"

A forceful young man with black curly hair, a pink shirt and a voice rasped by the Bondi Beach surf.

"I am a Russian," Zhukov said.

"Would you like a drink, sir?"

Zhukov grinned despite it all. Sir instead of shit. He thought this young Australian was probably very compe-

251

tent. He thought he was the sort of young man he might like to go out and get drunk with. "No, thank you . . . I have one here."

"But you're not from the Soviet Mission in New York, are you, sir?"

"Where are you from?" Zhukov asked.

"Melbourne. What do you think, sir, of the Soviet presence in Czechoslovakia?"

Presence. A nice word. "You should be a diplomat, young man."

Rebuff was no stranger to the Australian. "But what do you think?"

"I think that one day you will become editor of your newspaper."

He returned to the Security Council where the American delegate was comparing the Soviet presence in Czechoslovakia with the German presence. The presence which Zhukov had helped remove.

". . . Thus Czechoslovakia, wedged between more powerful states, has been the victim of two foreign tyrannies in succession: first that of Hitler and then that of the Soviet Union. Hitler's oppression, savage though it was, lasted for the comparatively brief span of seven years and ended with the downfall of the tyrant himself. But the Soviet tyranny that followed has lasted from 1948 to the present, for twenty years. And in this year 1968 when at last the national spirit of Czechoslovak people began to flame anew, the world waited through anxious weeks to see whether these few modest manifestations of freedom could be accepted by Moscow and its client states.

"Now we know the answer, which was written not in words but in the streets of Prague by the treads of Soviet tanks for all the world to read. . . .

"The question before us tonight is a vital one that has haunted mankind through the ages: Will the relations between men and nations be governed by the rule of main force and of rigid ideological conformity, or will they be governed by rules of fair play and tolerance which find their highest expression in the Charter of the United Nations?"

252

The words poured out while in the streets of Prague the guns snouted.

God knows how long the Russian talked. Or how he kept it up. History, politics, polemics, Vietnam, the Middle East, a spasm of irritation over the American member's comments on the Russian predilection for the word "imperialism." "It is to be found in every language in the world, and I believe that there are over twenty-eight hundred languages, according to the linguists, and imperialism is always imperialism, and the peoples of the world all abhor American imperialism whether or not the American representative likes it."

Muratov nudged Zhukov. "He is quite right. Such knowledge." He rubbed the hair on his cheekbones as if his fingertips were erasers.

"It doesn't seem to have a lot to do with Czechoslovakia," Zhukov observed.

"It was the American representative who raised it."

"I suppose so."

The Russian delegate produced a document from the "lawful legitimate authorities" in Czechoslovakia. An appeal for assistance from the Warsaw Pact allies. Again Zhukov leaned forward, hoping for the justification for everything.

The authors of the long document accepted responsibility for "rallying all patriotic forces in the name of our Socialist future and our homeland" and urged all Czechs to support the military units of the allies.

But, Zhukov thought, who are the authors?

"We appeal to all of you from Sumava to the Cierna Nad Tisov, from Karkonoszeto to the Danube, to understand the greatness and seriousness of these days . . . we ask that you be aware of your responsibility, that you keep confidence and be united in the future. Our guiding lines will continue to be foresight, order, progress, truth and Socialism, national sovereignty and solidarity. Long live and flourish the democratic, Socialist Czechoslovakian group of the Central Committee of the Communist Party and Government and National Assembly, which have addressed an appeal for assistance to Socialist countries."

The Soviet delegate said, "This is the appeal which caused us to heed it and to come to the assistance of Czechoslovakia and its armed forces. . . ."

But who the hell wrote it?

"There," Muratov whispered, "at last the imperialists have had their answer."

"Have you watched television lately?" Zhukov asked.

"I do not waste my time with propaganda, Comrade Zhukov."

The Soviet delegate talked on involving the *Wall Street Journal,* a Congressman from Florida, Undersecretary for Political Affairs Eugene Rostow, Senator Walter Mondale of Minnesota, German Foreign Minister Willy Brandt, Napoleon, Hitler, Truman and Churchill.

"Too much blood," he proclaimed, "too many heavy losses, too many victims—twenty million Soviet citizens —were sacrificed in Eastern Europe during the Second World War against German Fascism for us to remain passive when confronted with the attempts of the imperialist revenge-seekers to carve anew the borders of postwar Europe."

I fought, Zhukov thought. And, from the surprise of Muratov's face, realized that he had spoken his thought.

The American was speaking. He had just been handed a copy of a Radio Prague broadcast claiming that the Soviet military commander in Prague had issued an order that anyone seen on the streets at night would be shot. Said the American member: "Now that is one way to bring about tranquillity, because if this order is carried out faithfully it is quite certain that a number of very unfortunate Czechs are likely to become very tranquil indeed because they will be dead."

The Security Council resolution expressing concern over the dangers of "violence and reprisals" and the "threats to human rights" called for immediate withdrawal of troops and a halt to "all other forms of intervention in Czechoslovakian internal affairs."

During the debate on the resolution the American delegate said the world was disgusted by the Russian assertion that the invasion was merely "fraternal assistance." And, scoffing, cited opposition to the occupation from *imperialists* such as Indira Gandhi, Pope Paul VI, Ceausescu, Tito and Julius Nyerere.

The resolution was carried by ten votes to the inevitable two (Russia and Hungary) with three abstentions.

The futility of it all was finally emphasized by the Soviet Union which exercised its one hundred and fifth veto.

Zhukov reported back to the ambassador in Washington. But he sensed that Zuvorin was bored with such an inevitability and more concerned with the breakdown in his relations with the President: two men seeking autumnal grandeur for the history books.

Now the missile disarmament summit had been canceled. The United States was planning to bring forward military exercises in Europe and fly fifteen thousand troops to West Germany, thirty miles from the Czechoslovak border.

In this last accelerating phase of their careers the oceans between the continents were widening and freezing once more . . .

Zhukov watched the faltering Czech rebellion on a color TV set in a German bar on Third Avenue. The newscaster appeared in paintbox colors—bright-pink face and greenish background—while Prague appeared in black and white. More real, somehow, that way; like the frozen prints of the October Revolution.

It was Zhukov's simple aim to get good and drunk. Along the bar sat other men with similar objectives, adopting the traditional posture of the dedicated American drunk: crouched, both hands on the bar, drink between two paws, to be toyed with and stroked, before the compulsive gulp; drinks spaced at intervals, five or fifteen minutes according to your pocket; flick the empty glass forward and incline your head toward the aproned barman.

Zhukov drank a stein of draft German lager, straw-colored with winking froth, cold mist blurring the outside of the glass tankard.

He had been advised to stay that evening at the Soviet Mission on East Sixty-seventh, and Dmitri Muratov had invited him to supper with his wife. But to hell with them.

He had walked down the sidewalks of Lexington cooling in the evening, but the air trapped beneath the builder's helmet of smog was still tropical, the snared sunshine decaying a little. In the delicatessens salami curled its tongues and the hanging hams and sausages swung like relaxed elephantine testicles. Even lime-green milk shakes had a melted look about them.

Only the swank hotels managed coolness in the refined railroad terminals of their lobbies. Zhukov took himself to the Waldorf-Astoria because of its Hollywod familiarity. In its corridors men in thin snappy suits and women in silk met over cocktails, money still crisp from air conditioning in purse and pocketbook. Zhukov had in his pockets fifty dollars of limp capitalist money. He decided to spend none of it here; no workers of the world ever united here.

So he ended up in the German bar on Third as the first watering place.

Above the barman's head the Czechs who had allegedly welcomed the arrival of their Warsaw Pact allies shouted, jeered and climbed onto the implacable tanks. Buildings burned and gunfire crackled.

According to the newscaster with the blood-pressured complexion some of the tank crews had no idea that they were in Czechoslovakia when they climbed out of their turrets. Others were dismayed at the hostility that met them.

Zhukov wondered what Russian television was showing —if anything. A nice tableau, probably, in a quiet park. Tame girls embracing bashful soldiers, tank commanders ruffling children's hair.

The foam winked and he poured the beer that smelled vaguely of lions' cages down his throat. Another tankard and a shot of Smirnoff to go with it.

The drinkers ranged alongside him studied their glasses and their hands. A man beside him with a couple of chins, a bald head and ludicrous sideburns caught his eye and inclined his head, welcoming Zhukov into the fraternity.

Zhukov asked him if he'd like a drink.

"Sure, why not? You buy one and I'll buy one. Works out the same either way, I guess. So long as you ain't drinking no fancy drink." His eyes which had an eggy quality looked accusingly at the vodka.

"Only vodka."

"I reckon that's okay. I'll take a bourbon with you, friend." He placed the new glass of bourbon and ice in front of him for contemplation, as much part of the pleasure as the hangover was a remorse.

"What are you trying to forget, friend?"

"That." Zhukov pointed at the TV.

"That?" The drunk peered at the set. "What's that, friend? Another war or somethin'?"

"That's Prague."

"Uh-huh. That's in Europe someplace, ain't it?"

"It's in Czechoslovakia."

The drunk considered this, loose eyes following the movement of the ice under the whiskey. "Why should you be worried about what's happening a million miles from this bar?"

"Because I'm Russian."

The drunk accepted the confession without surprise. He would have accepted a drink from a camel. "A Ruski, eh? I knew a few once, when I was at sea. Now I'm all at sea." He laughed sloppily.

"Would you like another?"

"My turn, friend."

But Zhukov had ordered and his friend didn't resist.

The drunk tried to backtrack on the conversation, but the immediate past was elusive. "Why did you say you were drinking?"

"It doesn't matter."

"I'm drinking because there ain't nothing else to do. My wife left me, the kids grew up. I'm drinking because I like it, friend. What else should I do? Tell me that. Go for a walk in the park? Pick up some broad down Times

257

Square?" He shook his head. "I don't kid myself like some of these guys here. They'll give you some shit about a family sorrow or somethin'. Me . . . I drink because there ain't nothing else to do. Nothin'," he added with finality.

Zhukov decided to move on and toasted the drunk in Russian.

"What was that?"

Zhukov stood up and paid.

"Hey, friend, it's my turn to pay." The drunk slapped a collection of coins on the bar, willing to pay for another couple of minutes' escape from ulcerated loneliness. "I worked down in Florida once. They had a bar there where you could have any drink in the house for forty cents. How about that?"

But Zhukov was gone, walking down Third, surprised the liquor hadn't affected him at all.

He went into a bar called Costello's as easily as paper into a vacuum cleaner. A good honest bar designed for un-remitting boozing and extravagant talking; there were Thurber drawings on the walls and the breath of Brendan Behan who used to take drink there hung balefully over the bar. Zhukov warmed to it immediately; it reminded him of the Moscow beer halls where in the evenings tired men swilled beer and ate crustacean snacks the way New Yorkers gobbled peanuts.

Along the bar he recognized the Australian journalist in the pink shirt engaged in hearty argument. And a group of British journalists with a couple of tanned, long-haired American girls trying to understand their jokes.

Zhukov switched to whiskey because everyone else seemed to be drinking it. After he had drunk the first one, ice clanking against his teeth, he managed to dispatch the faces of Prague into the wings. Americans, British, Aus-tralians and one Russian drinking together in a noisy bar. This, Zhukov thought, is where the United Nations should meet. Who is the enemy? No one. No one at all.

Relaxation slid over him as smoothly as sleep. The world's leaders should meet in bars like this. Brezhnev,

Kosygin, the President of the United States, the Prime Minister of Great Britain, De Gaulle, the Germans, a little Chinaman tinkling his ice like wind chimes.

Down the bar the Australian recognized him and waved, not as deferential as he'd been at the UN. He came down and clumped Zhukov on the shoulders. The British smelling a story over the rims of their glasses wandered over, leaving the girls talking about clothes and diets.

The Australian said, "Have a drink, comrade."

Ah, the camaraderie of social contact. "Thank you," he said politely. "I'll have a scotch whisky."

The Aussie bought him one. And everyone else including an American at the bar who had presumed that he was alone.

A stocky Englishman with Byronic curls above his honest face said, "Introduce us to your friend, Dave." His accent reminded Zhukov of the diplomat at Massingham's party: a bit of coal dust there.

Dave said. "This is Vladimir. Vladimir, meet the press."

"How did you know my name was Vladimir?"

"As far as I'm concerned," Dave said, "all Russians are Vladimir. Drink up, mate, there's another round coming up."

The rounds came up with a wave of the conjuror's wand. No one seemed too worried about Czechoslovakia. Or the Presidential election or pollution or the gathering student revolt. They were talking about a racehorse owned by one of them which had just come in first—in the race after the one it had run in. And about girls, poker, expenses and stories. Zhukov liked them all, loved them.

He tried to buy a round and was waved aside. An amiable middle-aged American, who managed to look like a tourist in his own city, drank up gladly, agreeing with most things that were said.

One of the Englishmen, a man of great affection who reminded Zhukov of hugging vodka friends in Moscow, began to sing "Underneath the Arches." But no one joined him, too early yet for songs.

259

These are not the sort of Englishmen I have met, Zhukov thought. Maybe he had never met any nationalities —only diplomats.

The Aussie walloped him on the shoulders again and said, "How's it going, Vladimir?"

"It's going fine," Zhukov replied, feeling a grin crease his surprised cheeks.

"Good on you," Dave said, drinking the American's whiskey. "What are you doing over here, mate?"

"Observing," Zhukov said.

"Not much to watch. A lot of bloody talk that's not going to do anyone any good. What did you think of your guy's performance?"

Zhukov shrugged. "It's not for me to say."

"I thought it was a load of garbage," Dave pronounced. "A load of bullshit."

"You are an honest man," Zhukov said. "I like honesty very much."

"Pity the Kremlin doesn't like it, too."

A jovial British reporter with a wrestler's build and thinning blond hair said, "Come off.it, Dave. The American delegate came out with just as much self-righteous bullshit."

"Yeah? And what about my British lord, for Chris' sake?"

"What about him?"

"Please." Zhukov held up his hand. "Let us not argue about it. I insist on buying everyone a drink." The drinks were in their hands as if the barman had decided it was about time Russia put his hand in his pocket. "Let's not spoil the atmosphere. I would be disappointed. Because it seems to me that this is the sort of place where the problems of the world should be sorted out. In a bar called Costello's." He felt that he had made a contribution of some magnitude.

Dave the Aussie gave him a one-armed Australian bear hug. "I like that, Vladimir. Do you mind if we use it?"

"Use it?"

"Yeah—quote you on it. An anonymous Soviet called

260

Vladimir solving problems of the world in a bar within a quarter of a mile of the United Nations."

"I don't think that would be taken very seriously."

The wrestler, also with coal-gritted voice, said, "Why not? We don't work for *Pravda,* you know. People want to know what ordinary Russians think. We have no bloody idea what ordinary Russians are like. You never tell us. In London everyone thinks they're all crane-drivers or spies."

The foreign voice of the American spoke up. "I think you're both right," he said.

Another Englishman, smooth and gout-suffering, asked Zhukov what he really thought about the Soviet presence in Czechoslovakia.

"If the Czechs asked us to intervene then it is justified."

"Ah, but did they? And if they did—who did?"

The whiskey slipped down as easily as beer. A sort of shambling benevolence encompassed Zhukov, although he was saddened at the turn of the conversation.

The affectionate Englishman was singing about a street called the Old Kent Road, glancing at his watch as if the predestined moment for accompaniment was almost nigh.

Zhukov said, "I don't know, my friend. I have no idea."

What did the ordinary Russian think? The ordinary Russian didn't even know. But he, Vladimir Zhukov, knew, and if he wasn't very careful his thoughts would take wing. Because he wanted to tell them, wanted to tell someone; the alcohol oiled the ball bearings of his want. "Let's hear your friend sing another song," he said.

The singer bowed. "I'm 'Enery the Eighth I am. . . ."

Americans in the bar looked startled at the inhibited British who only got drunk at hunt-balls.

The Australian took the rostrum: "Once a jolly swag-man. . . ." Then songs from the north and the London end of England, and a couple from the Guinness heart of Dublin with Behan's echo in the rafters.

Student melody bubbled inside Zhukov, beneath the crust of long conformity. Bubbled and erupted with a pre-liminary belch. "The Song of the Volga Boatman"—a song they knew. "Yo-ho heave-ho." Such gaiety, such spontaneity. Wasn't this the way life should be treated?

A Canadian newcomer attempted a Cossack dance and fell on his back.

"Yo-ho heave-ho."

The Aussie punched Zhukov gently in the belly. "I like you, Vladimir. You're a good guy."

"I like you all."

"Pity it can't always be like this, old mate."

Zhukov agreed that it was indeed a pity.

"You don't mind if we do a little piece about it, do you? Quite harmless. Just showing how we all can get together if the politicians would keep their bloody noses out of things."

What harm could it do? The philanthropy of the common man overcoming the dogmatic hostilities of the overlords. The balloon of well-being expanded the membrane of reserve outside his consciousness.

Zhukov punched the Australian back. "Go ahead if you wish. But please—no names."

"No names," said the wrestler. "We'll call you Ivan— it's the only other Russian name we know. And we'll call you a tourist. Up for cup. Okay?"

"What cup is this?"

"Just a North Country expression. Don't let it worry you. Have another drink."

Another glass appeared on the bar.

They sang "The Lambeth Walk."

"And now," Zhukov said, searching for the slippery globes of words, "I must go."

"One more for the road."

"Just one more."

The faces blended into a single song to which he beat time with one hand, loosening his tie with the other. "There'll always be an England. . . ."

"And a Russia," he bellowed.

"You're a good guy, Ivan."

"You're all good guys."

He made his way elaborately to the door, apologizing to a chair which got in his way.

262

Outside, the glow of the day was suspended in warm dew. He bought a slice of pizza across the road and looked for the next bar, the last bar. A gray-haired black sat on the curb waiting for rain or a bus or a benefactor. Zhukov gave him a dollar which he took with a soft mumble. The old black made Zhukov feel sad with his waiting face that had bypassed hopelessness. He chewed on his pizza as if it were gum and hummed a song that wandered over the steppes in the fall.

Two cops stopped him on the corner of Forty-ninth. "Say, fella, isn't it about time you took a cab home?"

"No," Zhukov said. "Why do you ask?"

They were both young with smooth smart faces. "Because you're loaded, buddy," said the second cop. "That's why."

"Loaded? I have no gun."

"Say, fella," said the first cop, "where you from?"

"And where are you going?" said the second.

"I'm going to Prague," Zhukov said.

"That's a long way, fella. Do you have any papers on you?"

Zhukov produced his wallet, dropped it, picked it up, grazing a knuckle on the sidewalk and handed it to the cops.

The first cop showed it to the second. "Guess we'd better leave well enough alone."

"He ain't doing any harm anyways."

They saluted. "Watch yourself, comrade. If you take our advice you'll go back to your hotel before you get into any trouble."

Zhukov nodded. Nice young guys . . . kind behind their strutting manner.

He walked on mourning the loss of innocence, crossing a street against the lights and upsetting a cabdriver. The driver shouted a few obscenities and Zhukov waved back at him benignly.

At the next block he sidestepped into a bar packed with men and women picking each other up. In groups, couples and singles: something for everybody with not less than twenty-five dollars on them and an apartment within the

263

river boundaries. The barmen energetic and as swift with the change as shop-breakers with loot.

Zhukov bought himself a scotch, leaning with gratitude against a wall. Around him he saw the loneliness, felt the fear of it. If you had missed your knight or your damsel you came here and hoped that he or she didn't disgust you in the light of dawn. The bar was tactfully dark.

A girl of about thirty wearing a blond wig knocked his drink. "Sorry," she said, not looking sorry at all. She was thin and smart and unloved.

"Don't worry," Zhukov said.

"Say, do I detect an accent?"

"I'm Russian," Zhukov said.

"You're kidding."

"Why should I be kidding?"

"Wow," she said. "I really believe you are Russian. Say, you must be the first real Russian I've met. What's a nice Russian like you doing in a place like this?"

"Drinking," Zhukov told her.

"You can say that again," she said peering at him. "Did someone try to strangle you or something?" She pointed at his tie which was sliding beneath his jacket.

Zhukov replied that no one had tried to strangle him.

"You don't exactly make with the small talk, stranger. What's your name?"

He told her it was Vladimir.

"Vladimir. That's kinda cute. Would you like to buy me a drink, Vladimir? Or don't girls ask guys questions like that in Russia?"

"Certainly I'll get you a drink." He pushed off from the wall. "What would you like?"

"With you it'll have to be a vodka. A vodka tonic."

"You shouldn't mix tonic water with vodka."

"Okay then—I'll take it straight."

Zhukov pushed into the throng with a steady breast-stroke. Everyone was shouting, sweating with the effort of pickup cleverness. The men smelling of after-shave and deodorant, assessing how far they could go with suggestive openers; the women acting haughty to start with and talk-

264

ing intently to their girlfriends as if men were the last creatures they had come to meet in the market.

In Moscow the pickups used the National bar, but they were mostly KGB pickups.

When Zhukov got back to the girl she'd been joined by a friend with long lusterless hair and shortsighted eyes who tried to make up for her handicaps by wearing no bra. "This is Jean," the first girl said. "Jean, Vladimir. And my name by the way is Holly." Which Zhukov thought was unlikely.

Melancholy was fast overcoming Zhukov. It was like being on the subway in this bar, except that no one was going anywhere. Even the sexuality seemed spurious, the older women seeking someone to eat breakfast with rather than to copulate with; the younger ones seeking experience before they settled for a small car, husband and a mortgage.

"What part of Russia are you from?" the girl called Jean asked. Her voice was low and deliberately bored because she was used to losing men's attention.

"Moscow," he said, looking for the doorway through the bodies.

They sensed escape and Holly said quickly, "You know something? You're a very attractive guy. Different from all these creeps here." She dismissed all the creeps she'd come to meet.

"I suppose you're married," Jean presumed, because the men she met always were.

"Yes, I'm married." He felt a little sick. All those faces with the mouths opening and shutting. Beside him a man was stroking a girl's breast watching her face for reaction.

"And I suppose your wife doesn't understand you," Holly said.

"She understands me very well."

They both found this very funny.

Jean said in her funereal voice, "I like honesty in a man."

It seemed to Zhukov that they were now vying with each other for his attention; he wasn't flattered.

A young man built like a football player pushed his way up to them. "Say, what goes with you dames? I buy you a drink and you leave me holding them?"

"We didn't ask you for them," Holly said primly. "You just went and bought them. We didn't say we wanted drinks, did we, Jean?"

And while the young man complained Holly confided to Zhukov, "That's the kind of jerk you meet in this dump. One drink and they presume they can lay you. Still"— she glanced stealthily at Jean and the young man—"maybe they'll make it together and that'll leave you and me. Would you like that, Vladimir?"

"Oh, fuck off," said the young man. He had long brown hair and the beginnings of a beard on his sulky face; he wore jeans and a grubby sweat shirt and his biceps bulged like oranges.

"Don't you use language like that to me," Jean moaned.

"And who's this guy anyway?"

Holly said, "This is Vladimir. He's a Russian."

"A Russian? A white Russian or a red? Jesus, why did I have to buy drinks for two dumb broads like you. I suppose he's got snow on his boots."

"No," Zhukov said, "no snow." He smiled with relief because instinct told him that there would be a fight; he suspected that, for all his muscular plumage, the young man might try and back down. But you didn't take that risk; and the young man might have allies. In Army brawls in Leningrad the winner was the man who got in the first punch. And in any case Vladimir Zhukov, poet and diplomat, found that he wanted a fight: to drive his knuckles against the tanks lurking in the streets. He thought he felt sober.

"No snow, eh? What part of the Village you from, mister?"

"Village?"

The lout sighed dramatically, looking around for an audience. "The Village. Greenwich Village."

"I come from Moscow," Zhukov said, feeding him.

"Moscow, eh? Hear that?" Addressing a couple who

reluctantly began to pay attention. "This guy says he comes from Moscow."

"You don't believe me?"

"Hey, Vladimir," Holly said. "Don't try anything stupid. This jerk is half your age."

Zhukov was grateful for he concern: the decency beneath the sad smart face.

"Sure I believe you," sneered the young man, indicating that he didn't.

"Perhaps you would like to see my credentials."

"Sure. Why not?" But he sensed that he was losing face. "Show us your credentials, brother. Expose the whole goddamn works if you insist." He looked around seeking laughter. There was none, but a miniature arena had formed, the faces in the expensive seats silent and intent.

Zhukov showed him his identity card enclosed in yellowing plastic.

"Wow," Holly said. "You're a diplomat. A real Russian diplomat."

A hint of desperation was apparent in the voice of the young man who, Zhukov thought, hadn't got the guts to be a total hippie. "So you're one of the great team that just invaded the Czechs, uh? Shit. You must be pretty proud of yourself, comrade."

To his surprise Zhukov found himself defending the Soviet Union. His country, his belief. Snow smoked in the wind in the infinite white pastures of Siberia, guitars played martial music on the river beaches; the proud strut of soldiers' boots on the cobblestones of Red Square, the green and red splutter of anniversary rockets dripping from Kremlin skies.

How was this hooligan to know that his anger encompassed both his belief and his tears for the oppressed?

I have the right to criticize; not you, friend.

Zhukov said, "I am very proud."

Somewhere in the confused background the voice of one of the young man's allies said, "Aw, knock it off, man —he ain't doing you no harm."

His antagonist looked around for a more specific saving

267

grace but none was forthcoming. Desperately he plunged on through the minefield of his own laying. "Yeah, you must feel pretty proud. Beating up a few defenseless Czechs. I wish to God there was a Czech here tonight to show you what they think of the Russian bullies in Prague."

He looked around again. "Is there a Czech in the house? Please?"

Zhukov said, "Unfortunately for you there isn't. There's just you. And me."

Holly squeezed his arm. He thought he could love her just for her loneliness and for her decent, disguised ways. "Knock it off, Vladimir. He isn't worth it."

Zhukov pushed aside the snouting nozzle of a tank gun.

The young man combed at the belligerent streamers of his beard with broken fingernails. "Can you stand there in front of all these people"—he indicated the masses who showed no alignment—"and have the nerve to say you agree with what the Reds have done in Czechoslovakia?"

"By Reds I presume you mean Socialists?"

"Commies. Goddamn Commies—that's what I mean."

"The people of Czechoslovakia are Communists," Zhukov said. "And to answer your question, yes, of course I agree with them. We went to their help."

Creed against creed, nation against nation, village against village, neighbor against neighbor. What next? Planet against planet?

"You're a fucking hypocrite," said the young man, his voice as indecisive as his beard.

The bar was very quiet now. The gong about to sound. "Would you like to repeat that?"

Zhukov allowed him half a repetition. Then hit him hard just below the ribs, with all the power of the accumulated despair of the past few days gathered in his knuckles.

The young man doubled over. Then stretched up, sucking for breath. "You shit. That's the way you fucking bastards fight. Hitting the little guy in the gut. . . ."

Jean's voice rose an octave. "You aren't exactly little."

"You keep out of this." He swung like a pitcher, and

Zhukov dodged with brief alcoholic agility. His opponent's fist KO'd the wall. Zhukov clipped him neatly under the jaw and he fell to the floor.

When he got up he was holding a knife. "Okay, you son of a bitch. This is yours."

Zhukov kicked and sent the knife flickering over the mob like a leaping salmon. Then feinted with his left and clobbered protesting youth with a right that poleaxed him.

Now to get out. He patted Holly's arm. "Thanks," he said. And pushed his way through the crowd, sweat trickling down his face, heart stamping in protest.

The KGB were waiting for him outside.

Chapter 4

THE FIRES of summer began to cool and with them the fires of rebellion. The Czechs weren't crushed; they were suffocated. Press censorship was reimposed, the Czech Presidium reshuffled and it was announced that the withdrawal of Soviet troops would take several months. *Tass* continued to attack and *Pravda*'s Sergei Kovalev asserted, "The weakening of any of the links in the world system of Socialism directly affects all the Socialist countries which cannot look indifferently upon this." The President of the Czech National Assembly looked upon it differently. He said, "We never thought we would have to pay the price we paid the night of August 20–21."

But it was all academic: Freedom had received another kick in the teeth from a jackboot and wouldn't get up again for a long time.

World Communism was, by and large, upset by the invasion; the escapist future of equality had been jolted. Some parties protested and disassociated themselves from

269

the intervention; the Kremlin remained unapologetic and little moved by the disapproval because history had proved its transience: You didn't easily forgo shop stewardship in the capitalist factory.

In Washington, New York and London the futility of collective outrage was acknowledged: another defeat for organized idealism, another victory for bondage. If Russia were to be punished then best leave it to the Chinese. The shame was filed.

America returned to the Presidential elections and Vietnam (inseparable for the most part—especially during the antiwar demonstrations accompanying the Democratic Party convention in Chicago), student unrest and a forthcoming space shot in which three astronauts were to orbit the moon.

In Washington it was a delicate period for the society hostesses building the structures of election platforms beneath the cold buffets of their receptions and parties. With honey tans and spun-sugar coiffures, they presided regally over their screened guests, ensuring their husbands' futures —and terminating a few—and thus their own. Launching rehearsed rumors of villainous enemy activity with the pop of a champagne cork, casually disclosing sacrificial good deeds of the allies over a glistening lick of caviar.

In the Soviet Embassy in mid-September plans for the party to celebrate the Great October Socialist Revolution got under way. Booze: vodka of course, bourbon, scotch, brandy, Georgian wine, Russian beer and champagne. Food: caviar of course, chicken, pheasant, duck, veal, beef, lobster, sturgeon of course, ham, salmon, crayfish, shrimps, Russian salad, potato salad, turkey, chocolate eclairs, ice cream, chocolates and a sumptuous cake.

In other embassies reserves of aspirin and Alka-Seltzer were ordered.

Vladimir Zhukov continued to read his newspapers, but without appetite; waiting, without contrition, for his punishment; seeing little to celebrate this anniversary.

While the machinery of retribution clanked away, he was allowed one more reception, at the embassy of Kuwait—

six diplomats and a four-million-dollar headquarters off upper Connecticut built of brick and white marble with paneled walls and Islamic arches.

Neither Massingham nor his wife was there. As if, Zhukov thought, they had heard he could no longer be of any use to them. He drank two glasses of warm orange squash and left early.

At the embassy they left him alone, not wishing to be contaminated before the judgment. Although judgment seemed to be a long time coming, with psychology that he didn't attempt to analyze.

At home the atmosphere was as portentous as an autumn fog before a long cold winter. At first Valentina raged. Throwing away his future—their future. A common drunk, brawling, getting himself picked up by New York tarts, shooting off his mouth to strangers who were probably CIA agents. Compromising the Zhukov name, compromising the Soviet Union. But after she had laid the egg of her fury she went broody, behaving with the long-suffering of a libertine's wife.

Natasha stayed at home. She alone extended understanding but it was a remote quantity. Although he was not contrite about his protest he grieved for what he might have done to her.

One Sunday when Valentina was helping at a children's party he said to his daughter, "I'm afraid I haven't been a very good father, Natasha."

"You're a wonderful father," she said. She wore no makeup and her hair was captured in an untidy ponytail.

But he wasn't. And wondered if he ever had been. Their alliance had always been a bloc within the tripartite of their family. That was no way to bring up a child.

"This is a bad time for us," he said. "But"—he paused uncertainly—"is there anything else wrong? You seem very quiet. Like a girl whose lover has been sent to the wars maybe?"

She began to speak but Zhukov stopped her. Almost certainly there were ears in the walls now. "Let's go for a walk."

271

"Very well."

He noticed that she wore the Russian clothes she'd arrived with.

They drove to Potomac Park on the far side of the Tidal Basin where the dusty leaves were yellowing and the roots of the grass showed like string. Some boys played baseball, some old people watched, a circle of hippies lolled about counting grains of dry soil, couples necked. But it was an exhausted place.

They walked slowly, neither bothering to see if they were being followed. It didn't matter.

"Is there something else?" Zhukov asked his daughter.

"The usual thing," she said.

"A man?"

"A man."

"An American?"

She nodded, ponytail jogging.

Zhukov considered this, ashamed that he had consigned all his compassion to the Czechs and not retained any for his own daughter.

"And what are you going to do?"

"Nothing," she said.

He looked at her and saw tears gathering.

"You should have told me before."

"I was frightened. And, in any case, you have your problems. You act," she added, "as if you have all the problems of mankind."

"Does this American want to marry you?"

"He says he does."

"And do you want to marry him?"

"No," she said. The tears on her cheeks looked very wet this dusty afternoon.

"I don't believe you, Natasha, my daughter."

"How can I marry him?"

"It wouldn't be so difficult. You would probably have to choose between your country and your lover. I know it sounds dramatic but that's the way things are."

She lookeld at him in surprise. "You mean you'd encourage me to run away? To elope, to defect?

"It's a sad world when marriage is described as defection," Zhukov said. "But I'm afraid that's what it would be. And it would require a lot of courage. You'd be followed, and pestered by Soviet agents wanting your return. And you'd be pestered by Americans seeking publicity and prestige. Your love affair will be exhibited all over the Western world. But if it is love and not just another Georgi. . . ."

They sat on a bench a hundred yards from the hippies. To the right the flaccid waters of the Basin, ahead the barb of the Monument above the tired trees.

"Tell me," Natasha said, "would you have encouraged me, say, two months ago? Before Czechoslovakia?"

"Who knows? Maybe not. I believe in what we've inherited, Natasha. And I believe you do, too. But in a different way than your mother. Not the belief that becomes stupidity because of its blindness."

"I suppose so. But I also believe in the movement of youth, the energy for change. I believed in those young faces in Prague. I felt I should have been there with them."

"Ah so." That was all over, the bud blighted. "This young man of yours, what's he like?"

"He isn't my young man anymore," she said. "But he's very American, clean-cut, all the rest of it. And his ears are a bit too large for him. They listen too much," she added.

"What happened?" Zhukov asked, guessing the answer.

"He was spying on me. He isn't a professional spy, though—American Intelligence forced him to work for them."

"How did you find out?"

"He told me," Natasha said.

"I see." The attic door opened a fraction; inside a few pressed flowers from long-ago mountains. "He must love you very much, this American." He lit a cigarette. "Has it occurred to you, Natasha, what it must have meant to him to tell you? His instructions presumably were to seduce you, to get you so infatuated that you didn't care who you betrayed just to be with him. Your father even. But it seems to me he didn't try very hard. He doesn't sound like a very cold-blooded spy. It sounds to me as if he's the one who has had to do the betraying—because of you."

"All that time," Natasha said, "he was being dishonest with me. Even when we. . . ."

"Even when you slept together?"

"Yes," she answered quickly, "even when we were together like that."

"But he told you the truth. It must have been very hard. You don't realize, Natasha, what dishonesties men have to perpetrate to exist. To bring home food for their families and to pay the rent. Every clerk, every engineer, curbs his tongue when he's in the presence of a superior. That's a form of dishonesty. Some fawn and grovel to get the money to buy their wife new clothes, their sons toys. That's all dishonesty in different forms. It's not so disgusting, this dishonesty. You only despise it when you haven't had to use it."

"But you're not dishonest. You're the most honest man I know."

He shook his head. "I wish you were right."

"And Mother—she's not dishonest."

"No," Zhukov agreed, "I don't believe she is."

The hippies moved off leaving behind empty cigarette packs and spent matches. An airliner smoked laboriously overhead. A leaf spiraled from the tree under which they were sitting.

"What's his name?" Zhukov asked.

"Hardin. Charlie Hardin."

"The name is vaguely familiar. Perhaps I met him at one of my parties."

"He is an architect."

"Was an architect, probably."

"Why? Do you think he got into trouble because of me?"

"If he's told them that he confessed to you he's probably been sent to Alaska—if American Intelligence is anything like the KGB."

"That didn't occur to me."

"No," Zhukov said, "because you are inclined to be a prig."

"A prig!" The tears had dried. "How can you say that —after Georgi, after Charlie. . . ."

"I didn't mean it that way. You're a prig with human weakness. Such a prig that you can't see its strengths. You say he wants to marry you?"

Natasha said, "That's what he told me."

"Then I'm sure he does."

Natasha explained that, in her opinion, Hardin was more after a defector than a wife. In fact he'd said as much.

Ah yes, Zhukov advised his daughter, but the defection would be inescapable. The Americans loved a defector. "You might even be able to write your memoirs like Svetlana Stalin."

Never, said his daughter.

Zhukov, not yet sure that he was guiding his daughter in the right direction, said, "Did he really say that he regarded you more as a defector than a wife?"

Natasha said that Hardin had implied it. "No, perhaps he didn't. It just seemed that way to me."

Zhukov stood up and surveyed the overcooked parkland. "I think we should return to the car or else they will presume that we've both defected."

They walked in silence for a few minutes, close together. Then Natasha said, "If I ran away—eloped—what would happen to you?"

Zhukov shrugged. "Nothing much worse than what is going to happen anyway."

"I don't believe that. Nothing much will happen to you now. A reprimand, maybe." She held his hand for a moment. "At least Russians understand drunkenness. And they probably approve of you hitting that idiot in the bar." She laughed. "I approve very much. And I think secretly that Mother approved, too."

"No," Zhukov said, "she didn't approve."

"Anyway I don't think they'll send you to Siberia. But if I disappeared they really would punish you. Force you to appeal to me to return. Imprison you until I gave myself up."

"The way we talk of our own people," Zhukov mused.

"But that's what would happen. Look what happened to Georgi."

"Listen," Zhukov said as they neared the Volkswagen, a sand bug in the dying heat of summer. "I think Moscow will act very soon. I'm amazed they haven't acted sooner. I thought they'd send you back to the Soviet Union much sooner than this—so that they could threaten me with retaliation against you if I didn't carry out their orders. But I suppose they have their reasons—they always have. Perhaps they had an idea what you were doing. Then they could have shipped you back and held a real threat of punishment to you over my head. Perhaps they thought you might provide some sort of lead just as the Americans thought you would help them. I don't know." He leaned against the car, keys in his hand. "But I do know that they will act very soon. If you love this boy go to him. I know this is right. Don't worry about me—I can take care of myself. You do love him, don't you?"

Natasha said she did.

"Go to him but prepare yourself for the guilt you will endure. It's inescapable. But in time, with children and growing old together, it will fade."

She shook her head, flinging around the tears that had regrouped. "I can't. I know what they would do to you. That's the guilt I could never escape."

"Here." He gave her his handkerchief. "I promise that nothing will happen to me. I will even denounce you—if you tell me now that you will never believe what you read."

"Of course I wouldn't," his daughter said. "But I can't leave you. Unless"—the tears stopped flowing with the thought—"unless you defected, too."

To this Zhukov didn't reply. He opened up the oven of the car and they drove back to the apartment building near Du Pont Circle.

Ambassador Zuvorin thumbed the file on Zhukov with regret. He had a lot of respect for the newly promoted first secretary: a man he regarded almost as an equal, with Zhukov's years catching up on his (I was a teen-ager when Zhukov was born; when I'm a hundred he will be in his eighties). He paused on the last entry to the file, sighed and lit his first cigarette, enjoying the first gasp of smoke in his lungs.

His trust in Zhukov would be regarded as an error of judgment by the Kremlin. But not by Zuvorin himself; a man had a right to get drunk once in a while, and he could understand Zhukov's motives. He would also have liked to get good and drunk after the last explosive exchanges between himself and the Texan in the White House. But Zhukov should never have been a diplomat; he was too honest.

Zuvorin took himself on a tour of his palace because he thought well while he walked. The gold room, the green, the rose, the winter garden. He hoped that, before he left America, there would be time to reestablish his credentials, even if Czechoslovakia had frozen relations between Russia and America. He rather thought there would—tragedy was soon digested after the first painful swallow in diplomatic circles, successful deceit was acknowledged—after the deceived had got over the first resentment at being caught with his pants down and maneuvered a comeback. The President was good at coming back.

Soon there would be a new President. His last probably. A period of probing a new relationship, all according to the new man's viewpoint. If he were one of the Red menace brigade, then Zuvorin would be forced to withdraw into the old abortive frigidity; and his sense of achievement would be devalued, his retirement deprived of its glow.

Zuvorin looked through a window at Washington, the elegant nest of sincere endeavor with its cuckoo eggs of personal ambition forever hatching. My city. Sometimes the gold domes of the Kremlin were only distant notes of music.

Vietnam remained the barrier to the private negotiations of his soul, and any compromise of creeds; its presence forever bloodying diplomatic approach. If the Americans withdrew, according to the electioneering promises, then

277

there was a chance of neighborliness between the Red and White houses. The handshake that would invest his career with meaning. Election promises! Senile naïveté . . .

He adjusted his face to mask all private feeling and returned to his office, smiling at members of his staff. He reopened Zhukov's file and summoned him to his office.

Headmaster and errant student: Zuvorin didn't enjoy this seniority with such a man, a man who had also fought at Leningrad. "I'm afraid New York didn't work out too well," he observed.

"I'm sorry," Zhukov said without penitence.

"No decision has been reached yet." Zuvorin removed the last entry from the file and handed it to Zhukov. "But this doesn't help."

It was a feature, written with humor and compassionate journalese, from a London newspaper. All about a Russian called Ivan who thought the Security Council should be transported to a Third Avenue bar named Costello's.

Zuvorin watched Zhukov read it. Somewhere, perhaps, there was a file on Ambassador Zuvorin with contributions from M. Brodsky and others.

Zhukov handed it back.

"It's you, isn't it?" Zuvorin said.

"You know it is. I was followed the whole time."

"It's most unfortunate."

"Why?" Zhukov asked. "There's nothing anti-Soviet about it. Just a plea for an end to international hypocrisy. It's rather well done," he added.

"It implies that the case put by the Soviet delegate was so much hogwash—as the President of the United States might put it."

"It also implies that the Western protests were hogwash because everyone knew they would be ineffectual."

Zuvorin snapped the file closed. "You were very stupid. But I suppose you know that."

"Yes," Zhukov said, "I know it."

"Judges other than myself might consider you unstable."

"Perhaps they're right."

Zuvorin's hand went to his breast as a pain sharper than its predecessors needled him. He controlled the wince and took a tablet with a glass of water, murmuring about his asthma.

"I have to tell you," Zuvorin went on, "that it has been decided to curb your new duties while your case is considered. No more cocktail parties for a while, Comrade Zhukov." And no more Mrs. Massingham, he thought. "Instead you will take over responsibility for organizing the celebrations for the anniversary of the glorious Revolution."

"A very responsible job," Zhukov observed.

"You have been very stupid," Zuvorin said regretfully.

That afternoon the ambassador received a message from Moscow recalling him for talks to consider future Soviet policy toward the West and its application in Washington.

In his aseptic State Department office where integrity and intrigue were required to coalesce, Wallace J. Walden summoned once again the heads of Security and Consular Affairs, Intelligence and Research, and Politico-Military affairs; plus Hardin from the FBI and Godwin from the CIA. Charlie Hardin waited outside.

Walden poured himself ice water and said, "Gentlemen —and ladies—through circumstances beyond our control the Zhukov operation has gone adrift. As you know Comrade Zhukov has put his own future in jeopardy and we now have to reassess the operation in the light of events within the Russian compound."

"And events outside," Godwin asserted. "Like what happened to the FBI's big play with the Russian chick." Ash toppled from his cigarette onto his trousers and there was a tiny smell of burning.

Arnold Hardin said, I'll take care of that, Godwin."

"This was a joint operation," Godwin pointed out.

"Sure it was. But we both had our own responsibilities. I suggest you concentrate on yours which aren't exactly coming out smelling of roses."

Godwin nodded happily. "It's hardly the fault of the CIA if Zhukov chooses to torpedo his own career."

Gale Blair, Crawford and Bruno kept out of it.

Walden said, "I suggest we quit the squabbling. Sure it looks like a possible leak is going to be fouled up and we'll have to try and find another. But the way I see it we now have a chance of two highly prestigious defections. Okay, so young Hardin failed to persuade the girl to cheat on her father. So what? With her father in disgrace—on the threshold of a posting to Siberia, more than likely—she couldn't have got anything worthwhile anyway. But I do think that if the boy plays his cards right she may come over to us."

"I thought he *had* played his cards," Godwin said. "And lost. It wouldn't surprise me to learn that he'd confessed all to the girl."

Arnold Hardin said quickly, "The game is never lost, Godwin." Sunlight touched his face but the sleek health had left his cheeks. "These kids really love each other—something you probably wouldn't understand. I still reckon Charlie can pull it off. Which is more than can be said for the old bag you tried to get Zhukov in bed with. Jesus," he added, "what a hope."

The girl came in with tea which they stirred thoughtfully, the silence emphatic in the girl's presence.

When she had gone Walden said, "According to my sources Zhukov is in a highly nervous condition. It's my guess the Kremlin will pull him out. We certainly would if he was one of our men behaving like that in Moscow. Also his confidence in what's right and wrong has taken a beating over the Czech affair. He's so confused he's like a hypnotized rabbit." Walden walked over to the window and stood there, hands behind his back as if he were warming himself, his bulk dimming the light. "I figure it's only a matter of time before his daughter confides in him about her lover. If Charlie can really get to her then she'll tell Zhukov that she's going to come over to us. And I don't think it's outside the realms of possibility that he will follow her. If we play him right."

Gale Blair ventured a question. "Mr. Walden, how can we play him if we've lost contact?"

"Through his daughter, Gale. Once Hardin has persuaded her to defect then the next logical step is for her to try and persuade her parents to come over with her.

280

Hardin will have to work on that. Of course *we* know"—he was thinking aloud—"that Zhukov's wife is KGB. *We* know that she wouldn't come oven even if we publicly tortured her daughter. But I don't think Zhukov knows his wife's in the secret police. So somehow *we'll* have to let him know. And then, we'll be left with two defectors—father and daughter."

"How will we let him know?" Crawford from Politico-Military asked.

Walden shrugged. "A letter, an anonymous phone call. He might even find out himself. . . ." He turned and stared out the window, surveying a vast phantom crowd gathered to hear him. "A responsible Soviet diplomat and his daughter defecting. . . . The angle of the girl will really grab the kids in this youth-oriented age, especially those who might be flirting with Communism."

Crawford was enthusiastic; he usually was. "It could be a terrific coup. One of the best, especially with the romantic angle"—he saw it all in the pages of *Cosmopolitan*—"a beautiful Russian girl and a handsome young American guy. A real kick in the teeth for the Reds."

Godwin stirred his tea with the handle of his spoon. "You guys all seem to be overlooking one thing—this chick has given young Hardin the brush-off. That sounds to me like a pretty far cry from defection."

"She loves him," Hardin repeated. "She'll come over. But I wouldn't bet on Charlie's ability to coax her into persuading Zhukov himself to defect. She's got integrity, that girl."

"We'll see," Walden said. "Call young Hardin in."

Waiting outside, chatting to Walden's three secretaries who were as unattractive as they were available, Charlie Hardin, who never chased girls if they played it coy, tried to figure out a way of proposing marriage once more to Natasha Zhukova. Because he knew that she loved him and didn't even know how to act coy.

If that failed . . . the possibility sagged inside him. A physical pain. I love you, Natasha Zhukova. The honesty that withered any defensive half-smartness, your breasts in

281

my hands, the children we might have. Sunlight stuttering through tall trees . . .

He had told Walden about his confession to Natasha. Walden had reacted with fury; then calmed down as he began to reassess the chances of a defection, maybe two. Hardin had also told his father who had reacted pitifully inside his dapper husk. "You've got to get her to come across, Charlie. You've got to."

So, my Natasha, everyone wants you to defect, to become a traitor to your country. Probably Walden had always wanted this without even realizing it; one day he would pick his own pockets. He saw her again in the bookstore; after that first day he should have left her alone and uncontaminated. Natasha, what have I done?

A light winked on the desk of a secretary smiling at him. "Mr. Hardin," she breathed, "Mr. Walden wants to see you right away." (And I'll still be here when you come out.)

He entered the sanctum to hear Walden officially announce the substitute plans.

Charlie Hardin said, "I'll see Natasha one more time. And I'm going to play it straight with her. No more lies. But I can't ask her to involve her father. It's too dirty."

Walden hunched forward over his desk. "Not dirty, Charlie. Not really. You're getting the girl you love to be with you in the finest country in the world. And you're getting her father away from the secret police. In other words his wife."

Charlie, sitting on an upright wooden chair surrounded by Intelligence, said, "You seem to forget that they don't necessarily think America is the finest country in the world."

Walden made a gesture which implied: Impossible.

Hardin, Senior, warned, "Watch it, Charlie." (This sort of attitude isn't going to help me.)

"But," Walden conceded, "I know how you feel. I'd feel the same in your position. But look at it this way. The girl isn't going to come across if she thinks the Soviets will take it out on her father. Yet she wants to join you Charlie. I know it."

"I hadn't thought about reprisals," Charlie said quietly. "Maybe I shouldn't try anything."

Godwin said, "I still think Helen Massingham might get him over. She isn't playing a part anymore. She's got a real thing for Zhukov."

Bruno spoke and they listened because it was a rare occurrence. "The snag is Zhukov doesn't meet her anymore since his disgrace."

They paused to analyze the hidden wisdom.

Only Walden seemed to disregard him. "The way I see it, Charlie, it's best for everyone if Natasha persuades her father to seek political asylum. She'll be happy, you'll be happy and I figure Vladimir Zhukov will be as happy as he ever will be. And the United States of America will be very happy indeed."

Charlie walked to the window, dominating the proceedings and hating it. There didn't seem to be any escape from Walden's reasoning. Or, more accurately, I don't want to find the flaws. After a while he said, "I'll put it to her. But I'll put all my cards on the table. If, that is, I ever get the chance to see her again." He faced the conspirators. "But aren't we overlooking one thing?"

"What's that, Charlie?" Walden asked.

"Her mother."

Walden smiled reassuringly. "I think you'll find that will work out, Charlie." He lit his heavy pipe. "Maybe you should let her know about her mother. I'm not sure. I'll come up with something. Now you go home and figure out a way to meet her again."

"Like how?" Charlie asked. "Breaking and entering?"

"You'll find a way, Charlie. You love the girl." He glanced at his big watch. "Well, I guess that just about does it. I've got to get back to Bethesda. I've promised Sophie I'll address the ladies of the church this evening."

Her father's advice lingered joyfully with Natasha in her bedroom. Honesty was a quality you learned about, presenting itself in many forms, having many qualifications. Vaguely she thought she might have lost something by this reappraisal of Charlie Hardin. But the doubt was thrust aside by the release; honesty was a very malleable product when put to the test. But, she assured herself, Charlie had done his best to be honest in the circumstances. An impossible situation for absolute honesty. Eagerly she reaffirmed her naïveté in expecting the impossible and, without realizing it, stepped from youth into adulthood where many qualities are malleable.

The answer, she knew, was for her father to accompany her across the street from East to West. Hadn't he implied he was willing? Oddly, she didn't consider her mother's reactions, assuming that wife would follow husband because that was the marriage bond. Anyway, now that her father had spoken, she presumed that together they would make their plans accordingly; she presumed this because that was the way this new, unleashed impulse directed her. So she hugged her joy to herself, refusing to consider anything but the traditional course of true love, and wrote Charlie a note suggesting they meet the next afternoon in the bar of the Hawk 'n' Dove.

She also left a note for her father in view of the difficulty of discussing the subject in the apartment.

In the bedroom next door, while her husband was still at work, Valentina Zhukova wrote the last words of her report and wept.

Chapter 5

MIKHAIL BRODSKY met Vladimir Zhukov next day in the bookshop called Brentano's adjoining the National

Press Building. "The open air is the safest place for this sort of talk," he explained.

"You mean you're afraid of being bugged?"

"*Uh-huh.* Anything is possible, Comrade Zhukov. It pays to be cautious."

They crossed the road and walked past the White House, a building which adapted itself well to the seasons, a chameleon of atmosphere. Now it was Irish gentry, peering from behind sad trees at the mauve and russet Wicklow Mountains, soon it would be holly-berried, spiced, and rounded with snow, a jingle of harness bells on the frosty air.

Brodsky produced a new inhaler, black and gentle, and eased it into his nostrils affectionately.

"Are you sure that isn't bugged?" Zhukov asked.

Brodsky withdrew the black bullet and regarded it suspiciously.

The day was cool and vague, the sunshine filtered. Chrysanthemums grew raggedly in the gardens and the roses opened up fatalistically for the first frost. Soon the woods around Washington would glow with stained-glass reds and yellows.

They crossed Lafayette Square and turned down Sixteenth. Already some of the stores were showing ski equipment and clothes forecasting a long hard winter.

The secretaries in the street still wore minis fringing tanned thighs and the men wore autumn suits.

"The climate at this time of year isn't so very different from Moscow," Brodsky observed. "Soon there will be fogs and Sheremetyevo Airport will open and close like the doors of an elevator."

And the first tissue of ice will form on the lake in Gorky Park, Zhukov thought, to melt and freeze until the first skates sing in the falling snow.

Zhukov said, "What have you got to say to me, Comrade Brodsky?" He felt now as if he were in Moscow, closing his senses to the bargaining shops and the queuing cars.

"It's not good news, I'm afraid, Comrade Zhukov."

"I didn't imagine it would be."

"It seems to me that you have acted very foolishly."

"I think perhaps you're right, comrade."

Brodsky cataloged Zhukov's foolishness with pleasure. "First of all you appear to have been greatly influenced by the bourgeois press and your conversation has, to say the least, been unguarded. This worried us a bit but we attributed it to the baptism with the West which we have come to regard with tolerance. But you've been here a long time now, Comrade Zhukov, and you still draw unfavorable comparisons with the Soviet Union. We are not happy about that."

"We? Who's we?"

"You needn't trouble yourself about that," Brodsky said. He seemed to have been invested with new authority. "Your attitude over the plea from Czechoslovakia for military assistance from the Soviet Union and her allies was unforgivable."

"You will never understand this," Zhukov said, "but I'm a better Socialist than you, Mikhail Brodsky."

Brodsky thought about this, looking like a delicate schoolboy who'd never be any good at games. "It seems to me, Comrade Zhukov, that you are an enemy of Socialism." He continued cataloging. "Then there was your hooligan behavior in New York—an assignment which never had my approval."

"Should it have?"

The wariness Brodsky wore next to his skin revealed itself. "It was the ambassador's decision, of course. But there is no reason why I shouldn't entertain my own private approval or disapproval."

"No reason at all," Zhukov agreed.

They watched a cop apprehend a black crossing against a DON'T-WALK. Brodsky said, "Do you know they even put *race* on the warning ticket? The racial intolerance in this country is disgusting—an insult to mankind."

"I'm glad," Zhukov said as they approached the gallows of Brodsky's speech, "that I'm not a Jew living in the Soviet Union."

"This sort of talk won't help you, Comrade Zhukov."

"I am beyond help."

Brodsky went on, "According to Comrade Muratov of

286

the Soviet United Mission in New York your reaction to the Soviet case put before the United Nations with such articulate competence was one of profound cynicism. Comrade Muratov was shocked that a first secretary and apparent confidant of the ambassador himself should have expressed such doubt."

They passed the Statler Hilton, nearing the Russian Embassy.

Brodsky said, "And, of course, there was the inexcusable behavior in the New York bars. First newspaper interviews, then an attempt to pick up two prostitutes, then a vulgar brawl. Hardly what one expects from a diplomatic representative of the Soviet Union. . . ."

"They weren't prostitutes."

"Amateurs then. It doesn't matter. Then there is the question of your beautiful daughter."

Zhukov stopped walking. "What about my daughter?"

"She has not been discreet."

Please, Zhukov implored all deities, make indiscretion her greatest crime. "In what way, Comrade Brodsky?"

First of all, she deliberately eluded members of the staff who were assigned to protect her. This is a dangerous city —didn't you warn your daughter?"

"Young girls with spirit don't like to be followed."

"But I'm afraid that isn't all. It has come to our notice that she has been having a liaison with an American— although it would seem to be over now."

"What sort of liaison?"

"The usual sort. As is well known after the Alma-Ata episode, your daughter is not a girl of the highest moral caliber."

Zhukov grabbed the lapels of Brodsky's East German suit just above the first button. "I should retract that if I were you, comrade."

Pedestrians sampling the autumnal tranquillity in the air glanced curiously at the scene.

Brodsky's eyes rolled a little and his soft hair uncurled over his ears. "I'm sorry. I didn't mean to put it quite so explicitly."

Zhukov released him. "Say anything like that again, Brodsky, and I will kill you."

Brodsky tugged at his suit which resented ordinary wear let alone attack.

Zhukov said, "How do you know about this liaison? What lovers' tryst have you been polluting this time?"

"It came to our notice through a good servant of the Soviet Union at Black Walnut Point. A Ukrainian named Sokolov. He reported that your daughter was leaving the establishment at night and disappearing with a young man in a green sports car. Also that she was unduly interested in the American travesty of the intervention in Czechoslovakia as portrayed on the television here."

"This young man," Zhukov asked, "do you know who he is?"

"We're working on it," Brodsky said. "Probably CIA or FBI. Your daughter has been very foolish indeed. And we must get her out of harm's way. Perhaps," he said when they were inside the embassy, "we could go up to your office. I don't have one of my own. . . ."

"Third secretaries don't usually," Zhukov said.

"That was most unkind, Comrade Zhukov." They sat on either side of Zhukov's desk. "I'm only acting in your best interests."

"Come to the point, Brodsky. What are you going to do?"

Mikhail Brodsky said it wasn't what *he* was going to do—it was what the Kremlin was going to do. And the Kremlin had decided that Natasha Zhukova should return to the Soviet Union. In any case, wasn't it about time that she returned? Moscow had been very generous allowing her to stay so long.

"You had your reasons," Zhukov said.

Brodsky smiled, the school sycophant grateful for any small flattery. Of course—there had been reasons for everything, he said. First, they wanted to show good faith with Zhukov and to reward him for his efforts in espionage.

Zhukov interrupted, "And, of course, you wanted Natasha and myself to become close again so that the in-

288

evitable parting would be all the more painful and I'd be all the more worried about what you bastards might do to her in the Soviet Union. In short you worked it so that you'd have me at your mercy."

Accepting it as a compliment to his strategy, Brodsky conceded the psychology behind Natasha's stay. And he, personally, could see nothing wrong in that; no one suffered and the cause had been served.

"When is she to go back?"

Brodsky fiddled with blotter and papers so that it looked as if he were seated at his desk. "Tomorrow," he said. "That will give you time for a last dinner together. Her passage has already been booked," he added with finality.

"She isn't freight, you know," Zhukov said.

"Secretaries book flights for ambassadors, Comrade Zhukov."

"But an ambassador has some say in where and when he's going."

"Not always," Brodsky said. "And, by the way, could you please tell your daughter that she is not to leave home —for her own good, you understand. There's no knowing what American intelligence might try now they realize they've failed with this operator in the green sports car."

"You mean she's under house arrest?"

Brodsky shrugged. "Put it how you wish—she is not to leave the apartment."

Zhukov got up and walked to the window. The kids were out of school making their way to drugstores and soda fountains, to suburban houses with no fences around the gardens. Taxicabs fought and bullied; beckoning neon stammered into life in the light of the wasting sun. He asked, "And what do *they* propose to do with us, Valentina and myself?"

Brodsky opened the black Czechoslovakian briefcase he had been carrying. Inside was a folder bearing Zhukov's name in red ink. He opened this too, so that Zhukov could see the thick wad of papers. "This goes back a long way, comrade. Right back to Vladimir Zhukov schoolboy, Vladimir Zhukov patriot and heroic defender of Leningrad,

289

Vladimir Zhukov minor poet"—he glanced at Zhukov for appreciation—"and Vladimir Zhukov Foreign Ministry clerk."

"It looks thorough." Zhukov sat down. "Your organization must have had very good informants."

"The best." Brodsky left the file open on the desk.

"So what is to become of us?"

"It saddens me to have to tell you this," Brodsky gloated. "But Moscow has decided that you must return to the Soviet Union. Your little flirtation with the West is over, Comrade Zhukov. It has been decided that you are a security risk."

"When are we to return?"

"The day after your daughter."

"Can't we go together?"

"A decision has been taken against this course. By the time you arrive in Moscow your daughter will be in Alma-Ata."

"Doesn't the ambassador have a say in this?"

"The ambassador is already in Moscow. For talks," he added, giving the words his own special connotation.

"The minister, then."

"The minister has already approved Moscow's decisions."

At that precise minute—twelve minutes before five on his watch—Vladimir Zhukov decided to accept the ruling of his Moscow mentors. Whatever the compulsion, he had done the cause of Socialism a disservice.

By eleven minutes before five his decision was in fragments. Because the last report on the file lying on the desk was in the unmistakable handwriting of his wife. A surging Sibiryak hand that had been tutored to conformity between the rulered lines of Socialist bureaucracy and doctrine.

This autumnal evening, when there was a faint smell of fireworks and mist in the air, Vladimir Zhukov acted with desperate inspiration.

He left the embassy quickly, on the presumption that pursuers wouldn't be prepared for such a premature departure, and went first to a telephone booth on the ground floor of the National Press Building.

From there he phoned his Sibiryak.

"Hallo, Vladimir," she said. "Where are you?"

"It doesn't matter where I am."

"What's the matter, Vladimir?" The connection was so good she might have been in a booth beside him. Voice, he thought, doesn't alter with age.

"Is Natasha there?"

"No, she went out about an hour ago. She said she would be back by ten."

So he had five hours. "Valentina," he said, "I know."

"Know? What are you talking about, Vladimir?"

"About everything," he said. "About the drawer and the key and your reports."

A pause. Then the young voice from the mountains, "It was for your own good, Vladimir. For the good of . . . of everything. Do you understand?"

Of course he understood. Nothing. Who is the enemy?

"Vladimir."

"Yes?"

"Come home. Please come home."

His voice spoke. A voice spoke . . . it didn't sound like his. "All our life together," it said.

"A good life."

"A mockery."

"Please come home."

"For how long has this been so?"

"Not long. Please come home. I love you, Vladimir."

"Good-bye, Valentina."

Then he hung up, reminding himself that men didn't weep. Why this was so he had no idea.

He took the elevator up to the thirteenth to see if Richter or any of his new friends were there. Richter, crisp, pomaded and tough, was drinking in the big dignified bar.

"Where have you been keeping yourself?" he asked.

"Socializing," Zhukov told him. "I'm sure you've read about it."

"I heard that you gave some sort of interview in New

291

York. It sounded like a lot of fun." American slang clipped incongruously with Germanic precision. "What will you have to drink?"

"A scotch, please. A large one."

"Hey," Richter said. "What's up with you?"

Zhukov drank the scotch thirstily, as if it were beer, and ordered two more. Then he went to the phone and made two calls: one to the Madison Hotel booking a room for the night, the other to Helen Massingham.

In the bedroom at the Madison, Zhukov bought himself another scotch and waited. She arrived one hour after the phone call, wearing a green silk suit; very tanned with a tidemark just visible at the foothills of her breasts. She carried a cosmetic case and smelled expensive. But, he thought, despite all the costly trappings you still look like a whore.

"My," she said, sitting down, smoothing her skirt and lighting a cigarette, "what's come over you all of a sudden? We rather got the impression that our friendship was over."

Zhukov sat on the edge of the bed, jacket and tie on the chair. "What you mean," he said, "is that you thought I was *persona non grata* and therefore no longer of any use to you."

She looked shocked. "I don't mean that at all. You didn't turn up at any more parties and I assumed you'd grown tired of the decadent life."

"I have a proposition to put to you."

"Marvelous." She crossed her brown shaved legs, a little shiny at the shins.

"But we have to be honest with each other. I know perfectly well why you and your husband cultivated me. My motives were exactly the same. Can we please accept that?"

She walked around the modernistic bedroom with its double bed waiting to be used, her silk rustling, her breasts swinging a bit. "I don't know what to say, Vladimir. You're such a forthright person."

"This is what you have to do," Zhukov said, finishing

292

his scotch. "My daughter is at this moment with a young American acting for American Intelligence. She intends to defect but will return to the embassy before she does. If she does that she is finished. We must get a message to her now. That is what you have to do."

"But, Vladimir, how can I?"

"Please," he said. "Forget the pretense. Call your husband. Tell him to get in touch with American Intelligence. The young man is acting for the FBI. Tell them to reach him and stop my daughter from coming back to the embassy."

She looked at him uncertainly. "I don't know anything about all this. I just do what my husband asks."

"He will understand." He picked up the phone and ordered two more whiskies. "Also tell him that Natasha's father is willing to make a deal."

"And are you, Vladimir?"

"Please do what I've asked you."

"And us, Vladimir. What about us? You're the first man I've met in years to whom I feel really attracted."

Zhukov stood up and kissed her, opening strawberry-tasting lips. "We'll work something out," he said.

She picked up the phone and dialed. Half an hour later the phone rang. Zhukov heard his daughter's voice. The relief seemed to reach every part of his body and he grinned fiercely at the telephone. "Where are you?"

"At Charlie's apartment. What is it, Father? What's happened?"

He told her most of it, all that she had to know. "Wait there—I'll be over in half an hour." He hung up.

"Make it an hour," Helen Massingham said.

He turned around. She was naked, legs apart, like the expensive slut she was.

"All right," he said.

* * *

There were strangers in Charlie Hardin's apartment building that night who caused some comment from the other tenants. Strangers walking thoughtfully in the corridors, strangers resting in automobiles in the parking lot.

293

They watched Vladimir Zhukov with exaggerated uncon-
cern as he walked past the fountain in the garden and
waited for the elevator in the lobby.

In the apartment he embraced Natasha, his daughter.
The only positive product of his life.

The apartment had two other occupants. One a neat
middle-aged man who looked as if he'd stepped out of a
tailor's shopwindow; the other burly, crew-cut and holding
his pipe like a pistol.

"Please," Zhukov said, "I should like to be alone with
my daughter and my future son-in-law."

The two men looked at each other unhappily. The one
with the pipe who said his name was Walden said they had
a lot to discuss.

"Later," Zhukov said.

The other man who turned out to be Charlie's father
said, "Are you really coming over to us, Mr. Zhukov?"

"I said we'll talk about it later."

Walden extended his hand. "Neither of you need have
any fear. We'll give you every protection the United States
can offer." Zhukov felt the eagerness in his handshake.

Then there were the three of them. Charlie said, "A
drink, sir?"

"I've had enough. But one more won't do any harm."
He took the scotch and said, "Do you love her?"

Hardin nodded. "I do, sir."

"You both have a lot of trouble ahead of you. But you
realize that, don't you?"

Harding and Natasha stood close together, hands finding each other.

Natasha said, "But you, Father. What about you and
Mother? You know I can't stay unless you do too."

"We'll join you," he said. "First I have to collect some
things."

"You promise?"

"I promise."

He looked at Charlie Hardin and approved. As honest
as life allowed. A little self-important, perhaps, a little too
sold on the sporting, labor-saving, monied values of the

294

system; a university product and a little smug. But nothing that Natasha his daughter couldn't handle.

In fifteen years' time, he thought, they will have one house, two cars and three children.

Father and future son-in-law shook hands. Father and daughter embraced once more and he held her for a moment. Then he winked at her because he couldn't speak and left the room to talk with Walden.

They sat at a table in the lobby while Zhukov told Walden what he had to do. "Get Natasha out of here first thing in the morning. Get her as far away as possible—Alaska if necessary. But act quickly—there aren't all that many green MG's in Washington and they'll trace it."

Walden agreed with everything. "And you, Mr. Zhukov, when do you intend to join your daughter?"

"Obviously it will have to be as soon as possible because my people won't let me out of their sight once they realize my daughter has gone."

Walden offered cigars. "This has been a great victory for the future of international understanding."

Zhukov waved aside the cigar. "A great victory for the West, you mean. A victory over the Red menace, eh, Mr. Walden?"

Walden shook his head. "That's the way it might seem initially. But it will be part of the leveling process. If two Russians of the caliber of yourself and your daughter prefer the West then the equation balances just that little bit more."

"Ah," Zhukov mused. "The equation. You are trying to solve that one too, are you, Mr. Walden?"

"All my life," Walden said.

"And do you think it can be solved?"

"I'm an optimist, Mr. Zhukov."

"Perhaps one way of helping to solve it would be if you defected to the Soviet Union."

Walden said, "You have a wonderful sense of humor, Mr. Zhukov."

Chapter 6

THE NEXT MORNING, while Valentina frantically called the embassy and the police in search of her daughter, Zhukov began to pack. Methodically and deliberately, like a housewife making the beds after her husband has deserted her.

With care he folded his expensive mohair suit tailored for spying. And his new shirts and a silver tie bought on sale at Garfinckel's. Thoughtfully he regarded his bowl of matchbooks, then poured them into the wastebasket.

Outside the sun was molten red behind the gathering mist and he believed that he could smell bonfire smoke.

"Vladimir," she said, "why are you packing?"

"I think you know."

"I want to try and explain, Vladimir. But now we must think only of our daughter."

Gently he told her about Natasha. "And now I am packing to return home to Russia with you my wife because that's where we belong."

It seemed to be going smoothly. It was 10 A.M. and the black bulletproof Lincoln supplied by the CIA and driven by an FBI getaway chauffeur waited outside Charlie Hardin's apartment block, engine throbbing powerfully. Plainclothes men loitered around the lobby, outside the entrance and beside the wind-scattered fountain, as unobtrusive as football players at the ballet.

The Lincoln was to take Natasha Zhukova and Hardin to the National Airport where they would catch an executive jet to Newark. Another car would take them to a hideout overlooking the Hudson in upstate New York.

296

Charlie and Natasha came out together, ducking their heads into the rising wind. They sat in the back, close together, already feeling like bit players in a big production.

The FBI driver said, "Okay?" He looked Italian and everything about him was quick; his thin hands, his speech, his driving.

The CIA guard beside him—fair and Germanic with a school boy face—said: "Okay. It doesn't look like they traced the green MG."

But they had.

A couple of minutes before.

The gray beetle Volkswagen was parked fifty yards down the road. The driver told his companion to radio the embassy. "Where are they heading for?" the voice at the other end asked.

"We don't know yet." Five minutes later he said; "It looks like the National Airport."

The voice said, "That's what we thought. Our man there reports that there's an executive jet waiting on the runway and a lot of unusual activity. We're on our way."

The FBI chauffeur drove with disgust, fingers tapping on the wheel, foot restless on the gas pedal. "So why get *me* on a job like this?" he asked. "Why waste a car with two four-barreled Holly carbs, molded heads, the works—"

The guard glanced in the side mirror and tapped the driver on the shoulder. "That's why," he said, pointing his thumb over his shoulder at the three Volkswagens coming up behind them in attacking formation.

"Jesus," said the driver. He shoved his foot on the gas pedal, his fingers still light at the base of the wheel.

They were crossing the rain-feathered river. Not far to the airport. Most of the traffic was heading into the city, each car winged with spray. The whole wide road was aeronautical this morning: the wet sky pressing down, the jets lowering themselves from its base and feeling for the ground, the runways ahead, the black Lincoln airliner being buzzed by the Volks fighters.

Ahead lay an unbroken barricade of traffic across the lanes. Then a long clear stretch before the airport. The

Volkswagens behind were separated from the Lincoln by another formation of cars with careful drivers.

The guard, eyes cornflower blue in his college face, turned around. "Better keep down, ma'am. And you, Mr. Hardin. They say the glass is bulletproof, but who knows with some of this Soviet hardware. . . ." He took a Smith & Wesson from his shoulder holster.

The Lincoln lunged forward but the cars ahead didn't. The driver pressed the power brake too hard and they skidded, nudging a ceremonial Cadillac, full of outrage, before straightening up.

The driver took it out on the horn. But horns only sharpen outraged perversity; the single line of cars rode firm.

Behind them the fighters were weaving between the passenger craft and you expected to hear them open up with cannon at any moment.

All the time the driver talked, using words like chewing gum. "No sweat. But those babies can shift in traffic. They've gotten fifteen hundred engines in those, disc barkes on the front wheels, acceleration like a rocket taking off. And their cornering will make this old lady seem like a double bed."

The guard was radioing Washington, telling them to move at the airport. But there wouldn't be time—they all knew that.

Sitting on the floor, Hardin managed a smile for Natasha. She managed one back. "It's all right," he said.

"Yes," she said, hand tight around his fingers, hair touching his face.

"I don't always travel like this," he said with another actor's smile. He was astonished at their insignificance, like rare drugs being rushed to an emergency.

The driver took the Lincoln through a reluctant space in the cars ahead, nudging the Cadillac again and touching fenders with a Buick. Rain bowled across the clear stretch of highway; a jet felt its way out of the clouds.

But the fighters were with them now, two taking the line of traffic on the outside, one stalking the Lincoln from behind.

298

"Now we can show 'em," the driver said. "Now we can show those babies. Now we're on the straight." But as he stared through the windshield wipers a gray Volks got in front, just. "No sweat," said the driver.

He swung to the left but there was a Volks there, too. And to the right. The three of them taking the Lincoln into land. Each had a driver and a passenger, faces blurred behind the streaming windows.

The guard lowered the window and the car gulped in wind and rain. He held his Smith & Wesson without conviction, wondering about shooting Soviet diplomats.

The driver said, "It was the traffic that did it. The goddamn traffic. They couldn't have touched us on the open road."

The gray Volkswagen in front was braking, slowing them all down. The other two began to bump the Lincoln; the first two bumps not synchronized; the third giving them a squeeze.

The guard said, "Why don't you knock the bastards out of the way? You're big enough, for Chris' sake."

"Because we've got to turn here."

The two accompanying Volks swung out and back again, testing the bulletproofing. The leader had come down to forty and was still slowing.

"What the hell are they trying to do?" the drived asked.

Hardin said, "Trying to stop you."

"So they can grab the girl," the guard added.

"Here we go," said the driver, swinging the Lincoln down the airport exit, bouncing one of the Volks out of the way, the leader still in front.

The first car was braking hard, trying to block them. But there was plenty of space now, approaching the terminal buildings, and the Lincoln found a lot of it, accelerating so that it was level with the gray Volks. Then ahead. There was a lot of surprise around them as they headed toward the entrance to the tarmac.

But the barrier was closed. Beside it a man in a shiny raincoat was waving his arms as if he were parking an aircraft. The driver kept the horn going, swearing as he slowed down and the escorts caught up.

299

Finally the man in the raincoat understood. He went for the barrier and they hurtled through, grazing a fender. The escorts followed.

Ahead a Boeing trundled toward its lot, fresh from the sky, serpent face inquisitive. But there was no executive jet at the prearranged takeoff point.

Hardin sat up, keeping Natasha on the floor. "The wind's changed," he said. "It must be the other end of the runway."

"That's what the guy at the barrier was trying to say," the guard muttered.

"No sweat," said the driver. "I always wanted to be a pilot."

The Volks made one last effort, banking around the Lincoln, snapping and worrying. But they were on the runway and the Lincoln was accelerating toward the point of no return. At 100 mph. More. "Wow," said the driver. "Flaps down. Or is it up?"

Lights flashing, sirens wailing. A shadow came out of the clouds, hesitated, disappeared again. They thought they heard a couple of shots; they couldn't be sure. Behind them the Volkswagens became little bugs again.

The executive jet was waiting at the far end of the runway. Hardin bundled Natasha up the landing steps; the door shut ponderously.

The Volkswagens stopped and a lot of Russians got out. One with a nasal voice, gold-rimmed spectacles and a woolly scarf began to shout. "I demand in the name of the Embassy of the Soviet Union that you let Natasha Zhukova free. This is a gross violation of our liberties. . . ."

The jet moved away.

"Stop." The Russian tried to run in front of the plane but the guard restrained him. More cars encircled them now. The other Russians had given up. But this one continued to kick and struggle, almost petulantly, within the ballplayer grip of the guard. A white nasal inhaler fell out of his pocket and the guard, still holding him with one arm, bent down and replaced it in his pocket.

300

They kept Vladimir Zhukov and his wife for another three weeks in case they could use him to get his daughter back. But she had vanished in the Indian forests that shoulder the fat curves of the Hudson somewhere between West Point and Sing Sing.

And soon they heard she had married.

The car taking Vladimir Zhukov and his wife to the airport proceeded smoothly down New Hampshire Avenue. Zhukov tried to retain last impressions in the album of his mind. But they wouldn't stick.

River benches and silver ski trails leading the way through silver birch and pine. The forests content in their loneliness; the beaches robust with muscular happiness.

East equals West—but not yet.

At an intersection he asked the two silent guards if he might be granted a last favor. They shrugged and accompanied him into the supermarket, not quite holding his arms.

He took a shopping cart and filled it with goods from the capitalist storehouse. Frosted pop tarts (Dutch apple flavor), waffle and pancake syrup, imitation crumbled bacon, instant mashed potato puffs, lemon-flavored iced-tea mix with sugar added, kosher dill chunks, hot dog relish, creamy garlic dressing, lime after-shave, self-heating shaving cream, antistatic rug spray and a can of frozen pink lemonade.

And an electric can opener for Valentina.

Who is the enemy?

(Please turn page)